George David Boyle

The Recollections of the Very Rev. G.D. Boyle, Dean of Salisbury

George David Boyle

The Recollections of the Very Rev. G.D. Boyle, Dean of Salisbury

ISBN/EAN: 9783337218829

Printed in Europe, USA, Canada, Australia, Japan

Cover: Foto ©Raphael Reischuk / pixelio.de

More available books at **www.hansebooks.com**

THE RECOLLECTIONS

OF THE VERY REV.

G. D. BOYLE

DEAN OF SALISBURY

LONDON
EDWARD ARNOLD
37 BEDFORD STREET, STRAND, W.C.
Publisher to the India Office
1895

TO THE RIGHT HONOURABLE

SIR MOUNTSTUART ELPHINSTONE GRANT DUFF

G.C.S.I.

AN INDULGENT CRITIC, AND A MOST CONSTANT FRIEND

I DEDICATE THESE IMPERFECT MEMORIALS

OF DAYS THAT ARE NO MORE

PREFACE

DURING the progress of these Recollections, I have
been often painfully reminded of my inability to
give a suitable record of the eminent persons I
have had the good fortune to meet and know. I
can only plead in excuse for the appearance of this
volume, that I undertook to write it at the request
of some whose judgment was entitled to respect.
I trust that an effort to express simply what I feel
about some of the remarkable men I have known
may not be distasteful to those who hold their
memories dear.

G. D. B.

DEANERY, SALISBURY,
    January 8, 1895.

LIST OF CONTENTS

CHAPTER I

PAGE

Early days—Charles x. in Edinburgh—I see Sir Walter
Scott—Anecdotes of Sir Walter—Testimony to his
charm of character—A glimpse of De Quincey—
The Reform Bill, riots—The Queen's first visit to
Scotland.   1

CHAPTER II

Illustrious citizens of Edinburgh—Dr. Chalmers—
Professor Wilson—Henry Cockburn—Lord Rutherfurd—My first meeting with Thackeray—Dr. Muir
and Dean Ramsay—Some estimates of Mr. Gladstone—Sir Archibald Alison—William Mure of
Caldwell — The Edinburgh Theatre — A famous
bookseller.   18

CHAPTER III

1843-1853—I join Charterhouse—A first visit to Westminster Abbey—The De Veres—My first evening

PAGE

at school—My contemporaries at the Charterhouse—
Sir Robert Peel and Disraeli—The Opera—Macready
at Drury Lane—Three words from the Great
Duke. 40

CHAPTER IV

Recollections of the Oxford Movement—First meeting
with John Gibson Lockhart—The Iron Düke's
doctor—Lockhart and the *Quarterly Review*—Rogers :
his kindness, social success, and wit—Rogers and
Sydney Smith—Dean Milman and Bishop Blomfield
—Lord Coleridge. . . 54

CHAPTER V

The Oxford Movement—Frederick Maurice—Principal
Shairp—The last years of school life—Lord Byron's
early love—Mrs. Clive—Dr. Wolff—Stanley's *Life
of Arnold*—Matriculation at Oxford. . . . 75

CHAPTER VI

1847-1853—At Oxford—A visit from my father—Friends
and acquaintances—Balliol and Exeter—Charles
Marriot and Mozley—The great Vicar of Leeds—
Pusey, and the results of his teaching. . . . 100

CHAPTER VII

PAGE

The English Lakes—Hartley Coleridge; his criticisms
on literature, and conversation about his father—My
second term at Oxford—A. H. Clough—Henry
Smith—Rajah Brooke—Arthur Stanley.   116

CHAPTER VIII

Oxford in 1848—Excitement about Continental politics
—Bishop Wilberforce—Anecdote of Sir Walter Scott
—The true character of Wilberforce—His conver-
sation and witticisms.   129

CHAPTER IX

John Conington—*Essays and Reviews*—Goldwin Smith
—Halford Vaughan—Reading Party at Oban in 1850
—Sir William Hamilton's Lectures—Anecdotes of
Carlyle—Dr. Hannah—Macready—Baron Alderson
—The Great Exhibition Year.   145

CHAPTER X

Sir Henry Russell—Sir David Dundas—Death of my
father—Funeral of the Duke of Wellington—Lord
Aberdeen's Ministry—Ordination—Work in Wor-
cestershire—Lord and Lady Lyttelton—Matthew
Arnold—Robert Lowe—Sir Stafford Northcote—
Curate life.   163

CHAPTER XI

PAGE

J. S. Mill—Sir H. Maine—The Athenæum Club—Ireland
—Switzerland, Neuberg—The Carlyles—The Grande
Chartreuse—Fallen Royalties—*The Saturday Review*
— Theological Controversy — Incumbent of St.
Michael's, Handsworth—Cambridge—Thompson—
Whewell—Lightfoot—Marriage—Bishop Lonsdale
—Bishop Temple—Birmingham Life—George Daw-
son—Badham—Cardinal Newman.   .   .   192

CHAPTER XII

1861-1867—Lord Elgin and his sisters—Miss Harriet
Martineau; her conversation and recollections—
Lord Derby on Politics — Henry Smith — Dean
Stanley; his work and opinions—A Visit from
Maurice—Froude; and Newman and Manning—
Froude's *Carlyle.*   218

CHAPTER XIII

Vicar of Kidderminster—Bishop Selwyn and Bishop
Wordsworth—Canon Wood—Stanley and Pearson—
Death of Lady Augusta Stanley—The Parochial
System.   244

CHAPTER XIV

Nassau Senior's conversation—The criticisms of Bulwer,
Scott, Richardson, and Miss Austen—Coleridge—

PAGE

The Irish Church Question—Lord Arthur Russell
and Sir Louis Mallet—Hayward's stories—Bishop
Magee's Irish stories, theological views, and
preaching—Newman—Mozley, Dean Church, and
Liddon.   .   .   .   271

CHAPTER XV

L'envoi.   .   293

PORTRAIT OF THE DEAN OF SALISBURY.   . *Frontispiece*

RECOLLECTIONS OF DEAN BOYLE

CHAPTER I

Early days—Charles x. in Edinburgh—I see Sir Walter Scott—Anecdotes of Sir Walter—Testimony to his charm of character—A glimpse of De Quincey—The Reform Bill riots—The Queen's first visit to Scotland.

'LET the laddie see the King of France,' I distinctly remember hearing a good-natured man say, one fine summer morning at the corner of Castle Street, Edinburgh, and in a moment I was lifted in his arms to see two carriages and four driving along Princes Street. In the first was a stiff, grey old man, with a sad-looking lady at his side; at the window of the second carriage I saw a large, fat-faced boy. The old man and lady were Charles X. and his niece and daughter-in-law, the *filia dolorosa*; the boy was Henri Cinq, Comte de Chambord, of recent history. The royal party were on their way from Holyrood Palace to Hopetoun House, and I recollect how one or two passers-by touched their hats to the fallen royalties.

Standing at her window and looking at the carriages was Mary, Lady Clerk of Penicuik, a lady who was born in the year 1745, at Rose Castle, now the palace of the Bishops of Carlisle, and on whose cradle a white cockade was pinned,

A

in order that her mother might suffer no harm, by the captain of a party of soldiers who were on their retreat from Derby. It was said that Lady Clerk presented this relic to George IV. when he visited Edinburgh in the year 1822. She was not the only person associated with the year of rebellion seen and known by me. I have seen a very old man who held the horse of the Chevalier at Culloden, and I have often talked with a venerable lady, the great-grandmother of the present Viceroy of India, who, like Mary, Lady Clerk, was born in 1745.

Edinburgh, with all its historical and literary associations, was a pleasant place to pass one's childhood in. I remember how, a small, shy child, I was taken into my father's study, and saw sitting in an arm-chair an old man, with a stick between his legs. This was Sir Walter Scott, who came, I believe, to see my father on some business connected with his office, and I heard afterwards how shocked my father had been at the alteration in his old friend. Many years afterwards, when I saw for the first time at Mr. Cadell's, in St. Andrew Square, the well-known statue of Sir Walter, now in the Advocates' Library, I recognised at once, from the stick between his legs, the figure I had seen many years before.

The year of Sir Walter's death was a memorable one in my boyish life. My father had to go to Perth, on circuit, and I went with him, with my mother and two sisters, by the Queen's Ferry to my uncle's home in Perthshire, and it was then first I heard, as we passed Loch Leven, the wonderful story of Queen Mary's escape, and felt something of the beauty of the wild pass of Glenfarg, so familiar now to those who approach Perth after crossing the Forth Bridge. When the heavy carriage and four drew up at the door of Methven Castle, my uncle (the reigning laird) was standing at the entrance with a gentleman at his side. When my father saw this gentleman he clasped his hand and said, ' What news, Skene, have you of Walter?' A mournful shake of the head showed that there was no good news to tell. This was only a few weeks before Sir Walter's death, when, as I often have heard from several who knew him well, a great gloom and darkness seemed to cover all Scotland.

It was my good fortune, as a boy, to be on very familiar terms with one of Sir Walter Scott's most intimate friends, and in after years to receive much kindness, never to be forgotten, from his son-in-law and biographer ; and I think this is the place to record some particulars regarding that great writer, not, I hope, without interest. Sir Walter, in the delightful fragment of autobiography at the beginning of Lockhart's great work, mentions my father's name among the friends of his college days. My father was born in 1772, and had been a student at St. Andrews before he joined Walter

Scott's set at Edinburgh University. When Lockhart's *Life* appeared, he often spoke of the delightful days of his youth, and from him as well as from Mr. Murray of Simprim, I often heard many recollections of the days that were no more. Mr. Murray, I remember, told me that many of the features of the elder Fairford in *Redgauntlet* resembled the elder Scott, who, he said, was a far more genial person than he appears to be in the pages of Lockhart. The charm of Sir Walter's conversation, his command of proverbs and anecdotes, and his intense interest in literature, were often dwelt upon by Mr. Murray. Although my father was not in the secret of the authorship of *Waverley*, he told me that he never had a doubt about it after reading in *Guy Mannering* Mrs. M'Candlish's account of her change from the Burgher Meeting-house to the Kirk, a real paraphrase of what Walter Scott had told him, as an experience of his first circuit. Very early in his career as an advocate, my father had the good fortune to become well known to Henry Dundas, the first Lord Melville, and he has often told me that Walter Scott used to deplore the great hold that politics and his professional duties gained over him. ' You are not half so good a fellow as you were in the early days of the Club, when you were full of Horace and Virgil,' was one of Walter Scott's sayings, which my father told me when I expressed surprise that in his old age, though not a reading man, he could quote passages from the Georgics, and the Epistles of Horace.

In 1838 my father had a very severe illness, and I had from time to time to read to him portions of Walter Scott's *Life*. This led him to talk much of his college days. Some allusion to Sterne made him reach from a shelf in his study the volume which contains the story of Le Fevre, and when I had finished it he said to me, 'I shall never forget the first time I heard that read by Walter Scott, after supper at Murray of Simprim's. Clerk and Erskine were there, and we had a regular fight about the passage of the accusing spirit and the recording angel.' Many years afterwards, when I read Walter Scott's *Life of Sterne*, and came upon his reproof of the famous passage, I felt no doubt as to the side Walter Scott must have taken after that supper.

Although actual knowledge of the authorship of the Waverley series was supposed to be confined to a few, many outsiders were quietly admitted to the open secret. Charles K. Sharpe, so often mentioned by Lockhart, was permitted to allow the proof-sheets of many of the novels to be read by my mother and her sister before they were returned to Ballantyne. In this way the young ladies had the delight of racing through some of the most remarkable of the series. The memory of the younger sister was so excellent that she actually repeated the beautiful song from the

Pirate, 'Farewell, farewell,' to her elder sister after this hurried reading. All doubt as to the authorship of *Rob Roy* must, said the same admirers of Scott, have been removed when the verses which made the elder Osbaldistone so contemptuous were compared with the famous passage in *Marmion*.

Murray of Simprim, whom I often met in my boyhood and youth, was an excessively clever man. He was the son of the Lord Elibank who is so well known to readers of Boswell's *Johnson*, and had passed his life in what may be called intellectual epicureanism. His duties as a country gentleman sat lightly upon him, but I believe he was a kind and indulgent landlord. His wife was a Miss Murray, a descendant of the famous Susanna, Countess of Eglinton. She had two daughters and no son. A good deal of his time was spent abroad. When he visited Edinburgh it was his great pleasure to talk with his old friends on the two subjects he most delighted in, the Peninsular War, and the career of Walter Scott. For Wellington and Scott he had true hero-worship. A characteristic anecdote of the Duke I learnt from him. One of his aides-de-camp was found by the Duke at Strathfieldsaye reading a French book, in which it was said that the Duke did not win the battle of Toulouse. 'I do not care a straw,' said the Duke, 'what they say as to who won the battle; the French fought it to keep me out of France, but I got into France.'

But I am wandering from Walter Scott, who once

said to Mr. Murray, 'I am surprised, Peter, at my own success in life, and, to tell you the truth, I never look at anything I have written when it is printed without feeling ashamed it is no better;' and to Murray's rejoinder that at least he had given the world a good deal of pleasure, said, 'Well, I hope at least' (in the same spirit in which he spoke to Mr. Edward Cheney at Rome), 'I hope at least I have not done much harm.' On one occasion at my grandmother's house I had the pleasure of hearing William Clerk and Mr. Murray talk over the plots and characters of some of the best known of Scott's novels. Clerk, like the late Dean Stanley, put *Guy Mannering* in the first place. The art with which the characters of importance were brought into one room at Woodbourne was, he said, inimitable. Murray dwelt on the character of *The Antiquary*, and said he thought he would have rather been the author of Edie Ochiltree's talk than of anything that Scott had written. The evening was to me a memorable one, for it was the only occasion on which I ever heard my grandmother, who was the subject of one of Burns's best-known songs, 'Blythe, blythe and merry was she,' speak of her seeing Burns at Ochtertyre. The impression he had left upon her mind was not altogether a pleasant one. After supper the poet had been noisy, but on the following day he made amends by reading to the family party, while the ink was hardly dry, his lines on seeing the wild-fowl rise from Loch Turrit.

Mr. Murray of Simprim was one of the last of his generation who powdered his hair. I greatly regretted the disuse of this fashion, and disliked the brown wig which Mr. Murray wore in his latter days. When I was a young man, in my early Oxford days, I had a long walk with him in Hyde Park, and we ended in a visit to Murray's shop in Albemarle Street. 'I have not been here,' he said, 'since I came with Walter Scott to be introduced to Byron. People talk great stuff about getting over death. There are some deaths one never gets over. Life has been a different business to me since Scott's death. He was the most delightful man I have ever known.' A year or two before I had heard the same account of Scott from Miss Maclean Clephane, aunt of the present Bishop of Ely, who had known Sir Walter most intimately, and, many years afterwards, Mr. John Crawford, standing with me in the lobby of the Athenæum, after noticing a nobleman who was lame, and who was distinguished by a certain peculiarity of temper, said, 'I have generally remarked that men with congenital infirmities have some peculiarity, but there was one exception, Walter Scott, on the whole the most delightful being I have ever known.' Mr. Lockhart, of whom I shall have much more to say, once said to me: 'I have often wished that I could convey to people in words the irresistible charm of my father-in-law's character. He was utterly unlike, in his perfect simplicity, the rest of

mankind, and he made every one about him happy.'
Surely it is not too much to say that the *Life*, the
Journal, and the *Letters* so admirably edited by
Mr. Douglas, continue to impress all readers with
an affectionate reverence for Scott, such as few in
life or literature have ever inspired.

It is a distinction to have known men who were
honoured with Scott's friendship, and I must add
one trifling personal recollection connected with Sir
Walter. My eldest sister, Mrs. Hope, remembered
how Sir Walter Scott repeated to her 'Jock of
Hazeldean,' and the next time that she met him at
Sir William Rae's, when she was asked to sing, she
said, to use her own words, marvelling at her own
impudence, ' Sir Walter, I am going to sing Jock of
Hazeldean.' She sang it, however, so well as to win
praise from every one present, and many years afterwards I pleased her by telling her that Mr. Lockhart
had mentioned to me how Sir Walter himself had
written to his wife, ' I wish you could have heard
Miss Boyle sing " Jock of Hazeldean." ' A brother
of mine who is still alive, remembers well being
allowed to thank Sir Walter for his *Tales of a
Grandfather*. What a happy moment in many a
young life is the first acquaintance with that book,
perhaps on the whole the one which has given more
than any other book for children the title which
George Eliot in *Middlemarch* assigns to Scott,
' that beloved author.'

When the first volume of Lockhart's *Life* appeared,

the enthusiasm in Edinburgh was extraordinary. I had the good fortune to have as private tutor a man distinguished by a real love of literature. He came in the evening to help us to prepare our lessons for the Edinburgh Academy, a school which has had the honour of numbering many illustrious persons amongst its pupils. One day, at the close of our hour, our tutor said, ' I am going to give you a treat,' and he read the delightful account—fragment of autobiography—Sir Walter gives of his childish and boyish days. The tutor read uncommonly well, and he had a great delight in introducing us to his favourite passages in the Bible and in great authors. I can never hear Ruth's words to Naomi, the sixty-third chapter of Isaiah, and the fourteenth of St. John's Gospel, without a remembrance of his deep, strong voice, and his emotion when he came to a pathetic passage in Scott's poetry, such as the famous scene in Melrose Abbey when the book is delivered to William of Deloraine.

I must not dwell too much on the influences of Scottish history and poetry so often elicited by the romantic scenes round Edinburgh. There certainly could hardly be any purer pleasure than that enjoyed by boys who had made acquaintance with *Marmion* or the *Heart of Midlothian* than a ramble in the Queen's Park, and ascent of Arthur's Seat, or an occasional visit to the hill from which Marmion looked on Edinburgh and the Firth of Forth. Ill health for two years kept me from the Academy, and the tutor spent the greater part of the day with me, and in the course of our walks he talked constantly of Sir Walter Scott, Professor Wilson, and Dr. Chalmers, the three men to whom he gave the hearty homage of his well-stored mind. He inspired me with a real love for Ovid, Virgil, and Cicero, and although I daresay his scholarship was hardly of modern type, I do not believe that the inward strength, the pathos and the eloquent periods of these three great men were ever more enjoyed than by James Ferguson. He knew me thoroughly, often rebuked my desultory reading, and insisted on the claims of accuracy and criticism, and I hope I shall never forget what I owe to his pure taste and high feeling. He was in the habit of going to a watchmaker's to have his watch regulated. As I was standing on the steps of the shop, the watchmaker, Mr. Whitelaw, pointed out a little man, in a long shabby coat, and said, ' Yon's the opium-eater.' At that moment the wearer of the coat turned round, and I saw for the only time in my life the well-cut features of De Quincey. I had never heard of him before, but I was able after much persuasion to induce my tutor to read to me the wonderful passage in which he introduces the coronation anthem. When I was an undergraduate at Oxford, my translation of this passage, in an examination for the Hertford Scholarship, so pleased the late Dean of Westminster that he asked a friend, John Conington, to introduce me to him, and from that day he distinguished me by many acts of true friendship. When I told him I had once seen De Quincey, Stanley reminded me of Scott's one interview with Burns, and his application of the words of Ovid, '*Virgilium vidi tantum*,' and was pleased to find that my early love for Ovid enabled me to continue the quotation ' *nec amara Tibullo tempus amicitiae fata dedere meae.*'

When I again resumed work at the Academy I made the acquaintance of a friend with whom, since my Oxford days, I have lived in the closest intimacy, the ex-Governor of Madras, Sir M. E. Grant Duff. He has more than once reminded me that in the yards of the Academy I told him that my father, who was one of the trustees of Dr. Andrew Bell, had had a letter from Mrs. Southey describing to him the unhappy state of her husband, and suggesting that the life of Dr. Bell, which Southey was engaged upon when his malady commenced, should be finished by his son Cuthbert. I think a taste for history and general literature was imbibed by many of my school-fellows under the teaching of Mr. Cumming and Archdeacon Williams, the rector of the Academy. Williams was an eccentric but able man. His knowledge of the classics was extraordinary, and he certainly possessed the power of inspiring his pupils with a real reverence for them. His own contribution to the Homeric question was by no means worthy of his reputation. Under his successor, Dr. Hannah, the Academy achieved great successes. I was, however, transferred to the old Charterhouse before I had the full benefit of Archdeacon Williams' wide range of reading.

Before I left Edinburgh I was fortunate enough to possess a friend who was on very intimate terms with James Gibson Craig. Mr. Craig had a magnificent library. He was fond of lending books, and many a delightful treat I owed to his kind liberality. But the chiefest of all delights was when in the year 1842 I was permitted to read, before it was published, a copy of *The Lays of Rome*, sent to him by Macaulay. To read 'Horatius' and the 'Prophecy of Capys,' with the intense pleasure of those days is a satisfaction which is, alas! denied to old age. But the delightful ring of the verse still has its charm, and I was bold enough, at the suggestion of George Dundas, a judge with the title of Lord Manor many years afterwards, to ask Archdeacon Williams if there was any classical authority for the epithet 'ivory moonlight' in the last of the *Lays*. Dundas had much of the charm of his accomplished brother, Sir David, and could converse with young people in a way which made them feel that they were not such fools after all. He was one of the many ornaments of the Scottish bar, well known to me in my youth, whom it was a privilege to know, and a delight to remember.

Before I venture on my recollections of some of these remarkable men I must say something of the fierce political heat of my early days. It is something to have heard the farewell taken by an old nurse of an elder brother who was in the Navy, as with red baton in his hand he sallied forth to do duty as a special constable at the Reform Bill riots. When the Bill passed there was a general illumination. My father sturdily refused to put candles in his windows. The shutters were closed, and the thud of the stones thrown by the angry mob, and the smashing of the glass was often talked of in the nursery. I saw Jeffrey and Abercromby, afterwards Speaker, and Lord Dunfermline, chaired after their election. Abercromby was an old friend of my father's, who split his votes, giving one to the Tory candidate and another to Abercromby. Some of his brethren of the bench were highly indignant at his supposed departure from principle, but his defence was that Abercromby was a Canningite, and for him and his brother Lord Abercromby, he had always had a warm affection. When Jeffrey was raised to the bench, Sir John Campbell, the well-known Chief-Justice and Chancellor, was the Whig candidate. His wife had lately been raised to the peerage as Baroness Stratheden, and when the H. B. caricature of Adam and Eve in the garden of Stratheden came out, there was much laughter in the Tory camp. Three notable Edinburgh worthies, Lord Cockburn, Lord Fullarton, and Mr. Maitland, afterwards Lord Dundrennan, married three sisters, and in each family I had boy friends. We had a good deal of political wrangling. Some of them had buff and blue flags of magnificent proportions, but my modest Tory banner bore the inscription 'Learmonth for ever,' and was considered a great success. With shameful impudence I stood on the doorstep when Sir John Campbell passed in triumph, and waved my flag.

The Lord Advocate who succeeded Jeffrey, J. A. Murray, afterwards Lord Murray, had one very clever and charming son. He singled me out from other boys, and I often went to see him take lessons in the Riding-school, and spent many pleasant hours in his home, where he was the idol of his father and mother, and his uncle, William Murray of Henderland, who guarded him like the keeper of a fortress. There are some people in the world who seem to be born to give pleasure to others. Willie Murray was one of these. If he read a new book and liked it he instantly pressed it on you, and his enchantment at finding I enjoyed Miss Martineau's tale *Life in the Wilds* was so great, that he declared his intention of taking me to his father's country place, that we might enact the scenes of that story. One day I heard he was ill and that he wished to see me. He had only been in the house for a few days, but he looked thin and pale, and he told me he could not eat his porridge. I saw tears in the eyes of a Miss Carnegie, who was living with his father and mother, as she took me down-stairs, and in a very few days after this he passed away. I believe it was a case of rapid decline, and I know that for many a day I was sick at heart when I thought I should see him no more. Most of those who played together in the garden of Charlotte Square have gone into the silent land, but there are one or two still remaining, who will remember the look of sadness which came across the face of an old judge and his wife, as they remembered that they were speaking to some of the friends of the long-mourned Willie Murray. For many years I never passed the door of what was then the Lord Advocate's house in George Street, without thinking of his winning ways, his gentle smile, and his wish that all his friends had an uncle as he had, to give them a pony and lessons from Colonel Latham, the master of the riding-school.

The brother of Sir John Campbell, Sir George Campbell of Edenwood, lived in the house next to my grandmother. I heard the Attorney-General, as he then was, on the night of the election, address a number of his constituents from an open window. I never saw him again until the year 1851, when as Chief-Justice he was travelling with some of his family in Italy; but although many years had passed, he had much the same appearance as when he went through the streets of Edinburgh after his election, smiling as some opponents called out, 'Plain John, plain John.' Fortunately, among boys the strife of elections soon passes away, but an hour of revival came. When the Whig ministry clung to office, and Her Majesty was disinclined to part with the ladies of her house-hold, H. B. was again busy at work, and the Tory boys of Edinburgh had a good laugh at their Whig friends, after gazing at the caricatures in Le Sage's windows. We have passed through many crises of political feeling, but I do not believe that par-tisanship was ever more keen than when the London mail arrived one evening in 1841, with the news announced by the guard, that Her Majesty's Government, on the vote of 'No confidence,' had only a majority of one.

In the following year the Queen made her first visit to Scotland. It was impossible to describe the enthusiasm with which she and Prince Albert were received on their progress through the old town of Edinburgh to the Castle. Opposite them, in an open carriage, were Sir Robert Peel and Lord Aberdeen, and it was certainly marvellous, that the Conservative ministers, so soon after the Reform Bill, should have had the reception they enjoyed. From the windows of the Bank, where I saw this wonderful scene, I had also witnessed the proclamation of Queen Victoria in 1837. At the Jubilee service in Westminster Abbey in 1887, there were a few Scotsmen who may have, like myself, remembered the days of 1837 and 1842, in 'Auld Reekie.'

CHAPTER II

Illustrious citizens of Edinburgh—Dr. Chalmers—Professor Wilson—
Henry Cockburn—Lord Rutherfurd—My first meeting with Thackeray
—Dr. Muir and Dean Ramsay—Some estimates of Mr. Gladstone—
Sir Archibald Alison—William Mure of Caldwell—The Edinburgh
Theatre—A famous bookseller.

THE Edinburgh of my boyhood and youth could boast of many illustrious citizens. Occasionally vast crowds round one of the City churches on a Sunday morning gave evidence that Dr. Chalmers was to preach that day. In the years immediately before the Disruption of 1843 Chalmers was one of the most remarkable figures to be seen in the streets of Edinburgh. He walked rapidly, and always seemed pre-occupied, but his hearty greeting of some friend or old student was a delightful thing to see. There was power and benevolence in his look. I was too young to remember much of the two sermons I heard him preach, but the impassioned way with which he descended after a great rhetorical flight on his text was very remarkable. I saw him once in private life, when he came to preach in the church at Methven, two years before the secession of the Free Church. At that time he did not despair of a settlement of the great question which divided the Church of Scotland into two camps. Those who heard him preach in his later days to some of the poorest population in Edinburgh, have often dwelt on the charming mellowness of those sermons. Not long before his death he met Mr. Erskine of Linlathen in the streets of Edinburgh, and told him with what pleasure he had lately been reading one of Mr. Erskine's treatises. When he died suddenly, Mr. Erskine said to a friend : 'I asked Chalmers to come and see me in the autumn, and he answered, "The night cometh," somewhat sadly, and I gathered from these words that he had a presage that his days were few.' Chalmers certainly had the gift of impressing his own personality and the reality of his faith with extraordinary distinctness on his own generation. Dean Ramsay, who wrote an admirable estimate of Chalmers, once said to me, 'I have only known two men who had what I call real greatness of character, Chalmers and Lord Dalhousie.'

Professor Wilson, 'Christopher North,' was a great landmark in the Edinburgh of my boyhood and youth. As he marched along the North Bridge, leaning on the arm of a son, at a rapid pace near the hour of his lecture, every one turned to look at him. His somewhat shaggy hair and gleaming countenance gave him a look of enthusiasm such as his own rushing prose often carried into a reader's heart. I was once in a society of young students who were reading aloud Wilson's last article in Blackwood, with delighted looks. 'Is not this grand?' 'Well done, old Kit, there's life in the old dog yet,' rang out from their lips as a beautiful passage on posthumous fame was read out by Thomson, son of the well-known minister and landscape painter of Duddingston, who was one of the group.

Christopher North was honoured certainly in his own country, and the *Noctes*, as Brimley called them, the best magazine articles ever written, were often discussed with real enjoyment by men and boys in the days that are past. The Professor dined occasionally with my father, who generally contrived to have some of his own friends to meet him. He was certainly excellent company, and poured forth a stream of genial talk. 'I am a great corrupter of youth,' he said on one of these occasions, as he took me into the back drawing-room, and discoursed most eloquently on Wordsworth, Burns, and Carlyle. 'Thomas,' he said, 'is a grand creature; his descant on Edward Irving is delicious.' 'Oh, if he would always write as he does on Burns, what a difference it would make to all of us! It's a pity he is so crabbed, and his dear little wife had a bad time of it when he was living at Comely Bank. Jeffrey, who was one of the best of fellows in the world, was always trying to help Thomas and Mrs. Thomas, but Thomas was like the man who said "I will be drowned and nobody shall save me." He'll be very famous one of these days. *Past and Present* is wonderful. John Lockhart thinks his picture of Abbot Sampson as good as anything in Scott;' and in this way he would run on, always kindly, always encouraging, and delighting me with his praise and appreciation of my father, for whom he had a real regard. At a dinner given in honour of the famous portrait - painter, Sir John Watson Gordon, the Professor proposed my father's health, and wound up with the words, 'He is the very soul of truth.' I hope I may be pardoned for recalling this scene, at which I was not present, but which was referred to more than once in conversation by one of my father's oldest friends, Lord Meadowbank, as an admirable instance of Wilson's power of saying the right thing at the right time.

A delightful trait in Wilson's character was his hearty appreciation of great writers. He spoke of Milton and Spenser with an almost personal affection, and I have heard him predict what has certainly come to pass, that Wordsworth would one day be classed along with them, although, to use his own phrase 'he mixed too much milk with his cream.' There was something very infectious about his fun. 'Oh breathe not the name,' he said, when his brother-in-law, Sir John MacNeill, wanted to tell him the nickname his students gave him, and then with a droll aside, 'I daresay it is nothing more than old Kit North.' I once heard him say that he thought Lockhart's character of Scott at the end of the *Life* perhaps the most touching piece of English prose he knew. 'But I place very near it,' he said, 'the close of Southey's *Life of Nelson*, a grand bit of English.' I wish I could remember what I once heard him remark about Jeremy Taylor, but at the time I knew little of the rich treasures of that great Divine.

The biographer of Jeffrey, who has left interesting memorials of his own time, Henry Cockburn, was a man who never failed to impress boys and young men. There was a certain rusticity in his appearance, but he was in reality a true gentleman of the old school. He possessed that most delightful of arts, in common with many of the celebrities I have known, of putting you at once at your ease, and making you feel that you were talking your best. When he spoke of Ovid to a school-boy, or his favourite Tacitus to a youth from College, he managed somehow to convey his own real enthusiasm for the beauties of the authors he loved in such a way as to send you back determined to read more diligently and thoroughly. To see Lord Cockburn in his glory, skating on Duddingston Loch, was a grand sight. He thoroughly enjoyed the throng, the keen air and the admiration of old and young. Soon after the Eglinton tournament I met him in the Princes Street Gardens, and he insisted on hearing from me a long story of the last day, the grand procession, and when I had ended my enthusiastic account I remember how he said, 'I look on it as a great folly, but I think I should like to have been there after all.' Many years afterwards I had a long walk with him when he visited my father at his country place. He talked much of

Macaulay and Jeffrey, and gave me admirable advice as to reading, but 'Remember,' he said, 'I am like a young lady in Miss Austen's novel who was a capital hand in drawing up lists of books which she never read.' Although Cockburn was a keen partisan, he was thorough and kindly in his judgments of those opposed to him. He said good things with a quiet humour quite irresistible. On one occasion I heard him say of a young lady who had been recently engaged, and who was said to look pensive, 'Oh, she is only demure.' D. Mure, afterwards an eminent judge, was the happy man who had secured the hand of the lady.

Cockburn and his fame have passed away. The reputation of great advocates and judges is very transient, and there are few now living who can remember the shy and almost retiring Lord Mackenzie, the son of the 'Man of Feeling,' an eminent judge and a most delightful companion. He had two sons of great promise, who died early, beloved and lamented by many. Like his brother judge, Cockburn, Mackenzie was a real lover of books. He read regularly and steadily, especially history. Lord Fullarton was another distinguished man, brother-in-law of Cockburn, a most fastidious critic and real lover of the classics. Maitland, who was for a short time a judge, had a splendid and well chosen library. He was a most kind and friendly man, and delighted to find in me a friend of his son's, and a taste for books. I looked with awe and reverence on the complete set of Jeffrey's reviews, which long before any of them were reprinted he had made for himself, having got from the author a full list, and to achieve this result he must have destroyed a set of the review. His choice reprints of Herrick and Carew are witnesses of his taste and feeling.

But I must not linger longer among the recollections of these remarkable ornaments of Edinburgh society, happy then in the distinction of having among its members men of wit and spirit, like Peter Robertson, Charles Neaves, and Douglas Cheape, men of culture and learning, such as George Moir, Spalding, and Aytoun, and others such as Sir William Hamilton and James Forbes, professors whose lectures and conversation were often in the mouths of admiring students. I had every now and then a glimpse of Macvey Napier, the editor of the *Edinburgh Review*. I often heard of the troubles he had in adjusting the claims of Brougham and Macaulay. One night my mother, sitting next him at dinner, expressed her anger at the way in which Mr. Croker had handled Madame D'Arblay's Diary in the *Quarterly*. 'I shall write to Mr. Macaulay,' said Napier, 'and try to get him to give me a review of the book, which will, I hope, please you better.' When Macaulay's delightful article appeared, Mrs. Maitland, at whose house the conversation with Napier had taken place, rallied me on my mother having been the means of getting Macaulay to write the article, in which it

must be confessed the stinging sentences about
Croker preserve for ever the spitefulness of the
great historian. Lockhart, in my hearing, once
spoke of Macaulay's words in very strong language,
though Lockhart was by no means a great admirer
of Croker.

I must not fail to mention a very eminent man,
who in the later years of his life treated me with
great kindness, Lord Rutherfurd. For many
years Rutherfurd occupied an almost unique position as Lord Advocate and Member of Parliament.
He was an admirable speaker, and although his
manner was somewhat affected, he was able to cast
a spell over his hearers so that every fault was
forgotten in his earnest advocacy. One day I
heard him distinguish himself in a remarkable way
in a speech delivered before my father and his
Court. His opponent was John Inglis, who was for
many years Lord Justice-Clerk and Lord Justice-
General. When we walked home when the day
was over my father said to me, 'You have been in
luck to-day, two better speeches were seldom
heard; Rutherfurd was at his best, and Inglis
showed wonderful promise.' When in 1841 my
father became Lord Justice-General (a distinction
which would have been Rutherfurd's had President
Hope retired during the life of Lord Melbourne's
ministry), Rutherfurd, to the delight of all my
father's friends, proposed a resolution at the meeting
of the Bar, in touching and eloquent terms. Indeed

the friendly relations between him and my father were a proof that in the elder man political partisanship had been forgotten, and that Rutherfurd was absolutely incapable of entertaining any other feeling than warm affection. In private life he was delightful. He told stories admirably, and without any ostentation gave you the results of reading and his really wonderful scholarship. When Macaulay's *History* appeared he overflowed with admiration.

I sometimes lent Lord Rutherfurd books in which I was interested. Conington's *Agamemnon*, and Donaldson's *Antigone*, I remember, interested him much, and I was rewarded by being asked to his house to meet for the first time Thackeray, who was then delivering lectures in Edinburgh. The only other person present besides the present Lord Wemyss, who joined us for a short time, was a brother judge of Lord Rutherfurd's, Lord Ivory, and after luncheon I enjoyed such a treat as seldom falls to the lot of a young man. I never saw Thackeray more at his ease, and he gave us in the simplest and pleasantest way passages of his struggles as an author, and dwelt with real pathos on John Sterling's encouragement of him after reading *The Great Hoggarty Diamond*. Dryden, Marlborough, Pope, Carlyle, Dickens, Tennyson, were all reviewed and discussed. There was no asperity in Thackeray's estimate of his brother novelist, although he admitted what I suppose few will deny, Dickens' inability to deal with high life. Guthrie, who was at that time the most celebrated preacher in Edinburgh, Thackeray greatly admired. He was a favourite also of Lord Rutherfurd, who told us, I remember, that he had heard Chalmers preach a famous sermon on the 'Expulsive power of a new affection,' and that it had made him feel that there was after all no power like the power of the pulpit, no motive so strong as religion.

Lord Rutherfurd was an admirable Italian scholar. I have heard Sir James Lacaita declare that he and Mr. Gladstone were the only two Englishmen he had ever known who could conquer the difficulty of obsolete Italian dialects, and the late Lord Arthur Russell, many years after Lord Rutherfurd's death, gave me in letters which I still possess, much curious information as to some out-of-the-way Italian books Rutherfurd was fond of reading and quoting. Twice in his life the great prize of his profession seemed almost within his grasp. But it was not to be. With great dignity he submitted to his fate, showing no temper or disappointment. When my father retired in 1852 he received a most kindly and affectionate letter from the man who a year before would certainly have succeeded him, instead of the judge who was afterwards known as Lord Colonsay. In the Dean Cemetery at Edinburgh there is a classical memorial of this distinguished man. He had no children, but a nephew, Lord Rutherfurd Clark, still lives to remind many of one of the most illustrious of Edinburgh Whigs. Lord Robertson, the friend of Lockhart, a real wit and most delightful companion, once admitted to me in the course of a journey that there were very few men he had ever known so completely armed *cap-à-pie* as Rutherfurd.

I must now approach a subject which it is difficult to handle, the religious aspect of Edinburgh in my boyhood and youth. I am very anxious to avoid any exaggeration, but it is hard for those to whom religious questions have always had a peculiar interest to be moderate in expression. It was my good fortune in my own home to witness in both parents a strong power of belief and practice. My father attended the church of St. Andrew's in Edinburgh, where the services, conducted by two elderly men, were certainly not attractive to young people. Dr. Ritchie and Dr. Grant had been able men in their day, and the congregations were large and steadfast. I had relations who were Episcopalians, and the occasional visits to St. John's Chapel made me early in life an admirer of liturgical worship, and the very persuasive sermons of Dean Ramsay gave me an inclination for ministry in the English Church. I had, however, what I consider the great privilege of Bible teaching from Dr. Candlish and Dr. Muir, men who took different sides in the

Ten Years' conflict of the Established Church in Scotland, men, too, who by their intense faith and perfect knowledge of the Bible had the gift of unfolding the gradual development of truth in the Old and New Testaments in a way quite unequalled.

In my youth the transition from the Presbyterian body to the Episcopalian was easily effected. There were cordial relations maintained by the chiefs of both Churches. I have seen on the platform, where the cause of Ragged Schools was advocated, Bishop Terrot and Dean Ramsay side by side with Dr. Guthrie and Dr. Crawford. Occasionally my father would go to Dean Ramsay's church to hear an eloquent preacher, and members of my family educated in England became members of the Church of England, while they did not altogether desert the worship of their forefathers. Differences are now strongly accentuated, but I often feel that the generous and kindly spirit which animated Dean Ramsay, when he wrote for the Royal Society of Edinburgh an excellent memoir of Dr. Chalmers, and the kindly feeling which showed itself in the list of books given to me by Dr. Muir when I left Edinburgh for Charterhouse School, consisting almost entirely of books by English divines, and also encouraging a study of Pascal and Fénelon, were delightful evidences of true faith and a grand moral attitude.

Never can I forget the impression made upon

me by breakfasts at Dr. Muir's. At the time I knew him first he was a widower. A widowed sister and a cousin lived with him. He had two sons, both afterwards eminent as ministers of the Church of Scotland. The whole atmosphere of the household was calm and peaceful. Dr. Muir was a man of great dignity of manner, and his simple reverence in conducting family prayer made a deep impression. There was a gentle manliness if I may venture so to call it, about him, which made his simple counsels tell. 'Try to read a few verses of your Bible every day; say a short psalm like the twenty-third as you lay your head on your pillow; pray for your friends; do not forget me sometimes, I shall not forget you.' Words like these spoken to a boy, soon to be launched into a new scene, were not likely to escape the memory.

In after years I had many glimpses of this good man's life and conversation, and the kindness of his widow (he married a second time very happily) admitted me to the knowledge of a diary which he kept carefully for many years, and which if it had ever been published, would have heightened the high opinion which all men who knew Dr. Muir well, had of his character. He managed his great parish and congregation for years with wonderful fidelity and success. It has been thought by some, that in his old age he was not sufficiently tolerant of certain changes in the order of public service, and in doctrinal matters. But in the years when I knew him best, I saw nothing but large-heartedness and real breadth of feeling, and I well remember how he spoke of a service which he had been present at in England in the church of one with whom he had little in common, as showing a unity of devotion which we have not, he said, attained to in Scotland.

A talk with Dean Ramsay in his study was great delight. He was a very pleasant companion, and though perhaps somewhat timid in expressing his real sentiments, he was in the best sense of the word a man of real breadth. He had great influence with many persons of distinction and rank. I know instances of the fearless attitude he maintained when called upon to deliver his mind in family matters, when principle and morality were involved. At one time of my life I was deeply imbued with the views of Pusey and Newman, and began to have grave doubts as to the position of the English Church. A letter of Frederick Denison Maurice's in the *Christian Remembrancer*, at that time a monthly magazine, had attracted me, and I happened to mention it to Dean Ramsay, who strongly recommended me to read Maurice's *Kingdom of Christ*, which he said had been greatly praised by Mr. Gladstone. The character of Gladstone, his extraordinary interest in theology and his possible political future, were themes on which Dean Ramsay delighted to dilate. Although he had a sincere admiration for his friend, he said that he detected in him a vein of vanity, and on one occasion I heard him utter a remarkable prophecy— it was when Mr. Gladstone quitted Sir Robert Peel's government on the question of Maynooth— that William Gladstone would cause a good deal of trouble to a good many people before his career was over. Sir John Gladstone made a remark of a similar kind to my father, who expressed to him his regret at the step that his son had taken, in embarrassing Sir Robert Peel, 'I am afraid my son's mind is such, my lord, that he will give a great many people the same trouble he has given Sir Robert.'

At a dinner party at Dean Ramsay's, the late Duke of Buccleuch gave me an account of the way in which the Dean had helped him by advice, in all sorts of difficulties, public as well as private. The Duke, as is well known, stood by Sir Robert Peel on the question of the corn laws, and always entertained the hope that the schism in the Conservative party might one day be healed, by the return of the Peelites to the body of the party. 'Very shortly,' said the Duke, 'before Sir Robert Peel's death he expressed to me his belief that Sidney Herbert or Gladstone would one day be premier; but,' added the Duke, 'Peel said with sarcasm, "if the hour comes, Disraeli must be made Governor-General of India. He will be a second Ellenborough."' This, I think, was said in 1851, the year after Peel's death.

Every one except myself present at that dinner

party is now passed away. It was given in honour
of two English divines, Archdeacon Grant and
Ernest Hawkins, who came to Edinburgh to advocate the cause of the Society for the Propagation
of the Gospel. For many years Ramsay's house
was the pleasant meeting-place of many who were
widely separated in opinion. He numbered among
his friends all who were best known in Edinburgh
for learning and talent, and he certainly knew the
secret of imparting elevation of thought and faith,
as well as he did the stores of racy anecdotes which
have made him so familiar to many.

It is time for me to close my brief account of this
period of my life, but I must not forget the kindly
encouragement I had 'to read, mark, learn and
inwardly digest' great books of great men, from
Sir Archibald Alison, who sometimes paid my
father a visit at his country place, and who was
always a most kind adviser in literature. Alison's
generous appreciation of the writings of his contemporaries was a marked feature of his character.
Indeed, his eulogies were sometimes excessive. He
exhorted me to make the French Revolution a real
study. 'Carlyle's book, Burke, Thiers, and all the
memoirs you can lay your hands upon you ought to
make your own.' When I told him how I had
enjoyed his own early volumes, he said, 'They
ought to have been a great deal better, but I am
too busy to write them again.'

I remember another of Alison's sayings, 'There

is no style like Southey's, his *Life of Nelson* is almost perfect, and I love his *Wesley* and bits of *The Doctor* quite as much as I do Addison.' And again, 'I think *Eothen* shows more power in style than any book of travel I have ever read; but there are beautiful bits in *Anson's Voyage*. The passage which suggested Cooper's *Castaway* is quite perfect. I think *Letters from the Baltic*, and Borrow's *Bible in Spain* are gems of the first water.' But I must not say more of one who was a delightful host, and who was good enough when he last saw me to express a belief that I should live to be a bishop or a dean.

There was another remarkable man, a distant relation of my family, William Mure of Caldwell, who from a very early period of my life gave me the benefit of his wide reading and great culture. Mure's first publication *A Tour in Greece*, showing real familiarity with the authors, to whom he gave the best part of his life, I read eagerly, and when he found that I was interested he talked freely on the subjects next his heart. He was fond of telling what he dwells upon in his history of Greek literature, that he had once been a slavish follower of Wolf's, but had convinced himself at last that the *Iliad* and *Odyssey* were the work of one man, and that all other theories must be abandoned. Many years afterwards I was permitted to see the proof-sheets of the first three volumes of Mure's work. Those who saw him only in society formed a very

erroneous estimate of the real man. Under a cold
and perhaps haughty exterior there was real warm-
heartedness. He was never, when in Parliament,
an ardent partisan, and had perhaps rather what
was called a cross-bench mind. During many years
of residence abroad he formed a great friendship
with Bunsen. Bunsen guided his German reading,
and Mure diligently read everything illustrative of
Greek literature. He was unfortunately a slow
reader, and his book, alas! remains a fragment. It
has always been a great regret to me that I did
not keep an accurate diary, for if the many conversations I have had with William Mure on
Homer, the Greek dramatists and historians, had
been faithfully recorded, it would have been a
monument of his extraordinary reading and his
wonderful taste. In a long walk I once had with
him at his own place at Caldwell, he expatiated on
the undue neglect of Euripides, and made me
heartily ashamed of holding the popular superstition as to his merits.

Mure's taste in poetry was thoroughly catholic.
One evening at Caldwell a Mr. Dobie, a man of
some learning, repeated the greater part of Edgar
Poe's poem of 'The Raven.' The younger among
the company were half inclined to ridicule the
pretensions of Mr. Dobie's American poet, who at
that time was perfectly unknown in England, but
Mure said with some severity, ' Depend upon it
you are all wrong ; that is one of the most wonderful

things I have heard for many a long day.' When Tennyson had hardly achieved any great position, Mure said of his *Ulysses*, 'The man who wrote that has made himself perfectly master of Homer's characters, and he has made Ulysses to live again.' One of the last times I saw Mure was in London, and I went with him to the Prussian Embassy, where he left a card for the Prince of Prussia, who after the revolutionary troubles in Berlin had taken refuge in Bunsen's house. 'I'm afraid,' said Mure, 'that the career of this good prince is at an end,' but the end was not yet, and Mure would have been astonished if at that time some far-seeing prophet had foretold the unity of Germany, and the capitulation of Sedan.

The last days of Mure's life were days of sadness. He was worn by pain and his powers of speech failed him. The expression of his eyes, like those of the dying Agricola, desired something, and that something was found in a large printed copy of the well-known hymn, 'Rock of Ages,' which had been displayed a few days before by one of his family. He passed peacefully away after he had read the familiar words.

I had intended to say something of one of the great pleasures of my early days, occasional visits to the Edinburgh Theatre, where Mr. W. Murray (the brother of Mrs. Henry Siddons) for many years filled the part of manager and chief actor. But Mrs. Kemble, in her interesting records of her early life, has so well depicted the trials and successes of the Edinburgh stage, that it would be almost an impertinence to attempt any recollections. While life lasts, however, will last the memory of Murray's exquisite renderings of the parts of Sir Anthony Absolute, Dominique the Deserter, and Grandfather Whitehead. There was an ease, a grace, a playfulness, a gentlemanliness in Murray's acting quite inimitable. For years he kept a tolerable company together, and when Charles Kean appeared and acted all his great characters, or Helen Faucit came out in the *Antigone* of Sophocles, it was quite marvellous to see how the clever manager made the most of his materials, and condescended (for I can use no other word) to play himself a minor part, like that of a witch in Macbeth, in order to secure something like efficiency. He was greatly delighted when a special evening was devoted to what was called the Advocates' Play, and when the head of the Courts came to see *Redgauntlet* and hear the capital prologue, the joint composition of two of the wits of the Scottish bar, spoken by a well-known actor, Mackay, in the character of Peter Peebles. This goodly custom was continued, I believe, for many years during the management of Murray, who certainly conferred much enjoyable pleasure on the young people of my generation.

There is no place so dear to an inquisitive boy fond of books as a bookseller's shop, and on the very day on which I thought I must write to Mr. Stevenson to ask him if he had any objection to my mentioning him and his shop in Princes Street, I saw in the obituary of the *Times* a brief notice that his long life had ended. In the days when I knew him best, his shop, which was all but a cellar, was constantly visited by Charles K. Sharpe, James Maidment, W. Turnbull, and also by one who was at that time a young man engaged in business in Edinburgh, the now celebrated Sir Theodore Martin.

Sir Theodore Martin will not, I hope, object to my recalling a prophecy which Stevenson delivered, when Martin had shown him an article in *Tait's Magazine*, somewhat in the style of *Noctes Ambrosianæ*, and containing a few of the well-known ballads of the Bon Gaultier collection. 'That's a clever birkie, and he'll make himself a name like Christopher North, or John Lockhart,' and then he poured forth story after story of Wilson and De Quincey, and added 'Aytoun and Martin will keep the ball ganging.' Stevenson, however, was more than a mere reader of magazine articles. He had a real knowledge of Scottish history, and from him I learnt much of the wonderful lore, possessed by John Riddell, Thomas Thomson, Cosmo Innes, William Skene, and John Hill Burton, men who have made their mark as skilled antiquarians, and real delvers into antiquity. Stevenson once made me buy a copy of a little book called *Deliciæ Literaræ* which he told me was of great merit, but said that he must not disclose the author's name. I have lost the book, but I believe that it was really written by Joseph Robertson. I heard Stevenson, many years before the detection of the Payne Collier folio, express a doubt as to Collier's honesty, grounded upon a suspicion that Rodd the bookseller would never have let Collier carry away a book which contained original matter at a small price. Charles Sharpe and Stevenson had many a wrangle over old books, and I have often listened to the high-pitched voice of Sharpe exclaiming against the price which he was charged for some coveted treasure.

. Edinburgh has always been rich in physicians— men too who united love of literature with other studies. The high character of Abercrombie showed itself in the books which are now unknown to this generation. But the name of Dr. John Brown will be preserved for many a year, for there is a charm and a witchery in his writings, and indeed much of what Matthew Arnold calls true distinction ; and yet these graces can never give, to those who knew him not, the intense, the romantic feeling which seemed to hover like an atmosphere around him, and made many and many a hearer of his delightful conversation feel, as I heard Thackeray once express himself after a long eulogy on the goodness and greatness of Scott, 'it is good for us to be here.'

CHAPTER III

1843-1853—I join Charterhouse—A first visit to Westminster Abbey—
The de Veres—My first evening at School—My contemporaries at the
Charterhouse—Sir Robert Peel and Disraeli—The Opera—Macready
at Drury Lane—Three words from the Great Duke.

THERE is a beautiful passage in Southey's *Doctor* in
which he speaks of the chances and dangers of a
public school. The time came when I changed the
pleasant life of a day scholar who had all the full
enjoyment of a pleasant home, for the very different
experience of the old School of Charterhouse. Had
Arnold lived I should probably have gone to Rugby,
but in the year 1843, when I was nearly fifteen,
some doubt had been expressed as to the success of
Tait as a head master, and I was sent to Charterhouse, then ruled over by a great scholar, a friend
of some of my family, Saunders, afterwards Dean of
Peterborough.

No one can leave a school where he has made fast
friendships without regret, and the contrast between
an old life and a new was in my case very sharp.
Under the care of an elder brother, whose unbroken
friendship I enjoyed for many a year, on a dismally
cold morning on the 16th of January, and with a
heavy heart, I said good-bye to Edinburgh. At

that time the journey to London was a long
business. The misery of the long winter day, not
relieved by the sensation of crossing the Border for
the first time, the hastily eaten coach dinner, the
cold of Shap Fell, and the wretched cup of coffee
swallowed at one o'clock in the morning, before
entering the London train at Lancaster, stand out
vividly in memory after many years. London was
reached in twelve hours from Lancaster, and the
drive from Euston Square to an hotel in Cockspur
Street, the stir, the bustle, the roar of London life,
made me feel a new chapter in life had begun.

After an excellent meal we went to the National
Gallery, and I looked for the first time on the
'Banished Lord' of Sir Joshua, a Correggio and a
Gainsborough, with which I had long been familiar
in the engravings of the two volumes dedicated to
the National Gallery. That evening a most accomplished critic, Mr. Cautley, whom I met for the first
time at the house of an eminent engineer, where we
dined, rallied me on being far more enthusiastic
about the full-length pictures of John Kemble and
his sister, than the 'Market Cart' of Gainsborough,
and what he called the delicious landscape of
Rubens. The evening was a delightful one. The
host had gathered round him some friends who
went afterwards to hear his address at the Institu-
tion of Civil Engineers. Something was said about
Eton, and Mr. William Cotton, then Governor of
the Bank of England, quoted with admiration one

of the stanzas of Gray's famous ode. This brought out, in strong opposition to Gray's gloomy view of life, a protest from Professor Wheatstone, who was one of the guests. To my delight quotation followed quotation. Colonel Brandreth, I remember, said to Mr. Cautley, 'After all, there are very few poets like Gray, everybody ought to have the Elegy and this Ode by heart.' Mr. Cautley, who was a very little man, turned kindly to me and said, 'I daresay you know a good deal of it,' and I assured him that to learn the greater part of it by heart had been a real grief and pain in past years. 'There is a new poet arisen in England,' added Mr. Cautley, 'Alfred Tennyson,' and he expressed pleasure in finding that I knew 'Dora' and the 'Lord of Burleigh' well, from the review in the *Quarterly*. 'Ah! he said, ' that review was written by John Sterling, Edward Sterling's (of the *Times*) son ; poor fellow ! I fear he has not many months to live. He is a poet himself, too, and there is a charming song in his tragedy of *Strafford*.' I had never heard of Sterling before, but in after years, when I became familiar with the figure preserved for us by Julius Hare and in Carlyle's immortal biography, I remembered Mr. Cautley's words. Before he left the house that evening he most kindly offered to take me to Westminster Abbey next day, and told me that Monckton Milnes had lately said, very happily, that Westminster Abbey was a part of the British Constitution. 'I shall show you, too,' he said, 'Addison's tomb, for he, you know (which I certainly did not know), was what you are going to be, a Carthusian.'

I knew Washington Irving's paper on Westminster Abbey well, and was eager to see one of the tombs he mentions. The first sight of the Abbey is indeed to be remembered. From the door in the Cloisters, bearing the name of the Reverend H. H. Milman, the Canon himself walked out, and I looked with awe and reverence on the author of *The Fall of Jerusalem* and the hymns I had known in the small volume by Heber and himself.

When the visit to the Abbey was over, Mr. Cautley said to the daughter of his host of the former evening, 'Be sure and get young Aubrey de Vere's poems, the best things out since Alfred Tennyson's. The lines, "There was silence in the heavens," are quite exquisite.' I inwardly digested his words and resolved that the two first books I should buy would be Walton's *Lives*, strongly recommended to me by my kind Edinburgh friend, Dr. Muir, and *The Waldenses* of Aubrey de Vere; and in a month I carried out my intention. I have never been able to understand why de Vere's poetry has never gained a hold on the public. Henry Taylor, in a well-known review in the *Quarterly*, did his best to introduce the early poems of his friend to the general public, and if I am not mistaken, Lord Selborne, in the *British Critic*, praised highly the work of Sir Aubrey de Vere, and his son, Aubrey de Vere, has always had a certain audience, and at last, in the year I am writing in, a volume of Selections is becoming popular. Few men have ever in their generation shown such true critical insight as this gifted man, one of three brothers, distinguished by the purity of their taste and the elevation of their lives. With the elder brother of Sir Stephen and Aubrey de Vere, Sir Vere, for many years I enjoyed a true friendship, and many delightful walks and talks have we had, when Wordsworth and Tennyson, Montalembert and Lacordaire, were the themes of our discourse. The late Lord Emly once said in my hearing, 'The friendship of the de Veres is one of the greatest gifts God has ever given me.'

The contrast from the inspiring conversation of Mr. Cautley and what I went through in the next few hours, was a contrast indeed. My brother, who was unwell, was unable to go with me to Charterhouse. I arrived much too soon, and after a few kinds words from the head - master, who was playing with his child, I was dismissed to the care of the matron, who evidently wished me at Jericho, and who was counting over a vast mass of towels. The head-master had forty boys in his house, and by special favour I was added to the number, an addition which the worthy matron hardly approved, as she told me when we discussed a very scanty tea. There are desolations and desolations in the world, and I confess I felt the

full force of the word when I took my first solitary
ramble round the upper and lower green, and
entered the brick cloister, where many a good
game of hockey was enjoyed in after days. A
good-natured fellow who looked after the shoes
and clothes of the boarders showed me the chapel,
lately restored, and I looked with awe on the
quaint tomb of the founder, the worthy Thomas
Sutton, and the motto, '*Deo dante dedi*,' conspicuous
in the building. In 1863 I sat in the chapel on
Founder's Day, close to Thackeray, and as we went
up-stairs he said to me, 'What makes you look so
grave?' 'I was thinking,' I replied, 'of the first
time I saw the chapel twenty years ago.' He
spoke, I remember, with feeling, of his own early
days, as we went into the Governors' room to hear
the oration. When the dinner was over,—where he
made a capital speech,—I had again some talk with
him, and he asked me to come and dine with him
when I next came to London; but in a fortnight
after this the great novelist went into the silent
land.

The first evening of a new boy at school is not
altogether pleasant. Questions have to be answered,
and I soon discovered that a boy from Scotland was
looked upon with a certain suspicion. But in the
room where I found myself, number seven, were
some nice good-natured fellows, and nothing that
I have ever eaten in my life was more delicious
than the large cold mince pie distributed all round

by a cheery, pleasant grand-nephew of the famous Sir Astley Cooper, whose life, just published, was placed in the school library by the donor of the pies. By good luck I escaped the privileges of fagging, and was at once put into the Fourth Form, and had to make acquaintance with Horace, Homer, and Demosthenes, under the guidance of a genial and pleasant second master, Oliver Walford, who, during the whole of my schoolboy career, encouraged me with kindly friendliness. The head master's boarders dined along with those of the second master. I suppose, in these luxurious days, fault would be found with the fare, but we flourished under it; the old place was healthy, and I very soon began to feel that it was an honour to belong to a school so ancient and famous. Although our numbers were small, the distinctions won at the Universities were remarkable. In the same year two Balliol scholarships had been gained by the present Archdeacon of Oxford and another Carthusian well known in literature, and from time to time the news of a First-Class or a Hertford or Ireland scholarship procured for us a half-holiday. The three monitors of the head-master's house were all strong characters. One, admired by us all for his high principle, soon left for Oxford. He has been for many a year the faithful pastor of a parish, to which he has been constant: the boy was father of the man. Several years ago the second of the three passed away. He was a man of great power, but his unfortunate health prevented him from gaining high distinction at the Bar. He had a real enthusiasm for the beauties of the classics, and it was from him I first heard praise of Butler's sermons, and remember how he dwelt on Butler's famous description of ' compassion, which is momentary love,' but he never could see anything to admire in Wordsworth, and used to enrage me by quoting certain passages from Byron in support of his opinion.

There has been a completeness and strength in the life of the last of these three monitors, now Master of Charterhouse, altogether unique. At a very early age he found himself in the Sixth Form, where he was at once conspicuous for the thoroughness of his work, and his kindness to all juniors. I had not been many days at Charterhouse when he asked me if I was fond of reading, and it was by his advice that I took out Southey's *Thalaba* from the library, and during the quiet hour from eight till nine after supper, which we called 'sitting in banco,' when my school work was over, I read with keen enjoyment the wild and wondrous tale. But Richard Elwyn, for I must name him, did more for me than this. In his study I saw a well-read copy of Nichols' *Help to reading the Bible*. He advised me to get the book, to master it, and to read certain parts of both Testaments in the way the book recommended, and I can safely say that from the time I possessed it, and tried to follow his advice, I have found a never-failing source of real and intense pleasure from what has been the chief employment of my life. For a time this distinguished man reigned as head - master. Health gave way, but he recovered and did admirable work at York in the great school, and as Vicar of Ramsgate. As Master of Charterhouse he finds time to devote many an hour to public service for the good of the Church, and is held in high honour by all who know how to value noble character and true unselfishness.

We Charterhouse boys had many advantages. We were in touch with the outer world of life and literature. 'Going out' Saturdays and Sundays spent with friends in London or near it, were not only real refreshments but educational helps. Those were stirring years. Few, however, had such remarkable opportunities as I had, of knowing something of the currents of thought in literary, religious and political waters. In the three houses to which I had constant access, I saw, from time to time, men of science, men of letters, and occasionally clergymen, all men of mark, and all deeply interested in the progress of the Oxford movement.

I must add a few particulars of this deeply interesting time. At the house of an M.P., at that time a thorough supporter of Sir Robert Peel's, I sometimes saw members of the government, and heard much of the political gossip of the day. Faithful Conservatives as they were, they often regretted that there was no house where social pleasures could be enjoyed, and politics freely discussed, as in the palmy days of Holland House. Peel was admired and feared. In the judgment of some of his devoted followers, he kept himself aloof too much, although it was admitted by all that he encouraged younger men, such as Gladstone, Herbert, Lord Lincoln, Lord Dalhousie, and one or two more. Very soon after the height of his popularity as a Prime Minister had been reached, there came a reaction. Some determined Protectionists looked with suspicion on his attitude as regarded the Corn Laws, but the first symptoms of revolt showed themselves on the question of the permanent endowment of Maynooth, and many a discussion did I hear between some who supported the Premier, and those who followed the lead of Sir Robert Inglis and Colquhoun, at that time a prominent Conservative M.P., and a favourite at Exeter Hall.

Once or twice I was present at the House of Commons when there was good speaking. Graham and Follett seemed to my untutored taste the perfection of persuasive orators. Sir Robert himself did not make such an impression. The vivacity and charm of Charles Buller I admired so much, that Mr. Wodehouse, then M.P. for Norfolk, said once to me, 'Charles Buller will very soon make a regular Whig of you,' and told a good story of a visit Buller had paid at Oxford, when he said, 'a week more of All Souls', and I think I should turn Tory.' It was certainly very pleasant to hear, at my kind friend Mr. Packe's dinner-table, the free and unrestrained talk of the M.P.'s. When *Coningsby* appeared there were many attempts to name the originals of some of the characters, and lamentations were uttered about Sir Robert's determination not to offer office to Disraeli. History might have been different had Disraeli been made Under Secretary for Foreign affairs. For divers reasons George Smythe, afterwards Lord Strangford, was chosen. He was not a success as an official, and it is quite probable that if Disraeli had been in his place, his views as to Peel's great change might have been modified.

It was interesting to see Peel and some members of his government on Sundays at Whitehall Chapel, listening attentively to the sermons of the Oxford or Cambridge preacher. H. G. Liddell, afterwards Dean of Christ Church, preached once on the text 'Stretch forth thine hand.' 'One of the most remarkable sermons I have ever heard,' said Peel to a friend as he left the chapel, and on my telling this to Mr. Packe, he said, 'I daresay Sir Robert will put Liddell's name on his Bishop list.' During Peel's reign of office Archdeacon Lonsdale, then Principal of King's College, was made Bishop of Lichfield. One of the members of Parliament I met frequently at that time, after praising the appointment, said he believed Lonsdale would be a real 'Father in God.' Such indeed did I find him during seven years I passed in his diocese. He made me a Rural Dean, and to his good opinion I owed the offer of an important Bishopric in Australia, which I declined for various reasons.

Occasional visits to the House of Commons were not the only kindnesses I received from my M.P. friend and his wife. Devoted lovers of music and frequenters of the opera, it was their delight to introduce me to the pleasure of hearing the great operas, where Grisi, Mario, Lablache, and afterwards Jenny Lind, played their parts with matchless power. Under their auspices, too, I saw Macready in many of his best parts, at the time when he was making a gallant effort to improve the morals of the theatre, and raise the taste of the public. It was impossible to have *Much Ado about Nothing* more finely presented than I have seen it at Drury Lane, when Macready, Anderson, Phelps, Compton and Keeley were acting, and when the principal female parts were filled by Miss Fortescue (afterwards Lady Gardner) and Mrs. Nisbet (afterwards Lady Boothby), and when one of the gentlewomen, Margaret, was Miss Farebrother, known afterwards as the wife of a royal duke. When I add that on the night I saw this delightful rendering, the after-piece was Milton's *Comus*, with Miss Faucit as 'The Lady,' I think it would be acknowledged that the evening was one well worthy of being remembered, though '’Tis fifty years since.'

Once, as I was leaving the opera, a great piece of good luck befel me. Lady Shelley, who was on very intimate terms with the Duke of Wellington, asked me to go and see if the Duke's carriage was waiting. I found that it was so, and received from the Duke, who was escorting Lady Douro, 'Thank 'ee, sir.' 'What a lucky beggar you are,' was the exclamation of a Charterhouse friend to whom I told my adventure with high glee, 'to have had three words from the great Duke.' At conversaziones in the house of Mr. Walker, who was president of the Society of Civil Engineers, I once or twice heard a few words fall from the veteran lips. Mr. Walker possessed a fine head of Napoleon. The Duke asked who it was by, and said, 'I never saw him but at a distance.' I believe that occasion was at Waterloo, when Napoleon was surrounded by his staff.

At one of the Horticultural Shows at Chiswick, all the members of what was called the 'Young England' party were said to have been present, all in white waistcoats. The present Duke of Rutland is now, I think, the only surviving member of the small body, much ridiculed in *John Bull*, a paper which, however, had fallen from its high estate, when Theodore Hook wrote his stinging lampoons. Even in those days at Charterhouse, there were strong politicians who believed greatly in Disraeli, and predicted for him a brilliant future. I had been brought up to reverence Peel, and many a tussle did I have with school-fellows whose interests were with the clergy and squirearchy. We have lived lately through days of tension, but as far as I can recollect, the bitterness of those who considered themselves betrayed by Peel, was even greater than that which we have had evidence of in the days of a still greater change of opinion.

CHAPTER IV

Recollections of the Oxford Movement—First meeting with John Gibson
    Lockhart—The Iron Duke's doctor—Lockhart and the *Quarterly
    Review*—Rogers: his kindness, social success, and wit—Rogers and
    Sydney Smith—Dean Milman and Bishop Blomfield—Lord Coleridge.

MANY persons, I daresay, will think it highly improper, that Charterhouse schoolboys, whose days ought to have been given to work and play, should be interested in the religious movement which was in full force during my school-days. But it was inevitable. The newspapers were within everybody's reach, and the interest taken in subjects like the condemnation of Dr. Pusey, keenly felt by the under-masters, was shared by thoughtful boys.

I had a friend who spent some of his holidays in an ideal country parsonage, which sent out to Oxford three eminent men, one a great scholar and divine afterwards absorbed into the Church of Rome, another destined to be Lord Chancellor, and the model churchman of his age, and the third to be what he still is, a living ornament of his university. Advice given by one of these three cousins to study William Law's *Serious Call*, was not thrown away on my friend and on myself. We read it together, often went into one of the studies to read the evening psalms and lessons together, borrowed books such as Bowden's *Life of Gregory the Seventh*, read sometimes by stealth some of Newman's *Parochial Sermons*, and went, whenever we could persuade our friends with whom we passed the Sundays to take us, to Margaret Chapel, where Mr. Oakeley and his curate, afterwards the well-known Upton Richards, had introduced a service with Gregorian chanting, almost, with the exception of Portman Chapel and Christ Church, Albany Street, the spheres of work of Bennett and Dodsworth, hitherto unknown in London. I think I see the quaint chapel with its old-fashioned galleries, its queer old sexton, and its devout eager congregation, singing heartily, and distinguished, as an eminent Nonconformist once said, by an enthusiastic unity of devotion. There, sitting together, I once saw W. E. Gladstone, James Hope Scott, Edward Badeley, and Frederick Rogers, afterwards Lord Blachford, and heard, in the street, comments made by one of them on the scandal of Pusey's suspension, and the wrong done by the six doctors.

Oakeley's sermons were vivid and striking. I never heard Newman preach at Margaret Chapel, but I once heard him read the lesson with a wonderfully solemn effect. The impression made on my mind in those days by a rapid reading of James Mozley's essay on 'Lord Strafford' in the *British Critic*, deepened all my feelings and interest in the Oxford movement. I had the good fortune to be the private pupil of one of the under-masters, who encouraged and kept within bounds the tastes of forward pupils. Copies of the *Christian Year* and Newman's *Church of the Fathers* had been given to the library of the headmaster's house, by two brothers, of whose scholarship and attainments we were all proud; and they were eagerly read by those of us who took interest in religious matters. My tutor discussed with myself and a friend who is now an Irish Dean, the literary merits of Keble and Newman, and read to us choice passages from Wordsworth's *Excursion*, and from him we learnt much about the strange meteor of literature, whose *Past and Present* appeared in 1843 and had made men fully alive to the condition-of-England question. How astonished I was to hear that Carlyle was the only man living who could translate Tacitus properly! But I have often thought of my tutor's words when I turn to the close of the *Agricola*, one of his favourite passages. It is a delightful thing to be able to combine a sense of personal obligation with a reverent admiration for some of the best things that have ever been written. The *Bacchæ* of Euripides, the *Clouds* of Aristophanes, the great choruses of Sophocles, Canon Phillott taught me to admire and love; and I can now read with as much pleasure as when I was sixteen, the *Brutus* of Cicero and passages of Jeremy Taylor, which showed, my tutor said, how completely that great divine had entered into the spirit of the ancients.

In our examiners at Charterhouse in those days we were fortunate also. Thomas James, the author of many *Quarterly Review* articles, and a translation of *Æsop*, managed, in his papers of questions and passages set for translation, to show how wide was his reading, and his feeling for all that was attractive and new in literature. In Benjamin Harrison, chaplain to the Primate, we had a deep scholar and theologian. Praise from him was indeed distinction, and I remember his approving smile when I was once able to answer his question, 'Is Beelzebub ever mentioned in the Old Testament?' So good was his memory that, when I met him many years after in Convocation, he actually remembered that I had answered his question when in the fifth form at Charterhouse. Harrison, as the *Life of Pusey* shows, was connected with the early days of the Oxford movement. He was for many years the confidential chaplain of Archbishop Howley. His long residence at Canterbury, as canon, made him a familiar figure in the city and diocese, and Dean Stanley, though he differed from him, admired greatly his independence of character, and dedicated to him his well-known *Memorials of Canterbury*.

During the years of my school life I had many pleasant glimpses of John Gibson Lockhart. At the house of an old relation of my own, John Fullerton, he was a frequent guest. Fullerton was a remarkable man. Early in life he left Scotland and intended to practise as a medical man in India.

He had, however, marked capacities for business, and was taken into a great house where he made a considerable fortune. At one time he resided in Great Stanhope Street, and was fond of entertaining many people famous in literature and political life. He wrote political articles in the *Quarterly Review*, one of which, many years ago, I heard greatly praised by Hallam for its excellent English. Fullerton was obliged to go out again to India in consequence of some misfortunes which overtook the house in which he had an interest, but he returned to spend the latter days of life in London, and, though he could no longer afford to live in his fine house, he was able to indulge in a taste for rare old books, and to entertain his friends in very pleasant style. He was fond of travel, and was certainly one of the best-informed men I have ever known. His criticisms on books and politics were keen and searching. When he found how greatly I admired the *Life of Scott*, when I was his guest during my Whitsuntide holidays, he arranged the dinner at which I had for the first time the happiness of meeting Lockhart, and contrived that I should sit near him. Besides Mr. Fullerton's daughter and niece, two other ladies were guests on this occasion, one the wife of Sir Howard Douglas and the mother of a gifted lady, Mrs. Murray Gartshore, whose charming manner and delightful singing made her a favourite of every circle she joined, the second, Miss Raper, an admirable amateur singer; Mr. Shergold

Boone, a well-known London preacher, who at one time edited the *British Critic*, Dr. Hume (the Duke of Wellington's doctor), and an elder brother of mine, a barrister, completed the party. Lockhart arrived early, and he immediately, on my being introduced to him, began to talk about old days in Scotland, Sir Walter Scott, and various scenes in which my father and mother had taken parts.

The admirable print from a picture of Sir Francis Grant's, and the head which is prefixed to the best illustrated edition of the *Spanish Ballads*, hardly convey the full effect of Lockhart's appearance. He was an exceedingly handsome man, and when he smiled his expression was delightful. There was a lingering Scotch accent which came out as he told stories admirably. The conversation was general, but when the ladies had left the room Mr. Fullerton contrived to extract from Dr. Hume one or two very characteristic anecdotes of the great Duke. He spoke, I remember, of the intense emotion which the Duke showed on hearing of the death of Lord Aberdeen's brother at Waterloo, and said, ' I am not fond of hearing the Duke called the Iron Duke.' Lockhart praised the vigorous style of the Duke's despatches, and Dr. Hume said, ' It seems marvellous to me when I think how quickly they were written !' ' I wish,' said Lockhart, ' the Duke would read Napier's History, and tell the world what to think about it. I know he thinks poorly of Southey's book, and so did old Lynedoch, who declared he could find a mistake in every page.' This led to some talk about Southey, and made Lockhart say to me, when I told him I had never read Southey's *Life of Wesley*, 'I envy you, as I envy the man who has never read *Don Quixote*.'

Mr. Boone spoke to Lockhart of the delight he had experienced in reading the account of Scott's life at Abbotsford, and Lockhart said with great feeling, 'When I finished the *Life*, Mr. Boone, I thought I had made it too long; but when I think of the grand struggle of the last years, I sometimes feel I have been too short. No words,' he said, 'could give you any idea of Scott's pleasantness, and his modesty about his own writings. The only thing he ever owned to having written with any pleasure, was Wandering Willie's tale in *Redgauntlet*, but I think,' said Lockhart, 'he really had great satisfaction in writing things like "To the Lords of Convention," and,' he added with a twinkle in his eye, 'articles for the *Quarterly*.' Dr. Hume said that the only man he had ever heard Byron praise unreservedly, was Walter Scott. Lockhart heard with great interest that Charles Hope, who had been for many years President of the Court of Session, occupied himself in his retirement in re-reading the Waverley Novels, and said to his servant who told him that his carriage was waiting to take him for a drive, 'I must finish *Guy Mannering*.' Lockhart told us of a famous French writer, Villemain, I think, who said, 'I would rather have written the

Bride of Lammermoor than the Dialogues of Plato.'
'Will Scott live?' said Mr. Boone. 'I have no
doubt,' said Lockhart, 'he will suffer eclipse at
times, but I think he has a good chance of being
read by the next generation.' Afterwards, in the
drawing-room, Mr. Boone said to me, 'Johnson lives
in *Boswell,* and I think Lockhart will make Scott a
living figure for many a year to come.' Bishop
Blomfield also remarked to me, 'I think Boswell's
Life of Johnson is the best life in the language, and
Lockhart's *Scott* comes very near it.' But I must
not weary my reader with any more details of this
memorable evening when Lockhart was good enough
to say, 'I hope to meet you soon again, and you
must come and see me at some future time in the
Regent's Park.'

There was certainly in Lockhart a singular power
of creating interest in literature. His judgments,
which I had the pleasure of hearing from time to
time, always seemed to me sane and wise. When
I read a famous criticism on Goethe in the *Edinburgh Review* in 1850, afterwards re-published by
Herman Merivale, I was at once struck by the
resemblance it had to utterances of Lockhart's. He
deplored the influence of Goethe in Germany, and
the increasing strength of Goethe - worship in
England. When he heard that Lewis meditated
a *Life of Goethe,* Lockhart did his best to induce
Hayward to take up the subject, and I have heard
him complain that Hayward was prevented, by the

necessity of producing marketable articles, from undertaking the work.

Lockhart was fond of telling how successful he had sometimes been in obtaining contributions for the *Review* from new hands. He greatly admired the powers of Miss Rigby, afterwards Lady Eastlake, and used to refer to her article on ' German Female Biographies' as a specimen of what an article ought to be. When *Eothen* appeared, Lockhart got Mr. Kinglake to write the first of his two contributions to the *Quarterly*, on the 'Rights of Women,' in which Monckton Milnes's *Palm Leaves* was handled with inimitable drollery, and which contained at its close a passage of almost perfect beauty, often quoted by Lockhart, I believe because it recalled the memory of his wife. I have reason to speak with peculiar gratitude of the way in which Lockhart criticised some very imperfect attempts of my own, and I was indeed proud when he asked me to become a contributor to the *Quarterly*—a distinction, however, which my busy curate's life prevented me from securing. A short article which I wrote on the early poems of Matthew Arnold, and one of the poems of ' V.,' in another review, had the good fortune to attract Lockhart's notice, and win from him some praise. Henry Nelson Coleridge had many years before brought the *Nine poems of V.* before the public. Lockhart admired him greatly and I remember he said, ' V.'s poem on "The Grave' ought to find a place in anthologies of English poetry.' It has done so in Archbishop Trench's *Household Book of Poetry.*

The long list of Lockhart's contributions to the *Quarterly Review*, if ever given to the world, would astonish people by the variety of the subjects. His own early novels and his papers in *Blackwood*, he used to speak of with contempt and regret. I do not think it is at all fair to accuse him of having played the principal part in the *Blackwood* attacks upon Keats, Leigh Hunt, and the other writers of what is called the Cockney school. At least I know that Lockhart rejoiced in the great fame of Keats and Shelley, although he spoke with something like horror of Medwin's unfortunate *Life of Shelley*, and said he dreaded that the appetite for unhealthy gossip might injure the fame of the poet. We have certainly lived to see a most unfortunate revelation of much that even the warmest admirers of Shelley must wish forgotten. 'Literary biography,' Lockhart was in the habit of observing, 'is very ensnaring and ought to be kept within due bounds.' He was angry at the way in which Southey's son wrote his father's *Life*, and there are evidences of his feeling in the article he wrote upon the book, an article perhaps unfair to Southey's literary merits, although highly appreciative of his character as a man.

'Oh that Wordsworth had written less, and knew the difference between prose and poetry!'

was one of Lockhart's trenchant sayings. 'I am very fond of Rogers, but I cannot think that his poetry will last as long as the memory of his breakfasts—Sam is a hard hitter, but he has a kind heart, I know well,' said Lockhart; 'many an unfortunate chiel has he helped over a stile. Do read Mrs. Norton's lines to him, they are as good as the dedication of her *Dream* to the Duchess of Sutherland.'

I do not know if Lockhart was the first who ever uttered a witty saying I heard about a London magnate, 'He has more heart than head, and more manner than either,' but it came with telling force from his lips. He was always very amusing on the subject of Disraeli, and spoke very warmly of some of the political conversations about the change of ministry in *Sybil*. 'They are quite inimitable, and remind me,' he said, 'of a certain countryman of ours, who said when Peel came into power in 1841—"The question of questions is, who will go to the Mint?" and he also quoted a saying of his friend Patrick Robertson, at the same crisis in Scotland, 'The Writers to the Signet are in great perturbation, and one of them shakes his head and says "nothing can be done without a good 'Crown' agent"—the office which he hopes to fill.'

It is a great mistake to suppose that Lockhart was an indifferentist in religion, but I have heard it maintained by those who ought to know better. His friend G. R. Gleig, the chaplain-general, was in the habit of bearing emphatic testimony to the reality of Lockhart's religious opinions. He paid great attention to the progress of the Oxford movement and greatly deplored the influence gained by Ward and T. Mozley over J. H. Newman. 'Gladstone,' he said, 'writes hazily, but he is a considerable divine.' I have heard him say that he thought a chapter in Gladstone's *Church Principles*, on 'Rationalism,' profoundly interesting, and made him wish that Gladstone had taken orders instead of entering Parliament. When his son-in-law, James Hope, left the English Church and took Lockhart's only daughter with him, Lockhart felt the blow severely. Lady Davy told me that she had a terrible scene with him when he knew that the step was inevitable. 'It is going from light into darkness,' he said, 'and as a last attempt I told him (Hope) that I believed he would live to repent it, as I had known an old Oxford friend of my own do.'

The last time I saw Lockhart I told him I was about to take orders. He gave me admirable advice, and said that he believed that if the English Church and her sons would only remember Laud's words, 'The Church of England is not Rome, and it is not a conventicle,' a great future would lie before her. 'My son-in-law and daughter,' he said, 'are not the same as they were in the English Church. They have lost tone, they have lost character, and there is a sort of superstition about them; dear excellent creatures as they are, giving quantities of money away. God bless you, Boyle, and remember that you must never do anything unworthy of your father's son.' A few months after this, I had a letter from him, on my father's death, full of kindness, and soon after that another, telling me that his successor in the editorship of the *Quarterly* was Mr. Whitwell Elwin, ' a man of the truest literary taste.'

Lockhart was always on very friendly terms with Rogers, and indeed he was one of the very few who enjoyed the good opinion of the banker poet. I was twice in Rogers' famous house, and saw something of him in general society. He was certainly a strange mixture of caustic wit and kindly feeling. On one occasion, when his critical estimate of a famous London lady had been attacked, he said, 'There are spots on the sun, but there are very few spots on two of my suns, Lockhart and Milman.'

I think Rogers had a true affection for Walter Scott, and I know that when Scott's great difficulties took place, he generously proffered assistance. He regretted extremely the popularity of Balzac and George Sand in England, and declared no good could come from reading their books. His slow, deliberate way of talking was very impressive : 'I like to see young people eating strawberries and cream, it makes them really happy.'

Everything in his house was choice; the very

forks and spoons had an air of refinement, and the books, many of them bound in Russia leather, were peculiar and fragrant. I often heard of his deeds of kindness, how he would send game, fruit, and a carriage for the use of the wife of an afflicted friend, who only discovered by accident the source of those benefits.

'He is a real friend to many struggling men and women,' said Lockhart one day, when persons were expressing wonder at Rogers' love of society and great people. I have heard men who knew him well say, that he had really been far more courted by great and eminent people than he himself desired to be ; and that he often was sincere in his declaration of preference for a quiet, literary life. Those, however, who saw him the centre of a social circle, scattering his hard, dry sayings freely, as I have seen him at a private exhibition of pictures, could hardly credit this. Rogers has been the hero of many anecdotes. I only put down a few of his sayings, but I have an immense store of his sharp and severe words.

There was to be a fancy ball at Buckingham Palace, and when Monckton Milnes had declared his intention of going as Chaucer, Rogers was heard slily to say, 'I then, I suppose, must go as Dicky Milnes.'

'Mr. B. has red hair, a red face, and a red waistcoat,' said some one to Rogers. 'Everything red about him, except his books,' was the reply.

One day, when Wordsworth was his guest, he was late for breakfast. Rogers went up to see how he was, and said to his guests, 'He dined last night at Sir Robert Harry Inglis', and the consequences are serious. I prevailed upon him to repeat one of his own sonnets. He is recovering prodigiously and will be here directly.'

Although Rogers never spared the foibles of his brother bards, one day when Campbell and Moore were depreciating Wordsworth, Rogers said, 'Depend upon it, when the *Pleasures of Hope*, and the *Pleasures of Memory* and the *Loves of the Angels* are forgotten, Wordsworth's best bits will be remembered;' and on seeing how blank were the looks of the two poets, Rogers good-naturedly added, 'we three, however, enjoy a good circulation.' When Wordsworth had a great triumph at Oxford, Rogers said to Dean Milman, 'I rejoice in this, Jeffrey was quite wrong about Wordsworth; there is something very Miltonic about him.'

Lockhart told me that Rogers was the best judge of English style he knew, and that he once read him a passage, and said, 'Is not this beautiful? Who is it by?' Lockhart said, 'I guess Burke,' but Rogers said, 'No, it is Wordsworth's—from his pamphlet on the *Convention of Cintra.*'

There was always a good deal of sparring between Sydney Smith and Rogers. Rogers disliked any mention of the bank, and when Sydney Smith said to him, 'How are you, Rogers; how is Sharpe (his partner)?' 'He is very well,' said Rogers; 'I owe you half-a-crown, and if you go to the bank he will pay you every iota of it.' This retort could hardly have pleased the canon of St. Paul's, who had incurred some ridicule by saying in public that he believed every iota of the Thirty-nine Articles.

In spite of the jokes of the canon, Rogers had a most sincere admiration for his great powers. I heard Sydney Smith preach twice in St. Paul's, and one of the sermons was one of the most remarkable I ever heard; it was on the preaching of St. John the Baptist. In a very few words Sydney Smith brought out the features of the scene, and there was a manliness and power in his manner and language quite captivating. Archdeacon Hale, the Master of Charterhouse, told me, when I expressed admiration for this sermon, that he had heard it and thought it the very best he had ever listened to from Sydney Smith. Rogers, one of his nieces many years afterwards told me, said of this very sermon, 'South himself could not have beaten it.' One day Lady Dufferin found Rogers in a country house, with a volume of Sydney Smith's sermons in his hand, and said to him, 'What do you think of our friend as a preacher?' 'He is one of the very best I know, he always does me good.'

The contrast between St. Paul's when I heard Sydney Smith preach there and its present condition, is indeed striking. There was a coldness and deadness in the service almost overpowering. The choir boys were careless, the lay clerks looked bored, and whispered to each other, some of the windows were broken, and the vigorous old man in the pulpit was the only lively thing in the building. Happier times have come. St. Paul's is a real centre of noble worship and hearty preaching. The impression made by Liddon and others like him is as remarkable as that produced by Savonarola in Florence. What has been done at St. Paul's since the days when Dean Milman first established special services, and by his successors, Deans Mansel, Church, and Gregory, has raised the whole character of the religious life of England, and made St. Paul's indeed dear to the hearts of this generation.

At a marriage breakfast I once heard Dean Milman make an admirable speech. His sermons at St. Margaret's, when he was canon of Westminster, were often high-flown, but he was always equal to a great occasion. When the Emperor Nicholas was in England, Milman preached in Westminster Abbey a grand sermon full of historical allusions, and containing passages like those in his famous sermon on ' Hebrew Prophecy,' delivered in his old age as a sort of legacy to the University of Oxford. His conversation on literary subjects was most interesting. He too had a wonderful admiration for Scott. ' The *Bride of Lammermoor*,' I once heard him say at the Athenæum, ' has all the grandeur and dignity of a tragedy; it is Scott's noblest work.'

Lockhart was in the habit of saying that the world would never know how greatly it was obliged to him for having made Milman devote himself in his later years to Church history. Although Lockhart did not altogether like the way in which Milman treated the Gospel history in his *History of Christianity*, he was very indignant at the fashion in which Newman treated Milman in the pages of the *British Critic*. 'Some day,' he has often said, 'when Milman brings out his great book on the Papacy, the world will see how completely it has misjudged the writer.' When the essay on *Development* appeared, Milman reviewed it in the *Quarterly*. Lockhart was delighted at hearing that Bishop Thirlwall considered it a complete answer to Newman's argument. The essay has been reprinted in a volume since Milman's death. Lockhart did not live to see the great fame which Milman's *Latin Christianity* at once obtained. But I have often thought that his words were a remarkable instance of his literary insight. When I told him how some of Sir William Hamilton's essays in the *Edinburgh Review* were prized at Oxford, Lockhart told me that Milman had predicted, after reading some college essay of Hamilton's, that if he lived he would make for himself a great name in philosophy. I had the pleasure of mentioning this to Sir William Hamilton when I was attending one winter some of his lectures at Edinburgh. He told me that the praise of Lockhart and Milman when he was a young man had given him more pleasure than anything in his life. 'My opinion of those two men,' he said, 'I formed very early in life, and I have never changed it.'

The sermon preached at Charterhouse on Founder's Day in 1845 by Bishop Thirlwall, and which may be read in his *Remains*, is as vivid in my remembrance as that preached by Sydney Smith on St. John the Baptist. The first Lord Lytton, in speaking of the intellect of Herman Merivale, said that its characteristic was its massiveness, and it was the massiveness of pure gold. Something of the same impression was made on me by the solemn, majestic words of Thirlwall. Well did the Master of Charterhouse, Archdeacon Hale, say of this sermon, 'To treat our Founder's Day and its associations in such a fashion is a sign of true genius.'

Thirlwall lies in the Abbey close to his brother historian, Grote. They were both Carthusians.

It was the custom of Bishop Blomfield during the years when I knew London best, to preach at St. James's, Piccadilly, on the afternoons of Sundays in Lent. The congregations were always large, and the fine voice and excellent English of his sermons made them very attractive. Bishop Blomfield had a difficult part to play in the controversies of his time. His action regarding the strict keeping of the rubrics, and at the time of the Papal aggression in 1850, exposed him to much criticism ; but those who knew him best always spoke warmly of his generous temper and his unbounded charity. Sydney Smith made many jokes at his expense, and as the famous letters to Archdeacon Singleton show, Sydney believed that he was the ruling spirit of the ecclesiastical commission. The bishop may have made mistakes, but I have heard Bishop Wilberforce declare that the policy of Bishop Blomfield had done much to prolong the life of the Church of England as an establishment. He was often most sagacious in the dispensation of his patronage, and will be long remembered by his witty sayings, his great scholarship, and his noble use of his great income.

It was a surprise to many that Bishop Sumner was chosen to succeed Archbishop Howley, instead of Blomfield; but Lord John Russell, after hesitating for some time as to who he should appoint, gave the Primacy to Sumner as the favourite of Exeter Hall. The unpublished diary of Lord Carlisle reveals the fact that many of his friends wished to see Thirlwall at Lambeth. But whatever might have been the result of such a Primacy, the world might probably have been without the remarkable series of charges delivered, strangely enough, to the diocese of St. David's.

During my school-days at Charterhouse, the preachers were H. W. Churton and Folliott Baugh, both of them eminent Oxford men. Churton inclined to the Evangelical section of the Church. Baugh was a High Churchman, and Newman's influence was perceptible in his sermons. For deep devotional fervour few could compare with Churton, and a sermon of Baugh's on the Fast Day appointed for the Irish famine, on the words 'These sheep, what have they done?' was pronounced, by an eminent man who heard it, a masterpiece of eloquence.

With the exception of a single sermon, I do not think Baugh ever published anything; but Churton's interesting record of *Eastern Travel* enjoyed, before the publication of Stanley's *Sinai and Palestine*, a considerable reputation.

Baugh's father was Dean of Bristol, and when I left Charterhouse for Oxford in 1847 with some distinction, Baugh said to me, 'You have been head of your house, and you will never be so great a man again unless you are dean of a cathedral.' His words often occurred to me when Lord Coleridge, in his pleasantest and happiest vein, has more than once, when on circuit at Salisbury, rallied me on the great dignity of the Dean of Sarum. Among the many losses of the present year so fatal to great legal luminaries, I have to lament with many others that, whatever else life may have in store, it cannot bring the constant friendship, the extraordinary flow of anecdote, and the still more wonderful command of ancient and modern literature, for ever associated with the recollection of John Duke, Lord Coleridge.

CHAPTER V

The Oxford Movement—Frederick Maurice—Principal Shairp—The last Years of School Life—Lord Byron's early love—Mrs. Clive—Dr. Wolff—Stanley's *Life of Arnold*—Matriculation at Oxford.

So much has been written of late years upon the history of the Oxford Movement, that I hardly dare to approach the subject. I feel, however, that there is a certain imperfection in the records of Mr. T. Mozley, Bishop Charles Wordsworth, Dean Church, and Dr. Liddon, and I am vain enough to think that I am able to throw some light upon the history of the troubled days when Newman left the Church of England, and something like a panic ensued. I had heard from two very different men, J. C. Shairp and A. P. Forbes, well known as Bishop of Brechin, enthusiastic accounts of Newman's preaching when Vicar of St. Mary's; the former, in his essay on *Keble*, has given a vivid account of the effect produced by Newman upon him and many of his friends at Balliol, and Lord Coleridge has often spoken to me of Shairp's essay, and told me of the extraordinary power Newman exercised over men who were entirely indisposed to accept his teaching as a whole. I have also heard A. P. Stanley and A. H. Clough declare, that the grip which Newman seemed to get of the conscience, was greater and stronger even than that of their master Arnold.

When I was in the upper forms at Charterhouse, Oxford men came occasionally to their old school, and were fond of talking about Newman, describing his manner, and recalling particular passages, such as the famous one on music in the last of his University sermons. Thus Newman became quite a hero to two or three of us, and I well remember the shock I received on hearing from H. Hull, the son of a great friend of Dr. Arnold's, that it was certain that, in a short time, Newman would leave the English Church. When the last volume of sermons, published by Newman as an Anglican, appeared, all hopes of retaining him in the English fold vanished away from the minds of his most ardent supporters. A reaction had begun. When the *British Critic* stopped, W. Palmer started the *English Review*, intended to be the organ of those who had gone a certain way with the Oxford Tract writers, but were determined to remain loyal to the Reformation settlement, and to the teaching of the divines of the seventeenth century, S. R. Maitland, editor of the *British Magazine*, inserted articles against the *Lives of the Saints* and the devotional books adapted by Dr. Pusey from Roman Catholic writers. The *Christian Remembrancer* was transformed from a monthly magazine to a quarterly, and under the care of J. B. Mozley and W. Scott, became the organ of those who had been faithful to

Newman, until he showed unmistakably his Rome-ward tendency.

The publication of *Ward's Trial*, and the proceedings taken against him at Oxford, created an extraordinary interest in the Movement both in England and in Scotland. The action of the heads of Houses at Oxford, tyrannical and unjust in some degree, was simply the result of the strong feeling of repugnance aroused throughout the country at the possible secession of many of Newman's followers. The strong, vehement sermons of Christopher Wordsworth, in Westminster Abbey, had a powerful influence in London. I do not think any of those who have written upon the history of the Movement were sufficiently alive to the real alarm felt by many persons of great moderation at this time. Stanley's *Life of Arnold* produced an immediate effect. In spite of Arnold's exaggerated language about Newman and Keble, men felt that there was reason in what he said, and I am certain that there were many who, like myself, had been greatly attracted by what we had read of Newman, had admired the early numbers of the *Lives of the Saints*, and begun to entertain grave doubts as to the position of the English Church, were suddenly arrested and brought face to face with the question, Was the revolt of the sixteenth century justifiable or not? The intense interest felt for Richard Hurrell Froude, by those who came under the spell of his personal influence, blinded his admirers to the consequences of the publication of his *Remains*. I knew many people, disposed to be very favourable to the writings of the Oxford school, who were shocked by Froude's utterances, and withdrew entirely from any further contact with what they felt to be dangerous. The strong feeling evoked by Sir Robert Peel's endowment of Maynooth, directed by Christopher Wordsworth in a famous pamphlet, *Maynooth, the Crown and the Country*, was an evidence of the way in which the wind was blowing. It has been too much the fashion of late years to attack the Bishops for their charges at this period, and to look upon them as the aiders and abettors of popular prejudice. No doubt foolish and intemperate words were uttered, and kindly consideration might have done much to prevent secession. The instinct of recoil from approach to Rome was healthy and true, and what I venture to insist on is, that the theory of persecution is altogether exaggerated, and that the writers to whom I have already alluded were, to a great degree, ignorant of the strength of the antipathy aroused, when men like Oakeley claimed to hold and teach all Roman doctrine, and still retain preferment in the English Church. There were, I should think, many who found, as I did, a way of escape in Frederick D. Maurice's *Kingdom of Christ*, and who can never be sufficiently thankful for the inspiring and invigorating view which that remarkable book gives of life, society, and the Catholic Church.

Slowly has the influence of Maurice told upon English life and thought, but at last he has been recognised as one who has done more to elevate and sustain high ideals than any teacher of the last generation.

The first sermon I heard from Maurice was in Lincoln's Inn Chapel, upon the subject of 'Secession to Rome,' a sermon which contained much of what was afterwards published, as an answer to Newman's famous essay, in a preface to *Three Lectures on the Hebrews*. It may perhaps be asked what right or call had a boy at a public school to be interested in such deep matters? I can only admit my fault, and say how much I owe to the kindness of friends, who lent me books and did not check my aspirations, who bore with my imperfections, and often gave my inclinations a happy direction. I, too, like many another, was happy in possessing a mother who had real sympathy with wayward and tiresome extravagances, and whose admirable judgment as to books and men I learnt to appreciate more and more as I grew older. Some part of the obligations I owe to intercourse with J. C. Shairp. I have already acknowledged, in the volume of *Principal Shairp and his Friends*, the work of my friend Professor Knight. At the time when I was far more occupied with the subject of Newman and his secession than was at all desirable at my age, Shairp talked the whole matter over with me in the kindest and pleasantest way, and told me how much good he had received from men who had been hearty admirers of Arnold, and had caught something of his inspiring and enlivening power. Shairp was at this time an under-master at Rugby, and although he never threw off his allegiance to the Church of Scotland, he had great sympathies for those who had determined to make the ministry of the Church of England the work of their lives, and he encouraged me, as I was then looking forward to doing so, to try and preserve an attitude free from partisanship.

Every one knows how a strong, personal influence, at a critical time in life, often determines future thought and action. Shairp's love of literature, and especially his immense admiration of Wordsworth, gave me a taste which, I am thankful to say, I have never lost. I read at this time the whole of Wordsworth's poetry, with the delight a discoverer might have who gazed for the first time on some hitherto unknown island. Literary possessions which you have made in this way your own, acquire a certain sanctity. I longed to see the country where Wordsworth lived and wrote, and the effect of his poetry on my mind was soothing and elevating. When the one-volume edition of *Wordsworth* came out, I am afraid I often bored some of my Charterhouse friends, who were great admirers of Byron and Scott, by reading to them some of my favourite passages of Wordsworth, and insisting upon his claims to be ranked among the greatest of the English poets. From Shairp, too, I learned to value S. T. Coleridge's philosophy and religious thought. I am afraid that the influence of Coleridge is not what it used to be in the days when I first knew Oxford as an undergraduate, when tutors were in the habit of recommending *The Friend* and *Aids to Reflection* to such of their pupils as were reading for honours. The unwholesome atmosphere of ecclesiastical controversy seemed to melt away in the days when Wordsworth and Coleridge took entire possession of me, and I gratefully acknowledge the debt I owe to J. C. Shairp.

Shairp used to speak freely to me of his friends Norman Macleod, John Mackintosh 'The Earnest Student,' and the wonderful old man who exercised so much influence in Scotland, Thomas Erskine of Linlathen. Norman Macleod was a delightful companion, and he, like Shairp, had the happy faculty of taking younger men into his confidence, and discussing with them the deepest subjects. His enthusiasm was infectious. When he spoke of Leighton or Neander, he seemed to glow with generous feeling. Although he was a faithful son of his own Church, he had a great admiration for the Church of England, and when I once told him that I had thought out the question of the Episcopal form of government for myself, and held it to be really primitive, he said to me, ' I believe that what you say is true, and I often long for the day to come when Scotland may see her way to the moderate Episcopacy of men like Leighton.' I asked him if he had read Maurice's *Kingdom of Christ*, and he replied that the book had made a great impression on him, 'Though I do not,' he said, 'go as far as Henry Douglas (afterwards Bishop of Bombay), who puts it,' he said, 'very near Hooker.'

It is quite impossible for those who saw Norman Macleod in times of sorrow and trouble, to express in words the impression of his sympathy and tenderness. I only heard him preach once. It was a sermon which fully justified J. M. Ludlow's eulogy of a discourse he heard from Macleod at his own church in Glasgow, which he termed the perfection of a Christian sermon. It has always been a regret to me that I only saw Macleod four or five times in my life, but his looks, his words, his delightful outpourings on theology and poetry, remain for ever indelibly stamped on my mind. Especially do I recollect a conversation I had with him, at the meeting of the Social Science Association in Glasgow in 1860, upon the subject of Dr. Macleod Campbell's work on *The Atonement*, a book which has profoundly influenced many thoughtful minds. Many have been the tributes paid to Macleod's wonderfully versatile powers. Few men of his generation have had such an influence on minds very different from his own ; his reality, his geniality, and his delightful humour, made him the favourite of all who knew him, and he never for a moment forgot his work in life, and could give a rebuke, when rebuke was needed, with matchless skill and tact. On his return from India he spoke upon the subject of Missions in the General Assembly. An eminent English clergyman, who was present, said he never saw any impression so great as that produced by this earnest utterance. During the latter years of his life, he found the duties of his great parish and his literary labours a very heavy burden. I have heard J. C. Shairp often speak with deep regret of the weight which Macleod had to bear, and the noble struggle he made.

The last two years of school life are often most fruitful and important. It has been my fortune during life to enjoy the friendship of men older than myself, and when three of my school companions left Charterhouse for Oxford, I felt myself somewhat lonely. It was at this time that I began to make real acquaintance with Ruskin's *Modern Painters*, the first volume of which I borrowed from my tutor Phillott, who was an Oxford friend of 'the Oxford graduate,' and a new world of delight seemed to open out before me. I was successful in getting some kind friends to take me to Tottenham, in order to see Mr. Windus' famous collection of water-colours by Turner, and I made the discovery that by putting half-a-crown into the hand of the housekeeper at Turner's house in Queen Anne Street, one could obtain access to the long room, where some of Turner's most famous pictures could be seen. The second volume of *Modern Painters*

I also borrowed from Mr. Phillott, and took it to Scotland with me during my Charterhouse holidays. I read it and re-read it, until I knew some of its famous passages almost by heart, and, in short, experienced what I suppose thousands have felt, that Ruskin had opened one's eyes to the wonders of nature and art, and added much pleasure to life. In my first visit to Italy, Ruskin was living at Venice. He was well known to one of my fellow-travellers, who learned from him much about what we ought to see. Those delightful days, in the autumn of 1851, dwell for ever in memory, and return in full force whenever I open the pages of the *Stones of Venice*.

But I must now pass to a very different recollection. I was taken by a kind friend to a dinner party in Stratford Place, where I had a singular piece of good fortune. A lady who lived with the hostess, had been, in her youth, the intimate friend of Mary Chaworth, Lord Byron's early love. I took this lady to dinner. She began by asking me if I was fond of poetry, and if I particularly admired Byron. I told her that I tried to relish all great poets, but that I had particular admiration for some of Byron's minor poems, and especially *The Dream*. I did this perfectly naturally, but it led to her at once telling me the whole story of Byron's attachment to Miss Chaworth, in a most unaffected and simple fashion. She told me she had been on most intimate terms with the poet; that at that period of his life he proved a charming companion, and

that it had always been a great matter of regret to
her that her friend's affections had been given to
Mr. Musters, and not to Lord Byron. She believed
that this disappointment had changed and soured
his life. Never, she said, could she forget the time
when Byron discovered that all hope was gone, and
that Miss Chaworth's engagement would soon be
announced. He trembled all over, and exclaimed,
'Dear Miss Radford, little do you know what an
awful day this is to me. I knew that there had
been in Mary's heart some kindly feeling for me,
and I clung to hope.' Some years afterwards, she
met him accidentally at a London party. He was
then at the height of his fame, but when he saw
her he seemed to quiver again with emotion. 'I
believe,' said the old lady, 'that he was terribly
in earnest, and I have often longed that he had
been made happy by my friend.' Tears stood in
the eyes of Mary Chaworth's friend, as she spoke
of this scene. Those who were present, and who
knew her well, told me that she very seldom
mentioned those days, and that I was singularly
fortunate in hearing the story of her life at
Annesley Hall.

I had the pleasure of narrating this conversation
to one of the most remarkable women I have ever
known, the late Mrs. Archer Clive, author of *Nine
Poems by V.*, and the well-known novel, *Paul
Ferroll*. The small volume of poems, so highly
praised by Henry Nelson Coleridge, in a famous

review of *Nine Poetesses*, in the *Quarterly*, was written and published by Mrs. Clive before her marriage to the Rector of Solihull. For many years Mrs. Clive lived at Solihull, and there I paid a visit in the year 1846, full of enjoyment and charm. Mrs. Clive, though very lame, was a fearless rider, and greatly enjoyed a canter on horseback. Strangers at first found her manner odd and abrupt, but all this impression vanished away, and in a *tête-à-tête* she was an admirable and most agreeable talker. An uncle of mine who succeeded Mr. Clive in the living of Solihull, when the latter took possession of a property in Herefordshire, knew that I had heard Lord Jeffrey express a most favourable opinion of Mrs. Clive's poetry. He insisted upon my telling her the very words that Jeffrey had used,—' If I had not Mrs. Somerville's word for it, I should certainly have guessed that "V" was not a lady, but a gentleman. Three stanzas of *The Grave*, I think,' added Jeffrey, 'are as fine as anything in Gray's *Elegy*.' Mrs. Clive's eyes filled with tears when I told her this, and she said, ' This is praise indeed.' What struck me most in her, was the breadth and power of her literary criticism. Keble's *Lyra Innocentium* had just appeared. She had read it very carefully, and said to me, ' Though I think there are some things in this finer than anything in the *Christian Year*, there is a falling away. Keble is far too tender about Rome. Newman has done him harm. He was the poet of the whole

Church, but now he has become the poet of a party. There is a want of health about him. I read,' she said, 'the article on "Sacred Poetry" he wrote many years ago in the *Quarterly Review*, because Dr. Arnold praised it so. I did not care for it, because he spoke rather slightingly of Milton. The older I grow,' she said, 'the more I admire Milton. Reading him is like hearing an oratorio. How wonderfully the Bible comes home to one, after reading Milton! I hope young men at Oxford and Cambridge read Milton more and Keble less.'

There was, besides, in Mrs. Clive a deep satirical vein. Very few people have ever seen her *St. Old-ooman*, a very clever brochure suggested by the *Lives of the English Saints*. She had read widely, and was a great admirer of Whewell's writings. He had published some sermons preached before the University of Cambridge, which she highly praised, and she told me that Trench had recommended these sermons with the words, 'They are full of noble thoughts.' It was extremely pleasant to listen to her criticisms of Walter Scott's novels. Lockhart's character of Scott at the close of the *Life*, she could almost repeat by heart, and she told me that Mr. Rogers had said of it, 'Every word is true.' I heard from her, for the first time, that Scott's married life was not altogether happy, and she spoke of the exquisite tenderness in the use of epithets, by Lockhart, in speaking of Scott as 'a husband.'

It was a matter of regret to many of Mrs. Clive's friends that she ever published *Paul Ferroll*, a painful, though a most powerful book. The three other tales which she gave to the world were unequal. I have always wondered that her poems, especially the magnificent close of, 'I watched the heavens,' are not more generally known and prized. Dr. John Brown was a most hearty admirer of them, and his opinion is recorded in one of his remarkable volumes of *Horæ*. Archbishop Trench once told me that he had some favourite poems which he used as tests, and that Mrs. Clive's 'Grave' was one of them. Mrs. Clive died in a very sad way. Sparks from the fire fell upon the newspaper she was reading, and her powerlessness prevented her from summoning assistance. She had certainly one of the most powerful intellects I have ever met with, and she was a true and constant friend of many remarkable people.

There is, indeed, something especially captivating in the conversation of a really clever woman. At Edinburgh, at the house of Lord Medwyn, one of my father's brother-judges, I had the good fortune to meet more than once Miss Rigby, better known as Lady Eastlake. She was interested in finding that I considered myself greatly indebted, for advice as to reading poetry, to F. T. Palgrave and his brother W. G. Palgrave, distant relations of her own. The Palgraves had been reared in an atmosphere of literature, and they delighted to pour out their treasures, gained from unusually wide reading, to their school-fellows, and Miss Rigby spoke much of them and their mother, one of the many remarkable daughters of Mr. Dawson Turner. She was a real lover of books, music, and art. To me her judgment as to Schiller and Goethe seemed wonderfully searching and clever. She greatly deplored the popularity of Balzac and George Sand, and I was interested in hearing the same sentiments from her as I had heard from Mr. Rogers as to the effect of familiarity with what she called prohibited literature.

Dickens had been recently in Edinburgh, and Miss Rigby told me a good story of a lady I knew well, who said, 'I can never forgive you, Mr. Dickens, for the death of Nelly in the *Old Curiosity Shop*.' 'You would not have liked her,' he said in reply, 'to marry a butcher or a baker.' Of Professor Wilson's judgments about his own writings, she told me that they were the most curiously truthful verdicts ever pronounced by an author about his own productions. He had actually said to her, 'I have just been reading my three volumes of *Tales* over again, and I find them mawkish.' 'I was put in a great difficulty,' Miss Rigby continued, 'for it was the very word I would have used if I had been asked to describe the *Trials of Margaret Lindsay* and the *Lights and Shadows of Scottish Life*.' I had a long conversation with her on the subject of Newman's secession, and she told me that Archbishop Whately had once said in the Oriel Common Room, when the child's story of the *Three Wishes* was mentioned, 'If I had three wishes, they would all be for a " mind like Newman's." '   Every one who met Miss Rigby must have been struck with the variety of her acquirements and the strong interest in all sorts of different subjects.   She could write articles on music, dress, and, strange to say, drink ; and her contributions to art were alone sufficient to make her reputation.   I have always regretted that I did not see her more frequently in her later years.   At one time I tried hard to induce her to use once more the pen, which she had wielded with such vigour against *Rahel* and *Bettina* in defence of the faith, much misrepresented by a famous novelist ; but she pleaded her advancing years and lessening powers. She gave no sign or token of decay, however, in her contributions to periodical literature.

I spent a day once at Sunning Hill with Dr. and Lady Georgiana Wolff, very shortly before the famous expedition to Bokhara took place.   He was a most singular person.   His wife was a relation of an old lady, aunt of Sir George Murray, who lived at Sunning Hill.   I spent many days in her house, and often met remarkable people there.   Dr. Wolff, when I saw him, was beginning to look favourably on Oxford theology, and expressed some regret that his son, Sir H. D. Wolff, was at Rugby, where he thought Arnold's teaching still lingered.   There was a curious simplicity in his manner ; and his

anecdotes of Henry Drummond, and the circle
gathered round him at Albury, where Wolff had
often been a guest, were very racy. Mr. Drummond
had lately published a pamphlet in which there was
a sentence which Wolff repeated with great delight.
It was to expose the improper use of language in
England. 'A soldier of fortune was a soldier of
no fortune at all. A heap of cinders in the suburbs,
called Mount Pleasant. A man who threatens you
if you don't pay your rent, a solicitor, and a piece
of water in Hyde Park, which is neither the river,
or serpentine, called the Serpentine River.' Wolff
passed in a moment from gay to grave, and after
entertaining us with many stories of his adventures
as a missionary, said, 'It is now time for prayers, I
wish to give you to-night a short account of the
teaching of St. Paul.' 'Do not be lengthy, Dr.
Wolff,' said his hostess. But it was in vain. For
more than an hour did he pour forth a stream of
rather undigested exposition, and he received a
severe rebuke, when it was over, from his wife.
He turned round and said, 'I think this young
gentleman will thank me some day for what I
have said.'

It was impossible for any one to be angry with
Wolff long. Many stories have been told of his
simplicity. He borrowed my razor in the morning.
I had just begun to shave, and was rather proud of
two splendid razors purchased in Bond Street. I
suppose the one I lent him was packed in his

portmanteau, for I certainly never saw it again. When he took leave of me, he said with great fervour, 'I like you, and when you have become a clergyman I shall ask my friend Baring to give you a living'—greatly to the amusement of the old lady, who said to me when the Doctor and Lady Georgiana had driven away, 'I hope you won't build too much on Dr. Wolff's promise.' In his old age, when he became an incumbent in the West of England, Dr. Wolff became a firm friend and great admirer of Archdeacon Denison, who treated him with the greatest kindness. I have had the privilege of knowing the Archdeacon since my school-days, and have often heard him speak of Wolff's singular character, his energy, and the child-like nature of his faith.

It is difficult for me to say how completely Stanley's *Life of Arnold* took possession of me at this critical period of my life. When it first appeared in 1844, Dr. Saunders, the headmaster, presented it to the library of his boarding-house. I read it carefully at least twice, and when my mind was full of Arnold I spent Easter at Sunning Hill, at the house of the old lady where I met Wolff. W. H. Lyttelton, who was afterwards my rector in my second curacy, and whose friendship I enjoyed for many a year, was then curate of Sunningdale. In his Easter Day sermon he spoke of Arnold, and the doubt which he had felt at one time as to the reality of the Resurrection, in a way

which showed the strong hold which Arnold's life
had over him. When in Scotland I had frequent
opportunities of talking about Arnold with a
brother-in-law of mine, who had sent his eldest son
to Rugby, mainly, I think, in the hope that the
healthy vigour of Arnold's influence might linger
in the place. The biographer, too, had a very full
share of my admiration. Stanley was then Fellow
and Tutor of University College, and I heard from
a great friend, who went to Oxford a year before I
did, of Stanley's delightful lectures, and the inspiring effects of the sermons he was then preaching
before the University as select preacher, which
were afterwards published in his volume of *Sermons
and Essays on the Apostolical Age.*

With Arnold's particular views as to the Church
I had no great sympathy, but what attracted me, as
it has attracted thousands, was the evidence of his
intense desire to Christianise life, and make history,
poetry, and every province of thought subject to
the passionate power which true faith ought to
possess over the souls and minds of men. I had
found in Carlyle, with whose *French Revolution,
Heroes and Hero Worship,* and *Past and Present,* I
was now very familiar, the intense love of reality
and hatred of shams so distinctive of Arnold and
his teaching. Still I felt the powerful attraction of
Newman's sermons, and found myself often wonder-
ing what would Arnold's position have been had he
lived to see Newman's secession and the remark-

able rally of his scattered forces which, under the guidance of Pusey and Keble, established the Church party in a strong position. Dr. Tait, in a pamphlet written at the time when the question of Mr. Ward's degradation was agitated, had spoken of the existence of a third party in the Church, or rather a school of thought, bringing out from the treasures of Scripture many new things.

I have already spoken of my obligations to the writings of F. D. Maurice, and I remember well how a friend of my own pained me by calling him an Eclectic—neither flesh, fish, nor fowl—and how eagerly I declared that I would rather go astray with Plato than discover truth in the company of others. The intense spiritual fervour felt after long talks with Maurice I did not experience until, at the close of my Oxford life, I began to know him well, and felt many a doubt and difficulty disappear in talks with him after breakfast when he was living in Queen's Square.

In the spring of 1846 I was living in Warwickshire with an uncle who had the sole charge of the living held by his friend the headmaster of Charterhouse. I had always hoped to go to Balliol, but by some mistake my name was not entered properly on the list. It was then put down for three colleges, Christ Church, University, and Exeter, and I found myself, at a week's notice, summoned to matriculate at Exeter. I had never seen Oxford, and shall not forget the moment

when I entered it in a coach which started from
Henley-in-Arden.   An elder brother happened to
be in Oxford at that time to take his M.A. degree.
We walked about together, and I recognised to
my delight many Oxonians whose names I knew,
Arthur Stanley, A. H. Clough, Matthew Arnold,
Henry Coleridge ; and at a wine party given by my
brother at Mason's lodgings, I met for the first time
Edwin Palmer, James Riddell, P. Cumin, and one
whose name lives for ever in the records of the
English Church, J. C. Patteson, who was unknown
to my brother, but who was brought to his rooms
by a connection of ours, H. Broke, and who seemed
to me that evening, as always when I knew him
better, a man with the most delightful temper and
disposition, one of whom I have heard it said that
he carried about him an atmosphere of goodness.

Riddell, who had been well described in J. C.
Shairp's poem of 'Balliol's Scholars,' was one of
the most attractive men I have ever known.   I
wish that it were within my power to describe
him as he ought to be described.   From the time
that I came to Oxford as an undergraduate in 1847,
he distinguished me with kindness, and in his rooms
I met many men of mark, who have left their impress
on many minds besides mine.   An admiring friend
who knew him well called Riddell 'the Bayard of
Oxford.'   I have known instances of his kindly
reproof of folly and extravagance, conveyed in such
a way that lasting impressions were made.   Few

men have ever been more honoured in their college, or more sincerely regretted. Some of his translations into Greek are unrivalled. Shortly before his death he was busy with Plato, and when Gaisford died it was generally felt in Oxford that the Professorship of Greek which fell to Jowett was almost the right of Riddell. I was indebted to him for many pieces of good advice as to reading, and it was in consequence of his recommendation that I became a pupil of Conington, and by so doing laid the foundation of a very intimate friendship. Riddell was a great pedestrian. I have known him walk from Leamington to Oxford, and I met him once in Ireland, near Killarney, walking in a way which made me and my companion, Sir M. E. Grant Duff, feel that he was over-taxing a not too robust frame.

At this time also I made the acquaintance of C. E. Prichard, another Fellow of Balliol, a man who impressed every one who knew him with a sense of his pure and high-minded nature. Prichard, after spending many years of his life in the care of country parishes, passed away without leaving the mark which his many friends expected. Two small volumes of Commentaries on the Romans and some other Epistles, and an admirable paper on 'Theories of the Atonement,' in the *North British Review*, were evidences of the delicacy and skill with which he handled difficult themes. At the time when he was a Fellow of

Balliol, James Lonsdale, Frederick Temple, Wall, Lake, Woolcombe, Jowett, and the present Archdeacon of Oxford, Edwin Palmer, made the society conspicuous in many ways. Matriculation in the year 1846 was easily effected. At the head of one list was one who has been a faithful Scholar and Fellow of Exeter, C. W. Boase. It is not the fate of every College ·to possess in its historian 'such an honest chronicler as Griffith.' One often wishes that one could again taste the pleasure of the first visit to Oxford. Kindly welcomes of old school-fellows, the pleasant breakfasts and dinners in Hall, the stroll by the river, the first view of the boats, and all the sights and sounds that invest Oxford with romantic grace.

I had a cousin at Christ Church, a friend from earliest childhood, the late Earl of Glasgow, who was living in great intimacy with Lord Dufferin, with whom he had lately visited some places in the west of Ireland desolated by famine. The result of their tour was published, and generous sacrifices were made and contributions sent from undergraduate Oxford. I heard much of the horrors they had seen. Peel and his change of policy was a constant topic of conversation at this time. One of the circle of friends I met in my cousin's room, I remember to have heard exclaim, ' Your account of Skibbereen is a perfect justification of Peel's policy in abolishing the Corn Laws.' I am afraid, though, that he was almost hated by every other guest, as the tone of the society was Protectionist. I had not the courage to avow myself a follower of Peel. Lord Dufferin, however, did so.

Very shortly after my matriculation I paid another visit to Oxford, in order to stand for a Post-mastership at Merton. I did not succeed, and often think still of the terribly severe language discharged by the headmaster when I returned to school. In after years, however, all memory of his anger ought to have been forgotten; when he made me, what I have always thought the greatest distinction of my life, the offer of an under-mastership, vacant by the removal of Leonard Burrows to a post under Dr. Goulburn at Rugby. Dr. Arnold in his life dwelt much upon the fruitfulness of the years that followed the time that he took honours at Oxford. Friendships were formed, and books were read, and a happy impulse given to effort. Something of the same kind happens in the last year of school life, when a boy passes into manhood, Oxford lies before him, or it may be Cambridge. He finds out the real meaning and the responsibilities of school, and if he, as I did, had much pleasant intercourse with under-masters and younger boys, the days are days of pleasant memory. Two new boys came to Charterhouse as I was leaving. Their fathers, men of distinction, Mr. John Talbot and Canon Jelf, asked me to do what I could for their boys. I take a pride and satisfaction in thinking that one of these boys is the excellent M.P. for Oxford, the other is Canon of Rochester, the guide and helper of many, and in my old age I can still call them friends.

Old Charterhouse had this advantage, that it enabled school friends, on the going-out days, to make acquaintance with the families of their companions. At the house of Mr. Bransby Cooper, whose sons were friends of mine, I saw many remarkable ornaments of the medical profession, and I passed many delightful days in Kent at the house of Mr. J. J. Saunders, a London merchant of the old-fashioned cultivated kind. His wife was a daughter of Mr. Boyd, the man whose noble conduct in wiping off his former debts, at the conclusion of the great war, when he had retrieved his failures, drew from Walter Scott the just burst of eulogy which Lockhart has preserved in his *Life*. Mrs. Saunders was a favourite pupil of Madame Caradori Allan, whose delightful rendering of Scotch ballads dwells in my recollections for ever.

CHAPTER VI

1847-1853—At Oxford—A visit from my father—Friends and acquaintances—Balliol and Exeter—Charles Marriot and Mozley—The great
Vicar of Leeds—Pusey, and the results of his teaching.

THE changes in Oxford have been so rapid and remarkable that some account of the time between 1847 and 1852 may not be altogether without interest.

Whatever else may change, the feelings of an undergraduate in his first term, especially if that be summer term, must always remain the same. There are few things in life more enjoyable than the first introduction to the pleasant intercourse and conviviality of Oxford life; and the same good fortune which had hitherto secured for me pleasant friends of great ability followed me to Oxford. After attaining some success in school examinations, I went at once into residence at Exeter College in April 1847. The college was so full that I had only a bedroom in the college and a sitting-room in lodgings in New Inn Hall Street. In this small room, about a fortnight after I had been at Oxford, I had the pleasure of entertaining my father and mother, who came from London to spend the day with me.

My father, who was at that time at the height of
his judicial reputation as Lord Justice General of
Scotland, had received many marks of kindness and
distinction in London, and his account of dinners
at Lord Brougham's, Lord Eglinton's, and Lord
Denman's was extremely graphic and full of enter-
tainment.   At Lord Brougham's he had sat next
the Duke of Wellington, and heard from him many
characteristic sayings.   Sir Robert Peel, an old
friend, had also spoken to him very freely of the
political future, and my father had ventured to
express his hope that when the excited feeling
raised by the abolition of the Corn Laws had
subsided the Conservatives might again rally round
Peel.   Sir Robert himself, however, did not take so
sanguine a view.   He spoke very warmly of Lord
Dalhousie, in whom he knew my father was much
interested, and expressed his belief that, in a very
short time, Lord Dalhousie would be appointed to
the great office of Viceroy of India.

To my father, who had known well the first Lord
Melville, Sheridan, the Marquis of Hastings, and
others who figured in the earlier part of this century,
this glimpse of the political life of 1847 gave much
pleasure.   Lord Eglinton told me that he had been
extremely struck with the facility with which my
father talked to Lords Brougham and Lyndhurst,
and the way in which he answered their questions
upon the subject of Appeals from the Court of
Session to the House of Lords.   The Lord Advocate

Rutherfurd had, at this time, some scheme in his head for the appointment of a Scottish lawyer to assist in the legal duties of the House of Lords. Had this idea taken a practical shape, Rutherfurd himself would probably have been the man; but he once told a friend of his own, Sir David Dundas, that in the first instance it ought to be offered to my father. Lord Brougham, who was no lover of Rutherfurd, opposed the plan, and it was not until many years afterwards that the elevation of Lord Colonsay to the peerage solved the problem for a time. The present arrangement, of course, includes among the Lords of Appeal a Scottish lawyer.

Very early in my undergraduate life I made the acquaintance of the celebrated theologian, J. B. Mozley, and by his kindness I was able to take my father and mother to the beautiful service at Magdalen. It happened that on that day the venerable President Routh was in chapel. He had been Proctor when my father's elder brother had been at Oxford, and had shown him great kindness. My father would have called on the President, whom he had known in his brother's Oxford days, but the time was limited, as we had to pay our respects to the Warden of Merton and Lady Anstruther, an old friend of my mother's, and I thus missed my only chance of seeing Dr. Routh in his lodgings. More than once, in after days, I saw him in chapel, and I believe I was present on one of the last occasions on which he was at service. He died in his hundredth year. Lord Forbes, who lived in Oxford at this time, told me a curious story of the accuracy of Routh's historical memory. Something had been said about Claverhouse, Viscount Dundee, and it was remarked that he had no family. 'You are mistaken, sir,' said the President, 'he had a son, but he died in infancy.' Many a good story is told of Routh. One of the best is, that when a demy, afterwards very famous, translated extremely well the passage in the Odyssey, where Nausicaa washes the feet of Ulysses, the President said, 'There was nothing wrong in it, young gentlemen, it was the custom of the country.'

Sir Walter Scott speaks of the pleasure of sitting as a guest at his son's board, and my father, who knew that some very kind friends of mine had recently acquired an advowson with the idea of settling me one day in the living, said, as he partook of the luncheon I got for him from a pastry-cook's, 'I am afraid I shan't live to see you in a vicarage or a rectory, but at any rate I have had the pleasure of having one meal from you.' While he was with me, two Christ Church friends, one the son of the Dean, the other afterwards the well-known Ward Hunt, who were both friends of my cousin, the late Lord Glasgow, called upon me, and their pleasant, gentlemanlike manners made a great impression upon him. Hunt, one of the most excellent of men, was President of the Union. In my second term I made a speech about O'Connell, and very shortly afterwards Hunt put me on the committee. At his rooms I first met the present Lord Salisbury, then Lord Robert Cecil, and have the satisfaction of remembering many pleasant days, many keen debates, many earnest talks, when the promise which has been so wonderfully fulfilled, disclosed itself to all who were admitted to intimacy with that most distinguished man.

It is a fortunate thing for an undergraduate to be a man of many friends. This was my case. In my own college I had one most intimate companion, H. W. Sotheby, who had already given evidences of the scholarship and taste which gained him a first class and a fellowship at Exeter, and won for him, before he died, too soon for friendship, some literary fame. He was the grandson of the translator of Homer; his own literary preferences were similar to my own, and many an hour did we spend together in free and unfettered talk. A friend, who has also distinguished himself in various provinces of literature, T. E. Kebbel, if he ever chance to peruse this page, will remember the pleasant days of excursions to Godstowe and Whichwood, the eager debates as to the merits of Byron and Tennyson, the criticism of Latin verses and the wordy war of politics, all coming back into memory as I linger over my first summer term. Breakfasts at Balliol with F. J. Palgrave, Riddell, and Palmer, when I first saw Henry Smith, one of the most remarkable men of his generation, and renewed acquaintance with

William Young Sellar, the admirable Latin scholar, who did so much to revive the taste for Virgil and Lucretius, were among the delights of those days. At Balliol one seemed to be surrounded by an atmosphere of high-minded feeling and culture. Jowett's influence as a tutor was in full force. One often heard fragments of his pithy sayings in lecture repeated, and all my Balliol friends had many stories to tell of the pains he took with backward pupils and the kindness often concealed by his shy awkward manner. When October term of the year 1847 brought my old friend, Grant Duff, to Oxford, my knowledge of Balliol men increased, and I laid the foundations of firm friendship with Sir Alexander Grant, Henry Oxenham, and many others—men whom it was a privilege to know, differing in many ways, but all bent on acquiring distinction and making the best use of Oxford days.

At Exeter, among the Fellows, were several remarkable men. To one of them, William Sewell, scant justice has been done. At the time when I commenced my residence, Sewell was senior tutor. I was not his pupil, but I attended some of his lectures. He was excessively discursive, and would commence a lecture on Aristotle, in the usual way, but end with, perhaps, the Athanasian creed or the beauties of Gothic architecture. When Moberly was chosen to be headmaster of Winchester, Sewell was a candidate, and it was rumoured he was very nearly elected. He was a master of flowing English style, and a pamphlet of his, written at the time when the admission of Dissenters was first mooted, attained great success. In the Oxford movement he took rather an independent line, and an article of his in the *Quarterly Review* made a considerable impression. When Tract 90 appeared, Sewell publicly declared his own independent position, and in various writings on Christian Morals, Christian Politics, the Evidences of Christianity, and in his novel of *Hawkstone*, he asserted more or less the same views maintained by the High Church party who refused to follow Newman in the Romeward direction. Sewell was at times a fine and vigorous preacher. His delivery was not good, but he was sometimes pathetic and piercing. F. D. Maurice heard him preach a sermon on the Ministry, when he was reading for honours at Oxford, and many years afterwards heard the same sermon again when he came to Oxford as select preacher, and he told me that he thought the sermon one of the best he had ever heard, and that portions of it had lingered in his memory during the many years between the first and second hearing. I received many kindnesses from Sewell, and, although often provoked by the desultory character of his Plato lecture, freely acknowledge that he did possess the power of making his hearers recognise the intensity and glowing ardour of Plato's spirit. I am also glad to add here that a friend whom I knew many years afterwards, a real master of Greek and a true student of Plato, Charles Badham, once said to me that he could never be too thankful for the help he had from Sewell, when, as Professor of Moral Philosophy, he gave some lectures on Plato.

Numerous stories have been told of Sewell's eccentric and wayward opinion on many subjects, but I prefer to dwell on the recollection of his intense admiration of Butler and the insight he had into the great bishop's mind. He was capable, too, of generous admiration for men whom he did not always admire, and, after reading out the wonderful passage of Carlyle in *Sartor Resartus* about the minnow, Sewell said, ' This and a passage about the Creed in the *French Revolution* I call sublime.' When Sewell took the headmastership of Radley, most of his friends felt it was too late in life. He was unfortunately obliged to spend some years in exile, but when I saw him for the last time in 1870, on the eve of the outbreak of the Franco-German war, I had a most interesting talk with him upon the ' Four Gospels,' to which he was then devoting his attention. Although I differed much from him, in his view of inspiration, I was immensely struck with his extraordinary power of bringing out the characteristics of the Fourth Gospel and his anticipation of a great deal that has been admirably said by Bishop Lightfoot and Bishop Westcott, in their defence of the Johannine authorship. Sewell had also a true love and understanding for Shakespeare. He had been of great use to a son of Mr. Bartley's, who had died early in life at Oxford, and on two or three occasions Mr. Bartley read a play of Shakespeare's in the Hall of Exeter, in order to show his friendship for Sewell. To hear him was almost as great a treat as to hear Mrs. Kemble, and Sewell was never so happy as when he saw undergraduates chuckling with delight at Falstaff's speeches. Personally, I owe Sewell a great deal of gratitude. He knew that I was looking out for a curacy, and he named me to his friend Claughton, the vicar of Kidder-minster. Early in 1853 I received a letter from Claughton, and from the time I became his curate until the time of his death, I looked upon him in every sense as an elder brother.

At the house of Lord Forbes, on Sunday evening, a few friends were generally gathered together. There I saw a man who has been much mentioned in recent accounts of the Oxford movement, Charles Marriott, and another more distinguished as a writer and theologian, J. B. Mozley. Marriott had always, for me, a great attraction. He was absent in his manner and certainly sometimes 'swayed the great empire of silence,' but there was a purity and earnestness and a simplicity in all he said and did, which made me feel he was unlike other people. One evening he spoke of the commentary which Pusey was preparing on the minor prophets and the view he had as to the progress of criticism in Germany. The book, he said, when it appeared, would show the world something of Pusey's range of reading. Pusey's work on German Theology was also mentioned, and how the writer had retired from the position he assumed in that book. This, I remember, was rather a shock to me, as I had heard Archdeacon Burney, at one of the pleasant dinner parties of Archdeacon Hale, the Master of Charterhouse, speak in warm terms of the fairness and impartiality of Pusey's book.

Marriott took a great interest in the fortunes of the Scotch Episcopal Church, and spoke much of A. P. Forbes, afterwards Bishop of Brechin, who was at that time vicar of St. Saviour's, Leeds. I always heard Marriott preach with the greatest pleasure. He was master of the art of saying deep things in simple words. When vicar of St. Mary's, where he succeeded C. P. Eden, he often delivered admirable sermons, combining, as it seemed to me, the personal love for Our Lord, characteristic of a very different school of thought from his own, with great appreciation of the unique position of the English Church. I sometimes met him in after years in the Oriel common room, and have heard him maintain his own ground in argument with great force. Matthew Arnold, W. Y. Sellar, Burgon, Chretien, R. W. Church and Henry Parker, were present on this occasion, and when the question of University Reform was keenly debated, after the issue of the Report of the Royal Commission, Marriott contended that the original intentions of pious men to benefit the poor were in great danger from the overweening estimate of competitive examination. His own private means were freely bestowed in aiding needy scholars. He was well worthy of a place in Dean Burgon's series of the 'Lives of Good Men,' and as long as the records of the 'Oxford Movement' are read, his loyal friendship for Newman and his equally loyal attachment to the Church of England will be remembered.

Mozley was exceedingly kind to me. At his college, Magdalen, undergraduates were allowed to dine at high table by invitation, and many a pleasant evening have I passed in his society and that of William Palmer, elder brother of Lord Selborne, who also often asked me to Magdalen. Mozley was shy, but when you sat next him in common room, he would pour out his thoughts on men, books, and politics very freely. When his article on the 'Book of Job' came out in the *Christian Remembrancer*, he spoke to me about it, and said that he put all he could think of, as to the subject, into it. His feeling about Carlyle and Cromwell was certainly very strong. At that time I thought him unfair to both. When, however, I readily confess, I became better acquainted with the various accounts of the time, I admitted there was much more to be said in favour of Mozley's view.

When R. W. Emerson paid his first visit to Oxford, he somewhat surprised some of the young Oxford Liberals, who looked on Cromwell as a hero, by telling them of the effect Mozley had produced

in America.   Carlyle, it is well known, never
swerved from his original conception of Cromwell's
character, but there are evidences, in his correspondence with Emerson, that his American disciple
did not follow his master blindly.   Towards the
close of his life, John Forster, who had yielded
entirely to Carlyle's influence, admitted, to one who
told me, that the case against Cromwell had never
been put so powerfully as by Mozley.   For my own
part I have long thought, with the late Dean Stanley,
that Guizot's view of Cromwell, and indeed of the
whole history of the time, has never been properly
appreciated by students of English history ; but it
is almost an impertinence even to tread upon ground
so carefully traversed by Mr. Gardiner.   The high
authority of Bishop Stubbs is, according to Professor Palgrave in his notes to his *Visions of
England*, altogether on Mozley's side.

I once heard Mozley, who was an admirable critic
of poetry and fiction, say that he considered Miss
Austen's *Persuasion* one of the masterpieces of
English literature, and that the scene in which
Anne Elliot speaks of the real privileges of women
was absolutely perfect.   The author of the *Heir of
Redclyffe* may like to know, that when her early
book *Scenes and Characters* came out, Mozley
recommended it with the words, ' It shows that the
writer may became a first-class novelist.'   I once
heard him preach a University sermon, but it was
exceedingly difficult to follow it, and when he was

canon of Worcester in 1869, he preached in my church at Kidderminster one of the sermons contained in the volume that made his fame as a preacher, but very few persons in the large church heard him at all. When I last saw him I told him that in one of my visits to Cardinal Newman he had spoken much of him, the Dean of St. Paul's, and Mark Pattison. Mozley said with a sigh, 'Newman has never forgiven me my answer to his book on *Development*. I was obliged to do it, as no one else could be found.' I could not resist the pleasure of telling Mozley that Bishop Thirlwall had said to Archdeacon Moore, 'Since Pascal's *Provincial Letters*, there has been no such floorer as Mozley's answer to Newman.' Mozley looked pleased, but he said nothing. On the day on which it was announced that Archdeacon Manning and James Hope Scott had joined the Church of Rome, I had a long talk with Mozley, who then told me that he had grave doubts as to the wisdom of attacking the Gorham judgment. All who are interested in the *History of Doctrines* know now how independent was the line which Mozley took upon the subject of the 'Baptismal controversy.' The three publications in which he unfolded his own views, whatever else may be thought of them, are a wonderful evidence of the truth-seeking nature of the man, and the volume of letters, edited by his gifted sister, confirm even more strongly the belief in his absolute integrity, which I think all who knew him at all intimately, must have felt. Bishop Fraser once said to me, playfully, 'I believe in the transmigration of souls, and that Butler's has passed into James Mozley.'

In June 1847, on St. Barnabas Day, Dr. Hook preached the University sermon. The congregation was immense. He had been an exile from Oxford for some years. The effect of his sermon was extraordinary. He began by declaring his firm adherence to the largest scheme of toleration, and went on to assert, with hearty Anglican fervour, the peculiar position which he believed the Church of England occupied in Christendom. Mary, Queen of Scots, was not spared, and Elizabeth was certainly unduly exalted. The close of his sermon was an earnest exhortation to men, who believed the primal truths of the gospel, to enter the ministry, and I was not the only one, as I knew afterwards, who felt on that day that to be the 'son of consolation,' in any sense, would be a privilege indeed. Whenever I heard Hook preach, I felt that there was something Luther-like in his hearty faith and plain words. It is surely a great reproach to the English Church that Hook was not a bishop; we should not, however, have had his fine, vigorous *Lives of the Archbishops*, a book, as Freeman said, 'with grave faults, but full of a true, historic spirit,' if he had been bishop of a populous diocese. Once, when travelling near Leeds, in a second class railway carriage, I asked a Yorkshireman, who had reminded me of John

Browdie in *Nicholas Nickleby*, about the great vicar of Leeds. 'T'awd doctor is a good un. He rises at faive, lights his awn faire, and he is adoing summit all day long, and you may look at him with a microscope and he is never doing nawt wrong.'

Very soon after hearing Hook preach for the first time, I was told that Pusey was to preach at Mr. Hackman's church on a Sunday evening, and I and one or two friends got leave from the sub-rector of Exeter to be absent from Sunday evening chapel, in order to hear the sermon. It was one of Pusey's powerful moral addresses. I was repelled, I remember, by his stern view of post-baptismal sin; but his exhortation to live above the world and use Oxford life rightly, burnt into the mind. There was something awful in the deep monotony of his manner, and, after listening to him, I ceased to wonder at the veneration he inspired in some of the elder men, who were admitted to intimacy with him. I had frequent opportunities subsequently of hearing him, but I never met him in private life. I have felt, after long acquaintance with everything that he has written, that Pusey always had an excessive appreciation of what is noble and grand in the Church of Rome, and I have never been satisfied with the attitude he took on the subject of Biblical Inspiration: as Bishop Thirlwall said 'he has always been to me more or less of an enigma.' It is a strange thing that a man who certainly did lead many at one time in a Romeward direction, should also have been the means of deterring many others from taking the final road to Rome. I have, unfortunately, had many friends who submitted themselves to Pusey as a spiritual guide and fully adopted his theory of confession and direction, and in nearly every case I have seen traces of enfeebled intellect, and what I must call loss of real moral perception. If the system, so zealously advocated by Pusey, were ever to be generally adopted, a bad time would come to. English homes. There are indications of a healthier and higher spirit in the difficult province of dealing with souls which lead me to believe, at the close of my life, that the teaching of Maurice, Kingsley, Vaughan, Lightfoot and Westcott is gaining a firm hold over some of my younger brethren in the ministry. I am not unmindful of what Liddon, King, and Church have done, but I am certain that it is the teaching of the robuster school of thought which alone can influence the religious and thoughtful laymen who have an instinctive dislike of the confessional.

CHAPTER VII

I HAVE wandered away from my first term at Oxford, a time never to be effaced from memory. Many a conversation, many a pleasant hour, come back into memory, and the few who remain, doubtless, as I do, often think of the different way much of the pleasant undergraduate life might have been passed in. It is something, however, to be able to recall the recollection of inspiring influence gained in early Oxford days. In my first tutor, Frederick Fanshawe, and in one who was almost more than a tutor, R. Cowley Powles, I had the kindest advice in reading, and I went to my father's country place in Scotland with the determination to master Livy, and certain plays of Æschylus and Sophocles on a plan suggested by these two eminent scholars, and I worked so hard that my father resolved that I should have the indulgence of a fortnight at the English lakes.

I feel quite sure that the *Life of Arnold* increased the affection for the English lakes, originally created by Wordsworth, felt by so many of the more literary Oxford men, who were my seniors and contemporaries. Arnold's letters, in which he speaks of the hold the scenery round Fox How had upon him, are among the most attractive features in Stanley's delightful book. Fresh from a re-perusal of it, and with F. Garden's *Selections from Wordsworth* in my pocket, towards the end of September, I found myself in Gowbarrow Park, trying to realise the place where Wordsworth and his sister first saw the 'immortal daffodils' dancing in the wind. It was a delicious day, and, late in the evening, I went by Patterdale and the Pass of Kirkstone to Ambleside. I was soon transferred, by the kindness of some relations of my family, from the Salutation Hotel to a most pleasant home, known as 'The Cottage.' There I spent many days, made the usual excursions, and, to my great joy, it was arranged that, after morning service on Sunday, I should spend the afternoon with Hartley Coleridge, who was prepared, from a letter he had had, to see me and have a talk with me.

I went to Coleridge after luncheon and spent the greater part of the afternoon with this extraordinary man. He was small and odd-looking. The engraving in the first volume of *Essays and Marginalia* is exactly like him. His voice was peculiar, but, when he quoted poetry, seemed to acquire a sort of richness of tone, and the great number of passages from Wordsworth and Shakespeare he repeated, always now recall to me his penetrating tone and sweet expression, as I read them. He began at once, 'You are an admirer of Wordsworth, I know, and you will be glad to hear that, though he has been quite cast down by the death of his daughter, Dora, he is beginning to show that his interest in life is not altogether gone.' 'Southey and Wordsworth,' he said, 'are really as good as they are great,' and poor Hartley began to talk of his own troubled life and the unfailing kindness Wordsworth had always shown him. 'He keeps me in order,' he said; 'I am a wayward child, and I know I ought to be better; but enough of this. Do you know,' he said, 'Wordsworth's essay on Epitaphs? I think it shows that if Wordsworth had not been a great poet he might also have been a great prose writer.' Then, as we sat under the trees, he gave me a long and most interesting disquisition on the wonderful beauty of Shakespeare's female characters. 'Was there ever such a gallery, —Miranda, Imogen, Cordelia, Rosalind, Juliet, Ophelia, Isabella, and the divine Desdemona?' I told him how Alexander Dyce had expressed his opinion at a breakfast party at Rogers' that the finest thing in Shakespeare was Desdemona's lie when she was dying, and when she declared that she had done the deed herself and wished to be commended to her kind lord. 'Yes,' said

Hartley, 'Dyce is perfectly right. It is the triumph of Christian feeling. She knew that it was not her own Othello that did the deed, he had been practised upon. She wanted to screen him. She knew that he would find out that she was innocent and that the Almighty would pardon her deceit. Yes, yes, Dyce is quite right. I shall tell Wordsworth. You know how he loves "The gentle lady married to the Moor." Do you know, Mr. Boyle, I often think reading history is unnecessary. The whole lesson of history is in Shakespeare. Arnold used to say he should like to have to teach Shakespeare to a class of Greeks.' He then told me much about Arnold, his delight in his children, his talks with Wordsworth and his care for the poor. 'Everything about him,' he said, 'was great and noble. He could be stern,' and then he paused, while I wondered if Arnold had ever spoken of the thoughtless follies which, unfortunately, shadowed poor Hartley's career. He spoke much of the wonderful richness of English literature. 'I have been reading lately,' he said, 'Addison's delightful *Spectators*. Somebody lent me Macaulay's article, and I set to work. What nonsense people talk about the dignity of literature. These delicious things of Addison's came out weekly like newspaper articles, and will live for ever. Some of the best pieces in Southey's *Doctor* were written off after tea, when we were all chattering, and they are capital. I hope you love the *Doctor*.'

After a delightful ramble, in the course of which he quoted Wordsworth very frequently, we reached the Nab Cottage, where he insisted on giving me tea. The conversation then turned on his father and the influence he was having on men at Oxford and Cambridge. He said he could not at first understand his father's admiration for Leighton, but that De Quincey had shown him passages which quite justified all that Samuel T. Coleridge had said. He then spoke of his brother and sister. 'Sara,' he said, 'is a noble creature, and she guards my father's fame with real vigilance.' He showed me his copy of the *Biographia Literaria* recently edited by his sister and sent to him by her. He was delighted to find I knew it, and he read me the interesting concluding passage with great solemnity of feeling. 'I predict,' he said, 'a great fame for Tennyson. James Spedding repeated to me lately a beautiful poem about Lazarus,' and Hartley then gave me the few well-known stanzas in *In Memoriam*, which he had written down after hearing them from Spedding. 'This,' he said, 'is one of a series of elegies on the death of Arthur Hallam, and I hope some day they will be published.' So intensely interesting did I find Hartley's conversation, that I did not leave him until the dinner hour of my friends at Ambleside was over. My misconduct was, however, kindly pardoned. I had some refreshment, and heard from my host and hostess, who were greatly interested in all I had to tell them of my talk, many delightful stories of Wordsworth, Wilson, De Quincey, and Hartley himself. With these remarkable inhabitants of the Lake district the family at 'The Cottage' had lived for years in cordial intimacy, and it was their belief that Wordsworth and his family, by the sweet simplicity and purity of their living, had elevated the whole tone of society in the district and given a peculiar taste for literature to young and old. Mrs. Fletcher's autobiography, and a most interesting paper by her daughter Lady Richardson, as well as the somewhat grudging praise of Miss Martineau in her short life of Wordsworth's widow, fully confirm all that my friends had told me.

On the morning I left Ambleside for Keswick, Hartley Coleridge was waiting for me at the coach to say good-bye. 'Be sure,' he said, 'you see Wastwater, and do come back soon to Lake-land.' I did not, however, return to the Lakes till 1852, when, as all the world knows, Hartley had passed away, and was laid in Grasmere churchyard at Wordsworth's desire, close to the spot where, a few months afterwards, the great poet himself was buried.

I took Hartley Coleridge's advice, and, with the aid of a guide, crossed the hill from Borrowdale, and saw the stern grandeur of Wastwater. On our return a heavy mist came on, and we wandered for many hours, sometimes in considerable peril; but the evening was glorious, and the drive from Lodore to Keswick, unfolding at every turn the beauty of Derwentwater, remains, like many other possessions, a joy for ever.

I feel that I have given a most inadequate account of the richness and variety of Hartley's talk. One thing more I must record, his intense feeling about the poetry of the Old Testament—the rhythmical beauty of certain passages. He dwelt on Jacob's words, 'There they buried Abraham and Sarah his wife, and there I buried Leah.' He also quoted the words of Ruth to Naomi, and the beautiful passage in the Gospel of St. Mark, 'A parable of the fig tree: When her branch is yet tender, and putteth forth leaves, ye know that summer is near.' Lockhart once said to me, when I had written an estimate of Hartley Coleridge as a poet, 'I think you have praised him too highly, but I quite admit that his two sonnets on a " Proud Beauty " and the one that ends " I am a sinner " are as good as any of Wordsworth's, and I am not sure that I don't think Hartley's paper on Hamlet better than anything his father ever wrote.'

I saw Wordsworth himself for a few moments in the grounds of Rydal Mount. There was a homely dignity in his appearance, and, as he was arranging the chair in which his invalid sister sat, he seemed to me the very personification of kindly benevolence. From a working man in Langdale, I heard a wonderful testimony to the poet's care and interest in his poorer neighbours : ' He will walk miles to carry summat to a sick child, he is a good man the powet.' It may seem almost ridiculous in me to say anything about the education which the love of Wordsworth has been to many of the most distinguished men I have known.

In my second term at Oxford, I met for the first time, A. H. Clough, often very silent in general society, but, when certain subjects were mentioned, a most remarkable and powerful talker. I told him that I had seen Wordsworth, standing, like Matthew, with ' a bough of wilding in his hand;' and Clough said, 'I have seen him in that way again and again, and always thought of " The two April Mornings." ' He then broke out in a wonderful expression of praise about Wordsworth's view of nature and life ; and spoke angrily of Garbett, professor of poetry, who, in a lecture, had called Wordsworth a pantheist. Clough seemed to me to express exactly the peculiar position Wordsworth holds in poetry, and he spoke, I remember, of having heard that J. S. Mill had lately told some friend of his what a wonderful influence Wordsworth had had on his life and thought. The wellknown passage in Mill's *Autobiography*, which I read when it first appeared, reminded me of Clough's words.

Clough, though reserved and silent, was a very interesting man. It was known that he was passing through considerable changes of opinion and belief, and that he would soon give up his Fellowship at Oriel. Men, who had read with him in long vacation parties, were always greatly impressed by his character and personality. One of his admirers showed me some of the poems which were published in the small volume called *Ambarvalia*, which reflected completely the agitations and conflict of his spirit. One evening I heard him at a meeting of the Decade, which, by the kindness of Mr. Powles, I was permitted to be present at, speak for nearly an hour on the social questions so prominent at the time of the Revolution of 1848. It was a marvellous speech, and his words as to the duties of property sank into my soul. I have never forgotten them. He concluded with an allusion to a fine passage in *Sartor Resartus*, where the aristocracy are spoken of as preserving their game, and when he had done speaking, some one who was present, said 'These are words to think about, not to attempt to answer.' Matthew Arnold, in his poem on Clough, has described with inimitable grace his chief characteristics, and has succeeded in leaving an imperishable impression of one whose life was too short for friendship—not for fame. The recently published selection from his poetry will, I venture to think, be often in the hands of those who like to trace the effect of Arnold and Newman on a perhaps over-sensitive organisation. Clough wrote an interesting pamphlet on the Irish Famine, which had an effect of a certain kind, in moderating expenses and making some people save money in the midst of their dissipations in a summer term.

Before I went to Oxford in October, I passed a night at Rugby, to see a nephew who was then there, and I had a delightful talk with J. C. Shairp, who was looking after the boarders of his friend Bradley, now Dean of Westminster, who had recently been married. Shairp talked over my Lake experience with me, and heard with great interest my account of my afternoon with Hartley Coleridge. He had in his possession a translation of Hartley's from the *Prometheus Vinctus*, a beautiful fragment, which showed what Hartley might have done, had he persevered in this province. Shairp took a most kindly interest in my Oxford reading, and, by his advice and that of his friend, F. Fanshawe, on my return to Oxford I began to read with W. Marriott, a Fellow of my college, and to think seriously of standing for the Hertford scholarship. Through the good opinion of Marriott and some other friends I was elected a member of the Hermes, a small society which met for discussion in the rooms of its members, and which contained men whom I was proud to know. At one of these meetings, H. Smith gave us his views on Communism, and made every one who heard him feel that he was master of the subject. I cannot adequately express all that I felt about the greatness of Henry Smith. I first became thoroughly acquainted with him when my old friend, Grant Duff, came to reside at Balliol in October 1847. Trench's book on *The Miracles* had just appeared. Smith had read the Introduction, and I was certainly amazed at the wonderful power with which he examined the position, and enlightened us as to the view of Hume and certain Germans on the whole subject. He was as modest as he was great, and his humour was delicate and piercing. Few men have ever made such an impression as he did as an undergraduate; for years I looked upon him as an oracle, and his judgments of men and books were at once kindly and profound. His paper in the first volume of *Oxford Essays*, on the 'Plurality of Worlds,' seemed to me the very perfection of well-balanced criticism. Whewell and Brewster were weighed in his balance, and no faults could be found with his careful examination of their views; but, as I proceed, I shall have again to speak of the many great qualities of Henry Smith.

One remarkable feature of my second term at Oxford is worth recording. An honorary degree was given to Rajah Brooke, whose exploits in Borneo were at that time in everybody's mouth. The theatre was filled. The enthusiasm was, I think, as great as when Jenny Lind sang there. Brooke's quiet yet determined look was very fascinating. Through the kindness of a friend, I was introduced to him, and it was impossible to help feeling a thrill of pleasure, at the sight of one who seemed to repeat the story of England's great voyagers. Among the most prominent and enthusiastic Masters of Arts in the theatre was the keen face and small person of Arthur Stanley, who at that very time was issuing a pamphlet in support of Hampden, who had just been appointed Bishop of Hereford. The old anti-Hampden animus had revived, and Stanley, though never a warm friend of Hampden's, came chivalrously forward, along with F. D. Maurice, to champion the cause of one who never, I believe, recognised the efforts of those who did so much in his service. Indeed, it was said that the far more elaborate argument of Archdeacon Hare, who wrote a long letter to expose the unfair garbling of extracts from Hampden's *Bampton Lectures*, was never even noticed in any way by the Bishop himself. I think it is worth recording that, at this time, two volumes of sermons appeared, one by Keble, another by Stanley. The most interesting part of Keble's volume is the Preface, in which he makes an elaborate apology for the position he and Pusey took, as to remaining in the Church of England. Stanley's volume consisted of his University sermons on the ' Apostolic Age.' It did not command immediate success, but its freshness and vigour, as well as the incidental light it threw on the early history of the Church, made me feel that a new school of thought had arisen, and that the study of the Bible must be aided, to use Stanley's words, by employing the workmen of Tyre to build up the Temple at Jerusalem. The book itself seemed to some so dangerous, that Burgon, librarian of the Union, refused to order it in. A debate ensued, when the well-known Richard Congreve, then a master at Rugby, came up to fight for Stanley. 'I am not going to be frightened,' said Burgon, 'even by the explosion of a Congreve rocket.'

CHAPTER VIII

Oxford in 1848 — Excitement about Continental politics — Bishop Wilberforce — Anecdote of Sir Walter Scott — The true character of Wilberforce—His conversation and witticisms.

MANY years ago, Matthew Arnold said to me that he had been very much struck in reading again Stanley's life of his father, with the high-minded religious tone of the Corpus set, as they were called, and the great interest shown by them in literature. I had exactly the same feeling about the members of the Hermes and their friends, and this impression remains as strongly with me now as in the days of undergraduate life. The vicar of Malvern, J. G. Smith, always remarkable for his excellent scholarship, pure taste, and real practical power, was one of the most familiar figures of the circle. W. Marriott, a most truth-loving theologian, who has left some evidence of what he might have done had his life been longer, was another member of the group. Henry Coleridge, brother of Lord Coleridge, who made himself conspicuous in the Roman communion, which he joined, by the intensity of his character, and his insight into devotional theology, was to me a very attractive person. So, too, were F. Meyrick, who gave early signs of his interest in all Church questions, W. B. T. Jones, now Bishop of St. David's, and Tupper, a brother of M. F. Tupper, a man of noble character and great modesty. E. A. Freeman, busy then as always with history and architecture, came occasionally to Oxford, and I have heard him expatiate in 1847 on the unity of history, exactly in the same strain as in his Oxford lectures when Professor. I think all will admit that an undergraduate who had opportunities of seeing and hearing men such as these was a highly privileged person.

By Marriott's advice I remained during the Christmas vacation of 1847 at Oxford. The college was deserted. I and one other undergraduate were the only representatives of the junior part of the college ; but our solitude was relieved by sundry kind invitations to dinner in Common Room by such of the Fellows as were resident. The late Professor of Modern History gave numerous kind invitations, with G. Butler, to the two undergraduates, one of whom now looks back to the brilliant conversation, and the wonderful glimpses of the glories of German literature disclosed in the course of these memorable dinners. Mr. Froude had lately been at Bath, where he had met Walter Savage Landor. I had been for many years a fervent Landorian, and I listened with delight to the accounts of Landor's wayward proceedings, and his bursts of enthusiasm about his favourite authors. G. Butler, who was shortly to leave Oxford, to act as tutor at Durham, was an admirable scholar, and a man of wide reading. As he advanced in life his character deepened, and his interest in the highest subjects evinced itself in many ways. When on his marriage he returned to Oxford a few years afterwards, he and his gifted wife made their house in Beaumont Street a most pleasant place of resort. 'We can speak our minds freely here,' I remember C. Conybeare saying, and 'remember, Conington, nothing I say is to be put down in your diary.'

I think it is quite worth chronicling that at the end of 1847 the novel of *Jane Eyre* appeared, and was eagerly hailed by some of the resident Fellows as the mark of no common mind. I heard of the book, read the first volume and was completely fascinated. I then went down for two or three days to Gloucestershire, and was so anxious to get at the second volume, that I took a long walk of several miles to see if it had reached a circulating library in the nearest town. When I got back to Oxford, I went at once to secure the book, and was lucky enough to find it just sent in from the Principal of Brasenose, who had pronounced a most favourable verdict. Few books, I suppose, of the kind have ever taken possession of the public so completely as *Jane Eyre*; and when *Shirley*, the second production of Miss Brontë, was published, the interest, I think, was as great as when *Adam Bede* made its appearance.

With the year 1848, the year of revolution, many new actors came on the scene in my small theatre, and changes took place in my feelings on many subjects. I went to University College to put my name down as a candidate for the Hertford Scholarship. All candidates had to give in their names to A. P. Stanley, who was the chief examiner, assisted by Dr. Collis and W. Linwood. Stanley was not up when I knocked at his door, and J. Conington, who was quite unknown to me, but who had seen me at the Union Debating Society, kindly asked me to wait in his room till Stanley was ready. Conington had in his hands Newman's tale, *Loss and Gain*, which had just appeared. From his conversation on this morning may be said to date one of the great friendships of my life. In a few days he asked me to breakfast, and I began soon afterwards to take walks with him, and in a very short time I slid into the greatest intimacy with him.

My work in the Hertford examination was good enough to attract some special notice from Stanley, and I had the pleasure of meeting him soon also at breakfast, and although many years passed before I knew him in anything like the way I knew Conington, I had many evidences of his kindly interest and desire to help me.

Immediately after the publication of the *Saint's Tragedy*, Charles Kingsley came to Oxford. A friend of mine, who was a scholar of Corpus, asked me to come and meet him. I had already seen Kingsley in the rooms of his friend Cowley Powles, but the party was large, and I hardly heard him speak. At Corpus it was different. With the exception of Conington, who had taken his degree, we were all undergraduates, and Kingsley, thoroughly at his ease, talked to us freely about Carlyle, Tennyson, Luther, Charles Lamb, and all sorts of literary subjects in the most delightful way. Some of us were great admirers of the *Saint's Tragedy*, and the whole open-air effect of Kingsley's talk was most inspiring. I saw him several times during his stay in Oxford, and had a most kind invitation to visit him at Eversley; but I did not see him again until *Alton Locke* had been published in the year 1850, when an Oxford friend of mine had become his curate. I often regret the loss of some very valuable letters I had from him on the subject of some difficulties in the Old Testament history. They were sent by me, along with some of F. D. Maurice's, to a friend who died at Rome, and whose papers, in consequence of some scare of infection, were destroyed by authority. The world, however, now knows from the lives of Maurice and Kingsley how often these earnest and ardent spirits came to the rescue of those who were troubled, and gave wise and healthful advice. No greater benefit can be conferred upon those who are struggling and striving than to be in the presence and companion-ship of men who have passed through the waters to the firm land of belief. In these days of haste and over-work it will be well for the younger men of the generation if they can cherish opportunities of refreshment and strengthening. Retreats and quiet days may do something for the spiritual life, but I am rather thinking of the free and unrestrained intercourse with men older and wiser than one's self, which I have had the great privilege of enjoying, but have not, I fear, profited by as I ought to have done. Those who are intimate with *Sartor Resartus* will remember the passage in which Teufelsdröch speaks of his experience at Weimar.

The excitement caused by the unexpected revolution of 1848 was widely felt in Oxford. There are some still living who can remember Arthur Stanley's eager question as he entered the Union Reading Room, 'Is there any news of Guizot? I hope they won't kill Guizot,' and the excitement of the Bishop of Oxford, who had ridden from Cuddesdon to hear the last news. It was said at the time, I remember, that Mr. Alexander Dyce, occupied by some engrossing editorial work, had neglected for some days to look at the *Times*, which was duly brought to his chambers at Gray's Inn. A friend came to see him, who on hearing Dyce say that he must go to Paris to obtain special leave from the king to consult some treasure at Paris, said, 'My dear Dyce, there is no king in France now, he reached England as Mr. Smith last night,' greatly to the astonishment of the learned editor of Beaumont and Fletcher. The tenth of April and the collapse of the great Chartist movement, when Louis Napoleon acted as a special constable in London, were memorable events of the year. The Duke of Wellington certainly never stood higher in men's opinions than at this time ; and the action of Sir George Grey as Home Secretary was universally approved.

I heard much during the excitement of the time from J. Conington of the movement among Maurice and his friends which produced a now forgotten publication, *Politics for the People*. Maurice, Kingsley, Ludlow and Hughes contributed papers. Stanley wrote a most characteristic article on Lamartine, but the venture was not prosperous. I do not know who wrote the fine sonnet that wound up the little publication, which contained also stirring verses of Conington's, and some fine lines of Trench's. Christian socialism has certainly made many advances since those days, but it seems to me that its present upholders hardly equal in style and matter the telling sentences of Kingsley and the earnest words of Maurice.

Stanley, with some Oxford friends, visited Paris in the spring of 1848, and he and his fellow-travellers brought back to Oxford many interesting details of the strange and wonderful time. Pio Nono was for a short time the hero of the hour. '*Il est un vrai prêtre, mais il est trop faible,*' was the remark of a favourite French authoress at a reception, when Stanley and the late Sir Robert Morier were present. What Stanley used to call the greatest tribute ever paid to Walter Scott was told him by Guizot when he reached England. 'In the little room,' said Guizot, 'where I lay concealed there was a nearly complete copy of the Waverley novels, and I forgot my troubles.' Stanley was fond also of telling how he was endeavouring to find out the exact place where the hackney coach stood on the night of Louis the Sixteenth's flight from the Tuileries, when a carriage swept past containing more than one of the members of the Provisional Government. Many years afterwards, when his wife, Lady Augusta Stanley, was ill in Paris, he stood upon the same spot, and saw some of the passers-by touching their hats as Marshal Mac-Mahon rode past.

In the set in which I lived chiefly at Oxford, the interest excited by the state of things in France was marvellous, and at the Union and other debating societies many evidences were given of the intense feeling as to continental politics. The following year Stanley was appointed by the Vice-Chancellor, Plumptre, to preach the University sermon. It happened to be the anniversary of the day when the news of the French Revolution reached Oxford, and the preacher, according to his usual fashion, made several historical allusions. On the following Sunday Jowett was the preacher, and the contrast between his sermon, now embodied in his *Essay on the Character of St. Paul,* and that of Stanley, was as marked as the difference between the two contributions made by these two friends to the exposition of Pauline teaching.

I had the pleasure from time to time, during these years of undergraduate life, of enjoying the hospitality of the Bishop of Oxford. He had been a school and college friend of my eldest brother, and had always maintained a warm friendship with him. So much has been written about this remarkable man, that I feel diffident about expressing my own view of his life and character. He was extremely kind to me, and I always enjoyed a conversation with him more than I can express. To some his manner appeared artificial; I never thought it so, and the unreality which has been laid to his charge did not, I believe, exist. I have seen him in many circles, when he was the life and soul of the company, and I have always felt that, although his immense social powers might sometimes lead him astray, there was a depth of character and intensity of purpose, which did not reveal itself at first, but was, on nearer acquaintance, most marked. Whatever mistakes he may have made, in social controversies and political actions, the elevation of the episcopate, and the raising of the standard of clerical life and work, were never absent from his mind, and continually governed his actions. I have known him put aside engagements with royal personages, in order that he might do something to help an unfortunate brother in the ministry, or aid a distressed friend.

As a host he was charming. On the first occasion of my being his guest, Lady Davy, then a very old woman, was also there. The Bishop, knowing my father had been a friend of Walter Scott, introduced me to her, and managed to draw from her many telling anecdotes of Sir Walter's best days, his charming talk, and his kindness to his friends. One of these anecdotes is well worth recording, but it is of Scott in his sad decline.

When at Rome he was taken one day for a drive by a friend of Lady Davy's, who said to the gentleman who made the third in the carriage, when they reached a wayside pool, 'This is a wan water.' Sir Walter, who seemed to be dozing, revived, and with great spirit repeated the last verse of the ballad 'Kinmont Willie':—

> 'He is either himsel' a devil frae hell,
>   Or else his mother a witch maun be ;
> I wadna hae ridden that wan water,
>   For a' the gowd in Christendie!'

The Bishop was in the habit of gathering men of different ways of thinking together, and his tact and skill were most pleasantly exercised in bringing out characteristics of his guests. From Trench, his chaplain, he would extract much of his varied lore, and from others, like Archdeacon Randall, Hugh Pearson, and Burgon, he would manage to draw forth some particular story he wanted some great lady, or distinguished man, to hear. Lady Ashburton, who was one of the queens of society, was fond of describing the Bishop's conversation as a delicious trifle, with something very solid below it. The whole nature of the man showed itself when he was completely at ease, as I have had the pleasure of seeing him, in country houses and in company of those for whom he had a particular regard, such as the late Bishop Claughton of St. Albans. It was of course natural that a man who was fully aware of his ability to fill the highest posts in the Church should feel chagrined at the promotion of men younger than himself, and in his diary there are certain traces of the existence of this feeling. I can, however, recall more than one occasion when the Bishop, regretting he had spoken somewhat disparagingly of dignities, hoped that his hasty words might be forgotten, and uttered generous praise of those who had been the subject of his remarks. In 1866 he came most kindly to preach for me, on the completion of my church at Handsworth, and astonished a mixed multitude, some of whom were disposed to criticise, by a sermon on the words, 'Not as though I had already attained,' which long dwelt in the memories of those who heard it. Many and many a hearer of that sermon has thanked me for the privilege of that day. The Bishop had lately been staying at the Grange, and he told me a story of a walk with Carlyle, which in deference to his wishes I never mentioned till Carlyle's death. They had been walking together and talking of John Sterling, a man greatly loved by both. 'Bishop,' said Carlyle, 'have you really got a creed?' 'Yes,' was the answer, 'and it grows firmer under my feet every year, but I have a difficulty.' 'What is that?' said the sage. 'It does not make the progress I wish in the world.' After a pause, Carlyle said with some feeling, 'If you have a creed, you can afford to wait.' I told this some years ago, in the garden of Exeter College, to Lord Coleridge and Mr. Froude, who were both greatly taken with the question and the answer.

Bishop Wilberforce was accused by some of his early Evangelical friends of desertion. He was also attacked by men of liberal thought, for having thrown over the views of F. D. Maurice, evidently at one time greatly prized by him, and for yielding too much to the pretensions of extreme High Churchmen. I have often thought that he has been treated with great injustice. There are certainly passages in his famous article on 'Essays and Reviews' which I regretted to have read, and which I have no doubt the Bishop repented of having written. I believe that, in all the action of his later life, Bishop Wilberforce desired to make the true comprehensiveness of the Church of England more widely felt and known. I know that he regretted greatly the strong declarations made in moments of panic, on the subject of the Inspiration of Scripture, by men like his friends Burgon and Goulburn. This

led Carlyle and others who met him at the Grange
sometimes to doubt his absolute sincerity. But
those who heard him, as I have often heard him, in
the confidence of conversation, express his deepest
convictions and beliefs, know that he was a Christian first, and that his churchmanship, though strong
and pronounced, had no narrowing effect on his
sympathies and tastes.

In Greville's *Diaries*, there is a strange mistake
on the part of the accomplished writer, who seems
to have thought that the Bishop, in a meddling
spirit, was trying to gain an influence of a spiritual
kind. The truth is, that the Bishop, always ready
to recognise 'the man within the man,' often
yearned to impart, to those who seemed without any
feeling as to the things unseen, his own content-
ment and inward peace. In many cases he was the
means of bringing back some sense of the paramount claim of religion over the soul to those who
seemed absorbed in the present life. And there are
some now living who feel that the Divine Life
within the soul of man owed more than they can
express to his teaching.

Two men, very different, heard the sermon he
preached at Oxford on the Jubilee of the Church
Missionary Society, and resolved to give their lives
to God. One of these was Bishop French of Lahore,
the other was Bishop Patteson of Melanesia. To
have effected such resolves by a single sermon was
no common achievement. Whenever the weak-

nesses of Samuel Wilberforce are recounted, this triumph as a preacher should surely be remembered also. Hugh Pearson, who knew and loved the Bishop well, once said in my hearing, 'When Marlborough's avarice was mentioned to Bolingbroke, he said, "He is so great a man that I forget his foibles;" and I often think of this when envious people speak ill of S. Oxon.'

Every one who knew the Bishop well can recall instances of his ready wit. Stanley wrote the famous article in the *Edinburgh Review* in which he chivalrously pleaded the cause of the Essayists and Reviewers, and endeavoured to mitigate the severity of the Bishop's article in the *Quarterly*. A year afterwards, when dining at Cuddesdon, Stanley deprecated the Bishop's use of the word 'disingenuous,' in the case of one of the essayists. 'I cannot quote,' said the Bishop, 'as I am not so familiar with the book as I was a year ago.' 'Nor am I,' said Stanley, 'probably for the same reason.' 'Ah,' was the Bishop's rejoinder, 'so the two augurs have met each other.' What could be more adroit than his answer to Lord Redesdale, who expressed a wish that some place could be found for a dignitary who had married secretly, and resigned his post? 'We could give him the Bishopric of Ferns, for ferns are cryptogamous.' When he was told that a young man in whom he felt an interest was advised to become a curate of a very liberal vicar, the Bishop said, 'Is not that rather a massacre of an innocent?'   I once told him that Stanley had written to me that Liddon had preached a University sermon which had taken his hearers from earth for an hour, and kept them there; the Bishop said, 'No higher praise could be given, and it is admirably said.'   Of the Bishop's own confirmation addresses at Westminster Abbey to the boys of the school, Stanley said, 'I thought he never could surpass his last address until I heard his next.'

The Dean, to my regret, did not reprint from *Good Words* the sermon which he preached after the Bishop's death, feeling, perhaps, that the eulogy was somewhat strained.   But I have heard him say to his friend, Pearson, 'He often provoked me, but I felt when he was gone that a power had passed away from earth, and I never shall forget the kind letter I had from him on my mother's death.   He was very nearly a very great man.'   One secret of the Bishop's great success, and his power over younger men, was his evident desire that every curate, vicar, rector, canon, dean and bishop, should bring out into full relief the meaning of their vocation and work in life.   He preached once at Bridgnorth, in the church of a dear friend of mine, Mr. Bellett, a man of whom it may be said, briefly, that he made religion attractive to old and young by the perfect simplicity and consistency of his life.   Mr. Bellett was almost unknown to him, but the Bishop had an opportunity of hearing something of his labours as a parish priest; and his skilful allusion to this exemplary life drew from a churchwarden these words, ' Why, the Bishop spoke as if he had seen our vicar working away from morning till night, with a kind word for every one, and a word of advice about the Bible.' The preacher who could so impress hearers in a country town could speak home, as in his famous sermon before the British Association, so as to win from men like Murchison and Lyell the strongest words of praise. I have now said enough, I think, of this remarkable man, who more than once, in the kindest way, offered me work in his diocese.

CHAPTER IX

John Conington—*Essays and Reviews*—Goldwin Smith—Halford Vaughan—Reading Party at Oban in 1850—Sir William Hamilton's Lectures—Anecdotes of Carlyle—Dr. Hannah—Macready—Baron Alderson—The Great Exhibition Year.

I HAVE already spoken of my intimate friendship with John Conington. In the memoir of Mark Pattison, published after his death, there is a passage which gave to many of Conington's friends great pain. It must have been written in some irritation, and certainly conveys a wrong impression. Very different is the too brief account of Conington by Henry Smith, prefixed to Conington's *Miscellaneous Writings*. For many years Conington was a favourite figure in Oxford. He brought from Rugby a wonderful reputation. His memory was marvellous, and he was a devourer of books. He left his Demyship at Magdalen for University College, and as a Scholar and Fellow he was attached to that college for many years, until his election as Corpus Professor of Latin. He was a devoted admirer of Arnold, but the man to whom he owed most was Cotton, afterwards Bishop of Calcutta, and always one of Conington's most attached friends. What was surprising in Conington was, that with all his depth of scholarship he knew little of German. He had made a certain progress in the language, but he had none of the wide reading of Pattison and Nettleship. But there was a reality and strength in all his work, which made one feel that he was like a great sledge hammer in the world of literature. When you walked with Conington, you were obliged to feel that your intellect was on the full stretch. He delighted to talk of his favourite authors, and it was marvellous with what accuracy he quoted long passages. Under his influence, for at one time I was his private pupil, I made acquaintance with many books I should otherwise have been ignorant of. During the long period of my intimate friendship with him, I do not think a cross or angry word ever escaped him. In later years his religious views led him, perhaps, further from Arnold and his school, but his wisdom and moderation, in the troubled days when reforms at Oxford were keenly canvassed, gained for him the friendship of men with whom in earlier days he had little in common.

When I saw most of him, his admiration for Stanley was very great. He used to say, that to him and Goldwin Smith, and Henry Smith of Balliol, he owed more than he could ever express in language. As a critic of compositions he was unrivalled. During the years of his Professoriate he was in the habit of selecting younger men for reading parties, and among those who are now most distinguished in their various callings, there are many who I am sure will fully acknowledge what they owe to his encouragement and kindliness. By his advice I remained at Oxford for a considerable part of the long vacation of 1849, and read with Richard Congreve, who was then Fellow and Tutor of Wadham. Congreve's knowledge of history, particularly of Thucydides, was very great. He and Conington were on excellent terms, and many a pleasant evening have I spent in their society, listening to the exposition Congreve gave of the strange method and madness of Comte, who was beginning to acquire immense influence over Congreve's mind. It was most interesting to hear Conington's demurrers to many of Congreve's positions, and I daresay the mental gymnastics of that time were not without use, though I never felt at all the attraction which so many have found in Comte. It would be tedious to detail a tenth part of the obligations I owed to Conington. His advice was always sound, and he possessed the power of directing younger men than himself to the correction of faults and strengthening of weak places. I thought him a better Greek than Latin scholar, but when he was elected to the Professorship he made it his object to work his Chair in the way most useful to the University. His energy was immense. When once threatened with blindness, he began his well-known translation of Virgil's great poem, in order, as he said, to have resource, if his eyesight failed him.

After I married in 1861, he always paid me an annual visit, and though some thought that in his later years his sympathies had narrowed, I never found it so. In loyalty to his friends he never failed, and he could appreciate men differing widely from himself. During one of the last visits I paid him at Oxford, we went together to hear Liddon preach one of his most remarkable sermons, and as we returned to Conington's lodgings, he said to me : 'When that sermon was ended, I felt the truth of what Jowett says, that there is no power on earth like the power of religion.' One or two of his sayings I must endeavour to preserve. 'It is difficult to compare, but I think in Froude's History there are passages equal to anything in Thucydides, or Tacitus.'

Of Miss Martineau's *Deerbrook*, he once said, 'I love it. Christian forgiveness has never been better enforced than in the passage where Mr. Grey makes his little daughter repeat again Pope's well-known prayer with the verse :—

> " Teach me to feel for others' woe,
>   To hide the faults I see ;
> The mercy I to others show,
>   That mercy show to me." '

When I once read him a passage I copied from a review of Carlyle's *Latter Day Pamphlets*, by Goldwin Smith, Conington said : 'You will hardly find anything in Burke better than this.' I once searched, along with Conington, in the library of Hartlebury Castle, among Warburton's books, for the copy of Tickell's translation of the first Book of the *Iliad*, with Pope's annotations. Although it was in the catalogue we could not find it, and it must have been taken from the library, and have come into the possession of the Reverend John Mitford, as it was sold after his death. It was a great grief to Conington that he was unable to trace it, and give some account of it in his elaborate essay on Pope, originally contributed to *Oxford Essays*. I may mention here a curious fact connected with *Essays and Reviews*. I had written some portion of a paper on 'Clerical Education,' advocating the establishment at Oxford of a select school of theological students. Conington liked it, and wrote to his friend T. C. Sandars, one of the losses of this present year, who was the editor of *Oxford Essays*, and was told by him that the *Essays* had stopped, but that if my production was finished it would be inserted in a volume which afterwards became the famous *Essays and Reviews*; so that I had a narrow escape of notoriety. If I remember rightly, Archbishop Thomson had a similar escape, and actually afterwards edited the volume of *Aids to Faith*, the orthodox answer to *Essays and Reviews*.

Conington at one time was a candidate for the Greek Chair at Edinburgh. Bonamy Price was also a candidate. Professor Blackie was elected. Conington came to Edinburgh and made a great impression on some of the Town Council, who were then the electors. He dined at my father's house, and knowing that my father was intimate with Brougham, he managed to draw from him many anecdotes of Brougham's early days, and stories about Walter Scott, and the life at Edinburgh University, when he and my father were young men. When Conington had gone to his hotel, my father said, 'If your friend from Oxford gets as much from other people's heads as he did from mine to-night, he must have a vast store of stories.' This, indeed, was one of Conington's peculiarities. I have wondered at the way in which he would gradually coax men like Professor J. M. Wilson, Halford Vaughan, and Jacobson, to disclose much that had a special interest for himself and myself. I remember saying to him, 'How skilfully you led Vaughan on to talk about Michelet and French History.' 'Yes,' said Conington, 'I knew your laudable curiosity, and wanted to gratify it.' When a friend of ours, the much lamented W. W. Shirley, expressed his intention of taking orders, I said I was very glad to hear it, as he was a strong man. 'Ah,' said Conington, 'you like to see some one cross the plank before you. If it will bear him, it will bear you.'

The pithy sayings, the truthful aphorisms, the pleasant criticisms, that would fall from the lips of

Henry and Goldwin Smith and Conington, in the course of a Sunday afternoon's walk, would, if I had chronicled them at the time, in Boswellian fashion, have made these meagre recollections really valuable. To dig into your memory is one thing, but to reproduce the happy turns of expression, the powerful epigram and the ready wit, is another. I have read somewhere that the famous Lord Holland did at one time, in imitation of Boswell, make a faithful chronicle of actual conversation; and I have heard Sir David Dundas, who was a guest at Bowood, speak of a long morning, when Charles Austin and Macaulay talked to the admiration of listeners for hours, and express his regret, as I am now doing, that there had been no Senior present to act as chronicler. I have heard in my time many good talkers, but I have known few who for variety of topics and power of memory could match John Conington. But in him there was something higher and nobler than mere literary power. It was a delight to him when I took orders, to hear of my activities, especially among pupil-teachers and young folks, and many a helpful hint did I get from him, and many a talk have we had over the message of the Bible to man, and the enduring claims of religion on the soul. When he read an interesting tract of R. H. Hutton's, he said to me: 'What a happiness it is to bring a great doctrine a little nearer the hearts of men!'

University Reform had a warm advocate in

Conington. Before the Royal Commission had reported, he was fond of contrasting the condition of Magdalen with that of Trinity, Cambridge. 'The incomes of the two colleges are exactly the same, but the results are different.'

Strangers who made acquaintance with Conington were astonished at his memory, and the extraordinary variety of his reading. Percy Smythe, afterwards Lord Strangford, who had been formerly a 'postmaster' of Merton, and had gone into the diplomatic service, came sometimes to Oxford to see his friend Sir Alexander Grant. After a pleasant dinner at Oriel, where Grant had assembled many of his friends, some revelation was made by Conington of the width of his reading. When he left the party Smythe said, 'I have always looked on my chief, Stratford Canning, as a sort of political cyclopædia, but Conington beats him.'

The presence of Smythe in Oxford, I may here say, was a real refreshment. He foresaw the coming struggle in the East, long before the outbreak of the Crimean War, and his anecdotes of Sir Stratford were most amusing and racy. I had many opportunities of meeting him in the rooms of his friends Grant and Roundell. He was one of the select few whose merits and wisdom were only known to his intimate friends, and when he passed away it was then known how different a part he ought to have played in the drama of life.

It would be improper of me to say anything of the benefit I derived from walks and rides with Goldwin Smith, who returned to Oxford towards the close of my undergraduate life. At that time there was no one who interested the thoughtful men of his University more. A great career seemed before him, and his powerful thought, aided by a most vigorous style of writing, gave him an almost unique position. Lord Sherbrooke once said, after reading Goldwin Smith's book on Irish history, ' If the writer of this chooses a great subject, he will be one of the greatest historians the world has ever seen.' Many, I suppose, have often regretted that there will be no monumental work by this gifted man, of whom a famous lady once said, ' that he and Carlyle were the only two men she had ever known, in her great experience, who had the true elevation of genius.'

When Halford Vaughan delivered his inaugural lectures as Regius Professor of Modern History, new life and interest were imparted to the subject. In my first term I used to go with my cousin, the late Lord Glasgow, to hear really interesting lectures on French History, read by Cramer, Dean of Carlisle, to ourselves and one other hearer, in the drawing-room of the Principal of New Inn Hall. The contrast between this select body and the throngs who listened in the Taylorian Buildings was complete. Vaughan, in spite of his great power, hardly fulfilled the promise of his first lectures. He was a very remarkable man, and had been a Fellow of Oriel. His manner in conversation was somewhat dogmatic. An eloquent pamphlet on the Professoriate, and some rather singular volumes on Shakespeare, are all that remain of his writings. It was said that a work on *Man's Moral Nature*—the work indeed of his life—was destroyed by some accident, and that he never had the heart to resume his task. Some years after he quitted the Chair of Modern History, I saw him gazing at Holman Hunt's picture of the 'Finding of our Lord in the Temple,' in a way which showed how completely he was entering into the spirit of the painter. He too, it was hoped, might have enriched English literature with a great history. Most men have known in their lives some who have departed and left behind them no trace of their great promise.

In the year 1850 a serious change took place in my life. I left Oxford in order to read quietly at my father's country place in Ayrshire. A solitary life tempts one to read more than is good for health, and I paid the penalty. At the end of my seclusion, I was joined by my friend, Grant Duff, and after a few days of rest and quiet, we joined the party of an Oxford tutor at Oban. The late Master of Balliol, who had with him the present Speaker, Lord Cottesloe, H. Lancaster, too early lost to literature and the Scotch Bar, and D. Owen, was then also at Oban. He preached frequently in the upper room where the Episcopal Church service was conducted, and I believe I could now, if specially required, write out much of what he then said. Certainly there are passages in the Epistles I never read without recalling some of Jowett's pregnant sayings, in after years re-cast in his essays for the two volumes on St. Paul's Epistles. There is one, once spoken at Oban, still as fresh as it seemed to me then :—

'To the poor and uneducated, at times to all, no better advice can be given for the understanding of Scripture than to read the Bible humbly with prayer. The critical and metaphysical student requires another sort of rule for which this can never be made a substitute. This duty is to throw himself back into the times, the modes of thought, the language of the apostolic age. He must pass from the abstract to the concrete, from the ideal and intellectual to the spiritual, from later statements of faith and doctrine to the words of inspiration which fell from the lips of the first believers. He must seek to conceive the religion of Christ in its relation to the religions of other ages and distant countries, to the philosophy of our own and other times : and if in this effort his mind seems to fail or waver, he must win back, in life and practice, the hold on the truths of the Gospel, which he is beginning to lose in the mazes of speculation.'

The pleasures of a reading party are not easily forgotten. The long walks and talks, especially those with Grant Duff, the exquisite effects of sunset in the delightful region of the West Highlands, glimpses of J. C. Shairp, E. Poste, and Fitzjames Stephen, who came for a brief sojourn at Oban, made the time very memorable. *In Memoriam* had just appeared, and was in everybody's hands. Warm praise of it from Jowett, I remember, surprised me.

I had the misfortune to fall into bad health at the close of my stay at Oban, and was forced to abandon all idea of entering the Honour Schools. Disappointments of life are sometimes seen in after years to have been blessings in disguise, and although my failure in health prevented me from becoming what I had at one time hoped to be, a resident in Oxford like one or two of my lifelong friends, I have at least the satisfaction of thinking that active ministerial life has many channels of usefulness, and some compensations denied to a mere student. I spent the winter of 1850-51 chiefly in Edinburgh, and attended regularly Sir William Hamilton's lectures. In consequence of infirmity he was only able to read for half an hour, but he was still most vigorous in expression and language. It was a great treat to hear him expound Kant, and on the days on which he lectured on Logic he was perfectly admirable. He was good enough to allow me to ask him questions about Hume and Butler. He had heard with great interest of J. M. Wilson's lectures at Oxford, some of which I had heard and was able to report to him. One day he gave a very diverting account to his class of the principal argument of Sewell's *Christian Morals*, a book which he said was hardly worthy of the great University, ' of which I am an unworthy member.'

During the course of this winter, I frequently met Bishop Terrot and Dr. Hannah, both of them capital conversationalists, and capable of drawing from each other rich stores of anecdotes. Bishop Terrot was a friend of Mr. Carlyle's, and had much to tell of the Sage of Chelsea. ' I consider,' said Carlyle on one occasion, ' the apostle Peter and his following to be the representatives of dogmatic theology, and if Peter were to come here to-night, I should say, Peter, my good Peter, you may go, you're done with.' This utterance of Carlyle's was made, I am afraid, at the table of the famous Thomas Erskine of Linlathen. Emerson's relations with Carlyle were mentioned. Carlyle was at times rather tired by Emerson's optimism. One evening an admirer of Carlyle's called at the hour when he and his wife were at tea. He was much astonished at the delight with which he was received by Mrs. Carlyle, and when she had left the room to make some addition to the fare, Carlyle said, ' She's rale glad to see you, she thocht you was Emerson.' The Bishop had a real pity for Mrs. Carlyle, and knew that Carlyle talked about what he was writing to certain persons, Lady Ashburton being one of them, in a way that he had never done to her. He knew the passages that had taken place between Mrs. Carlyle and Edward Irving, and had actually heard her say, what is, I think, recorded by Mr. Froude, that if she had married Irving, there would have been no 'tongues.'

Dr. Hannah was thoroughly well read in English literature, and was indeed an admirable specimen of the Oxford first-class man. His success in Edinburgh, at Glenalmond, and as vicar of Brighton, was very great; and it is, I think, a great reproach to the dispensers of patronage that he died an Archdeacon. As Bishop Terrot said of him, 'Few men know the insides and outsides of books like Hannah.' It was my privilege often to meet him at Methven Castle, where my uncle, William Smythe, who was himself an Oxford first-class man, and a true lover of the classics, delighted to hear Hannah expatiate on the books he knew and loved so well. His *Bampton Lectures* and a small volume of sermons, deserve to be far better known than they are.

Early in 1851 I was suddenly obliged to go to London. There was great excitement in the political world. Lord John Russell, in consequence of the complications arising out of the Papal Aggression question, resigned. The Queen sent for Lord Stanley, who was unable to form a Government, and the Whig Ministers returned to office. I was fortunate enough to be present in the House of Commons when elaborate explanations were made, and heard good speeches from Lord John and Sir

James Graham.   The excitement in London was
very great.   It was known that Lord Palmerston's
conduct of Foreign affairs, which led to his quitting
office at the close of the same year, was distasteful
in high quarters, and Arthur Stanley, who was at
that time busy with the affairs of the Oxford Royal
Commission, told me that he had heard rumours as
to the great political changes.   He greatly approved
the line which the Peelites had taken on the Papal
Aggression.   Strange to say, he considered that
Cardwell was likely to assume a more prominent
position than Gladstone; and that Macaulay had
expressed great anger at the growing indifference
of people to what he called true Whig principles,
and had added, 'I believe the future is with these
nasty Peelites.'   I heard all this with great interest,
as I had at that time a thorough-going admiration
for Gladstone.

I had also at this time the pleasure of being
present when Macready played Macbeth for the
last time, and took his final leave of the stage.
Most of his great friends and admirers were
there.   Bulwer Lytton, John Forster, and Tal-
fourd, sat near each other.   The enthusiasm was
great.   Macready played with great dignity, and
his faltering voice in the last scene showed his
emotion.   After a short pause, he appeared again,
in plain clothes, and spoke with great feeling of his
efforts to purify the stage and encourage dramatists.
Two years before this I had seen him play

Wolsey, when the Queen came in state, just before he left England for America. There was a disturbance in the gallery, and Macready, having obtained gracious permission to speak, spoke a few words with great dignity, and the turmoil fell. No actor that I have ever seen impressed me like Macready. His voice was harsh, but it was commanding. There was an elevation in his tone, and a thorough mastery of the part he played, which made you feel you were in the presence of a man of real mind, who knew the depths of the human heart, and could play upon every chord of feeling. His Lear was magnificent, but upon the whole, I think his best part was Richelieu. I do not know if Mr. Henry Irving ever saw Macready in Richelieu, but his personation of the great cardinal reminded me of Macready, especially in the powerful scene when the wretched king implores him to return to office, with most absolute authority.

Would that all plays could have the effect that Macready's renderings of Shakespeare have had on me and on so many. The stage must exist, and the stage must be purified. Arthur Helps says somewhere, finely, that a man who has come away from a fine representation of Hamlet or Macbeth is in no temper for a low debauch.

So much has been written on the subject of the Great Exhibition in 1851, that I need do no more than say that the whole effect on London life and society was of the most extraordinary kind. Great people of all kinds were to be seen in Hyde Park. Many really believed that a new epoch had commenced, and that European wars were at an end. But the *coup d'état* of Louis Napoleon, at the close of 1851, and the conduct of the Emperor Nicholas as to the Eastern question, soon gave evidence of another state of things.

In the summer of 1851, when returning on horseback from the consecration of a friend's church, I had the misfortune to break my collar-bone. I passed the night at Lewknor, and was most kindly ministered to by Lady Alderson, and her daughter, now Lady Salisbury, who were the guests of my friend Mr. Dean. To this accident I owed an acquaintance with Baron Alderson, the charm of whose conversation and ready wit made him famous in society. Anything happier than the after-dinner speeches of Baron Alderson and Sir Cresswell Cresswell I never heard. At the Founder's Day at Charterhouse they were particularly happy. The most delightful feature in Baron Alderson's conversation was his real interest in religious questions. He spoke with a wise and thoughtful tolerance, which made one feel he might have been as admirable a bishop as a judge.

In the autumn of 1851 I spent a few delightful weeks on the Continent. The first sight of Paris with all its wonderful associations, days at Florence and Venice, delicious lingerings on the Italian lakes, a glimpse of Switzerland, and the delight of the

Rhine as we returned home, in most pleasant company, have often made me wish that it was possible to recover the first rapture of the first time. The moment when, aided by Sir F. Palgrave's admirable handbook of Northern Italy, one realised the greatness of the pictures in Florence, the exquisite beauty of Giotto's Campanile, and the dignity of the Duomo, is indeed an event in life, to be ever gratefully remembered.

CHAPTER X

Sir Henry Russell—Sir David Dundas—Death of my Father—Funeral of the Duke of Wellington—Lord Aberdeen's Ministry—Ordination—Work in Worcestershire—Lord and Lady Lyttelton—Matthew Arnold —Robert Lowe—Sir Stafford Northcote—Curate life.

In his famous drama, Sir Henry Taylor says the world knows nothing of its greatest men, and most men know from their own experience how men of great ability often pass their days in obscurity. One of my most intimate friends at Oxford was Sir George Russell, now M.P. for Berkshire, and at his father's place at Swallowfield I spent many a pleasant day. Sir Henry Russell had filled most important posts in India. His father had been Chief Justice in Calcutta. Bad health compelled him to live a very quiet life, but he was never idle, and always continued to take an active interest in Indian questions. The letters of ' Civis ' originally appeared in the *Times*, and were afterwards published as a pamphlet. They showed how complete was Sir Henry's knowledge of India, and the style bore traces of the diligent student of English literature. A conversation with Sir Henry on the merits of Johnson, or the power of Hazlitt's criticism, was a real enjoyment. He was particularly kind to me, and I treasure the recollection of his sanity and wisdom. He possessed a charming library, often used by his neighbour, the authoress, Miss Mitford, who dedicated one of her latest writings to Lady Russell, a French lady, whose spirit and pleasantness were inherited by her children.

Baron Rolfe, afterwards Lord Cranworth, was living near Swallowfield when I was paying one of my frequent visits there. We went over to spend an evening, always remarkable to me, as I then for the first time met Sir David Dundas. Greville has sketched Sir David's character in a somewhat caustic fashion. He has done no justice, however, to Dundas's power of conversation. His career was a singular one. At one time he had practice at the bar, but it left him; and when he was Solicitor-General, he had very little. He refused an important office from the feeling it was too much of a sinecure; and although odd, and in some ways eccentric, he did not deserve to be called what Greville calls him—a humbug. He honestly believed Macaulay's view of Whiggery to be the true rationale of English politics; and no man admired Mackintosh, Horner, and Romilly, more than Dundas. He was always seen at his best in the company of Lord and Lady Cranworth. It was my own fault that I missed being present at some of the pleasant evenings with the Miss Berrys, in Curzon Street, where Dundas had expressed his

readiness to take me. The secret of these ladies'
success, he said, lay in their unfailing desire to
think well of all human beings, with the exception of Sam Rogers, who for some reason of his
own, for a very considerable time, avoided their
society.

In the year 1852, my connection with Oxford
came to an end. It was the year of my father's
retirement from his judicial office. After a long
and almost unexampled career,—forty-one years,—
to the astonishment of his brethren, who thought
him at eighty in full vigour, he placed his resignation in the hands of Lord Derby. He had,
however, unmistakable evidences of failing health.
It is not perhaps proper for me to dwell on the
remarkable testimony, given throughout Scotland,
to his character and work. I had intended at one
time to accept a very kind offer of a place in the
party of Dean Stanley to the East, and had almost
made up my mind to spend some money of my own
in the tour which produced *Sinai and Palestine*.
Stanley himself was most kind, and his companion,
Theodore Walrond, an intimate friend of my own,
would have made everything easy, but my elder
brothers felt, and I felt also myself, that it was
right that I should spend the winter of 1852-3 at
home, in order to be of use to my father. I never
regretted the abandonment of my eastern project,
as in 1853, in February, my father passed away,
soon to be followed by my youngest brother, who

had passed through Haileybury with great distinction, but, unfortunately, fell a victim to severe
pulmonary disease. His tutor, Mr. Buckley, thought
so highly of his scholarship, that he wished him to
leave Haileybury and go to Oxford.

I ought to have recorded the fact, that I saw, in
1852, that most striking sight, the funeral procession
of the Duke of Wellington. The sight of the
crowded streets, and the quiet reverence of the
multitudes, was most impressive. I had a ticket
for St. Paul's, but preferred the procession; and, as
it turned out, by skilful management I might have
seen both sights.

During my stay in London at this time, I saw
Maurice and Lockhart frequently. Maurice was
most helpful to me in discussing some Bible difficulties, and I never saw Lockhart so interested in
anything as in hearing my accounts of my breakfasts
with Maurice in Queen Square. He had heard of
Maurice from John Sterling, and expressed great
reverence for his character. The short-lived administration of Lord Derby was drawing to its close.
Lockhart, Hayward, and his friend Robert Hay,
had all expressed their belief that Disraeli's career
was at an end; but Lord Strangford, who knew
Disraeli well, predicted that, in spite of what had
taken place, 'young Ben' would live to be Premier,
and a very great one too. Lockhart, in giving me
an account of this, said, 'We laughed him to
scorn.'

Lord Strangford's epigram on the Queen's speech,
is, I think, worth preserving—

> ' The Queen tells of triumph on Africa's shore,
>   Bights the tropic without, bights the tropics within ;
>   But why does she not mention one triumph more,
>   That wonder of wonders, the bite of Ben in ? '

I happened to know several persons who were in
the secret as to the negotiations which ended in
the formation of the coalition government of which
Lord Aberdeen was the head. The history of the
time has been told so fully, that it is almost impossible to add anything to what has already been
published. It was a time when accusations were
freely made, by the Tadpoles and Tapers of politics.
The Peelites were accused by the Whigs of grasping
at too much, and the Whig Memoirs certainly give
a poor idea of the public spirit of some great men.
Lord Aberdeen most reluctantly took the reins of
premier. I heard a very shrewd observer predict,
what really came to pass, that Palmerston was not
unlikely to assume more prominent position.

The whole history of the administration, the
drifting into war, and the miseries of the Crimean
winter, made the retrospect of those years no
pleasant page in English annals. It was felt, I
think by many, that if Sir Robert Peel had been
alive, the unfortunate vacillations which led to the
Crimean war would never have taken place, and
Lord Stratford de Redcliffe would not have been
permitted to control the situation in the East.

More than forty years ago the examination of

candidates for Holy Orders was a very perfunctory affair. Bishop Wilberforce had the merit of introducing a new state of things, and now, at the most solemn time of a young man's life, every care is taken to deepen religious conviction, and infuse true ideas as to the greatness of the ministry. Bishop Pepys of Worcester had no ordination when I entered the diaconate in May 1853. I was sent by letters dimissory to the Bishop of Rochester, who held his ordination in Archbishop Tenison's chapel in Regent Street at an early hour on a Sunday morning, in order that the usual congregation might not be interfered with. There was no sermon on the duties of the ministry, and the Bishop wore a wig, so that the whole service seemed like a survival of a past state of things. It happened, however, by a fortunate chance, that, in the afternoon of the same day, I heard from F. D. Maurice, in the chapel of Lincoln's Inn, a most wonderful burst of eloquent reasoning, on the duty of those who, as ministers of Christ, were bound to consider themselves successors to the prophets. I have heard many sermons from Maurice, but on this particular occasion he seemed to rise into a diviner air than usual, and his words often came back to me when I first began to do battle with the various forces one encounters in a manufacturing town.

I was certainly most fortunate in beginning my new life under the leadership of my vicar, Claughton. I very soon began to be on very intimate terms with him. He had a singular power of winning the affections of those who worked under him. He had no particular method in the direction of our work. Every one had a considerable district intrusted to his care, and every one, I think, felt that he enjoyed a certain liberty of action, and this had the effect of deepening the sense of responsibility.

When a difficult case came before us, the vicar was ready to aid with advice, and, if there were need, to go with the curate, and give him a practical lesson how to act. He was fearless in rebuke, and could still preserve a loving and fervent spirit. I delighted in talking to him of the peculiarities of my people, and I very soon began to feel, under the inspiration of his guidance and friendship, the engrossing interest of parochial life. The object of the vicar of Kidderminster was to give every one of his curates a full share of work. We had our mornings in the schools, and were trained to catechise publicly in church. Sermons were not generally required much from those who were in their first year, but I, owing to circumstances, had to undertake the charge of a small chapel, and to preach frequently to a small number of simple country folks, among whom was a rare specimen of a true old English farmer, as genuine and true in his simple faith, and loyalty to the Church of England, as Sir Roger de Coverley himself. Many a pleasant walk did I have on Sunday mornings, through a romantic valley, to the little chapel, where there were a few shrubs, brought by the pious care of Leopold Acland, the first curate of Trimpley, from his father's Devonshire home.

There is an order in life which often surprises one, and I was often astonished to find how soon the interests of other days had passed away; and how thoroughly and completely the tasks of new life had become paramount in my affections. There had already been in Kidderminster many good workers, and I found, in my town and country district, constant experience of the truth that it is character, and character alone, which impresses on working men the lessons of religion. Consistency in life, and the knowledge that a man is really in earnest, are far more effective than emotional appeals, and rigid inculcations of particular truths.

There are those now alive who remember the present Bishop of Wakefield when he first worked as curate in Kidderminster, and who could speak feelingly of what they owed to his cottage lectures, and the sweet simplicity of his life.

Very soon after my entrance on curate life, the vicar, in his pleasant, playful way, told me that he had no time to prepare a lecture which he had promised to give at Bridgnorth, and that I must take his place. There was no help for it, and so I did my best to put into shape all I had heard from A. P. Stanley on the subject of the Black Prince. Stanley was at this time Canon of Canterbury, and was ready to pour forth for the benefit of his friends the historic lore which he gave to the world in the shape of his *Memorials of Canterbury.*

The commencement of my career as a lecturer led to my forming a friendship with Mr. Bellett, one of the vicars of Bridgnorth, a man of whom Osborne Gordon once said to me, ' you may look through the list of the higher clergy, and you will find no one more fitted to be there, from character, ability, and true literary taste, than Bellett.'   Mr. Bellett was an Irishman, and of a family well known for literary taste and great religious fervour.   He was one of those who may be said to have thoroughly enjoyed the privileges of a religious life, and who made that life attractive to others by the grace of his character. He was a true lover of great authors, and had, like his friend S. R. Maitland, an almost romantic love of truth.   After many years of faithful work at Bridgnorth, he was placed by the present Bishop of Hereford in an easier country living, where he died some years ago at a great age.   A privately printed memoir has told his friends what manner of man he was.

My visits to him from time to time, and his to me, are among the golden recollections of my life.   I never heard a better reader of poetry, except Bishop Claughton.   Mr. Henry Cheney, who had a great admiration of Mr. Bellett, used to declare that as some temperance lecturers were said to have a shocking example ready to produce, Mr. Bellett ought to be shown as a perfect specimen of the unambitious clergyman, whose whole soul was in his work. On hearing that a celebrated prelate was somewhat vexed that he had not received higher preferment, Mr. Bellett was heard to murmur: ' What does he want? has he not food and raiment?' —a remark which was thoroughly characteristic of the man. He had a true enjoyment of Irish humour, and I have jogged along with him in a pony carriage on Shropshire roads, while he read out some of the most amusing passages, in the now-forgotten Irish story, *Irish Men and Irish Women.*

For many years he undertook the duty of acting as chaplain at a very remarkable school, founded by his friend Mr. Whitmore, for the benefit of work-house lads. I have sometimes passed pleasant days at Mr. Whitmore's, where men like the late Lord Wrottesley, and others interested in education, visited the school, and were astonished by the really wonderful knowledge Mr. Bellett and a very intel-ligent master imparted to these boys.

In consequence of a certain aptitude for lectures, elicited by my kind vicar, I added to my general work, instruction of pupil-teachers, and in this way formed many most pleasant friendships with young men who have taken prominent places in training colleges, and under the Education Department.

Worcestershire was happy at this time in having amongst its clergy men like Canon Woodgate, Canon Melville, Archdeacon Lea, Canon Lyttelton,

Dr. Collis, and many others, who, aided by the impulse given by Mr. H. W. Bellairs, the Government Inspector, established prize schemes, gathered schoolmasters together, and in many ways elevated the whole tone of primary education, and conferred lasting benefits on their neighbourhoods. In these labours I was permitted to take some part, and I look back upon four years of town work in Kidderminster, and three years in the country parish of Hagley, with a feeling of intense thankfulness, that I was the intimate friend, and I may say fellow-labourer, of men who brought to the solution of the educational problem their great intelligence and earnest love of reality. Preparation of lectures was, in itself, a real education; and many a good-humoured laugh did my vicar, Claughton, give as he saw my pupil-teachers leave the Old Chantry of Kidderminster, from what he called—the Boyle lectures.

One day, as I was lecturing, the vicar brought Freeman to see the parish church. The architecture of the Chantry led Freeman to think it was so late that it could hardly have been used for the purpose of a chantry, and in the same year it was discovered that it had actually been planned in the year when Henry VIII. first agitated the divorce question.

The vicar of Kidderminster kindly permitted his staff to avail themselves of invitation from neighbours. In this way I had many pleasant relaxations, and among the chiefest of these was an occasional visit to Hagley. Lord Lyttelton took a great interest in the educational work of the diocese as well as in all theological questions. He was the unfailing friend of all the younger clergy, and a day or two at Hagley—where we were sure to meet some notable and interesting people—was a most pleasant break in the usual routine work. I wish I could properly describe the charm and grace possessed by Lord Lyttelton's first wife, the only sister of Mrs. Gladstone. To see her in the midst of her numerous young family, the boys busy at cricket, and the girls eagerly watching the game, shedding a radiance peculiarly her own on the whole scene, is a cherished recollection of those days. She was the kindest of hostesses, and had a real pleasure when she saw her guests walking under the shades of Hagley, enjoying her brother-in-law's outpourings on Homer and Dante, his hearty appreciation of Newman's sermons, Butler's *Analogy,* and Carlyle's *French Revolution.* There was great freedom of speech at Hagley. As the Dowager Lady Lyttelton once said to me, 'George makes people speak their minds. I have always felt strongly the blemishes in Shakespeare, but I never, till to-night, heard people dare to speak so freely about his coarseness.'

I am sure all who knew that venerable lady would feel as I do that it was one of the great privileges of one's life to know her. She was quite unique, and in my humble judgment perfectly realised the ideal

of a well-bred, courteous, Christian gentlewoman.
Although she had been for many years accustomed
to Court life, she never, except on rare occasions,
gave any evidence of her intimate acquaintance with
great personages. Her power of expression was
remarkable. She had a real insight into character,
and her judgment on politics and books showed the
vigour and intensity of her mind. Whenever she
spoke on religious subjects, she convinced every one
who heard her that the governing motive of her
life was a real love for Divine things. She was a
constant and unfailing friend to all who had the
privilege of her acquaintance. For many years she
was in the habit of treating me with perfect confidence, and on the last occasion when I saw her
she spoke with delight of the happy and successful
lives of her grandchildren, ending with the remarkable words, ' Very few people in this country have
more reason to say than I, " Goodness and mercy
have followed me all the days of my life." ' I wish
indeed that I had the pen of a Clarendon, to convey
to those who read these pages the elevating and
purifying influence so widely felt by the family and
friends of this venerable lady. Her letters, full of
grace and sparkle, resemble those lately given to
the world by the son of Lady Granville.

Lord Lyttelton was an earnest student and a
devoted classical scholar. His official career had
been a short one. He was an admirable Lord-
Lieutenant, always ready to take the chair at public

meetings, and a most liberal dispenser of the means at his disposal to all good works. I never knew any one who so thoroughly and heartily enjoyed his religious privileges. His manner was peculiar. Those who were intimate with him soon found out his intense kindliness, and felt absolute reliance on him as a friend. He very soon admitted me to great intimacy, and from the year I first knew him, until his death, I had constant tokens of his kindness and friendship.

When, in the year 1867, I was appointed by the Crown, Vicar of Kidderminster, Lord Lyttelton assured me that he would always be ready to come and give a helping hand to any cause that needed aid; and it is quite impossible to say how much all those who were interested in educational matters were indebted to him. Grave differences on important subjects in no way interfered with the kindly relations he maintained with all his neighbours. The school at Hagley, where he taught every Sunday, was maintained by him, and always bore a high name for efficiency. He was one of the nursing-fathers of the Saltley college for schoolmasters; and was as ready to read a paper to a clerical society, or give a lecture to a village audience, as to translate Comus into Greek verse, or play a game at chess with a regular adept.

I had, when bailiff of King Edward's School, Birmingham, a difference with him upon the subject of a new scheme for that great foundation. Lord

Lyttelton was commissioner of Endowed Schools, and was responsible for the scheme which was rejected by the House of Lords. I thought it was a remarkable evidence of the generosity of his temper, that very soon after this he sent me the proofs of a translation he was busy with, with the words, 'I count on some corrective comment from you.'

Monckton Milnes had been his guest at Hagley, and had talked over with Lord Lyttelton the character and works of Walter Savage Landor. Very soon after this, I gave Lord Lyttelton a copy of a little volume called *Typical Selections*, to which I had contributed a short memoir of Landor. He read it and said, 'Milnes and you seem to me to spend your days in trying to wash a blackamoor white.' When an old friend had attempted to stand up for Fielding, as on the whole not an immoral writer, Lord Lyttelton remarked, 'Two men I never can forgive, Swift and Fielding. They have written things which ought never to have been written, and, great as their genius is, I think they have done infinite harm to mankind.'

In Lord Lyttelton's literary judgments there was a remarkable union of sanity and strength. His knowledge of Shakespeare was profound; he was an earnest student of Dante. The last time I saw him he was reading a volume of Madame de Sévigné. Carlyle's *French Revolution* was a favourite book; but the book of which I have heard him speak with the greatest enthusiasm was Newman's *Anglican Sermons*. In a volume of 'Ephemera,' there is a paper on some books of devotion, which fully indicates the high tone and purity of his mind. The Church of England never had a more loyal and devoted son than Lord Lyttelton.

There are objections to what are called family livings, but those who witnessed the cordial and pleasant work in the parish of Hagley must often have felt the advantage secured by the co-operation of Lord Lyttelton and his brother. William Lyttelton, whose curate I was for three years, was a high-souled and original man. He had great independence of mind, and, though not possessed of the accurate scholarship of his brother, was an earnest and diligent student. His sermons, though sometimes deficient in form, were always impressive. One, preached during a meeting of the British Association in Birmingham, was greatly admired by the late Lord Derby, who asked him to print it. Every plan for the moral and social improvement of his parish was heartily embraced by William Lyttelton, who was perhaps only too ready to listen to the suggestions of men of very different views, and to every new method of teaching his parishioners. Before I was his curate, and until the moment of his untimely death, I had the fullest and freest intercourse with him on all sorts of subjects. I have never known any one who submitted so entirely to the criticism of his own productions, and he was a most kind and indulgent critic of the writings of his friends.

He had a most thorough veneration for F. D. Maurice; a new book of Maurice's was to him an intense enjoyment, and he looked forward confidently to, what he called, a time when men's thoughts should be leavened by Maurice; a dream which has in some degree been realised. Lyttelton was, however, always ready to adopt whatever he thought good and edifying in public service. He was a warm advocate of daily prayer, and weekly communion, and was happy in seeing the healthy growth of Keble College, under the fostering care of its first Warden—the husband of his niece. The beautiful patience with which he bore the painful malady, which ended too soon his useful, honourable life, endeared him more than ever to his family and friends. He felt, to use his own expression, ' the wonderful mystery of pain,' and his thoughts on scientific subjects, in which he was always interested, had brought him a grand conception of the awful order of nature. I do not suppose there ever was any one who rejoiced more heartily in the advancement of his friends than William Lyttelton.

It was a supreme felicity to me that the vicar and rector of my curate days were such firm and kindly friends as Claughton and Lyttelton. To enjoy the friendship of men older than myself has been one of my most remarkable privileges in life; but when they are gone into a world of light, it is then that the touching words of Landor, in one of his dedications, come back into memory. He speaks of Dr. Parr, who had shown him much kindness, 'with such feelings as that man's are, who has shaken hands with those who followed him to the ship, and who sees from the vessel, one standing wide apart, whom he never can hope to see again.'

Even at the risk of seeming egotistical, I ought to say something of the intense refreshment and pleasure I sometimes had in those days, when Matthew Arnold came to inspect a Nonconformist school at Kidderminster. I once heard a famous preacher at Oxford compare a student's first acquaintance with Bengel's Commentary to the admission of a ray of light when a shutter was opened in a darkened room! The arrival of Matthew Arnold at my lodgings was not unlike this. He brought with him a complete atmosphere of culture and poetry. He had something to tell of Sainte-Beuve's last criticism, some new book, like Lewes' *Life of Goethe*, to recommend, some new political interest to unfold, and, in short, he carried you away from the routine of every-day life with his enthusiasm and spirit. He gave me most valuable advice as to the training of pupil-teachers. 'Open their minds,' he would say, 'take them into the world of Shakespeare, and try to make them feel that there is no book so full of poetry and beauty as the Bible.' He had something to tell me of Stanley and Clough, and it is really difficult to say what a delightful tonic effect his visits produced. He was living at that time at Edgbaston, and he appreciated thoroughly the intellectual life he found among many whose tastes and acquirements took him by surprise. One of his pleasantest characteristics was his perfect readiness to discuss, with complete command of temper, views and opinions of his own, which he knew I did not share, and thought dangerous. Many and many a conversation have I had with him at the Athenæum, and never did an unkindly or peevish word fall from him.

No one ever heard Arnold complain of the drudgery of his life. All who knew him constantly regretted that a man of such wonderful gifts should have spent his life in the laborious duties of an Inspector. He contrived, however, to throw light and culture into his ordinary occupations, and he had much gratification in his later years, in the general appreciation of his poetry and criticisms. I often met him at Dean Stanley's, and had the pleasure of hearing the Dean and him talk of old Rugby days, when Dr. Arnold was the life and soul of the school and of his own family circle.

Nothing gave Matthew Arnold so much pleasure as tributes to the influence of his father, and a passage in one of Dr. Temple's sermons at Rugby, containing a beautiful allusion to Arnold's life and death was often quoted by him. When his friend and helper, Theodore Walrond, died, Arnold told me that he felt as if part of his life had been taken from him. Walrond was the head boy in the house when Dr. Arnold died, and had shown great presence of mind at a time of great confusion.

Matthew Arnold's place as a poet is safe, and it will be long before the *Forsaken Merman* and the *Scholar Gipsy* are forgotten.

The consequences of the Crimean war were bitterly felt in Kidderminster. It was a terrible time. Some of the manufacturers failed, and in my district I often saw men, women, and children nearly starving. Great efforts were made to relieve the distressed. Noble sacrifices were made by many who could ill afford to give freely. The energy and spirit of the vicar, aided by the great liberality of his brother-in-law, Lord Ward, seemed to arouse kindly efforts and sympathy in all directions. Lord Ward did his utmost to assist some of the distressed weavers to emigrate. I never heard a better speech than he made, after his failure to secure a grant from the Government. By a kind loan he enabled some of the manufacturers, who were anxious to introduce steam-power, to carry out their object, and at a most critical time in the fortunes of the town, when the population was declining, his timely assistance recovered the trade, and brought back happiness to many a working man's home.

Lord Ward, better known as Lord Dudley, was

a most kind-hearted and generous man. He knew how to sympathise with men who were trying to do their work as clergymen in the murky regions of Staffordshire. The cathedral at Worcester would never have been ,fully restored, unless he had come forward with his munificent gifts. I had from him the most kind encouragement, and most valuable help, during the thirteen years I was vicar of Kidderminster, a post which I owed to the favourable recommendation given by him and Bishop Claughton to Lord Derby, with whom the appointment rested.

At the time of the distress in Kidderminster, Robert Lowe was member for the borough. He was always ready to help those who needed aid, and I knew how often he gave, in a quiet way, most valuable assistance. Lowe was seen to great advantage in his visits to Kidderminster. He astonished me when I met him, at some of the houses of his friends, by his extraordinary information on all sorts of subjects. His judgments were fearless and independent. He had the power of telling in a few words the whole story of a man's life. When he was dining one day at the house of one of his supporters, Turgot was mentioned. 'Who was Turgot?' asked one of them who was present. Lowe immediately, in the pleasantest way, gave a sketch of Turgot, which might have been inserted at once in an encyclopædia. Oxford reform was one of the leading subjects of the day, and upon this Lowe was especially great. He gave his experience as a coach, and told many capital stories of the days when he was in full work. Lowe was not fortunate in his addresses to the people of Kidderminster ; and I think the unpopularity which led to a horrible attack upon him in 1857 was in some measure due to the contemptuous tone of his address at his nomination. He behaved with great dignity and courage, and nothing was more remarkable than the fine temper he showed when nearly killed by the violence of the mob. Two years afterwards he abandoned a contest when he found that there was much corruption among the electorate.

We move fast in these days, and the fine speeches of Lowe in the year 1866, on the Reform Bill, are nearly forgotten. He was unfortunately too late in the field, but, had his wise counsels prevailed, much that many now deplore would have been altered. He was one of the few who had the courage of their convictions, and although he cannot be said to have been on the whole a successful statesman, his independence and character will long be remembered.

I once heard him tell a pleasant story, illustrative of the cleverness of the London *gamin*. After some function at Buckingham Palace, Lowe wanted to cross the Green Park in his Windsor uniform, but was prevented by a policeman, who had been told to allow no one to pass. Lowe told who he was in vain, and an urchin cried out: 'Don't be 'ard on him, Bobby, 'e 's 'ad no eddication.'

At a public meeting at Kidderminster, the want of a good room for meetings was mentioned. 'I think,' said his worship, the mayor, 'we could manage to build a shell.' 'Your best course in the long-run,' said Lowe, 'will be to shell out.'

Many a story can be told of his readiness in retort.

On one occasion I heard some one say, 'Our imports are more than our exports, and that is not healthy.' 'I don't see that at all,' said Lowe. 'If I take a box of beads to Africa, and get instead gold dust and ivory, I get what is useful to me, and the savage gets what pleases him. My import is more than my export.'

After hearing a sermon from Mr. Claughton, Lowe received the Holy Communion. Something was said by his host, and Lowe replied, 'After such a sermon as that I could not but remain.'

Although he, as Jowett said, sometimes dissembled his love for the classics, and declared his preference for scientific education, no man ever valued them more, or could quote them more aptly.

The last conversation I had with Lord Sherbrooke was in the Jerusalem Chamber, when we were waiting, on the 25th July 1881, to go in procession to the funeral of Dean Stanley. In a very few telling sentences he gave a sketch of Stanley's work and character, and I always treasured a few of his words.

'I think,' he said, 'he had a real faith of his own, and that it is very unfair to call him names because he chivalrously tried to defend men who were down. I heard him once preach,' he continued, 'a sermon at Oxford, about what young men ought to do, when they took curacies, and it made me think of Claughton, and the way you and your friends worked in the bad days at Kidderminster.'

I was very much struck at the time with Lord Sherbrooke's words, and, indeed, the very words of Stanley which he mentioned, I had often read and quoted.

On one of the last occasions in which I had a long conversation with Jowett, he spoke with warm admiration of Lord Sherbrooke, and said he was one of the few men who had a true appreciation of Aristotle and Thucydides. Lord Sherbrooke was as remarkable a specimen of the cultured Oxford Liberal as Sir Stafford Northcote was an example of the Oxford Conservative, who had, however, strong Liberal instincts.

It was at Himley Hall, where Lady Ward, with the kindest hospitality, often invited me, that I first met Northcote, who was at that time the Peelite member for Dudley. Mr. Henry Cheney was also there, and the impression made upon me was, that it would be difficult to find two men more thoroughly representative of the highest English culture. Northcote made no secret of his desire to see Mr. Gladstone again in the ranks of the Conservative party. Mr. Cheney had lately had, at Badger, Mr. Charles Greville as his guest, and during a long walk in the park at Himley I heard him and Northcote discuss the future of English politics with great freedom. Palmerston was in power, but it was well known that his majority in the House of Commons was not to be depended upon. Mr. Cheney shared Northcote's desire that Gladstone should become a prominent leader in the Conservative party. His task, he said, ought to be to make a new Whig party, and to resist the inroads of the Manchester School. Northcote and Mr. Cheney surprised me, by the high opinion they entertained of Disraeli's ability. Mr. Cheney knew him well, and said that he believed that he was capable of great magnanimity. I was at that time no admirer of Disraeli, but, two years after this conversation took place, during Lord Derby's second administration, I was not surprised to hear that Sir Stafford had been re-united to the Conservatives, and had succeeded to a seat at Stamford, and taken office. 'There is a quiet efficiency,' said Mr. Cheney to me, 'about Sir Stafford, that must tell in the House of Commons. If he ever becomes leader, he will be trusted like Lord Althorp,' and he then proceeded to tell me many stories of the way Lord Althorp was trusted in the House of Commons, and how, on several occasions, he had seen him triumph over opposition by the pure force of character.

It was to Mr. Lockhart's good opinion that I owed my entrance to the kindness and hospitality of Badger Hall. Mr. Cheney, and his brother Mr. Edward Cheney, were most agreeable men. They had known a multitude of interesting people, and were proficients in the art of conversation. Mr. Cheney was an excellent host, and everything at Badger spoke of comfort and ease. A stroll with Mr. Cheney in 'The Dingle' was a great treat. He sometimes admitted large parties from Wolverhampton to his grounds. The liberty was seldom abused; and one day, in a summer-house, he found the following four lines :—

> 'The man who comes this pleasant place to view,
> Admires its owner, generous, kind, and true,
> And then returning to his dull town prison,
> Exceedingly regrets it is not his'n.'

Mr. Cheney wrote much in the *Quarterly*. He was at this time much occupied with Church questions, of which he took a moderate, yet independent view. He was a great admirer of my vicar, Mr. Claughton, and he said to me, and a great friend of mine and fellow-curate, Alfred Peel, who had been telling him of our pleasant evenings at the vicar's, the free discussion of parish matters, and the vicar's admirable readings of poetry,—'You young fellows are fortunate indeed. You have one of the most delightful men in England for your chief; what you tell me, makes me long to be young again, and take a curacy at Kidderminster.'

Mr. Cheney told stories admirably. In his youth he had seen much of Walter Scott, and said that he had only one fault, that he was too ready to play the lion at Lydia White's parties, or wherever he was asked. He was too good-natured. 'Mrs. Lockhart,' he said, 'had a great deal of her father in her, and her husband had never been the same man since her death.'

Whenever I met Mr. Cheney, he told me of some interesting book worth reading. I once shewed him the late Dean of St. Paul's article on Dante, and he told me that he thought it one of the finest pieces of criticism ever written. He thoroughly appreciated Macaulay's powers as a narrator, and I remember his chuckle over a passage in Samuel Lucas's review of Macaulay's later volumes. 'Dundee scrambled down the Castle rock.' 'No doubt,' said Lucas, 'a Whig would have descended more gracefully.'

In manner, Mr. Cheney had a certain oldfashioned politeness, but on the whole I have always looked upon him as perhaps the most finished specimen of an English squire I have ever known. In knowledge of literature, and especially of English novels, he was nearly equalled by his brother Edward.

Northcote too, was a real lover of literature. He was one of a band of Oxford men who started the

Guardian newspaper, but I do not think he was one of the proprietors.

When, in the last year of his life, after his elevation to the House of Lords, I had again the pleasure of meeting him, he spoke of the days at Himley as amongst some of the pleasantest he had known, and asked me, with a smile, if my admiration for the writer of a certain article on the ' Idylls of the King' was as great now as it was then. The writer was Mr. Gladstone, and I was obliged to confess to Lord Iddesleigh that that eminent statesman had long ago overdrawn his credit at my bank. 'Ah!' said Lord Iddesleigh, 'in those old days, you and I had hopes that he would liberalise the Tories, and did not expect to see him throwing sops to Cerberus.'

The method of work now pursued by clergy in large towns has grown most exacting, and some who read these pages will be inclined to think that short absences, even amongst elevating associations, were not healthful. I have no doubt we ought all to have worked harder, but I returned to my visits among the poor, my cottage lectures, and evenings with pupil-teachers, with great zest, and with the feeling that although social life has its pleasures, there are compensations in active ministerial work which make up for drudgery. The real power of religion, during the hardships of a distressed time, was seen in the patience with which poverty and sickness were borne. It is something to have known, as I have known, a bed-ridden woman, who never left her miserable garret for twenty years, but who fed on the great truths of the Gospel with an intensity and glow of feeling such as is seen in the pages that tell of the faith of true saints.

I ought to say how much the curates of Kidderminster were indebted to the hearty support they had from some true-hearted laymen, who were often almost too indulgent in furthering our schemes, sometimes not very practicable, for the improvement of the young.

From the friends of the vicar, who were often his guests, Bishop Wordsworth of St. Andrews, and the Earl of Selborne, we caught something of the enthusiasm for the noblest causes so distinctive of these two men, united with Bishop Claughton in lifelong friendship. The days of my curate-life in Kidderminster were indeed golden days.

CHAPTER XI

J. S. Mill—Sir H. Maine—The Athenæum Club—Ireland—Switzerland, Neuberg—The Carlyles—The Grand Chartreuse—Fallen Royalties—The *Saturday Review*—Theological Controversy—Incumbent of St. Michael's, Handsworth—Cambridge—Thompson—Whewell—Lightfoot—Marriage—Bishop Lonsdale—Bishop Temple—Birmingham Life—George Dawson—Badham—Cardinal Newman.

My friend Sir M. E. Grant-Duff has always been fortunate in becoming the friend of most interesting and distinguished people, and he has been also most kind in making them known to his friends. The pleasure of having seen and heard J. S. Mill I owe to him. We found Mill in his room at the India House, and were most kindly received. The delicate-looking, and gentle, shy man, who shook hands with us warmly, was very different from the Mill of my imagination. He had a look of great refinement, and I was at once struck with his extreme felicity of language, and the natural way in which he talked on the many topics of our conversation. It was in 1854, I think, that this interview took place. Louis Napoleon was then in everybody's thoughts. Mill spoke sadly of the prospects of France, and contrasted the state of things with the first few years of the Orleanist dynasty, when Armand

Carrel and his friends were revelling in freedom of thought and political vigour. He spoke harshly of Thiers' Histories, and attributed, of course, much of the Napoleonic illusion to his influence. I had never before heard so much about the early days of Louis Philippe's reign, and was immensely struck with the way in which Mill managed to give us a clear view of the situation. He spoke strongly of Guizot's weakness in the management of the Chamber, and told us how Sir William Molesworth, two years before 1848, had predicted a great catastrophe, unless the Reform question was grasped like a nettle. I longed to hear Mill speak about his friend John Sterling, but the mention of Frederick Maurice led him to give us some account of his ability as a student of philosophy. In fact, I heard that afternoon from Mill an expression of opinion as to Maurice's power in almost the same terms he employs in his autobiography. In deference I suppose to my white neckcloth, he did not, as at another time he did, to Grant Duff, regret that Maurice should ever have written his famous *Subscription No Bondage*. Mill spoke somewhat contemptuously of Lord Derby, whose advent to power as Premier had been talked of as not unlikely. ' Has he ever said anything in any speech that you remember five minutes afterwards ? ' but he added, ' his son, Lord Stanley, is a very different man, and we may look for great things from him.' I was sorry when, at the close of our interview,

Mill and Grant-Duff began to talk of the ' Flora ' of Greece, a subject I did not care for, as I longed to hear Mill say something about S. T. Coleridge. His article on Coleridge, now reprinted in his *Dissertations*, was a great favourite of mine, and I knew that Mill had always a considerable weakness for Coleridge's writings. A thorough acquaintance with Mill's *Logic* and *Political Economy* was one of the benefits I had from reading with Richard Congreve. Although always more or less in rebellion against Mill's teaching, I was completely subdued by the sincerity and elevation of his tone. His great book, written against Sir William Hamilton, to my mind, whatever may be thought of its conclusions, exhibits more of his mental power even than his earlier ones. There is a strange pathos in his book on the *Subjection of Women*, the full force of which I have felt, when I saw, many years afterwards, Mrs. Mill's tomb at Avignon, and read the inscription, which, like that on Mrs. Carlyle's grave at Haddington, tells something of the true feeling of the man. I once heard Mill speak in the House of Commons, and was pained at the indifference with which he was treated. He did not seem to me at home, and certainly had not caught the House of Commons' tone. It was a little like a professor addressing a class.

It was through Sir M. E. Grant Duff also that I had the pleasure of once hearing Sir Henry Maine lecture at the Temple. The substance of his lec-

ture was afterwards embodied in *Ancient Law.*
It was perfectly admirable. His lucidity, as I
have heard a good judge remark, was only equalled
by his modesty. He was the most unassum-
ing of men, and, if I may venture to express an
opinion on such a point, he always seemed to me
to have taken into his own mind what was best in
Liberalism and Conservatism. I once had a long
railway journey with him, during the course of
which we travelled over a vast field of mental
ground. We began with Miss Yonge's novels, one
of which, my favourite, *Heartsease,* I was reading,
and we ended with Jowett's *Plato,* which had just
appeared, and was occupying Maine greatly. I had
the pleasure of having him as my guest at Salisbury
the year before he died. He enjoyed the quiet
and calm, and hoped to come again the following
year. The wall of the Close was built by warrant
of Edward the Third. When Maine, Sir M. Grant
Duff, and I returned from a drive, my dog 'Fop'
was sitting on the wall: 'There,' said Maine, 'is the
nineteenth century criticising the time of Edward
the Third.'

The Athenæum Club, to one who, like myself,
has been a member ever since 1865, is tenanted by
many ghosts, and as the door from the library into
the drawing-room opens I am sometimes led to think
that Dean Stanley, Mark Pattison, or Sir Henry
Maine may enter, as I have so often seen them,
steadily making for the receptacle of the new books,

and sinking into a sofa with the object of their search.

In 1855 I went with my friend Grant Duff to Ireland. From Dublin we went to Cork, and after seeing the charming Glengariffe, made for Killarney. There is a great charm in all lake scenery. Scotland, the Italian and Swiss lakes, and our own lake region, have their distinctive features, and seem to suit particular moods of mind, and evoke associations all their own. A fine day at Killarney is like nothing else in the world. There is a tenderness and softness in the air utterly unlike the atmosphere of any other place I have ever known. Tennyson's glorious lyric, ' The splendour falls on castle walls,' with all its eerie effect of the blowing bugle, it is said, we owe to Killarney. I saw it once again, and do not wonder that a living poet, Aubrey de Vere, should again and again resort to that loveliest of lovely regions as a well of inspiration.

1855 was a remarkable year. It saw the birth of the *Saturday Review*, and Tennyson's *Maud*, our companion in travel, with its war verses, was the subject of a critique in the first number, by a very distinguished man of letters.

Travelling in Ireland was a real pleasure, and one comes across instances of humour which make one feel the life-like pictures of Miss Edgeworth and Carleton. In the following year, in the course of a pleasant trip up the Rhine and what may be called the usual Swiss tour of the Oberland, I had as my

fellow-traveller for several days the attached friend
of Carlyle, Neuberg, who is so frequently mentioned
in Mr. Froude's *Life of Carlyle.* Many of the strange
revelations which startled the world so much were
not new to me, as Neuberg, in the course of long
Swiss rambles, made me perfectly familiar with the
curious relations between Carlyle and his wife. At
Carlyle's wish Neuberg left England, in order to
verify some tales as to Frederick the Great. On his
return he found, from Mrs. Carlyle's account, that a
moody silence had been pursued by Carlyle during
the greater part of his three weeks' absence. It was
the dead season in London, and hardly anybody had
come near them. In two minutes after Mrs. Carlyle
had told this, the sage appeared on the scene in the
highest good humour, and in a few minutes more Mrs.
Carlyle was laughing heartily at some old Scotch
stories. Neuberg had an immense admiration for
Mrs. Carlyle, but spoke with great regret of Carlyle's
failure to interest her in whatever work he was
engaged on. 'He is not a tyrant in intention, but
they do not understand each other,' I remember was
one of his sayings, and it was extremely interesting
to see how, in spite of all his oddities and the habits
of the peasant never shaken off, Carlyle still maintained a firm hold over Neuberg, who venerated
him for his great moral qualities and his hatred of
unreality. He admitted, however, that Carlyle had
a certain dislike to witness the success of other
authors, and spoke very strongly of his ill-treatment

of Sir Walter Scott. Neuberg seemed to me, from his long residence in England, to combine the best excellencies of English and German character. He had been on intimate terms with Dean Alford, at the time when he was busy with his Greek Testament. He had a real love of English poetry, and was quite enthusiastic about Matthew Arnold's stanzas from the Grande Chartreuse, which I had with me, and which had made me resolve to go with my companion, the son of a clerical friend, from Chambéry to spend a night at the monastery. We did so. It was a never-to-be-forgotten day of unusual splendour. The grand *cul-de-sac* of wooded hills, and the almost awful solitude, leave a wonderful impression, and the solemn midnight service, so powerfully described by Arnold, is like a relic of the Middle Ages. Two days after I had been at the Chartreuse, I journeyed to Paris with the celebrated Abbé Mermillod, and from morn to dewy eve, in Latin, we discussed the whole case of the question between Rome and England. He astonished me by his knowledge of English theology, and his defence of Mariolatry was one of the cleverest I have ever heard. Some days after I had met him, I heard him preach in Paris, and he did me the honour to allude to some hearty words I had spoken of Fénelon and Pascal, ' dear even to the prejudiced English,' he said, ' who are outside the Catholic Church.'

Louis Napoleon was at the height of his popularity

in 1856, and I heard him and the Empress warmly cheered in the Bois de Boulogne. Three years ago, the train in which I was going from Salisbury to London stopped at Farnborough to oblige the Empress Eugénie. In the elderly lady leaning on a stick I at once recognised the remains of the brilliant Empress I had seen in Paris. My thoughts went back to the sight of fallen royalties I had had in Edinburgh at a very early age, and to the only experience I ever had in Worcestershire, of the dignified composure but somewhat sad expression of the Duc d'Aumale.

In the year 1870 it was my fortune to be abroad when war was declared between France and Germany. I was sitting in a hotel at Geneva, when the landlord came and told me of the disasters which had overtaken the French army. 'The doom of Louis Napoleon has come.' I had in my hand my constant travelling companion, Palgrave's *Golden Treasury*, and the words I had just read were those of Wordsworth's sonnet on the extinction of the Venetian Republic :

> ' Men are we, and must grieve when even the shade
> Of that which once was great has passed away.'

When the *Saturday Review* first appeared, it was felt by many that a fresh and vigorous spirit had been imparted to newspaper criticism. Many of my friends wrote in it. My own part was a very humble one, but I have sometimes looked back with amusement on the determination of the editor

not to print an article of mine on the first volume
of Robertson's Sermons, a book which seemed to me,
impressed as I had been with what I had heard
of Robertson's teaching, to mark an epoch. The
ecclesiastical adviser of the editor thought my
estimate of the volume ridiculously high, and
though a very eminent man, one of the most valued
contributors, stood my friend, the article never
appeared. It was some consolation to me, however,
in after years, to see what a wonderful circulation
this and the succeeding volumes had enjoyed; and
at one time the sermons were the only work of the
kind ever reprinted by Tauchnitz. When Stanley's
Sinai and Palestine was published, the author
acknowledged that a great impulse to the sale of
the book had been given by the reviews in the
Saturday, written by one who throughout his life
combined a true love of geography and history, Sir
M. E. Grant Duff.

Nothing is more instructive in the retrospect of
a life than a reflection on the rise and progress, the
decline and fall, of theological controversy. In the
Church of England, during the first years of my
clerical life, one wave seemed to overtake another
before we had time to breathe. Archdeacon Denison maintained with characteristic vigour doctrines
regarding the Eucharist, which became the subject
of litigation, ended mainly on technical grounds.
F. D. Maurice's position as to the meaning of the
word 'eternal' led to his dismissal from King's

College, and for many years affected his estimation as a theologian. Professor Jowett's views on the satisfaction of Christ, contained in the volumes published by him in 1855, united men who are often found in different camps in defence of the doctrine they believed to be in danger. The controversy which arose on the publication of Mansel's *Bampton Lectures* was bitterly waged for some years. Dr. Rowland Williams, afterwards better known as one of the Essayists and Reviewers, was attacked on account of his views on Inspiration, and chose to encounter Bishop Thirlwall in a memorable conflict, when the Bishop certainly proved himself a formidable opponent. In Scotland the Bishop of Brechin was brought to trial for the views he held upon the subject of the Eucharist, and the strife was memorable on account of the action of Mr. Keble, who espoused the cause of the Bishop. The appearance of Lightfoot as a calm and impartial critic, when Stanley and Jowett gave to the world their volumes of exposition, seemed to many to prove that a new school of English theologians was again to manifest itself in Cambridge. Men who are content to be debtors, not slaves, to German criticism, and who combine reverence for the past with due appreciation of what is valuable in the present, have never been wanting in Cambridge. The gradual rise of the influence of Lightfoot and Westcott in English theology, and the labours of Hort, Perowne, Vaughan, Farrar, and others who could be named, have revived true Biblical study at Cambridge. At Oxford also this good work has prospered, and the professoriate, in the hands of Liddon, Wordsworth, Cheyne, Driver, and Sanday, has given evidence of great activity. Results, not always apparent, of the intense interest created by the careful prosecution of Biblical studies at the Universities, are to be found among the younger clergy, in their various spheres of work. Unfortunately for England, far too great an influence has been possessed by what are called religious newspapers. In the days when I was a curate, owing mainly to efforts made in London, attention was called to the want of interest in religion among the masses. Special services, begun at St. Paul's and Westminster Abbey, became the custom throughout the country, and I remember well how elderly men really seemed to believe that an era of peace and tranquillity was dawning, when a general desire for High, Low, and Broad to work together should banish the spirit of partisanship. Much disappointment, however, was felt when the question of the Confessional, and the riots at St. George's-in-the-East, fanned the embers of controversy again into a blaze. Minor matters of dispute died away and were forgotten, when the long strife regarding *Essays and Reviews* occupied for some years the minds of many most prominent in the Church of England.

In the year 1859 Dr. Hook was made Dean of

Chichester. A very kind friend of mine, Mr. Wood-gate, brought my name—I was then curate of Hagley—without my knowledge, before the trustees who had to elect a new vicar of Leeds. I sent in some testimonials which I had collected for another purpose. The present Bishop of Hereford was chosen ; but, singularly enough, when he and his successor, Dr. Woodford, were promoted to the bench, the far too favourable opinion of friends did subsequently place this great post within my reach. The first time this very flattering distinction was named to me, I had only been a short time vicar of Kidderminster, and when it was again in my power I had taken root, and had begun to feel the effect of some years of hard work. In the year 1860 I had three offers of new work at once. One was to labour in London under the very able rector of St. James' ; another post at Wolverton had special advantages, and the last was the care of a district close to Birmingham where there had been some difficulties. I consulted my kind friend Claughton as to which of these I should choose. His advice was delightfully characteristic. ' I have not a doubt, my dear Boyle, you must take the hardest of the three, and I shall come and help you with a sermon whenever I can.' I took his advice, not without misgivings, and, in August 1860, undertook the charge of St. Michael's, Handsworth, where I was afterwards incumbent and rural dean, and spent seven busy and most fruitful years, close to Birmingham, and in full touch with many of the great interests of that centre of life. 1860 was a marked year. In the spring, very shortly after the publication of *Essays and Reviews*, I went to Cambridge to see a nephew of mine, Sir Charles Dalrymple, who was at that time an undergraduate of Trinity. I dined at high table with a friend, Mr. H. Hotham, and met for the only time the famous Professor Sedgwick. Thompson, afterwards Master of Trinity, was also there. He was a friend of Conington's, and with him I had a great deal of conversation. Next day my nephew and I went to Ely, where the Bishop of Oxford was to preach in the Cathedral. Archdeacon Mackenzie, whose death as missionary bishop excited such profound interest some years after, was present, and a great gathering of the Fen country, under the auspices of Dean Goodwin, took place. Thompson was a canon of Ely. He kindly insisted on our spending the day with him. We saw the grand scene and heard the fine sermon of Wilberforce to great advantage. The cold reserve of the great Greek scholar gradually disappeared. I grew so bold as to ask him many questions about Plato, and I listened to his *dicta* with profound reverence. He had edited Archer Butler's lectures on Greek philosophy, and he spoke with great admiration of his powers. F. D. Maurice had lately published a sequel to his book about Mansel, and had shown, Thompson said, what all his intimate friends knew, that he was a great thinker. 'The germ of the whole matter, however,' he said, 'is in the Parmenides of Plato. Our master, Whewell, has said some admirable things about this controversy in a sermon lately preached in our chapel.' Many years afterwards I found in Todhunter's *Remains of Whewell* the telling extract from this very sermon, which I subjoin.

'As I have said, my anxiety to warn you against this doctrine, false as I hold it to be in philosophy, does not arise mainly from its bearing on philosophy, but upon religion—not because it makes natural theology impossible, but because it makes revealed theology equally impossible. If we cannot know anything about God, revelation is in vain. We cannot have anything revealed to us if we have no power of seeing what is revealed. It is of no use to take away the veil when we are blind. If, in consequence of our defect of sight, we cannot see God at all by the sun of nature, we cannot see him by the lightning of Sinai, nor by the fire of Mount Carmel, nor by the Star in the East, nor by the rising sun of the Resurrection. If we cannot know God, to what purpose is it that the Scriptures, Old and New, constantly exhort us to know Him, and represent to us the knowledge of Him as the great purpose of man's life, and the sole ground of his eternal hope?'

Thompson was shy and sometimes difficult to approach, but whenever I met him I ventured to ask him some question about books which I knew he was master of, and many a pithy saying have I heard from him as to the merits of certain authors. He certainly did not spare such. More than once I have heard him say, 'If Gladstone had read Löbeck we should have had no bulky book on Homer.' On the day which I spent with him at Ely, he keenly dissected some passages in the *Essays and Reviews*, and spoke of Lightfoot as a man who would do more for the better understanding of St. Paul than Jowett or Stanley. He spoke with great approval of the 'Life of Christ,' written by Thomson, afterwards Archbishop of York, in the *Dictionary of the Bible*; and said, 'he is on his way to the bench.' Many years afterwards, when Thomson was Archbishop of York, I heard him preach in Westminster Abbey a sermon which Dean Stanley pronounced to be one of the very best he had ever heard. Next day I saw the other Thompson at the Athenæum, and I told him what Stanley had said of the Archbishop's sermon. He said, 'I am not surprised. I heard him once in the Abbey myself, and I thought it was the best sermon I had heard since I heard Julius Hare preach at Cambridge.'

During my stay at Cambridge I breakfasted with Lightfoot, and laid the foundation of a real friendship. He too talked much about *Essays and Reviews*, and expressed a hope that the book might not receive much notice. For some time it seemed as if this hope was likely to be fulfilled, but in the autumn of the same year a real storm arose. A long controversy was maintained, for at least three years, and it is hardly perhaps easy even now altogether to forget the anxiety and perplexity of those years. Early in the year 1861 I married. For seven years I was the tenant of Mr. M. P. W. Boulton, and had the pleasure of receiving at Soho House many remarkable people as guests. As my parishioners were all more or less Birmingham people, I was very soon immersed in the many interests and occupations of that busy town, then containing, as it does now, men of energy, public spirit, and ability, such as very few communities can boast. I shall have something to say of its clergy, its men of letters, and its men of business. Handsworth was in the county of Stafford and diocese of Lichfield, of which Bishop Lonsdale was then Bishop.

He was a man of truly fatherly character, and very soon after I went to Handsworth he was my guest, and gave me the most valuable advice as to the people under my charge. There were Nonconformists of different kinds, followers of George Dawson, some very ardent Churchmen, and some who took a strong Protestant line. The Bishop's advice to me was, 'Take your own line, be careful to consult your chief people about any change you make, visit every body, try and show yourself their friend, and encourage them to talk about the subjects they are most interested in.' I took his advice to heart, and aided by the kind encouragement I received from many excellent people, among whom I must mention Mr. Twells, an admirable specimen of the old-fashioned churchman, I overcame some difficulties, and passed some most happy years. I had also, in the friendship of Mr. Morse, one of the most eminent of the Birmingham clergy, a constant source of invigoration. Dr. Miller, who was then rector of St. Martin's, Birmingham, although a strong partisan, always treated me with great consideration and kindness. All moderate people had their own difficulties, during the years of controversy of which I have spoken, and when I succeeded in getting Dr. Temple to come and preach at the opening of a new school, I was assailed by many anonymous letters, as well as by the reproaches of friends, as a traitor of the deepest dye. We have travelled far since those days, and the head-master of Rugby has become, as Bishop of London, a warm friend of many who in those bitter times misread him so completely.

Very few persons have ever in any age reached real greatness. Bishop Temple has many claims on the admiration of his fellow-countrymen. Nothing in his long career has seemed to me more admirable than the way in which he met the pitiless raging of the storm when the winds were high. The sermon which he preached in my church had some remarkable results. It made a young layman who heard it leave a considerable position, and after taking his degree at Cambridge he became a most earnest and hard-working clergyman. ' I am very sorry I called

Dr. Temple a heretic,' said the highest churchman in Birmingham to me. 'I never heard the Incarnation of Christ more beautifully put in a sermon. Dr. Temple's sermon will make me read my Bible more than ever,' was the dictum of a layman who was considered one of the most prominent Evangelical Churchmen in Birmingham. I greatly enjoyed the success of my experiment, as I had been one of those who had seen the testimonials collected by my friend Theodore Walrond, when Dr. Temple was a candidate for Rugby school, testimonials such as Dr. Scott, the Master of Balliol, said he believed no man had ever before had. Dr. Temple refused at the time to look at these tributes of his friends' opinions. I do not know if he has ever seen them.

There was something infectious in the life and public spirit of Birmingham. The energy with which all the good works of the town were supported was very striking. I was soon enlisted as a worker in two of the hospitals, and on the committees I found men working who soon became great friends of mine. At the meetings of the committee of the old Library, men of very different opinions were gathered together, and books old and new were often discussed in a most pleasant way. George Dawson, a very remarkable man, and a true lover of books, attended these meetings regularly. It would be very difficult to define exactly Dawson's precise position in religious matters. He had left his own community, and drawn round him a wide circle of friends, some of whom had been Unitarians, while others had belonged to various communions. I had many most interesting conversations with him. His intellect was keen and piercing. He got at the heart of a book in a wonderful way, and, with the exception of Froude, and A. J. Scott of Manchester, he was the best lecturer I have ever listened to. His after-dinner speeches at the gathering of a Shakespeare Club, where I was often a guest, were inimitable. His address at the opening of the Free Library at Birmingham was indeed worthy of the occasion. At first sight you thought him a little rough, but nearer acquaintance revealed true tenderness of spirit, and a power of appreciating characters and opinions very different from his own. Dr. Badham, who knew him well, and admired him greatly, once said to me, ' If Dawson had had in his youth such training as you and I have had, he would have been the first man of his time. Among my own parishioners there were many who owed their spiritual life entirely to Dawson, and who spoke of him with the deepest and truest affection. He knew that I was on terms of intimacy with Dr. Newman, and I was the medium who led to Newman's sitting to a Birmingham artist for the very remarkable picture, the original of which is now in the National Portrait Gallery, and the replica at Birmingham. I often discussed the peculiar position of the Church of England with Dawson. The famous words of de Maistre, as to the possibilities

of the future union of Christendom, and the part
which the Church of England might play, affected
him greatly. 'If you only knew how to play it,' he
said, 'what a game you clergy have in your hands !
You have not broken entirely with the past, and
you really might work out a grand church of the
future.' 'Why don't you join us ?' I said : 'there
is but a hand's-breadth between us.' 'I have often
thought of it,' he replied, 'after our conversations ;
and I am sure you and I, on most of the great
questions, are at one.' I repeated what I have just
written to two very different men, one, a leading
Evangelical clergyman, the other, the venerated
pastor of the old Unitarian congregation, Mr. Bache,
and their replies were almost identical. 'Dawson
believes a great deal more than people believe he
believes.' As far as I have seen, the sermons, the
prayers, and the lectures which have been published
since his death, more than confirm what I have
said ; but they utterly fail to convey any idea of the
powerful eloquence, the sweep of thought, and the
genial vigour of the man himself. In actual knowledge of theology Dawson was excelled by Vince,
the minister of the chief Baptist chapel in Birmingham, a man of delightful temper and true Christian
manliness ; and he did not possess the keen political
insight and the true attributes of a divine, so
marked and prominent in one who is still among
the distinguished men of Birmingham, my ever
generous and cordial friend, R. W. Dale, whose

writings are text-books in many of our theological colleges.

Badham and Dale were the life and soul of a graduates' Club, where I passed many a pleasant evening. Our rules unfortunately prevented us from having among our members a man whose knowledge of literature is almost unrivalled, to whom Badham gave the name of nature's graduate, the true friend of Free Libraries, Samuel Timmins.

In 1851, during the time of the great Exhibition, the Bishop of London wished sermons to be preached in different churches in French, German, Italian, and English. Dr. Badham was then living at Blackheath, and it was said he was ready to preach as the Bishop required. Had a sermon been wanted in Attic Greek, he would have been equal to the occasion also. He was one of the readiest and wittiest of men, but at the Edgbaston School he was in the wrong place. At last he found a post in Australia worthy of his powers, but at Oxford or Cambridge a scholar like Badham, who had belonged to both universities, ought to have had a niche. I have had long letters from him in his exile, full of emendations on Plato and Thucydides, and when he met men like Conington at my house he would pour forth his ideas upon Greek texts and Shakespeare readings with astonishing profusion. Sometimes he could be sharp and incisive, but when he liked his company no one could be more pleasant. It is difficult to say how much I owed to my intimacy with him. He was not like Mark Pattison, a mine into which you could dig with the certainty that the nugget you wanted would come up at the first motion of the spade. But he was rather like a deep vein of precious stones, every one of which glistened with strange brilliance. Cobet declared to my friend, Lord Reay, that Badham was more like a modern Erasmus than any scholar he had known. He was like Erasmus too in depth of feeling. He had made application for a post vacant at Oxford when Lord Derby was Premier, and with true friendliness he desired to withdraw when he found that a friend whom he valued greatly had some chance of receiving the appointment. Bunsen used to long for five minutes of patronage, that he might give great preferments to Hare and Maurice. I often longed to be able to make Badham Greek Professor in some University in Utopia.

To turn to a very different person, Cardinal Newman. Before I had actually made his acquaintance, Father Bittleston, one of my colleagues at the ' Discharged Prisoners' Aid Committee,' asked me if I were brother to a Mr. Boyle who had been Dr. Newman's pupil at Oriel, at a time when Samuel Wilberforce, Sir George Prevost and Sir Charles Anderson had also been there, and that he would be glad to make my acquaintance. I think I went for the first time to see him with Sir M. E. Grant Duff, and whenever I had any guest who was anxious to renew acquaintance with him we made our way to the Oratory. In the *Apologia*, the Cardinal speaks of the feeling which came over him when Keble took him by the hand on his election as Fellow of Oriel. When I first saw the man of whom I had heard so much, and looked on the bird's-eye view of Oxford which hung on the walls of the little room, with the words 'Can these bones live?' I felt something of the same feeling. The kindly manner and penetrating voice very soon put one at ease. His interest in all that concerned his old friends was unmistakable, and his felicitous choice of language, a characteristic so often noticed, gave a great charm to his conversation. The state of religion in France was first mentioned, and he spoke with great interest of Montalembert, and one or two others more or less known. When I once visited him along with Sir Vere de Vere he regretted that he did not know German. One of Döllinger's books had lately been translated by one of his friends, Mr. Darnell, and he spoke with great admiration of the way in which heathendom was described in its pages. Once or twice I visited him along with Mr. Woodgate, a very old friend, and I listened with delight to their recollections of old days, and especially to their stories about Whately. One of them I must record.

Whately took a strong line about Queen Caroline's trial, and when one of the Fellows of Oriel said in the common room, 'Whately, there is more about the Queen in the evening paper,' Whately said,

'My dear fellow, don't think that because I don't want to see a dirty puddle stirred, I delight in the odour.' After Whately had left Oxford, Woodgate said that the Provost of Oriel asked him, 'When you preached University sermon, did you preach to young or old?' 'Always to the young,' said Whately, 'I never try to galvanize corpses.'

Knowing what the relations of the Provost and Newman had been, I was hardly prepared to hear the hearty praise Newman gave him. Readers of the *Apologia* will, however, remember Newman's evident desire to do justice to that remarkable man. I was much struck with his kindly criticism of Scott and Miss Edgeworth. When I took Conington to see him, he talked much of Virgil and Crabbe, and to my surprise he told us how much he regretted that he had seen so little of Arnold. Newman's judgments of character always seemed to me remarkably fine. On the last time I saw him he gave sketches of J. B. Mozley, Dean Church, Mark Pattison, who was then dying, and J. A. Froude, and they were masterpieces. Of Hurrell Froude he once said to me, 'I have known no such intellect as his, so clear, so piercing, so charming.' He spoke tenderly of his brother, and said he should like to see him again. Very soon after this Froude came to stay with me, and I told him what Newman had said. I believe he made an attempt to see him, but I do not know if he succeeded.

I could fill pages with my recollections of Newman's talk, but I must end by saying that when I last saw him he thanked me much for coming and seeing him again, and said, 'The blessing of an old man will do you no harm. Give my affectionate love to dear Bishop Moberly. Often do I think of him.' Newman's was a happy, peaceful old age.

I had the pleasure of telling him that passages in the *Grammar of Assent* had been greatly prized by a member of the Royal Family, and I asked his leave to reprint them. At first he consented, but afterwards he yielded to pressure and withdrew for some reason his assent, but he expressed great satisfaction at what I had told him. 'It is the first time,' he said, 'I have ever been in touch with one of the family, in whom I take true interest.' 'I came into this part of the world to see Mr. Keble, whom I had not met for at least twenty-one years, there I found Dr. Pusey, whom I had not seen for nearly as long a time, and Mrs. Keble being ill, we three dined *tête-à-tête* together, a thing which perhaps we never did before in our lives. His wife, I am sorry to say, was too ill for me to stay, but if all is well I am going to him again next Monday.'

This is an extract from a letter, dated September 15, 1865, in answer to one in which I had ventured to ask Newman to meet one or two old friends, Lord Stanley and Henry Smith, who were then my guests. The Cardinal's letter was written immediately after this strange meeting of long parted friends, and the passage has a real interest. Bishop Moberly gave me a most interesting account of a dinner at the Deanery at St. Paul's, when he and Bishop Jacobson of Chester met the Cardinal after many years' estrangement. The concluding words of the *Apologia*, so full of pathetic tenderness, tell us what his friends were to Newman, and even those who could hardly boast of intimacy could not fail to feel how the true man in all his charm of character made one entirely forget the barriers of separation, and the way in which differences melt in love, in such a presence.

CHAPTER XII

1861-1867—Lord Elgin and his sisters—Miss Harriet Martineau ; her conversation and recollections—Lord Derby on Politics—Henry Smith—Dean Stanley: his work and opinions—A Visit from Maurice—Froude ; and Newman and Manning—Froude's *Carlyle*.

I HAD in the autumn of 1861 a very special opportunity of knowing something of a very remarkable man. Lord Elgin was shortly about to leave England for India, and by a happy accident I was his companion in long walks at my uncle's country place in Perthshire. He had been on intimate terms with the two last Governors-General, Dalhousie and Canning, and while a Fellow of Merton, he had known much of Oxford and Oxford men. Like most of his family, all distinguished for charm of manner and ready sympathy, he entered fully into the feelings and opinions of those with whom he conversed, and I have rarely passed pleasanter days than those in which he gave me the experience of his very interesting life. When he was Governor-General of Canada, he went on a special mission to Washington, and he told me that when he heard the bells ringing in consequence of the result of the Kansas and Nebraska question, as he stood on the steps of the Capitol, he said to Mr. Seward, 'This is the knell of the Union.' He felt strongly nothing but a Civil War could settle the slave question.

From having been absent in the Colonies for many years, Lord Elgin had assumed a very independent position in home politics. He had a great desire that at Palmerston's death, Gladstone should form an independent party, and he looked with considerable anxiety on the reform methods of Bright and his friends. Interesting as his talk on politics was, what he had to say on other subjects was even more agreeable to me.

His mother, Lady Elgin, was a woman of remarkable character, and had been greatly occupied with many of the religious movements in Scotland. She was an admirer of Chalmers, and the intimate friend of Thomas Erskine of Linlathen. Of these two men, Lord Elgin had much to tell. He was a great admirer of Milton's prose writings: when a boy, Chalmers had praised them highly, and it was on his advice he read them first. 'I always feel braced,' he said, 'when I read two books, Milton and the *Christian Year*. I believe I was the first person to bring the *Christian Year* to Scotland.' Two years afterwards, when he was passing away, Keble's beautiful poem on St. John's Day was repeated to him by his daughter. The advantage a man like Lord Elgin had enjoyed in meeting all sorts of persons was very apparent in his varied talk. His observation was keen, and I was particularly struck with the way in which he noted the difference in a friend who had joined the Church of Rome. 'In his youth, he was delightfully tender in conscience, and I often admired his evident desire to rule his life, but I was surprised to find when we met many years afterwards, that he looked on dinner as the great event of the day, talked a great deal too much about vintages, and snuffed immoderately. We came to close quarters, and he told me he lived under direction, had his life mapped out for him, and had very little trouble. I marvelled at the change, and was not edified.'

For Lord Dalhousie, Lord Elgin had high praise, and he spoke very warmly of the calm attitude of Lord Canning in the Mutiny.

'The cleverest man I have ever known is Laurence Oliphant, but he has some curious ideas. I should not wonder if he became a Jesuit.' I have often thought of these words, when I read some of Oliphant's submissions to a very different teacher from Ignatius Loyola.

Some people possess the art of making people tell all they have worth telling. An Edinburgh bookseller, Mr. Stillie, was at Methven Castle, cataloguing the library, when Lord Elgin was there. Stillie had often as a boy taken proofs from the printers to Walter Scott, and Lord Elgin drew from him exact descriptions of how Scott talked, looked, and how hearty was his praise when the work was done to his mind. It is sad to think that Lord Elgin's career ended at fifty-two. As Miss Martineau has said of the three friends, Governors-General of India, ' In the noble line of rulers of India, they will, in their order, form a group of singular interest, standing on the boundary line of the old and the new systems of Indian rule. Thus they will always be remembered together, and regarded as apart.'

It was singular enough that in the same year that I knew Lord Elgin, I grew into very much greater intimacy with Arthur Stanley, who two years afterwards married Lord Elgin's sister, Lady Augusta Bruce. I was at Oxford, and in the course of a walk, I told Stanley how interested I had been in meeting Lord Elgin, and I praised most heartily the three sisters, Lady Charlotte Locker, Lady Augusta Bruce, and Lady Frances Baillie. When the Dean wrote to me to tell me of his engagement and his Deanery, he said, ' I have not forgotten your glowing words about Lady Augusta, when you spoke of your talks with Lord Elgin.' Indeed, I have always thought, that as there was but one Arthur Stanley, there was but one person that was truly fitted, from her perfect sympathy and ready interest in all his life, to be his wife.

In the following year I was again at the Lakes. Conington gave me an introduction to Mrs. Harriet Martineau, as she liked to be called, and I spent two evenings at her cottage at Ambleside. She was a perfect mistress of monologue, and she talked so freely to me upon all sorts of subjects, that when I read her autobiography I found that I was already master of the principal events in her remarkable career. I had always been an admirer of her writings, and had just finished her *History of the Peace*, when I made her acquaintance. She had lately performed an astonishing feat. In order to give the writer of the 'Money Article' in the *Daily News* a holiday, she had undertaken his work for a certain time, and by the aid of telegrams had actually achieved it. She was glad, I think, to talk on general subjects, and she gave me most interesting and amusing accounts of the many people of eminence she had known. The account of her first meeting with Charlotte Brontë was exceedingly interesting. She was staying in London with her brother, and sat alone in the dining-room on a Sunday afternoon, to receive Currer Bell. She was astonished, when a little, sharp-looking, bright-eyed woman entered the room, 'and in three minutes we were talking,' she said, 'as if we had been brought up together.' She then gave me a most graphic account of Matthew Arnold's meeting Miss Brontë at her house, a meeting which has been commemorated in the striking poem on Haworth Churchyard, originally published in *Fraser's Magazine*, and not, I think, improved by some alterations and omissions. Stanley had been recently at Fox How, and she had had a long conversation with him. This led her to speak of Arnold and his sons. She predicted, I remember, a great fame for Matthew as a poet.

Lord Brougham was not a favourite, and his curious conduct when in office brought out many stories.

I am sure Miss Martineau exaggerated her own influence as a writer, but I am bound to say that she spoke with great modesty of the books which I think she is the most likely to be remembered by, *Deerbrook* and the *Playfellow*; but the marvel of this wonderful woman's talk, when she warmed into enthusiasm about Comte and his system, it is impossible to express. She really spoke as if she was inspired with a desire to convert the world from every opinion and belief to an absolute acceptance of Comte as the hierophant of the coming age. When I ventured mildly to say something of the strange aberrations of Comte's later writings, she told me that these were not to be remembered, but entirely put aside as the coruscations and exuberances of a great heart. I was much struck with her evident interest in all her neighbours, and the enthusiasm with which she spoke of Dr. Arnold's widow, a most constant and unfailing friend. W. E. Forster had a very high place in her regard, and she told me that she believed that very few people ever had such reverence and homage as Mrs. Wordsworth, the poet's widow. Her description of the efforts made by Mrs. Wordsworth to console the poet after their daughter's death was very touching, and she also dwelt upon the wonderfully unselfish spirit she showed in her care for

Dorothy, who was for many years a sad burthen in the household at Rydal Mount.

One of the most remarkable features of Miss Martineau's conversation was her power of giving in a short sentence a sketch of a character. What she said of Arthur Stanley dwelt in my mind. 'He has the same vivid interest in history as a boy has in *Beauty and the Beast* or *Jack the Giant-Killer*. If he lives he will carry into old age the freshness of youth, and that, you know, Coleridge says, is genius.' Of Wordsworth's poetry she remarked, 'When he is at his best you feel that what he has said is inevitable. Is there anything in the English language better than the " Wishing Gate "?' I replied I liked his verses at the grave of Burns almost as well as anything he ever wrote. 'Ah! that,' she said, 'is because you are Scotch. I have often seen in your countrymen a great love for Wordsworth, because he appreciated Burns and Scott.' Her praise of Carlyle, Mrs. Somerville, and Mrs. Jameson was very hearty, but the person she mentioned with the greatest admiration was Lord Durham. Charles Knight, and his efforts to make Shakespeare popular, she spoke of also in high terms. Every now and then she wandered into the strange world of mesmerism, and it was marvellous to hear this gifted woman, who had thrown away all the beliefs of her youth, speak quite calmly of the power with which certain clairvoyant friends of her own had anticipated the turns of the Money

Market, and had made successful speculations. When I bade her adieu, she spoke as if her life was soon to end. The loss of her niece, two years after I saw her, was a terrible grief to her.

The volume of *Short Lives* contributed by her to the *Daily News* is a very remarkable monument of the unique power of Harriet Martineau. Her estimate of Professor Wilson is exceedingly happy. One who knew him well, the late Lord Neaves, a man of the very highest culture, told me that he thought two sentences of Miss Martineau's about Wilson were quite perfect. 'He made others happy by being so extremely happy himself, when his brighter moods were on him. He felt, and enjoyed too, intensely, and paid the penalty in the deep melancholy of the close of his life. He could not chasten the exuberance of his love of Nature and of genial human intercourse, and he was cut off from both long before his death. The sad spectacle was witnessed with respectful sorrow, for all who had ever known him felt deeply in debt to him.' During some long years of seclusion, Miss Martineau, in her *Life in the Sick-Room*, has dwelt most feelingly on the enjoyment she had in Wilson's bounding, vigorous, inspiring prose.

The meeting of the British Association in 1865 was at Birmingham. I was one of three secretaries —one of them a man of rare gifts, the late John Henry Chamberlain, an architect of great ability and an earnest student of literature—and the work of preparation for the meeting was a most interesting one. I had some men of mark as guests during the week: Lord Stanley (afterwards Lord Derby), Sir H. Acland, Professors Henry Smith and Canon Rawlinson, Mr. A. Vernon Harcourt, Lord Lyttelton and his brother. Never did I see H. Smith to greater advantage. He found in Lord Stanley an 'answering mind,' and the talk of these two men, ranging over a vast variety of topics, made the week memorable. At first Lord Stanley seemed reserved and difficult to approach, but he grew more at ease with us, and it is not easy to describe the interest of his conversation. I kept notes at the time of some of his observations on politics. 'I go with my father's party, and feel that it is not a bad thing to be a drag chain now and then when things go on so rapidly as at present.' When some one spoke disparagingly of Disraeli, he said, ' Well, you must know him as well as I do to appreciate him thoroughly. He seems to be a charlatan, but he is not. He has great ideas as to the future of England, and, if he has a chance, he will be thought more of than many who are more prominent.' The general election had just taken place, and Gladstone had lost his seat at Oxford. ' I am bound, I suppose, to rejoice,' said Lord Stanley; 'but I wish you had kept him in. He will make a great show of Liberalism now, but he is more of a Conservative than a Liberal.'

After a luncheon given by the Mayor of Birmingham, we were joined by Lord Houghton ; and I had the satisfaction of hearing some very interesting conversation. 'What will happen when Palmerston goes (the end was very near, as he died that autumn)? I think Gladstone won't like to play second fiddle to John Russell. Since Cornewall Lewis's death he has been bidding for the first place.' 'And he must have it,' said Lord Houghton ; 'the first commoner since Chatham.' 'If I were not here,' said Lord Stanley, 'I should say a Brummagem Chatham. I don't care for Gladstone's speeches in Lancashire. They want Bright's go and purpose. They are the speeches of a man who is beginning to play a new part and does not do it quite naturally.' Mill had just got in for Westminster. 'He has given us great books, but he is too late for the House of Commons. I doubt his ever finding his feet. He will not attract young men, and their opinion goes for a good deal in the House of Commons.'

On the Sunday of the British Association week, my friend W. Lyttelton preached a fine sermon in my church, and Lord Stanley admired it and asked him to print it. In the evening he spoke much of Jowett's writings, and told us that he admired him much, and liked his style and way of treating some subjects. I quoted some words of Walter Bagehot's about Jowett, and we talked of Bagehot and R. H. Hutton. 'I think some of the *Spectator* articles,' Lord Stanley said, 'are about the best things going.

Hutton has a very interesting mind. He is really a man of candour. He is the Lord Grey of literature.' When the visit came to an end, he thanked me for the pleasure he had enjoyed; 'one of the greatest,' he added, 'is having seen something of your friend Smith, the most modest man of notability, I think, I have ever met.'

At this I did not wonder. Never had Henry Smith appeared in so remarkable a light as at this time. The *Essays and Reviews* of Church, a volume very little known at that time, was discussed. H. Smith praised very highly the Essays on Dante and St. Anselm. Lord Stanley read them and admired them both greatly. In the following year Professor Shirley, a man of great promise, died. Many Oxford people thought that Church ought to be his successor, and I was strongly urged by some of my friends to write to Lord Stanley and tell him that if his father gave the post of Professor of Ecclesiastical History to Church, it would be very popular in the University. I wrote to Lord Stanley, and, in the kindest way, he said he had done what he had never done before, and had mentioned Church to his father. He said he had not forgotten Henry Smith's character of Church, but he feared that the appointment was already disposed of. It was given in fact to Mansel, who, though eminent in other ways, was not the man especially designed for the Chair of Ecclesiastical History; but who, it should be remembered, during his short tenure of the office, did some really good work. One of Henry Smith's remarkable characteristics was a power of appreciating those who were opposed to him on many questions. His moderation and fairness were as conspicuous as his ready, playful wit. What could be happier than his exclamation, when some one expressed a wish that laymen, like Matthew Arnold, might sometimes deliver University sermons: 'I think Mat's text would be, "Philistia, be thou glad of me," ' or his quiet reproof to a boastful man of science : 'Do not forget that though you are the editor, you are not the author of Nature.'

When Oxford was incensed on the appearance of Mr. Froude's earlier volumes, the only man who seemed to preserve a true equilibrium was Henry Smith. 'Froude,' he said, 'may have been mistaken in many ways, but I believe him to be absolutely sincere in thinking the Reformation the best thing that ever happened in England.' The memorials of Smith, prefixed to two volumes of his special writings, give, far better than I could do, a real picture of this great spirit. 'There is but one Henry Smith,' was a saying of Dean Stanley's.

One of the most delightful surprises I ever had in my life was when Stanley appeared, just as I was finishing a sermon on Sunday morning, with the words, 'Here I am, ready to preach.' It was Hospital Sunday when, in all churches and chapels in and near Birmingham, collections were made for hospitals and kindred institutions. My congregation, fortunately, was large, but it would have been overflowing had it only been known the Dean was to preach. He never preached better; and into his sermon, on the words, 'Peace I leave with you,' he inserted some admirable sentences, in which there were some words of Thirlwall's on a similar occasion, about the hospitals of England being the true palaces of the land. He had come to Birmingham for a special purpose, and could only spend a short time with me. He was anxious about the future of a friend who at that time thought of leaving the Church of Rome, and he disclosed to me his own real sentiments as to the future of our church, and the necessity for a wide toleration, in a way that I can never forget. He did not always admit his friends to such complete confidence as he did that day; and though I am perfectly well aware that he may sometimes, not unfairly, be charged with indifference to dogma, and thought to be too anxious for an impossible compre-hension, I am certain that those who knew him most intimately must have always felt, as I did, what a grand vision of Christian unity lay at the bottom of his heart.

During his first years of the occupation of the Deanery of Westminster, he strove most earnestly to bring together men who, he felt, ought to be at one in the great struggle to elevate and improve society, but who were too often found in different camps. I always felt strongly that Bishop Colenso's attitude was one inconsistent with his position in the church, and felt sorry that the Dean defended him so chivalrously. I remember telling him that it was in my house that Bishop Gray heard of the unfortunate resolution of Colenso, to publish the first volume of his work on the Pentateuch, and that the grief of the Bishop of Capetown was one of the saddest things I had ever witnessed. Colenso had also refused to meet in conference Bishops Thirlwall and Jackson at Bishop Wilberforce's house. Stanley said, 'If that meeting had taken place, and that book had not been launched, a great deal that is painful might have been spared us, but I cannot help admiring a man who was ready like Luther to go on his errand though it rained Duke Georges.' I must be pardoned for saying that, many years after this, when I had spoken somewhat hotly on the subject of Bishop Colenso, the Dean showed how little he thought of my opposition by putting in my hands his last book, 'from his friend of many years.'

In the first years of his married life, the Dean made his home in London a most pleasant centre of hospitality. Lady Augusta Stanley, knowing my admiration for Browning, asked me to meet him one afternoon. Browning was in great force, and a lady who was present drew from him some very characteristic criticisms of Burns, Shelley, and Milton. I was pleased to hear him say that he thought Johnson's criticism of Milton, though carping and cold at times, did full justice to Milton's greatness. 'I like,' he said, 'praise from a man who, like Johnson, knew the depths of human nature. What he says of Milton and Shakespeare seems to be drawn out of him per force, and is very valuable.' When I lamented to Browning that I thought it terrible that three men who had lately died, Dr. Maitland, A. J. Scott, and T. L. Peacock, had left so little worthy of their reputation behind them, he grasped my arm and said: 'Terrible, if this life were all.' He made a deep impression on me, and his words about the wanton exuberance of certain popular poets in France and England, gave me a great insight into his views of life. I was never on intimate terms with Browning, but I have had some very pleasant talks with him on the subject of Walter Savage Landor and Carlyle. His knowledge of Landor's writings was wonderful. The dialogues he liked best were also, I found, my own chief favourites: the ones between Roger Ascham and Lady Jane Grey, and Penn and Peterborough. I was one of many who were made very welcome at the Deanery at Westminster, and although full justice has been done to the Dean's kindly desire to bring men of different ways of thinking together, and make the special sermons at the Abbey representative of the various schools of thought in the English Church, I think it is only those who knew him thoroughly well who can bear proper witness to his generous wish for great toleration and comprehension. I am quite aware that he stretched this desire too far, and that he might even be sometimes accused of indifference to points of doctrine very dear to many. But the charming nature of the man, his appreciation of persons differing as widely as Keble and Kingsley, his intense interest in every fresh discovery of historic interest in the great Abbey, carried you completely away, and made you feel that he was the right man in the right place.

Some years before the late Dean of St. Paul's had been appointed, I met him at the Deanery at Westminster. The Dean had shown him and two ladies some portions of the Abbey they had never seen before, and the conversation at luncheon turned upon some of these points of historical interest. ' How can you find time, Stanley,' said Church, ' for your sermons, your writing, and lionising country folk like ourselves?' 'The result is,' said the Dean, ' that everything is badly done, sermons, writing, and lionising.' Here the two ladies strongly exclaimed that they had no fault to find with their cicerone; and, indeed, all who had any experience of the lifelike, vivid touches which the Dean would throw into a tour of the monuments, felt that a new pleasure had been added to life. For his brother Dean of St. Paul's, Stanley had a great admiration. A perfectly upright man, I have heard him call him, after telling the story of Dean Church's action as proctor, when a censure on Tract 90 was attempted by heads of houses at Oxford. The satisfaction of the Dean when Temple, Fraser, and Maurice had severally preached in the Abbey, was very great.

'I saw a man there to-night,' he said, 'who had come to hear Temple, who had not been to church for years. This, I think, is a delightful result.' He chuckled over Lord Ebury's praise of a sermon of Bishop Fraser's, given in the words: 'I never heard anything better at Exeter Hall.' When Maurice preached, a good old lady who attended the Abbey regularly said to the Dean, 'I thought Mr. Maurice was not orthodox, but his sermon was exactly like one of Archbishop Trench's.' When the present Bishop of Ripon preached, I think, for the first time at Westminster Abbey, the Dean wrote to me, 'One of the most eloquent and reasoned sermons I have ever heard, reminding me of Melvill, but far more logical.' One who knew Stanley well, said to me that he thought the most delightful feature of his character was his intense realisation of some of the most beautiful passages in literature. Again and again, during an intimate intercourse of many years, I have had reason to feel the justice of this remark. There are passages in Macaulay's writings, and in Walter Scott, ever to be associated with rapid walks round St. James' Park, or luncheon parties at the Deanery. The special sermons, too, which I heard from him from time to time, with their illustrations and applications of the Bible, elicited by the circumstances of the time, dwell for ever in memory. Who that heard his sermon on 'the just shall live by faith,' preached at a great crisis in the Franco-German war, could ever forget it ? One of the last he ever delivered, on the death of Lord John Thynne in 1881, with its fine quotation from Tennyson's *Ulysses*, and the ring of his voice as he spoke of the everlasting gospel of Christ, abides with me as a most solemn remembrance. Stanley in his preaching reached the hearts of men who were not often susceptible of any influence from the pulpit. 'I think it quite impossible to overstate the effect Stanley has produced in London,' said a most remarkable man, Sir Louis Mallet, to me very shortly before his death, and I believe that many others have felt as he did. The power of the Bible, always before the age, and what he called its modern spirit, was constantly present to Stanley's mind.

I had the good fortune, when living near Birmingham, to induce F. D. Maurice and J. A. Froude to come and lecture at the Midland Institute. Those who have had the privilege of receiving Maurice as a guest, must always look back with intense satisfaction to the elevation which he seemed to give to the society around him.

At Birmingham there were a few faithful ones who were delighted to meet him at my house. Badham, who had a warm admiration for Maurice, said : ' I want you to repeat to us a striking anecdote you told me many years ago, when you told me of your and Hare's visit to Bunsen.' ' I remember,' said Maurice, ' we were sitting in the garden of Bunsen's house at Berne. It was the habit of the house to have the dessert in the open air in order to enjoy the view of the Oberland, but the afternoon was dull, and nothing could be seen. While we were talking, the mist rose like a curtain from the stage, and the snowy peaks came out in all their beauty. Bunsen sprang to his feet, and in a way I shall never forget, called out " Revelation ! " ' ' Yes,' said Badham, ' I wanted you all to hear this delightful story of Bunsen.'

Maurice spoke that evening of a scene he had witnessed at Lucerne, when the Catholic authorities had actually allowed the English communion service to be used in the Cathedral after High Mass on Sunday, as the usual place set apart for the English congregation was under repair. The Roman Catholic worshippers were actually on their knees, while the English sang ' My God, and is Thy table spread,' before the service.

' This,' said Hare to me, ' is as it should be. Differences melt before the Sacrament of love.'

Maurice dwelt much that evening on the healthy influence of Hare at Cambridge. He said, ' I believe Hare was the means of getting Wordsworth read at Cambridge. Jeffrey's view of Wordsworth was accepted like a gospel, but Hare was never weary of trying to make men see Wordsworth's beauty. He was perfectly delighted when he heard that Wordsworth had been rapturously received in the theatre at Oxford.' Of Augustus Hare, he said, ' He would have made a perfect bishop. His early death was a calamity to the English Church.'

Maurice lectured on Milton, and the lecture is to be found in the *Friendship of Books*. When he left us, it was impossible to help feeling that he breathed a different atmosphere. There was about him a wonderful distinction and dignity, and though he could not be called eloquent in conversation, he was certainly capable of making those about him feel that they were in the presence of a man who had the highest view of life. He spoke with immense admiration of some of his brother clergy in London, and of the efforts Mr. Kempe, of St. James', and Dean Stanley, were making to interest the younger clergy in the questions of the day. What had struck him most, he said, in Newman's *Apologia*, was the intense hold Thomas Scott, the commentator, had gained over Newman's youthful mind. It was, he said, perhaps the greatest tribute Scott had ever had paid him, that his writings should have had such binding force on a mind like Newman's.

As I drove Maurice to the station, we met Newman walking with a friend. 'That,' said Maurice, ' is Copeland, to whom Newman dedicated his last volume of Anglican sermons.' Copeland edited the re-issue of the whole set of sermons, with Newman's permission, and continued till his death on the most intimate terms with him.

While I have been gathering these ' Recollections ' together, Mr. Froude has passed away, and I can now speak very freely of two visits I had from him when he, too, came to lecture at the Institute, on Erasmus and Luther. Conington came from Oxford to meet him. We had a most pleasant time. The two old friends, who seldom met, enjoyed their meeting greatly. Many subjects were discussed, and many old memories revived. Froude heard that Manning was to be in Birmingham, and he said, 'I am afraid there is no chance of his coming to hear me lecture.'

'When I was at Littlemore with Newman, Manning came up to Oxford to preach the 5th of November sermon. He preached in so Protestant a tone, that Newman said, "If Manning comes to Littlemore, I shall not see him." Mark Pattison and I were sitting with Newman when he was told that Manning had come. Newman said to me, "You must go and tell him, Froude, that I will not see him." I went and told Manning, who was greatly distressed, and I walked along the road some way with him, bareheaded, to give him what comfort I could. I never saw Manning again, until he was Archbishop, when a great lady took me up to him at a London party. I was tempted to remind him of our last meeting, but I refrained.'

'Do tell us,' said Conington, 'if you have no objection, something of these Littlemore days.'

'There is very little to tell,' said Froude. 'When I knew where Newman was going, I was at first greatly distressed, but I had begun to read Carlyle, and felt that to Rome I could not go. There were

two parties at Littlemore, one set wanted Newman
to take the final plunge earlier than he did. I am
inclined to think he would have listened to those,
who, like Charles Marriott, urged longer delay. But
at last a sort of panic overtook him. I never saw
him to such advantage as in those Littlemore days.
He always felt certain that Pusey and Keble would
remain in the English Church, and I think he felt
severance from them most keenly.'

I told Froude that I had heard of the bitter grief
Pusey showed when Newman's sermon on the 'Parting of Friends,' was preached.

'Yes,' said Froude, 'I have heard that also.
Pusey lifted up his voice and wept. It was a
terrible scene. All who heard that sermon knew
that with Newman it was only a question of time.'

'What,' said Conington, 'would have happened
if he had remained ? '

'No one can tell,' said Froude, 'but I think, with
Stanley, that if Newman had read German, things
might have been very different.'

Froude spoke with deep regret of the correspondence with Kingsley, out of which the *Apologia*
grew. His final verdict, however, admirably written, is to be found in his *Short Studies* in one of
the letters written on the Oxford Movement.
Froude spoke exactly as he wrote, and when I read
these letters I recognised the very turn of expression, in his conversation with Conington and myself.
So too, is it in his four volumes of the *Life of Carlyle*.

When he spoke of his great intimacy with the sage of Chelsea, he used the very words with which he pictures Carlyle's wealth of thought and language. Conington, when Froude left the room, said to me, 'If Froude carries out his intention, some day we shall see a *Life of Carlyle*, as good as Stanley's *Arnold*. Cromwell will be painted with the wart.'

At the time that Froude was with me, I was very full of Lightfoot's edition of the Galatians. I had lately had, in my church, services for brother clergy, when Claughton and Lightfoot had preached on the subjects of 'Meditation' and the 'Moral Power of Scripture.' Froude was anxious to see some notes I had made of Lightfoot's sermon. He read them with interest, and said, 'I think this man has the making of a great theologian in him.' Many years afterwards I reminded Froude of what he had said, and told him that W. G. Ward had stated lately, the English Church has three theologians, Pusey, Lightfoot, and Llewelyn Davies. At this, Froude smiled and said, 'I quite agree with Ward.' Whenever I met Froude at the Deanery at Westminster, or at my friend Theodore Walrond's, he was always good enough to talk to me with great familiarity. 'I think,' he said, 'you ought to write on the Oxford movement, as you have heard Newman speak freely, and have heard what I and Mark Pattison have had to tell. I confess I have been wrong about the present development. I don't like it, for I like the Reformation more and more. A good deal, however, of this ritual is unreal. While the clergy are busy about their clothes, working men in London are asking if there is a God.'

And now I must deliver myself of an utterance which I have ventured to think interesting!

The Carlyle books had all been published, and the criticisms upon Froude's conduct had been somewhat fierce, when I met him at Oxford, at the Exeter College Gaudy. After breakfast in the college hall, as I was walking with Lord Coleridge in the garden, he said, 'Here comes Froude, and I am determined to have it out with him about this Carlyle matter. You shall be a witness.' We walked up and down the garden for some time, and Froude gave us his view of the whole matter. After telling us how completely Carlyle had vested an absolute discretion in him, Froude said, with great solemnity, 'Now, I assure you, Coleridge, I have written what I have written, and printed what I have printed, in the full belief that, a hundred years hence, there will be no more interesting figure in literature than Carlyle's, and I believe that what I have done he would approve.' He then left us, and Lord Coleridge said to me, 'You must put this down, and if you survive Froude and myself, you must let the world know it. Whatever error of judgment he may have made, I believe he is perfectly sincere.' I feel tolerably certain that I have quoted the very words Froude used. I told what had happened to Mark Pattison, the rector of Lincoln, and he charged me if I survived Froude to do as Lord Coleridge enjoined me. It may seem to some a small matter, but at the time when I write, when so much is being said about Mr. Froude's want of accuracy, sometimes I think unfairly, I am anxious to preserve what he said upon this subject. I have no right at all to attempt to criticise his position as an historian, but I feel certain that in his attempt to paint a great picture of Carlyle he used every endeavour to preserve proportion, and to represent truly. I happen to know that the relations between Carlyle and Mr. Erskine of Linlathen are described in Froude's biography with consummate fidelity, and that the account of Carlyle's early married life at Edinburgh is exactly the same as that which was given by Wilson and De Quincey.

I have spoken of the pleasure I had when near Birmingham, of being sometimes the host of eminent men. Before I end what I have to tell of this part of my life, I ought to say something of my kind and excellent bishop, Bishop Lonsdale. It was his habit to hold an annual meeting of his rural deans at Eccleshall. The meetings were full of interest, and when the work of the day was over, and discussions on schools and church matters were ended, the Bishop, who was a true scholar and lover of books, delighted to draw out all the powers of his guests. Then Archdeacon Moore, generous, impulsive, vehement, would pour out his choice stories of Cambridge dons, and show his knowledge of the literature of the last century, and his acquaintance with the politics of the present. Then Charles Wilbraham would delight his hearers with racy stories of his eastern travels, and others, some living, many, alas! now dead, would rejoice to think that they had spent such an evening as seldom fell to the lot of men. I have known many charming hosts, but I have never known one who combined such fatherly interest in his clergy and diocese with such true appreciation of all that was great in ancient and modern literature, and in theology, as my kindest friend, Bishop Lonsdale.

A very few weeks before his death in 1867, I helped him to arrange his letters, on one of the days of the Wolverhampton Congress. I had just left his diocese, and had begun my work as vicar of Kidderminster. 'Do not forget,' he said, 'that you are the vicar of everybody. Remember that you have duties to dissenters as well as to churchmen. Try to bring men together.'

CHAPTER XIII

Vicar of Kidderminster—Bishop Selwyn and Bishop Wordsworth—Canon Wood—Stanley and Pearson—Death of Lady Augusta Stanley—The Parochial System.

IN 1867 I left my charge at Handsworth for the vicarage at Kidderminster, and felt much of the diffidence which a pupil ought to feel when he is called upon to take his master's place. The years I spent there were years of some importance in the history of England and Europe. The leap in the dark, as the Reform Bill, passed by a Conservative Government, was called, was a great political change. The disestablishment of the Irish Church was another. The results of the Franco-German war in 1870-71, had told remarkably upon Europe. Any one who looks back on a considerable period of years and thinks of the wonderful changes that have taken place, must feel what Sir Charles Bell expresses in a pensive page of recollection, when he says, ' That whoever sits by a stream, and comes back to the same place after a great many years, and can think of himself otherwise than a straw cast on the current, has more conceit than I.' It is indeed humbling to look back on what might have been a great opportunity.

244

The position of a vicar or rector, in a considerable place, has many advantages, and ought to be a very happy sphere of labour. A man who holds this place, if he has with him a hearty band of younger men, working with him, has much to learn from them, and ought not to shut his eyes to the new setting which old truths often require.

'Do you manage your curates, or do your curates manage you? There is no third course,' said a worthy old Worcestershire clergyman to me, after I had been some years vicar of Kidderminster. I think my reply was, 'Give and take, is my motto.' But if I spoke somewhat lightly, it was not because I did not feel the immense responsibility of a parish where secular duties sometimes conflict with spiritual ones, and where tact, judgment, and temper, are often needed.

If I were giving a lecture to younger clergy, embracing my own experience, I should say that on the whole I had been a singularly fortunate man. Some difficulties I had, when questions involving controversial opinion occasioned difficulty, but I had loyal and kindly gentlemen to deal with, and, in the relation of vicar and curate, firm friendships were formed, and ties of the most enduring kind established. To one large-hearted curate and his sisters, the parish owed the generous gift of a chapel of ease, much wanted in a country district, given as a memorial of the bounty of parents, taken away from earth within a few days of each other. In the very worst part of the parish, the brother, at his own cost, built another small church.

I must not, however, dwell on the many helps of an efficient kind I enjoyed during these years, in the building of an infirmary, and in various works of restoration, and improvement of schools, through the bounty of Lord Dudley, and the large-hearted men who, by their enterprise and energy, have done much for the town of Kidderminster. I enjoyed, too, the special advantage of being able to rely on the fatherly advice of one of the most single-hearted prelates ever known in the Church of England, the late Bishop Philpott, who treated me with almost parental kindness. He was ever ready as a friend and neighbour to give help and aid. He entered fully into every difficulty, and was as sagacious as he was kind. When I was asked, along with a retired manufacturer, to act in a difficult question of arbitration, between the principal employer of labour with his men, I consulted the Bishop as to what I should do. ' Do not hesitate,' he said, 'for a moment ; no greater honour on earth could be conferred on you, than to be the choice of master and men ;' and by timely concession on both sides a great strike was averted ; and I retained the hearty friendship of all concerned.

New plans for deepening spiritual life, Bible classes of working men, and thorough instruction of pupil-teachers, originated with some of my younger fellow-workers, some of whom are still to be found in Kidderminster and the neighbourhood, others winning distinction in positions of importance, and all, I believe, animated with the true spirit of devotion to work, which, in spite of our unhappy divisions, is the characteristic of this time. Some have been taken by death and illness from active employment.

Days and years pass quickly, and the excitement of the time when W. E. Forster's great measure was carried is fading from men's minds, only to be recalled when fierce School Board contests bring passions into play. For many years I was Chairman of the School Board in Kidderminster. We had ups and downs, and after one election, I was left out in the cold, by a mistake in marking the cumulative vote ; but I soon found myself reinstalled by the generous effort of Churchmen and Nonconformists, who treated me with remarkable kindness.

Two pieces of advice were given me by my dear friend, Bishop Claughton, when I succeeded him : ' Do not put it out of the power of any of your parishioners to call upon you for help, whether they are churchmen or not ; and do not lose your temper at a meeting. I did both, and have often regretted it.'

I often thought of his words, and, indeed, of all his counsels, for it is not too much to say that during the whole time of my vicariate, busy as he was in his great and important diocese, he was ever ready to extend to me some of the treasures of sympathy, which his intense and glowing mind abounded in. When we met, which we frequently did, he would listen with intense interest to the details of the illnesses of old friends and parishioners, and hear from me accounts of hindrances and helps in my work.

I have already said that Worcestershire was rich in men of culture and high feeling, especially in matters of education. Had the wise counsels of Canon Melville, at last sanctioned by the Lower House of the Convocation of Canterbury, as to the adoption of a definite religious basis, such as the Apostles' Creed, Lord's Prayer, and Ten Commandments give, been adopted as the policy throughout the country, much of the strife now agitating England would have subsided. Unfortunately, the desire to find a common ground of agreement has faded away before the advent of the new spirit of spoliation, which is now so openly advocated by many public men, and has confused the relations between Churchmen and the Nonconformists who are on many points of doctrine agreed with them.

The remarkable character and fine presence of Bishop Selwyn have often been described. Very soon after I went to Kidderminster, he came to speak at a meeting, when the Bishops of Rochester and Worcester were also present. He had actually refused to leave New Zealand for Lichfield, but when he was requested by the highest authorities in Church and State to re-consider his decision, he consented to leave the scene of his great labours and succeed Bishop Lonsdale at Lichfield. When he was with us he spoke, in a way never to be forgotten, of his own work in New Zealand, and dwelt with great admiration on the work done, especially by Wesleyans, in the Southern Seas. I had known a simple-hearted missionary of that community who always spoke of the Bishop with great reverence; and the account given by the Bishop of this good old man's work in Fiji was generous and touching. I had heard Bishop Selwyn preach in 1854, and always felt that he was a man to whom the epithet 'chivalrous' could be properly attached. There was an air of absolute sincerity in everything he said, and when he told you that he considered the essence of Christianity to be what you could make an uninstructed savage or a child in a Sunday School understand, you felt at once that he spoke from a true spiritual experience. He distinguished me by many acts of kindness. His words, after a conference at a Home Reunion meeting at Wolverhampton, I have always cherished. 'Do not speak of failure; failure and despair are out of place in a Christian's mouth. There is a good time coming, though we may not live to see it. The kingdom of Christ has a future.'

Some have spoken of Bishop Selwyn's English episcopate as a failure compared with his New Zealand work; but those who have read the excellent account of his later days, by Canon Curteis, who thoroughly appreciated the Bishop, know that this is an entire mistake, and that Bishop Selwyn breathed life and vigour into all the work which his excellent predecessor had most at heart. We owe to him much of the feeling which has called together clergy and laity in more hearty co-operation; and when he passed away, with terrible suddenness, all England mourned.

Parochial festivals sometimes brought to our aid great and eminent preachers. Dr. Vaughan, Dr. Lightfoot, and Bishop Woodford came to help us. It is pleasant to remember that at the time of Dr. Vaughan's visit, for the first and last time, I had under my roof Dr. M'Leod Campbell, whose son was a curate near us. At Dr. Vaughan's request, Dr. Campbell told us the very moving story of the last days of Edward Irving, who came to see Campbell at Glasgow, when, as he said, the hand of death was upon him. 'He was like a man in a dream, full of tenderness. He knew I had no faith in the spiritual manifestations, but he spoke little of them, and his kindly, brotherly words sank into my soul. I felt certain that I should see his face no more. All that Carlyle says of him was true. It was indeed a sad parting.'

Dr. Campbell spoke of his friend, Mr. Erskine, with intense feeling: 'The purity of his mind is as striking as its dignity. He delights in everything that is noble, and his love for Mr. Carlyle is most genuine. I think, too,' he said, ' it is returned.'

In Dr. Campbell's writings, difficult as they sometimes are, there is what Matthew Arnold was so fond of mentioning, a note of distinction.

Archdeacon Moore told me that Bishop Thirlwall had said to him : ' The best thing produced by the *Essays and Reviews* is Dr. Campbell's " Thoughts on Revelation." Think of that man being deprived of his living by the General Assembly, because he said our Lord died for all men !'

J. B. Mozley met Bishop Lightfoot when he came to Kidderminster, and when I was the Bishop's guest at Auckland Castle, in the year of his lamented death, he showed the wonderful power of his memory in recalling much of the ground over which he and the newly-appointed Regius Professor of Divinity had travelled. This very year was realised one project of which Mozley spoke. In speaking of Stanley, he said : ' Some one ought to make a volume of extracts from Stanley's books. He is just the sort of author you can do that with.'

Mozley returned. to Oxford with a deep sense of the change that was overtaking theological opinion in England. His sermons and lectures raised him to an almost unique position, and the volume of his letters is a lasting evidence of the high and noble view he took of his position at Oxford.

One of my most frequent visitors was the late Bishop Wordsworth of St Andrews ; his eldest son was one of my curates, and whenever the Bishop came to us he preached, as he had often done in the time of Bishop Claughton, sermons full of fire and eloquence.   No man ever carried on his Oxford culture so completely through life as Charles Wordsworth. He had a real love for literature, as his book on *Shakespeare's Knowledge of the Bible,* and his edition of the historical plays, abundantly testify. He delighted in keeping up his great power of Latin verse.   In his youth he had been one of the great athletes of Oxford ; and I have seen him on a loch in Scotland, show the same skill in skating which was the admiration of his contemporaries in Oxford days. I always regretted that he had not been raised, like his brother Christopher, to an English bishopric. Although he threw himself keenly into the interest of his northern work, the sphere was a small one, and I confess I sometimes thought of him, as Goethe said of Hamlet, 'as an oak in a china pot.' He has done, however, great service to Scotland by his persistent endeavour to bring men back to a unity of belief and Church order, which is sure one day to take possession of the earnest-minded men who are labouring for a greater unity than divided Britain at present possesses in matters of faith.   Ever since I knew him in the days when first he went to Scotland, Bishop Wordsworth treated me with almost paternal kindness, and it was a great satisfaction to me to think that a notice which I wrote of the volume of the *Annals of his Life,* gave him some pleasure.

During one of Bishop Wordsworth's visits, Canon Wood, an old Oxford friend of his, told us an experience of his own which, the Bishop said, must be preserved.

Canon Wood was chaplain to the Queen Dowager, who was the guest of Lord Howe at Gopsall. He left London when the Duke of Wellington was supposed to be hopelessly ill; a few years before his actual death. When he arrived at Lord Howe's, Sir Robert Peel, who was one of the guests, took him aside to hear the last news of the Duke, and on hearing how desperate his condition seemed to be, burst into tears, and said : ' He is the truest man I have ever known.'

In 1850 Mr. Wood and his wife saw Sir Robert Peel fall from his horse. He at once went up to him, secured the carriage of a doctor, and took him home. He was witness of the terrible meeting of Lady Peel with her husband, and remained in Whitehall Gardens until Sir Benjamin Brodie had come and pronounced Sir Robert's state to be almost desperate. The Duke of Wellington arrived very shortly afterwards, and one of the family requested Mr. Wood to see the Duke. He found him at the door, and when he told him of Sir Robert's condition, the old man said with a husky voice : ' He was the soul of truth,' mounted his horse and rode away.

After I became Dean of Salisbury, Canon Wood paid me two visits. I entreated him to put this striking story down, but he said : 'No, you must do it. You have heard me tell it more than once ;' and I think I can safely say I have recorded it as I heard it. What is still more strange is, that the horse had an evil reputation, and that there is a friend of mine now alive who once suffered from the same trick which was fatal to Sir Robert.

Canon Wood was one of the kindest and most hospitable of men. He had been at one time tutor to the present Duke of Cambridge, and all who knew him found him ever courteous, ever kind, ever hospitable.

At the Ember seasons for some years, I had celebration of the Holy Communion, and addresses or lectures by men of distinction. I think we were most fortunate. Bishops How and Barry, Archdeacon Norris, and his brother (Mr. Foxley Norris), Canon Bernard, the Vicar of Malvern (Mr. I. G. Smith), Mr. Morse, Mr. Ll. Davies, Mr. Pennefather, and others, were good enough to come and give life and animation to our gatherings. I am sure that the meeting of friends who can agree to differ on some points, and yet discuss Church questions freely, ought to be encouraged more and more. Little differences often melt away.

For some years I took part, as an examiner, in the examinations for the Indian Civil Service. This made a pleasant diversion from my ordinary work, and brought me into contact with many men of mark. Sometimes I had to examine men of the highest ability. An essay on the words, ' The virtue of Paganism was strength,' seemed to me of such extraordinary ability that I ventured to call the attention of Sir Edward Ryan to it. He pronounced it to be admirable. It was the work of a young Scotchman, who had already done much credit to his college at Oxford. One day as I was going to examine for the army, a lady stopped me and said, with a strong Irish accent, ' I am a widow woman, sir. Be merciful to forty-two.' Forty-two needed no mercy, for he was a most brilliant fellow, and is no doubt high in the service.

When I asked a young fellow from Dublin a question about the dedication of Bacon's *Advancement of Learning*, he said, ' It is full of flattery of the king. Men of letters flattered the king then just as they flatter King Mob now.' This reminded me of Bishop Magee's words at a Church Congress at Southampton. He was addressing working men, and he said, ' The people who flatter you, and tell you you are the finest, thriftiest, soberest people in the world, in the last century would have been found in the waiting - room of some great man, with bag-wigs on their heads, swords by their sides, and in canary-coloured continuations.' It was in the year 1870, that memorable war year, when so many hopes were destroyed, and so many prophecies falsified. At Pontresina, where I was when war was declared, I heard an American man of letters say with full confidence, 'The French will be at Berlin in a fortnight.' But on the afternoon of the same day, I went with that shrewd observer of men, Alexander Knox, to see the last telegrams. When he saw that the Prince of Prussia was to command the army of southern Germany, he turned to me and said, 'This is the doom of Louis Napoleon.' All who remember the events of that autumn must have had similar experiences.

I had the honour of being made a governor of the great foundation of King Edward's School, at Birmingham, and during the thirteen years I was vicar of Kidderminster, I was still able to take an active part in its affairs. The first scheme of the Endowed Schools' Commissioners was, I think, rightly opposed and rejected by a vote of the House of Lords. When Mr. Disraeli's government in 1874 had been some little time in power, an amended scheme was passed. The governing body was joined by men of great eminence. Dr. Lightfoot, Dr. Dale, Mr. Green, the able professor of Moral Philosophy at Oxford, and Dr. Harper, the Principal of Jesus College, brought their remarkable powers to bear on the enlargement and improvement of the foundation. Dr. Lightfoot, until he was called to fill the see of Durham, was a constant attendant at our meetings, and much did I glean from him in the intervals of work. I learnt, as all who knew him well learnt, that he was always ready to communicate his wonderful stores of reading, in a most pleasant and lucid fashion. We should certainly have been richer, had he not been called upon to leave Cambridge, in some ways ; but his episcopate, memorable for many reasons, was a signal proof of the devotion which a great scholar and theologian can bestow on the practical work of a diocese. No man ever felt the responsibilities of his office more heavily, or bore his great honours more meekly.

The restoration of the old church at Kidderminster was the means of discovering a text on the pillar near which Richard Baxter's pulpit stood. For some time there had been a great wish to erect some memorial of Baxter's work ; and at last a fine statue, the work of Mr. Brock, was placed in the centre of the town. The Dean of Westminster, who had always had a most affectionate regard for Baxter's memory, came and delivered one of his most characteristic addresses when the statue was unveiled. The Bishop of Worcester, and the Lord-Lieutenant of the county, Lord Lyttelton, were present, and the eminent Nonconformist, Dr. Stoughton, and many others, cordially united in doing honour to Baxter's memory. This was in the year 1875, when I was recovering from a very severe accident.

The long and anxious illness of Lady Augusta Stanley had told much upon the Dean. He was looking forward, however, to the possibility of her removal to Bath, where he hoped to see something of Bishop Thirlwall, who had lately resigned the bishopric of St. David's. The day of the unveiling, alas! brought the news of the Bishop's death; and in the evening, as the Dean was talking to myself and a friend (Canon Melville) upon the history of the English Reformation, there came a telegram requesting that the Bishop might be buried in the Abbey. The Dean at once acceded to the request, and on the following Sunday he preached one of his most interesting funeral sermons.

Bishop Bowlby, Canon Morse, and Mr. W. Lyttelton, had all assembled to meet the Dean, who appeared, as he always did, to the greatest advantage, when he was surrounded by congenial friends. Morse asked him if Arnold's sermons produced a great effect on the School, and the Dean gave us an account of his own experience. It was like a page from *Tom Brown's Schooldays.* The memory of his great master always seemed to call out a wonderful enthusiasm. 'I know,' he said, 'Arnold could be stern, but his very sternness was attractive. A cold shudder,' he said, 'used to come over Arnold, when he had to speak of any moral fall.' It was so with the Dean himself. I have never known any one who was so keenly alive to blemishes of character. I have never known any one also, more anxious that opportunity should be given for recovery.

It was during this visit that he told us a delightful story of Kinglake. In a sermon preached at the request of Bishop Wilberforce at Oxford, the Dean had quoted a passage from Kinglake's *History*, and he had also alluded to the wonderful etching of the ' Chess Players,' where the guardian angel overlooks the game. He sent a copy of the sermon to Kinglake, who wrote back that he was indeed grateful for the sermon, because it had given him, in the passage about the ' Chess Players,' a thought which would never leave him. I pleased the Dean by telling him that I had shown the passage to the historian Motley, who expressed his admiration at the use the Dean had made of Retsch's etching.

My intimate friendship with Stanley was cemented and increased when I became intimate with Hugh Pearson, who had been, since undergraduate days, the Dean's dearest friend. When I first knew Bishop Wilberforce, he asked me if I knew Pearson, the vicar of Sonning; and he said, ' When you come to know him, as you surely will, as he is a friend of Stanley's, you will find that a great pleasure has been added to your existence.' It was so. There is such a thing as friendship at first sight. I at once seemed to find in Pearson distinctive qualities such as few men I have ever known possessed. He was, in truth, one of the most loveable of men ; and during the short intercourse I had with him, in the last years of his life, I do not remember anything connected with him that does not give me unmixed pleasure in recollection.

Readers of the charming letters of Miss Mitford

will remember the way in which she speaks of Hugh Pearson, who brought to her, at the close of her busy life, the truest and best consolation. Very few parish priests have ever reigned so completely in the hearts of their people as Hugh Pearson did, in his forty years' sojourn as vicar of Sonning. His friendship for Stanley was of the most romantic character. He delighted in his literary and social success, entered into all his difficulties, and he became as intimate and dear a friend of Lady Augusta Stanley, as of her husband. But the remarkable feature of Pearson's mind was, that he could thoroughly appreciate the characters and aims of men who were very far from sharing his own opinions. He was the dear friend of High Churchmen, Low Churchmen, and Broad Churchmen. He had a wider and deeper interest in literature even than Stanley himself. 'There is no man,' said the late Master of Balliol to me, 'whose judgment and taste I valued more and miss more than Pearson's.' Indeed, the tribute which the Master paid his friend in the funeral sermon he preached at Sonning in 1882, in its simple words, better indeed than any eloquence, is as touching a memorial as friend ever rendered to friend. There is a certain irony in one's fate ; and when I think of the intense pleasure I derived, during the years I knew Pearson well, I have often regretted that our meeting had not taken place years before it did.

When I was provided with a curacy at Kidderminster, in 1853, Stanley said to me, ' I know you wanted work in a town, or I would have advised you to go to my friend Pearson's.'

My visits to Pearson began in the latter years of my vicariate at Kidderminster, when he was Canon of Windsor. It was on a visit to him that I made acquaintance with Dean Wellesley, who at once was good enough to admit me to friendly intimacy, and from whom I received many kindnesses. Pearson had the warmest affection and admiration for the Dean—a man, as he called him, fearless, judicious, and sober-minded. These visits to Windsor were not only pleasant in themselves, but were the means of making known to me much of the delightful neighbourhood, some of which in my boyhood I had been familiar with. Pearson had some peculiarities. He did not share Stanley's admiration for the *Christian Year*, and was certainly, to my mind, an inordinate admirer of the first Napoleon. Few men knew Walter Scott and Miss Austen better than he did, and quotations from Miss Austen constantly flowed from his lips in the freedom of conversation. He was a great reader of theology, and every work on the relations of science with religion he studied with intense interest. American writers he greatly prized, and his enthusiasm for Phillips Brooks was boundless. He took the most genuine interest in the affairs of his parishioners ; and I have known him leave a country-house in Scotland, where there was abundance of everything he most prized,—

pleasant friends, and a delightful neighbourhood, with excursions planned for every day—in order that he might not disappoint a good old woman whose niece he had promised to marry.

In the year that Dean Stanley died, it had been agreed that he and I should join the Dean and a medical friend of his at Rome, where I had never been. Pearson wrote, 'I look forward, G. D. B., with childish delight to showing you what delighted Arthur and myself, years ago;' but the untimely death of Dean Stanley put an end to this project. Pearson followed his friend to the grave in the next year, and in the autumn the Dean of Windsor passed away. He had been with me at the funeral of Dean Stanley in the Abbey, and unconsciously addressed to me—almost the same words used by Walter Scott, at the funeral of Ballantyne—'You and I will have less sunshine in our lives from to-day,' as we turned from the grave of the Dean. 'What a scene it was,' he said to me. 'We might have touched Lord Shaftesbury, Sherbrooke, the Duke of Argyll, Claughton, Archdeacon Harrison, and Dr. Martineau, as we stood in Henry the Seventh's Chapel.'

It is impossible for me to convey to others a distinct impression of the unrestrained freedom of speech and thought which I enjoyed frequently at Methven Castle and Megginch, when Stanley, Pearson, and J. C. Shairp, were there. There were others, too, occasional guests, like Principal Tulloch, Professor Knight, and Dr. Cameron Lees, men in whose company and conversation Stanley and Pearson delighted. Everything that was interesting in Scottish literature had a great charm for Stanley. I went once with him and Pearson and Tulloch to see some old church plate at Perth. There was some doubt as to whether we could see it, as we were a small party. 'Tell him,' said Stanley, enumerating all the various titles we possessed, 'that we must see it.' He then told us how Sydney Smith, who was going down to the west of England the day before Dr. Bull, who had asked him to order dinner for him at a certain inn on the road, did order it for a Canon of Christchurch, a Canon of Exeter, the Rector of Staverton, and some other livings and preferments all held by Bull. Preferments were a frequent subject of jest with Stanley. 'Pearson,' he said, 'you ought to write the history of preferments. It would look very well: by the Reverend Canon Pearson, with appendices by the Dean of Salisbury.'

There was a latent spirit of drollery in Stanley. He had a keen relish for all Scotch stories, and no man appreciated the rich stores of Walter Scott more highly. In his lectures on the 'Church History of Scotland,' there is a beautiful passage in which he speaks of Scott's power as a great moralist. He went further, and I have often heard him speak strongly of the mistake men made in thinking Scott's views of religion shallow and conventional. 'Look,' he said, 'through the whole range of Scott's writings, and you will find passage after passage giving clear evidence of the depth and feeling which Lockhart brings out so finely in the *Life*. For my part, if a being came to me from another planet, and asked me, " What is your religion ? " I should be very much tempted to say, " The religion of Walter Scott." ' Once, when Matthew Arnold was saying something of the haste with which Scott wrote, Stanley said : ' I do not care about the haste when the whole result is so genuine and noble. When Goethe speaks of Walter Scott to Eckermann, how fine his tone is ! He may not have had the perfect temper of an artist, but I place many of Scott's characters very near Shakespeare's.'

After Lady Augusta Stanley's death, a change came over the Dean. He made great efforts to recover his interest in life, and was fully sensible of the exertions made by his sisters, his sister-in-law, and the kind cousins, who had been so much with Lady Augusta during her last illness, and brought sunshine and social ease to his Deanery. Whenever I saw him, as I had known Lady Augusta in my early days, he used to question me as to the impression she made ; an impression, I may add, that she had a truly sympathetic nature, and a power of interesting herself in everything that her friends cared most for. During the last visit he paid me at Kidderminster, he spoke of his singular good fortune in having, in his mother and wife, the uncommon union of the truest sympathy and the keenest criticism. 'His mother,' he said, 'had plainly told him that the fearless expression of his opinion had hindered his promotion to the highest post in the Church; but that she did not lament this, as she hardly thought him fitted for the work of a bishop.' 'I used to think this hard,' he said; 'but I now see she was right, although I am quite willing to admit, that when a man becomes a bishop, he can rise, like Fraser, to an extraordinary height of usefulness and power. Tait,' he added, 'is another instance of the wonderful development of latent force and statesmanship the office brings out. Sometimes,' he added, with a smile, 'I should have liked to hold an historic see like Salisbury. I remember visiting Bishop Denison there; and I thought much of Burnet, his strangely mixed character, his Pastoral Care, and his love for Leighton.'

Some persons have an impression that the great concourse at Lady Augusta's funeral was highly prized by Stanley as the tribute to her character, from persons of the highest station. I think this is an entirely erroneous view.

The Dean enjoyed the confidence and respect of many whose notice is courted by all men. All such distinctions he took at their proper value. They came to him unsought, and never had the effect of withdrawing him from the closeness of familiar friendship, or elevating him unduly. He had in him nothing of the courtier. He had a real delight in perceiving noble traits of character, and felt most gratefully the sympathy and kindness he received from those to whom he said he could make no return.

I have a great dread, in what I have said of Dean Stanley, of representing him, in character or opinion, untruly. I shall never forget that on the last day I saw him, shortly before his death, he spoke much to me—I had been speaking to him of Arnold's life —of the wonderful hold Arnold's teaching had over his own life, and he also declared that his defence of the *Essays and Reviews*, in one particular portion, exactly expressed his own feeling as to the great subject of St. Paul's preaching. He spoke also of the Essay by Herman Merivale, which concludes his volume of *Historical Studies*, and told me that it had produced an immediate effect upon Edward Twisleton, who was the principal contributor to the memorial of Keble in the Abbey, which we had just been looking at.

I could fill many pages with anecdotes of the wonderful charm which the Dean's character and nature imparted to conversations on all sorts of subjects. But I must refrain. There are many, though the circle is getting smaller every year, who will gladly admit that if they have been ever able to take large and just views of the comprehensive character of the English Church, and to look forward to a time when she will become the rallying-point of many who long for a suspension of hostilities and real reunion, they owe much of this feeling to the writings and the counsel of Arthur Stanley.

I met at the Deanery, at the time when England was agitated by the discussions on the Public Worship Act, W. E. Forster, and have a very vivid remembrance of the view which he gave of the excitement in the House of Commons. The Premier, it will be remembered, spoke of this Bill as being intended to put down Ritualism. Mr. Gladstone left his temporary retirement, and strongly opposed the measure as impolitic, and likely to create confusion. Mr. Forster, who, from his peculiar position, was able to look on the matter dispassionately, told me that he thought that a panic had seized on the House of Commons, and that the effect of the agitation would be prejudicial to the Church. The years which followed were years of trouble. The Bishops, who felt compelled to let the Act work, were loudly abused when the result of litigation led to the imprisonment of clergymen. At one time it almost seemed as if a strong party might possibly succeed in breaking up the Church of England. Although Archbishop Tait had at first shown a strong inclination for repressive measures, his statesmanlike spirit moderated much of the rancour; and the appointment of a Royal Commission, upon the subject of the Church Courts, in 1881, did much to calm the tempest and prevent mischief. Many were surprised to find that the taste for ceremonial, hitherto unknown in England, gradually grew stronger. It was difficult at times to discriminate between those who were really anxious to assimilate Anglican services to Romish standards, and those who, though really faithful to what they believed to be allowed ritual, were strongly opposed to Roman teaching.

A very wise and shrewd observer, who always looked unfavourably on the Public Worship Act, the late Bishop Moberly, said to me when Archbishop Tait died: 'That although he did not always agree with particular acts of the Archbishop's, he believed that, mainly owing to his wise policy, the disestablishment and disendowment of the English Church had been wonderfully deferred.'

Mr. Forster took very much the same view. 'The parochial system,' he said, 'has this one great advantage, it gives a man a royal road to every house in his parish. If you clergy are wise, you will make much of this, and not talk too much of your right to your endowments; if you do, you will find that you won't carry many jewels with you out of Egypt.' In these later days I have often thought of his words.

A national Church is best vindicated by taking the highest ground; and when the endowments of a Church are looked upon as possessions held in trust for the benefit of the nation, and as the best means of preaching the Gospel to the poor, men are more likely to refrain from taking possession of the revenues of the Church, than from any scruples about the original intentions of those who granted tithes and property.

How small and petty, after a few years, the controversies which had their hour of empire often appear! I have no wish to be thought a cynical latitudinarian, or to uphold as absolutely perfect the Prayer-Book and system of the Church of England; but ever since I read in a very remarkable pamphlet of Mr. Gladstone's, on the Royal Supremacy, the striking words of Joseph de Maistre, that whenever a real desire for reunion should arise in Christendom, it is to the Church of England, touching Old Catholicism on the one hand, and Protestantism on the other, that men will turn their eyes, I have felt persuaded more and more, that if men can only afford to wait, the Church of the future may owe much to England. The experience of Colonial bishops, and the utterances of American prelates, all point in this direction.

'What a wonderfully interesting time is coming for the Churches of England and America! I wish I could live for forty years to see what will come from these interesting young fellows at Oxford,' said Phillips Brooks to me two years before his untimely death. Many a tribute has been paid to this powerful divine and delightful companion.

When he was staying with me at Salisbury, on the evening of the Sunday in which he had preached in the Cathedral, he went with me to the Training College for Schoolmistresses, spoke to them of their future lives, and of the power that common duties possessed when done in a high spirit. I have heard many addresses to teachers, but I never heard one so perfectly human, so replete with simple and touching appeals to the highest instincts. It was, indeed, a privilege to spend some hours with one who elevated every subject he touched on by the sweet reasonableness and purity of his thoughts.

CHAPTER XIV

Nassau Senior's Conversation—The Criticisms of Bulwer, Scott, Richardson, and Miss Austen—Coleridge—The Irish Church Question—Lord Arthur Russell and Sir Louis Mallet—Hayward's Stories—Bishop Magee's Irish Stories, Theological Views, and Preaching—Newman—Mozley, Dean Church, and Liddon.

LADY ST. JULIAN, in *Sybil*, makes some severe remarks upon people who go out to breakfast in London. If she had ever been present at any of my friend Sir M. E. Grant Duff's agreeable breakfast parties, she would have found that the people talk even more freely at that meal than at dinners. Such, at least, is my experience. I have met many old friends, and made many new ones, at my host's well-assorted gatherings. Perhaps the most distinct figure among the celebrities I have seen there is that of William Nassau Senior, the friend of Whately, and indeed of most of the distinguished men of his time. He enjoyed special opportunities for detailing, as he did in his published and unpublished conversations, some of the most interesting facts and opinions of his busy life.

When I first met him he began a very interesting conversation in this way. 'I am a trustee of a charity to distribute books. A bishop's son—himself a clergyman—sent us in a list of books he wanted for his parish. The first on his list was Bulwer's *Pelham*. I thought this droll. I must say, however, the rest of the books he wanted were very different. I have been reading a good deal of Bulwer lately,' he continued, 'and I think he is a very wonderful man. A German said to me the other day, " Your best play-writer and your best novelist is Bulwer ; " and I can't help thinking myself,' he said, 'this new poem, "St. Stephen's," is uncommonly good.' Some one who was present—I rather think, Lord Acton—praised the good English of Bulwer's later novels. ' Yes,' said Senior ; 'and, after all, it is by the style that novelists live. Look at Scott and Miss Austen.'

Senior was the reviewer of most of Scott's novels in the *Quarterly*. The delightful volume called *Essays on Fiction* is not, I think, sufficiently prized. ' *Waverley*,' he said, 'I think, on the whole, the best of Scott's novels. There are very few things better than the life of Tullyveolan ; and the Prince is admirable.' Some one spoke warmly of *Guy Mannering*, and this drew Senior on to speak of Scott's historical novels. He gave the highest praise to *Quentin Durward*, *The Abbot*, and *Ivanhoe* ; 'although,' he added, 'Sir Francis Palgrave has shown that Scott was altogether wrong in some of the details of his history. But Rebecca,' he said, ' is a charming creation. People don't value half enough *St. Ronan's Well*.' Lowe had been staying lately at

Chevening, and he praised *St. Ronan's Well* so much that all the young people were mad to read it, and the copies in the house were in great request. ' I heard Macaulay,' said Senior, ' tell the story he was fond of telling about *Clarissa*. He took it with him to the hills in India, and made everybody, by his description, long to read it. His copy was handed about from one reader to another. What a pity it is,' added Senior, ' people don't read Richardson more. I said something to a lady the other day, who sat next me at dinner, about the sorrows of Clementina. " Do you mean," said she, " Lady Clementina Villiers ? " " Oh dear no ! " I said, " I mean Clementina in *Sir Charles Grandison*," and she acknowledged she had never read a line of it.'

He then again mentioned Miss Austen, and said to me, ' Mr. Collins and the clergyman in Miss Austen's novels are very different from the vicars and curates in the novels of to-day. How inimitably clever also Thackeray is in Tom Tusher, in *Esmond* ! *Esmond* is a wonderful feat ; Thackeray a real genius. Mr. Elwin has written admirably on Thackeray in the *Quarterly*. We have few critics like Elwin. His articles on Gray, Sterne, Cowper, and Johnson are first-rate. I tell Murray they ought to be reprinted.' To this, I am sorry to say, Mr. Elwin himself has never yet given his consent.

From English novels and critiques, Senior passed to French politics. ' The Emperor,' he said, ' is in a most difficult position. He has not strengthened himself by the Savoy and Nice affair, and he must soon find something for his army to do. What France wants is men of the old Whig temper. The Emperor, if he could only get men of character round him, might do much for France. He is hampered by his friends. Kinglake was wrong in writing as he did about the *coup d'état*, but a great deal of what he said was true.' I wish I could remember the very emphatic praise of Guizot's *Memoirs*, which Senior had lately been reading ; but I only recollect that he said, ' How history repeats itself ! Guizot was very like Neckar. By-the-bye, everybody ought to read Louis Blanc's French Revolution *History*, although he is monstrously unfair to Marie Antoinette.'

When I next met Senior he spoke a great deal about Shakespeare. ' Schlegel's criticism was on the whole very good. It has filtered into the English mind. Coleridge got a great deal from Schlegel, and never acknowledged his debts properly.' Some one mentioned Matthew Arnold's saying ' Coleridge had no morals.' ' It is quite true,' said Senior ; ' opium destroyed him. Lockhart used to be quite pathetic when he spoke of Coleridge's total absence of moral restraint. Southey and Wordsworth did everything that two good men could do to help him. But he was for ever slipping through their fingers. He made fair promises of amendment, and broke them over and over again. He reminded me of an Irish story I heard at Mount Trenchard. Great pains had been taken to put a cabin in order, and the landlord made Paddy promise to keep the pigs out. When he went to see it he found a hole in the floor, which had been carefully mended, and the occupant and a friend threshing corn with flails. "Do you call this keeping your word ?" "I promised to keep the pigs out, but I never promised not to touch the place." Coleridge would keep his promise as to opium, but allowed himself to indulge in other ways of drowning care.'

'How,' said Senior, 'people neglect to read good things ! Did you ever read Green's *Diary of a Lover of Literature* ? It is full of capital things. He was one of those who found out Turner's genius as a painter before the rest of the world did. The book ought to be reprinted; very few people have read it. Another neglected book, a very small one, is *Remarks on some of Shakespeare's Characters*, by the father, I think, of Archbishop Whately. It is a little volume of real criticism.'

'The Irish question,' said Senior, 'is a very difficult one. The Romanists ought to have their own way to some extent about university education. I fear, what Macaulay calls "the bray of Exeter Hall" will prevent English statesmen taking any part of the Irish Church revenue for the priests. That would be the real panacea for a good deal of Irish discontent. The old Knight of Kerry pressed it upon Pitt in vain. I believe Pitt would have done it, if he had not feared the king's state of mind. I had a long talk with Stephen de Vere upon the subject, when I met him at Lord Monteagle's.' So Senior spoke some years before Mr. Gladstone found that the Irish Church question must be settled. Bishop Thirlwall, the only prelate who voted for the Irish Church Bill, always consistently maintained that the endowment of Maynooth ought to have been followed by a generous treatment of the Romish priesthood. But when the question was raised by the Duke of Cleveland in the House of Lords, it was thought to be too late to think of concurrent endowment.

It was at one of these breakfast parties that I first met a man who possessed a singular charm of character, and great intellectual distinction, the late Lord Arthur Russell. Lord Beaconsfield has often said that he thought the mother of three such sons as Hastings, Odo, and Arthur Russell, a woman much to be envied. Lord Arthur had a wonderful knowledge, I think I may say, of all European literature. He had lived much abroad ; and, when you had grown accustomed to his shy, diffident manner, you found in him a wealth of knowledge, a nice and judicious political judgment, and a most real appreciation of all that is highest and most elevating in philosophy and sociology. He was for many years a member of the House of Commons, and held, I suppose, a good deal of the old Whig creed. The surrender to the advanced Irish party

he regarded with strong moral indignation; and
when I saw him for the last time, he deplored with
almost passionate bitterness what had taken place,
and said he felt like a man walking on a shore
covered with wrecks. He had a quiet humour of
his own, very attractive. 'When the Dean appears
in the Athenæum,' he said of me, 'I know the Convocation is sitting, and that I consider a personal
benefit.' I tried to persuade him one day to come
and hear the present Master of Trinity speak
upon the subject of Parochial Councils, but I did
not succeed. I owe to him the opportunity of
reading some admirable French writings, which I
should not have seen but for his kindness; and I
felt, when he passed away, that one of the kindest
of oracles on many subjects most interesting to me,
was hushed for ever. Every one understands what
it is to have known men whose peculiar gifts make
you long to see more of them, and regret when
they are gone into the 'silent land,' that you did
not value them enough, and use the great advantage
of their life and thought more.

Such, too, was my feeling about another of my
friend's guests, Sir Louis Mallet. Very few people
have possessed the gift of lucid exposition so richly
as he did. He could, in a few words, make you
master of some position of Cobden's or Bastiat's,
and show its bearing on political life and national
development. He would discuss writings like De
Quincey's with freshness and relish; give you an

exact account of Arthur Young's work, and speak in the most instructive way about his own official experience, especially of the India Office. Very shortly before his death I saw a good deal of him at Bath, and heard from him a full account of the great part Sir James Hudson had played in Italy, and also a most vivid narrative of the time when, in 1834, 'the hurried Hudson' left Brighton for Italy in search of Sir Robert Peel, who was called upon suddenly to the premiership when King William dismissed the first reformed government.

It has always seemed to me there must be something defective in our system when men like Sir James Stephen, Herman Merivale, and Sir Louis Mallet, spend the greater part of their lives in subordinate, though influential, places. Some few have been raised to the peerage, and it is possible, I suppose, that if the House of Lords is to be strengthened, our public offices may supply life peers with great advantage.

Hayward I have met at dinner, but I do not think he was often to be found at breakfasts. He was an admirable *raconteur*. He had a wonderful gift of telling a story, without addition or ornament. Caustic he could be, and sometimes coarse. He admired strongly, and hated strongly. His literary gifts were very great, and the volumes of his republished essays contain many excellent things. What could be better than his saying of a great Lord Chancellor, 'a few more drops of Eldonine and we should have had the people's charter'? This was written a good many years ago, and we have had considerable instalments in that direction. It is a great pity that Hayward was obliged to devote so much time to periodical writing. He might have added some great work to literary history, for he had read immensely, and was master of all he read. He had a most sincere admiration for Lockhart, who had treated him with great kindness. 'Get Murray,' he said once to me, 'to give you a list of Lockhart's articles in the *Quarterly*, and you will be surprised to find what a wonderful critic he was. I think his taste was greater even than Jeffrey's and Macaulay's, and his *Lives* of Burns and Scott are both first-rate. Very few editors are as good as Lockhart was, although Croker was round his neck, like the old man of the sea.' I had a letter from Hayward shortly before his death, in which he told me a good story. Old Lord Strangford was dining with Quentin Dick, a very rich man, who called his attention to the soup, and said 'it was turtle for the million.' 'Good enough,' said Lord Strangford, ' for the million, but not for the millionaire.' He was fond of telling the good things of Lord Chelmsford's. One of his great favourites was, ' When Lord Westbury appeared for the first time in the House of Lords after his fall, in plaid trousers, " There he is," said Lord Chelmsford, " scotched, but not kilt." ' I think I must add another. When Lord Chelmsford was Sir Frederick Thesiger, a clerical friend consulted him as to the restoration of a church rate, which he had dropped, but was now from want of means obliged to restore. 'Ah!' said Lord Chelmsford, 'yours is the case of the man in Horace,

> "mox reficit rates,
> Quassas indocilis, pauperiem pati." '

A dinner at the Athenæum, with Hayward, Sir W. Stirling-Maxwell, and Sir Edmund Head, was a thing not to be forgotten. Anecdote followed anecdote in pelting profusion. Hayward said that, among the many witticisms of Sydney Smith, he thought one of the best was, 'Man is certainly a benevolent animal. A. never sees B. in distress without thinking C. ought to relieve him directly.' 'Helps,' he said, 'declares that the king of proverbs is, "Nobody knows where the shoe pinches but the wearer."' After a profound silence, Stirling-Maxwell and Head, both masters of proverbs, declared that they believed he was right. Haywardiana ought to have been attempted by some one who constantly dined in his company. I heard Thackeray say that he had counted on one occasion fifty-five stories, and he did not think he had ever heard Hayward tell one of them before. It has been said, that if the original of the first part of *Faust* had perished, it might almost be recovered from Hayward's prose translation.

It may seem strange to connect a bishop with Hayward; but the only man I have ever known who could match him, in abundance of anecdotes, was

the late Archbishop of York, better known as Bishop
Magee. To spend some days in a country house or
an episcopal palace with that versatile prelate, was
no ordinary treat. A volume of Irish stories, like
Dean Ramsay's famous book, might easily have been
compiled by those who heard Bishop Magee as I did,
at the invitation of Bishop Claughton, give some
specimens of Irish humour. 'When you have told
the Bishop of Peterborough your story about the
old woman and the Pope, he must give you his story
of the old woman and the catechist.' My story was
simply the reply of an old woman in Scotland, on
hearing from a young lady that she had been to
Rome and seen the Pope. 'And did ye see the
Paip himsel', miss, honest man ; and has he ony
family ?' The Bishop laughed heartily, and then
told us how a Connemara woman exclaimed, after
hearing from the catechist the not very appropriate
Scripture which tells of Solomon and his wives, 'To
think of the privileges them early Christians had !'
But anecdotes like these, poured forth in profusion,
were only a very small portion of the pleasure to be
gained from a long evening in Bishop Magee's
society. I have heard him at Danbury, and at
Selsdon, speak on the highest themes : the conflict
of belief and science, and the difficulties of contend-
ing manfully for definite truth in the nineteenth
century, in a way which recalled the wonderful
words of Carlyle, when he says in *Sartor Resartus*,
'The conversation took a higher tone, one fine

thought called forth another; it was one of those rare seasons, when the soul expands with full freedom, and man feels himself brought near to man.'

Upon the subject of Bishop Butler's influence the Bishop was very great. 'Goldwin Smith,' he said to me, 'says that he has lived in a university where Butler was almost worshipped like a fetich. Well,' he added, 'fetich-worship is wrong, but I am very much of Bishop Fitzgerald's mind, who said, "that every year he lived, he thought more of Butler." There are two aphorisms, "compassion, which is momentary love," and "resignation to the will of God is the whole of piety." How complete, how embracing they are! A quiet bishop in the eighteenth century dares to say, "that reason is indeed the only faculty we have wherewith to judge concerning anything, even revelation itself;" and ignorant fellows in this nineteenth century will tell you that Butler was timid and no thinker. David Hume knew better, and thought himself highly fortunate when he got Butler's approval for his essays. I once met,' said the Bishop, 'an old man in Ireland, who told me Edmund Burke had said to a lady who asked him what book he would have liked best to have written, "Butler's *Analogy*, and Johnson's *Vanity of Human Wishes*."'

As a preacher, Bishop Magee had few equals. I heard him once at Leicester preach, without a note, a sermon on the text 'God is a Spirit.' It was a wonderful argument for real worship. A commercial traveller, who had heard the Bishop preach the same sermon a few days before at Edinburgh, told me that, with the exception of a sentence in which the Bishop mentioned the liberality of a former curate of mine, in whose church he was preaching, the sermon was exactly the same as that preached in Scotland. This power may be a gift peculiar to Irishmen. I have heard that a clergyman who, in his youth, had been greatly impressed by a sermon preached by the late Dean Boyd of Exeter, went into the Cathedral, when the Dean was eighty years of age, and heard him deliver, after forty years, a sermon which he believed to be identical with that which had changed his life and thought. I told this to Bishop Magee, who said, ' Surprise is sometimes expressed at the small results of preaching. There is no greater error. A friend of mine once spoke, in a second class railway carriage, some careless words on this subject. There were three men in that carriage who positively declared that they had been made serious by Spurgeon's preaching. Fitzgibbon, afterwards Lord Clare, went, rather against his will, to hear a famous preacher in Dublin. He left the church a changed man; and I think Bishop Jebb mentions that he used to go to receive the Holy Communion quietly in a country church. After this, I could not resist telling the Bishop that a sermon of his own at the Chapel Royal, on the text, "Be not deceived, God is not mocked," had been pronounced by three very different men, Lord Ossington, Lord Cardwell, and Lord Sherbrooke, to be one of the best they had ever heard, and that I should like to read it. "It was never written," he said. "I was ill coming over from Ireland, and unable to write, and had to do the best I could."'

It has sometimes happened, that preachers of eminence have passed away without knowing anything of the effect produced by their teaching. I remember when I and some of my brethren were talking in a despondent way of the little effect produced by sermons, Mr. Bellett, a friend whom I have mentioned before, said, 'Do not be discouraged, and listen to my two experiences. When I first went to Bridgnorth, I found myself in the house of a very thoughtful man. He told me that he owed his soul to two sermons, preached in my church by my predecessor. "I was a regular infidel," he said; "and I went, after many years, to St. Leonard's, heard a sermon which gave me a week's misery. Next Sunday I went again, and heard another. I began to read the Bible thoroughly, and at last I found peace." "You went and told that clergyman, I hope, and encouraged him." "No," he said, "I never spoke to him in my life. I lived in another parish."'

The other story was this. On a Good Friday evening Mr. Bellett expected a friend to come to preach for him. He never came; and he went into the pulpit himself, and made, as he thought, a thorough breakdown, in an attempt to expound the first lesson. His wife assured him that he had failed utterly. Next day, however, a young lady, who had been actually hostile, called upon him and told him that she was entirely convinced by his feeble words that her life had been an entire mistake; and the sequel of the story was, that she became a most remarkable helper of every good work at home and abroad.

Mr. Gill, vicar of Tonbridge, once preached a set of mission sermons at Leeds. A young man, a favourite disciple of Bradlaugh, came to the first sermon to scoff. At the end of the week a change came over his spirit; and his life has since been given, in the place where he unsettled many, to very different labours. It is impossible, when one thinks of the wonderful influence wielded by men like the late Dr. Liddon, Archdeacon Farrar, and Dean Vaughan, to believe that the power of the pulpit is not as great as in the days when Wesley addressed the colliers at Kingswood, and Whitefield charmed Lord Chesterfield. I once sat, on the Founder's Day at Charterhouse, next to the Rev. T. Mozley, who talked very freely on the power of the press, and on the power of the pulpit. He had been reading the account given by Principal Shairp of the effect produced by the preaching of Newman on the undergraduates of the Oxford of the early days of the forties. Mozley admitted the general truth of what Shairp had said, and declared his belief that it was the manner, even more than the matter of Newman's preaching, which exerted such a charm. 'Newman,' he said, 'had a greater command of the Bible than any man I have ever known. He could bring together a cento of passages, drawn from both Testaments, in a way that showed how thoroughly the moral force of Scripture held him in a vice. His English,' he added, 'is almost perfect. I think his sermons on particular characters like Elijah, are his best.'

It was curious to hear Mr. Mozley, who had edited the *British Critic*, and been for many years a writer in the *Times*, speak of the Oxford Movement in a dispassionate way, and discuss the question as to what might have happened if the Heads of Houses at Oxford had let the leaders have their own way entirely. To my surprise, he admitted that Newman and Pusey had shown themselves unable to direct the stream of tendency, and had been overcome, to some extent, by the extremists of the party. Ward's ability he spoke of very warmly, and told me what has now become known to the world, of the singular relations maintained by him with John Stuart Mill.

Mr. Mozley spoke of his connection with the *Times* newspaper; and told me how old Mr. Walter, after dinner at the office, had made Rogers (afterwards Lord Blatchford) sit down and write an article, which so pleased him as to make him at once make an offer of constant employment. 'Rogers,' he said, 'was unlike me. I could work in harness; he could not, and soon gave up his connection with the paper.' At this very interesting moment the after-dinner speeches of Founder's Day began. I never met Mr. Mozley again, or heard more of his revelations. He had a dry, donnish manner, but his language was wonderfully felicitous; and his short account of Hurrell Froude was almost exactly the same as that which I had heard from Sir George Prevost, who had known Froude when he was an undergraduate at Oriel.

The four volumes published by Mr. Mozley in his lifetime are most valuable records of the period in which he played a prominent part, but they are not so interesting as the volume in which Dean Church showed his marvellous power of presenting character, with all the grace and beauty of his matchless style. There is a sweet reasonableness in the Dean's writing entirely different from the acrid way in which Mr. Mozley serves up his dishes. Dean Church was a man who really shrunk from public life in any shape. He was drawn with great reluctance from the care of his country parish, to the Deanery of St. Paul's; and although fitted in many respects for much higher positions, he felt strongly a dislike for great ecclesiastical activity. His countenance showed the delicate, and yet strong, expression of a character in which austerity and sweetness, intense belief, and the highest tolerance were wonderfully blended. He most kindly came to Salisbury shortly after my appointment, and in a lecture on Bishop Butler, too subtle, perhaps, for an ordinary congregation, gave us an admirable specimen of the way in which he could sound the depths of unbelief and unrest, and yet hold firmly the old truths. In his power of appreciating all new ideas, and yet clinging resolutely to the great foundations of revealed religion, Dean Church always seems to me, in his writings, to occupy a place filled by no other writer. Of his sermons we may say, as Dr. Johnson somewhat too liberally said of Baxter's writings, they are all good. I think I may venture to add that I induced him to republish three ordination sermons, which I had been in the habit of giving, as long as copies were procurable, to younger men; and I think any one who reads them in the volume called *Human Life and its Conditions*, must feel they have a reality and value entirely unique. In his monographs on Spenser and Bacon, the Dean balances with wonderful power the merits of the poet and the philosopher. In his *Life of St. Anselm*, he has entered completely into the struggle of the time, and the character of the man. But it is in the two volumes of *Village Sermons*, published since his death, so rich in the gradual disclosure of great truths in familiar language, that the exquisite character of Dean Church is most evident. He seems to have delighted in bringing back that which was dearest to his heart within reach of the capacities of his country congregation. I have heard

Kingsley preach at Eversley, and, wonderful as it was, one could not help feeling that in his desire to make his meaning clear, he was sometimes a little too familiar. This impression too, I think, his published sermons convey. But in Dean Church's case, as in the altar sermons of Augustus Hare, although there is simplicity, there is also the felt presence of elevation.

When Dean Church turned to ordinary topics in literature, as in his searching criticism of Montaigne, the noble and elevating tone of his mind is very apparent. A paper which he wrote on Ritualism, in 1881, had an extraordinary effect in making people think more tolerantly of changes in worship. The Dean himself had no taste for ritual excesses; indeed, I have heard him use very strong language on the subject; but he was anxious that leniency should be shown, and that men should have no excuse for saying that they had been persecuted. In his evidence before the Royal Commission on Church Courts, he showed great ability in laying down the lines of Anglican polity. I do not think that he quite appreciated the position of men like his brother Dean of Westminster, who always had a tender feeling for Nonconformists. Dean Church never forgot the early days of the Oxford Movement; but it must be remembered that he looked with indignation on the outcry made against Dr. Temple, even though it had the support of one whom he revered, Dr. Pusey. He was for many years Mr.

Gladstone's warmest adherent, but he was opposed to the surrender to the Irish cry for Home Rule. He was one of the men I always longed to see more of. He gave me advice, when I became a Dean, of the most valuable kind; and I shall never forget a conversation I had with him, at the Deanery at St. Paul's, upon a subject of which he was master, the merits and the evils of habitual confession and direction. One sentence I record here: 'Some natures may be strengthened and braced by habitual resort to confession; but the highest spiritual condition is impeded by it.'

I must say a few words about another very distinguished member of the Chapter of St. Paul's, Canon Liddon.

In the year 1850 I was a private pupil of Canon Rawlinson's, and I went to his house three times a week, at twelve o'clock. Liddon had the time from eleven to twelve o'clock. I knew him by sight, but did not know his name. I asked Canon Rawlinson, and he told me, 'His name is Liddon, and I think he will make a noise in the world.' Very shortly after this I met Liddon in the rooms of a fellow of All Souls. We talked together upon church matters. Mr. Allies was about to leave the Church of England, and Liddon expressed his great surprise that a man who so thoroughly understood the fallacy of the Papal supremacy, and had actually published convincing arguments in favour of the English Church, should at last have yielded. I was strongly con-

vinced, by the extraordinary knowledge Liddon
showed, that his career would be a very great one.
I very seldom saw him during the next twenty
years, during which he had been curate at Wantage,
vice-principal of Cuddesdon College, and chaplain
to Bishop Hamilton of Salisbury.

In 1870 I met him abroad. He had just come
from Munich, and seen much of Döllinger ; and in
the wonderful variety of his knowledge, in his wit,
in his unrivalled command of literature and theology, I had such a treat as those only who knew
Dr. Liddon well can fully understand. I have always
felt that if he had given his full powers to literature
he might have been a Macaulay or a Froude. His
whole soul, however, was in theology. He delighted
to show the bearings of a particular truth on life
and character. I think he was often timid, and I
also believe that Dr. Pusey repressed in him certain
liberal tendencies. To Stanley I think he was
unfair and unjust. But there have been few such
high-souled, high-toned preachers in any age as
Liddon. His humour was delightful. When he
told me that Döllinger was pleased to find that the
English Communion Office had the prelatory absolu-
tion, I looked greatly pleased, I suppose, and Liddon
said : ' Ah, I should not have told you this ! You will
make a bad use of this, and tell it to Stanley.'
Stanley valued Liddon more than Liddon knew.

Very shortly before Stanley's death, a Romish
ecclesiastic ventured to circulate a fable regarding

Liddon. Stanley heard of it, and took good care that the error was detected and exposed.

It is almost superfluous to say anything of the effect produced by Liddon's sermons at St. Paul's. I heard very few of them; but there was one, when the Lord Mayor and Judges came in state, so moving, so solemn in its effect upon the great multitude, that it stands out in my memory as the most remarkable instance I have ever known of a perceptible relief shown in the countenances of the congregation when the sermon was ended. Men seemed to me to look as if they had been subjected to an intense strain and tension, and were relieved when the pressure was removed.

When Liddon was made a D.C.L. at Oxford, Lord Salisbury spoke of him as one who had almost as great claims on literary as well as theological grounds to distinction; and I believe that those who met him and Dean Church at the meetings of the Literary Society Club felt that these two divines were most worthy successors to the social reputation of Bishop Wilberforce and Dean Milman. Long may the union between literature and theology be maintained in England!

CHAPTER XV

It has, I suppose, often happened, that when the work of life seems fullest of interest, and opportunities for correcting mistakes open on the view, a change is at hand. It was so with me. In 1880, when my fellow-workers were all engaged in a cordial spirit of endeavour, and I had had a most pleasant experience of the kindly confidence of my parishioners, I was most unexpectedly offered the Deanery of Salisbury. I had however begun to feel that it was time to think of a less laborious office than the cure of a great parish, and it was somewhat strange that I should go to a place of whose charm I had often heard from friends. The Bishop of Liverpool had been appointed to the Deanery, but before his installation, Lord Beaconsfield nominated him to the Queen as first Bishop of Liverpool. I virtually succeeded Dean Hamilton, a man of great reputation in his youth at Cambridge, who had held the Deanery for thirty years, and had been a most munificent friend to the Cathedral, and an encourager of every good work in the city of Salisbury. Once upon a time, having lately heard from a college friend, whose father had been Dean of Salisbury, of the charms of the Deanery garden stretching to the clear water of the Wiltshire Avon, I had laughingly written in a book of ' Likes and Dislikes,' a wish to have a river at my garden's end, and to be Dean of Sarum.

Very few people, at the age of fifty-two, which I had reached in 1880, have ever been received, on entrance to a new office, with such kindness as I experienced from the four members of the residentiary Chapter, all older than myself, and from the venerable Bishop Moberly, who during the four years that I was his neighbour, conferred upon me such kindness as I can never forget. Bishop Moberly had always been to me a most interesting character. As an undergraduate I had listened with delight to some of his admirable University sermons, admired the silvery accents of his voice, and valued most truly his generous and feeling letter in Stanley's *Life of Arnold*. His Winchester sermons had for me an especial charm. He had been the intimate friend of Keble and Sir William Heathcote, and I had often the pleasure of hearing him speak of old Balliol days, when Tait and Manning were his pupils, and when the great Oxford Movement was beginning to stir men's minds. He was for many years head-master of Winchester, and although his promotion was delayed until the year 1869, when he succeeded Bishop Hamilton, he was able, during the greater part of his episcopate, to draw the clergy and laity of his diocese together in his Diocesan Synod in a very remarkable way. He was a true scholar of the old type. His love for Pindar was great. On my installation as Dean he presented me with his translation of Pindar, a book which, like many of Bishop Moberly's writings, has never, I think, been properly appreciated. The Bampton Lectures, and his sermons on the 'Beatitudes,' contain a great deal of very beautiful writing, and a volume of *Parochial Sermons* published since his death—a sequel to one which he issued himself— is a beautiful specimen of his power as a preacher.

When I first came to Salisbury, Bishop Moberly told me that the then Lord Justice General of Scotland, John Inglis, had been his pupil at Balliol. His powers were great, but he was lazy, and only took a third class. 'When I took leave of him,' said the Bishop, I said, 'Inglis, you will either be at the top or at the bottom of your profession.'

So many of my old friends had been known to Bishop Moberly that I at once found myself able to draw from him most pleasant recollections. Whenever he spoke of Keble, he seemed to glow with enthusiasm. Many of his clergy had been his pupils at Winchester, where his personal influence was always great. The Bishop could say in a few words things which dwelt in the memory, and he could sometimes be severe; but his judgments were weighty, and he had a really noble, tolerant spirit. Salisbury has been fortunate in a succession of such

Bishops as Denison, Hamilton, and Moberly—and the present occupant of the see has hereditary claims as well as personal ones, to distinction and eminence.

Whenever in England a clergyman is appointed to an office like a Deanery, he must always, I think, be inclined to remember how fortunate he is, while there are so many learned and excellent men who are obliged, and often content, to live in the shade. It was, however, I confess, a very great pleasure to receive kind words from many old friends. Conington, one of my greatest Oxford friends, passed away in 1869, but Henry Smith, who was not taken from his University until 1883, was one of the very first to wish me joy of my new dignity. On the same day I had kind letters from Archbishop Tait, Dr. Dale, and the friend of many bishops and deans, A. K. H. B.

In 1881 I had the pleasure of welcoming at dinner my old instructor in music, Mr. Hullah, who was delighted to find me as fond of Cathedral music as I had been in the days when he taught the Charterhouse boys. Mr. Goldwin Smith has well said, ‘Wells and Salisbury are perhaps the two best specimens of the Cathedral Close, that haven of religious calm amidst this bustling world, in which a man tired of business and contentious life, might delight, especially if he has a taste for books, to find tranquillity, with quiet companionship in his old age. Take your stand on the Close of Salisbury or Wells on a summer afternoon, when the congregation is filing leisurely out from the service, and the sounds are still heard from the Cathedral, and you will experience a sensation not to be experienced in the New World.'

Every year brings more pilgrims to Salisbury from America. It is a real pleasure to see how thoroughly they enjoy the Cathedral, Stonehenge, and Bemerton. It has often amused me to find that the Deanery garden has a charm for many as having been known to the 'Angel in the House,' 'The very garden where Honoria walked,' said one lady in great glee—an utterance which much amused my friends, the late and present Professors of Poetry at Oxford. The record, alas! which a Deanery guest-book can show, in fourteen years, has a certain sadness. Many names of well-known persons who have gone from earth are there. Here we have had many friends, all filled with admiration for a cathedral whose beauty seems to grow as year after year passes away. 'Do not over-value your west front,' said my friend, Professor Freeman, to me. 'It is only a device for the exhibition of sculpture.' I am glad, however, to say that there are some experts who think that the Professor was not altogether right.

I hope I am not presumptuous in thinking that cathedrals have still an office to perform. The maintenance of a stately and well-ordered form of worship, with ritual attracting all, and repelling none, is in these days a desirable object.

Cathedrals may be great centres of diocesan work. The gatherings we have in many of them for choral festivals, missionary meetings, and special services for children and schools, such as the present Bishop of Salisbury has called into life, are of inestimable value. I have often wished that those who scoff at cathedrals could have listened to the words of the late and present Chancellors of Sarum, spoken in lectures and sermons during the fourteen years of my residence. It has indeed been a high privilege to enjoy such teaching, and the time is coming when, in days of haste and unrest, men will value more and more the deliberate utterances of those who have leisure to think and meditate.

In 1881, when I first became a member of Convocation, I was introduced by Dean Blakesley to the historian, Dean Merivale, as the youngest member of what he called the 'Order of Deans.' I felt, as I ought, the pleasure of standing by the side of one whose 'kingly intellect' was prized by Tennyson, and being introduced to the historian, who led me through his long and noble gallery of portraits. 'You will find,' said the Dean of Lincoln, 'something to do at Salisbury. I once found Thirlwall reading a volume of sermons, sent him by a dean, and he expressed a wish that deans would not publish so much, as he felt bound to read what they sent him. "What would you have them do?" said I. "Give a tone," was Thirlwall's reply.' Dean Merivale laughed heartily, and said, 'The Dean of

Sarum must not forget this story.' He reminded me of it many years afterwards, when I dined with him at Ely, and enjoyed his memories of the days when he and other Cambridge friends hailed the light of Tennyson before it had shone on the world.

The life of a dean is not always a life of leisure, and I soon found that in the well-ordered diocese of Salisbury there was plenty to interest those who have some leisure, and in lectures to the Training College for School-mistresses, and the Theological College students, as well as in occasional sermons, there was abundant occupation. There have been during the last five-and-twenty years two very re-markable movements in the English Church,—the organisation of special missions and the temperance movement. In spite of the mistakes sometimes wrought by zealots, an immense deal of good has been done by the last of these movements. There is a steady advance. Moderation and good sense are having sway, and in a very short time public opinion will be declared in favour of wise measures for the mitigation of our national disgrace.

Ten years ago I took a humble part in the great East London Mission at Hackney. What I saw and heard there made a lasting impression on me. I had some satisfaction in learning from time to time, from some of those who heard me speak, that all had not been entirely in vain. I have seen and heard something of missions in other places, and feel strongly how wisely and sagaciously Bishop Lightfoot acted, when he gave Canon Body, a man of true evangelistic spirit, a place in the Chapter of Durham. The mission movement is, after all, only one aspect of the great and vital struggle now made in the Church of England. Often and often am I reminded of those noble words of Dean Church's : ' In one sense, indeed, what is gained. by any great religious movement ? What are all reforms, remedies, restorations, victories of truth, but protests of a minority,—efforts, clogged and incomplete, of the good and brave, just enough in their own day to stop instant ruin,—the appointed means to save what is to be saved, but in themselves failures ? Good men work and suffer, and bad men enjoy their labours and spoil them : a step is made in advance,—evil rolled back and kept in check for a while, only to return, perhaps, the stronger. But thus, and thus only, is truth passed on, and the world preserved from utter corruption.'

It is well, perhaps, for those whose office it is in a humble spirit to revive and restore the idea of a great foundation, to have such passages as this sometimes in their mind. A great cathedral has an inspiring effect. When, as at Sarum, in the long list of worthies are found names like Hooker, Barrow, Pearson, and Butler, men may be pardoned for sometimes feeling proud of being in any way connected with such a foundation. ' There,' said Macaulay, when on a visit to Lord Radnor he saw again, after many years, the Cathedral of Salisbury, ' there stands the spire of Salisbury,' and he expatiated, so I have heard, on many of the historic scenes in which Salisbury had a part. ' It will stand, I hope,' said Sir David Dundas, who heard him, ' for many a year still, in a certain page in a certain history, beside the towers of Lincoln.' This pleasant allusion, I have heard, greatly delighted Lord Macaulay. The spire is still standing, and although the finest view of it is from the bishop's garden, there is another from the deanery garden, highly prized and remembered by many of the illustrious persons who have honoured me with their company during the fourteen happy years I have lived under its shade.

It is time to close these rambling Recollections, only, I fear, to be considered as the garrulous outpourings of one who is rapidly approaching threescore years and ten. But I shall end with words worthy of being remembered, which often come into my mind as I watch the peregrine falcons whirling round the spire. They are the words of Mrs. Archer Clive, at the close of the first canto of her unfinished poem, ' I watched the Heavens.' They express the spirit which ought sometimes to animate those who look back, not without sadness, on the little done, the vast undone :

> ' For 'tis not only in the sun to bask,
> Nor by bright hearths to shun the tempest's rage,
> That man is summon'd to his earthly task,
> And shown afar his native heritage.
> More glorious labours are assign'd the race
> Whose future home is all the breadth of space,

And who in many a fight must win the strength
Which nerves their spirits to that height at length ;
E'en as the falcon, when the wind is fair,
Close to the earth on lagging pinions goes,
But when against her beats the adverse air,
She breasts the gale, and rises as it blows.'

THE END

Printed by T. and A. Constable, Printers to Her Majesty
at the Edinburgh University Press

SELECTIONS FROM
MR. EDWARD ARNOLD'S LIST

THE BRITISH MISSION TO UGANDA IN 1893.
By the late Sir GERALD PORTAL, K.C.M.G. Edited by RENNELL RODD, C.M.G. With an Introduction by the Right Hon. Lord CROMER. Illustrated from Photographs taken during the Expedition by Colonel RHODES, with a Portrait by the Marchioness of GRANBY. One vol. demy 8vo, cloth, 21s.

RIDING RECOLLECTIONS AND TURF STORIES.
By HENRY CUSTANCE, Thrice Winner of the Derby. Cheap Edition. Eighth Thousand. One vol. 8vo, cloth, 2s. 6d.

'An admirable sketch of turf history during a very interesting period, well and humorously written.'—*Sporting Life.*

SEVENTY YEARS OF IRISH LIFE.
Being the Recollections of W. R. LE FANU. Third Edition, one vol. demy 8vo, 16s. With Portraits of the Author and J. SHERIDAN LE FANU.

'It will delight all readers—English and Scotch no less than Irish, Nationalists no less than Unionists, Roman Catholics no less than Orangemen.'—*Times.*

RECOLLECTIONS OF LIFE AND WORK.
Being the Autobiography of LOUISA TWINING. One vol. 8vo, cloth, 15s. With Two Portraits of the Author.

'There is much to interest our readers in this autobiography. Miss Twining looks back over her work and the changes that have passed over society with the calm reflection won by long experience.'—*Guardian.*

ECHOES OF OLD COUNTY LIFE.
Recollections of Sport, Society, Politics, and Farming in the Good Old Times. By J. K. FOWLER of Aylesbury. Second Edition, with numerous Illustrations, 8vo, 10s. 6d.

*** Also a large-paper edition of 200 copies only, 21s. net.

'A very entertaining volume of reminiscences, full of good stories.'—*Truth.*

STUDENT AND SINGER.
The Reminiscences of CHARLES SANTLEY. New Edition, crown 8vo, cloth, 6s.

'A treasury of delightful anecdote about artists, as well as of valuable pronouncements upon art.'—*Globe.*

ENGLAND IN EGYPT.
By ALFRED MILNER, formerly Under-Secretary for Finance in Egypt. Fifth Edition. With a Prefatory Chapter on 'Egypt in 1894' by the Author. Large crown 8vo, with Map, cloth, 7s. 6d.

'An admirable book which should be read by those who have at heart the honour of England.'—*Times.*

WILD FLOWERS IN ART AND NATURE.
By J. C. L. SPARKES and F. W. BURBIDGE. With 21 Full-page Coloured Plates. Royal 4to, handsomely bound, gilt edges, 21s.

'The collaborators are to be congratulated on having produced so useful, as well as so ornamental, a book.'—*Spectator.*

THE LIFE, ART, AND CHARACTERS OF SHAKESPEARE.
By HENRY N. HUDSON, LL.D., Editor of *The Harvard Shakespeare*, etc. 969 pages, in two vols., large crown 8vo, cloth, 21s.

LONDON: EDWARD ARNOLD, 37 BEDFORD STREET, STRAND, W.C.

Publisher to the India Office.

Mr. EDWARD ARNOLD'S

AUTUMN LIST OF

New *and* Forthcoming Books

AND EDITIONS.

1894.

MEMOIRS of the RIGHT HONOURABLE SIR JOHN ALEXANDER MACDONALD, G.C.B.,

First Prime Minister of the Dominion of Canada.

By JOSEPH POPE

With an Introduction by the Baroness MACDONALD of Earnscliffe.

Two vols., demy 8vo., cloth, 32s.

With two Portraits of Sir JOHN A. MACDONALD.

These two volumes contain the authoritative record of Sir John Macdonald's life. Mr. Joseph Pope, the eminent Canadian barrister, who was present for the Dominion of Canada at the Behring Sea Arbitration, was for many years private secretary to, and an intimate friend of, Sir John Macdonald ; and it was in accordance with Sir John's own directions that Lady Macdonald requested Mr. Pope to undertake the work of writing her husband's life, and put at his disposal a large collection of letters and papers which Sir John had carefully preserved. Mr. Pope has made free use of this correspondence, and some valuable appendices accompany each volume. A study of the life and policy of Sir John Macdonald, who for some forty years was the predominant influence in Colonial politics, and to whose genius the Dominion of Canada is in the main due, is essential to anyone who desires to be conversant with the affairs and history of Greater Britain, and these Memoirs—a faithful and authoritative record of the political and private life of the 'Colonial Beaconsfield'—may fairly claim to be the most important work on Colonial politics hitherto published.

LONDON :

EDWARD ARNOLD, 37 BEDFORD STREET, STRAND.

Publisher to the India Office.

THE LIFE AND LETTERS OF MARIA EDGEWORTH.

Edited by AUGUSTUS J. C. HARE,

Author of ' Memorials of a Quiet Life,' ' The Story of Two Noble Lives,' etc.

Two vols., crown 8vo., cloth, 16s. net.

This Memoir of Maria Edgeworth, by her step-mother, Mrs. Edgeworth, was privately printed in 1867, but is now published, by the kind permission of the Edgeworth family, for the first time. The letters of Maria Edgeworth, which form the greater part of this work, are full of literary and human interest, and many of them are of great historical value. The talented author of 'Belinda,' 'Castle Rackrent,' 'Moral Tales,' etc., was residing in Paris, 1802-3, during Buonaparte's consulship. In Paris, through her relationship with Abbé Edgeworth, Louis XVI.'s confessor, Maria Edgeworth came in contact with the most celebrated French people of the time, and gives in her letters a vivid description of their conversation and manners. Again in 1820 she stayed for some months in France, moving in the best society of the monarchy, and gives anecdotes of Necker, Madame de Staël, Madame Recamier, Dumont, Madame de Genlis, Duc de Broglie, and of other leading characters whom she met during her visit. Miss Edgeworth was intimate with most of the literary celebrities of the day in England. She visited, or received at Edgeworthstown, Sir Walter Scott, Lockhart, Sir James Macintosh, Lord Lansdowne, Lady Byron, Joanna Baillie, Hallam, Luttrell, Mrs. Barbauld, and her sketches of their conversation and life are bright and full of interest. The pictures of Irish life during the period have also their historical value; she was at Edgeworthstown during the rising of '98, and had to fly with her father from the house. These volumes are edited by Mr. Augustus Hare, who also contributes a Preface to the work. While omitting any letters and other material of a personal nature which have ceased to be of interest, Mr. Hare has carefully preserved in these volumes all that is of value in the original Memoir.

THE RECOLLECTIONS OF THE DEAN OF SALISBURY.

By G. D. BOYLE, M.A.,
Dean of Salisbury.

One vol., demy 8vo., cloth, 16s.

With Photogravure Portrait.

The Recollections of Dean Boyle cover a period of over sixty years.   His father, who was Lord Justice General of Scotland, was an intimate friend of Sir Walter Scott and of the brilliant set of literary men who then resided in Edinburgh.   In this volume many anecdotes are related of Sir Walter Scott and his friend Lockhart, Dr. Chalmers, Dean Ramsay, De Quincey, Professor Wilson, Jeffrey, with all of whom the Dean was brought in contact as a lad in Edinburgh.   In England the talents of Dean Boyle soon brought him the notice and acquaintanceship of most of the more brilliant men of the last generation, and into close intimacy with Dean Stanley, Thackeray, and the best of his contemporaries. This volume will prove of interest not only to that wide class of general readers who like to learn at first hand the characteristics and conversation of the men whose names are familiar to them in politics and literature, but to those who value literary criticism, and the opinions of a man of talent and learning and close observation on the various social and ecclesiastical movements of the time.

ALPHONSE DAUDET.

A Biographical and Critical Study.

By ROBERT H. SHERARD,
Editor of ' The Memoirs of Baron Meneval,' etc.

One vol., demy 8vo., cloth, 15s.

Mr. Sherard is fortunate in being well acquainted with M. Alphonse Daudet, the most popular of French novelists.   A resident in Paris, a master of the French language, a friend of Alphonse Daudet, Mr. Sherard has every qualification to fulfil the task he has undertaken, to make English readers acquainted with the life and character of the brilliant author of 'Tartarin.'

MORE MEMORIES.

Being Thoughts upon England Spoken in America.

By DEAN HOLE.

One vol., demy 8vo., cloth, 16s.

The wide popularity of 'The Memories of Dean Hole' ensures a cordial welcome to this further volume of Reminiscences by the Dean of Rochester. The Dean again has much that is instructive and amusing to say on many subjects—on Art, on Sport, on Horticulture, and on matters Ecclesiastical. The material from which this book is formed has been collected by the Dean of Rochester for a series of Lectures in America in aid of the restoration of Rochester Cathedral, but every care has been taken that this shall not detract from the readable character of the book, in which Dean Hole treats, with the same light but pungent pen as before, of things grave and gay, past and present.

BY THE SAME AUTHOR.

A LITTLE TOUR IN IRELAND. By AN OXONIAN. With nearly forty Illustrations by JOHN LEECH, including the famous steel Frontispiece of the 'Claddagh.' Large imperial 16mo., handsomely bound, gilt top, 10s. 6d.

ADDRESSES TO WORKING MEN FROM PULPIT AND PLATFORM. One vol., crown 8vo., 6s.

Twelfth Thousand.

THE MEMORIES OF DEAN HOLE. With the original Illustrations from sketches by LEECH and THACKERAY. One vol., crown 8vo., 6s.

A BOOK ABOUT THE GARDEN AND THE GARDENER. With steel plate Frontispiece by JOHN LEECH. Second Edition, crown 8vo., 6s.

Twentieth Thousand.

A BOOK ABOUT ROSES. Crown 8vo., cloth, 2s. 6d.

COMMON-SENSE COOKERY

For English Households, Based upon Modern English and Continental Principles, with Menus for Little Dinners worked out in Detail.

By A. KENNEY HERBERT ('WYVERN'),

Don of the Order of the Cordon-Rouge, and Author of ' Fifty Breakfasts,' etc.

One vol., large crown 8vo., cloth, 7s. 6d.

Colonel Kenney Herbert, the Director of the Common-sense School of Cookery, has written in this volume a standard work on Cookery and the Management of the kitchen. The chapters of this book include 'To Housekeepers,' 'Kitchen Requisites,' 'The Menu,' 'On Roughing it,' etc., and chapters dealing with Soups, Sauces, Fish, Entrées, Braising and Roasting, Boiling, Vegetables, Game, Réchauffés, Fritters, Luncheons, Salads, Eggs, Macaroni and Rice, Toasts, Hors d'Œuvres and Savouries, Pastry, Pies, Curries. A complete and careful index concludes the volume.

BY THE SAME AUTHOR.

FIFTY BREAKFASTS. Containing a great variety of new and simple Recipes for Breakfast Dishes. By Colonel KENNEY HERBERT ('Wyvern'), Author of 'Culinary Jottings,' etc. Small 8vo., cloth, 2s. 6d.

'Colonel Herbert's book is one of the best of its kind, for it is thoroughly practical from beginning to end.'—*Speaker.*

'All who know the culinary works of "Wyvern" are aware that they combine a remarkable conviction and excellent taste with an exceptional practicalness and precision in detail. His "Fifty Breakfasts" will well sustain this reputation.'—*Saturday Review.*

'Distinctly it is a book to be read and studied.'—*Pall Mall Gazette.*

'Excellent from beginning to end, and should be in the hands of every cook in the kingdom.'—*The Hotel.*

SELECT ESSAYS OF SAINTE BEUVE,

Chiefly Bearing on English Literature.

Translated by A. J. BUTLER,

Translator of 'The Memoirs of Baron Marbot,' and late Fellow of Trinity College, Cambridge.

One vol., 8vo., cloth, 5s. net.

The literary criticisms of Sainte Beuve are acknowledged to be unequalled in delicacy and authority. The object of this volume is to collect the essays which bear upon English Literature, and also the references to English writers which are scattered through the works of Sainte Beuve. Mr. Butler's name is sufficient security that the translation is above reproach. The essay 'Qu'est-ce qu'un Classique?' is included.

THE DRAUGHTS POCKET-MANUAL.

By J. GAVIN CUNNINGHAM,

Editor of 'Boy's' "Chess and Draughts Corner," etc.

Small 8vo., cloth, 2s. 6d.

A complete handy guide to the rules and best methods of play for beginners and students. A large number of carefully selected games are given ; and the English, Italian, Spanish, Polish, and Turkish forms of the game of draughts are explained and illustrated.

A Companion Volume to the Chess Pocket-Manual.

A COMPANION VOLUME TO THE ABOVE.

THE CHESS POCKET-MANUAL.   By G. H. D. Gossip,

Author of 'Theory of the Chess Openings,' etc.   Small 8vo., cloth, 2s. 6d.

'Combines brevity with fulness perhaps more successfully than any similar work to be had.'—*Pall Mall Gazette.*

' Useful alike to the novice and the master.'—*World.*

' Well fitted to serve as a manual of reference.'—*Athenæum.*

'At a pinch it will tuck into the waistcoat pocket, and its information is neither too much nor too little to be mastered by anyone who lays himself out to be a good player.'—*Saturday Review.*

'The gambits and openings are very clearly put, and withal succinctly, but perhaps the best part of a really useful book is the pages devoted to ends of games.'—*Chronicle.*

THREE NEW STORIES OF ROMANCE AND ADVENTURE FOR BOYS.

A Romantic Tale of Crown and People.

THE DOUBLE EMPEROR.

A Story of a Vagabond Cunarder.

By W. LAIRD CLOWES,
Author of ' The Great Peril,' etc.

With Illustrations by FRED. T. JANE.

Handsomely bound.　One vol., cloth, 8vo., 3s. 6d.

A Stirring Narrative of Strange Adventure.

SWALLOWED BY AN EARTHQUAKE.

By E. D. FAWCETT,
Author of ' Hartmann the Anarchist.'

With Illustrations by H. SEPPINGS WRIGHT.

Handsomely bound.　One vol., cloth, 8vo., 3s. 6d.

An Exciting Story of Travel and Incident.

THE REEF OF GOLD.

A Story of the South Seas.

By MAURICE H. HERVEY,
Author of ' Dark Days in Chile.'

With numerous Illustrations.　One vol., cloth, 8vo., 5s.

BAREROCK; or, The Island of Pearls.　A Book of Adventure for Boys.　By HENRY NASH.　With numerous full-page and other Illustrations by LANCELOT SPEED.　Large crown 8vo., over 400 pages, handsomely bound, gilt edges, 5s.

' A book vastly to our taste—a book to charm all boys, and renew the boy in all who have ever been boys.　There are all kinds of delights—a shipwreck, a desert island, a Crusoe-like life enjoyed by two boys, a "surprise party" of savages, and a wonderful coil of exciting incidents among West African blacks.'—*Saturday Review.*

WILD FLOWERS IN ART AND NATURE.

By J. C. L. SPARKES,

Principal of the National Art Training School, South Kensington, and

F. W. BURBIDGE,

Curator of the University Botanical Gardens, Dublin.

With 21 beautiful Coloured Plates of Flowers from water-colours specially drawn for the work by Mr. H. G. MOON.

In a handsome binding specially designed by Sir JOHN STIRLING MAXWELL, Bart.

One vol., royal quarto, cloth, gilt edges, One Guinea.

This splendid volume was issued in six parts during the year 1894. While the parts were being issued the following appreciative notices, among many others, appeared in the Press :

'The lithographic representations of these flowers (in Part I.) in colour are very successful, and the work promises to be an attractive as well as useful one.'—*Field.*

'Part II. of this handsome publication lies before us, and we have nothing for it but praise. The letterpress is excellent, and drawings, in colour, by H. G. Moon, are admirable, and, we rejoice to add, they are printed in England. We await future numbers of the series with interest. If they are as good as the last specimen, the volume, when completed, should be widely popular.'—*Black and White.*

'May be recommended to all who love flowers, and to all who love flower-painting. . . . The illustrations are really beautiful. They are of the natural size, excellently grouped, and the colour-printing—done, we are pleased to note, in England—is exceptionally good. There will be six parts, and we cannot doubt that they will command, as they certainly deserve, a very large sale.'—*Guardian.*

'A really delightful and instructive study of art and natural history combined. Nothing appears to have been spared that can contribute towards making this work as perfect as it is possible to make it. . . . The plates are justly described as a triumph of British colour-printing.'—*School Board Chronicle.*

'A happy combination of literary and artistic beauty of a very high order.'—*Schoolmaster.*

'A daintier present than this book when complete, at the moderate price of one guinea, comprising as it does science, poetry and art, it would be difficult to imagine.'—*Hearth and Home.*

'In point of technique, absolute faithfulness in drawing and colour-reproduction, these prints are the finest of the kind probably ever produced at the price.'—*Yorkshire Post.*

'To judge by the part before us, so artistic a volume on the subject has never appeared before.'—*Morning Post.*

WINE GLASSES AND GOBLETS

OF THE SIXTEENTH, SEVENTEENTH, AND EIGHTEENTH CEN-
TURIES.

By ALBERT HARTSHORNE.

With many full-page Plates and smaller Illustrations.

This important work is in course of preparation, and will be
largely illustrated with full-size plates and outline drawings,
grouped and classified in such a manner that the owner of an
antique glass or goblet will be able at once to ascertain its
nationality and date.

DIANA'S LOOKING-GLASS, AND OTHER POEMS.

By CANON BELL, D.D.,

Rector of Cheltenham and Honorary Canon of Carlisle.

Crown 8vo., cloth, 5s. net.

BY THE SAME AUTHOR.

POEMS OLD AND NEW. Crown 8vo., cloth, 7s. 6d.

'Canon Bell's place among the poets will, we feel sure, be finally settled by this volume.
In the amount of his workmanship, in the variety of it, and in the excellence of it, he
makes a claim which will hardly be disputed for a place, not simply among occasional
writers of poetry, but distinctly for a place among the poets.'—*The Record.*

THE NAME ABOVE EVERY NAME, and Other Sermons.
Crown 8vo., cloth, 5s.

'A series of sermons which will prove a model of excellence in preaching.'—*The Rock.*

WINCHESTER COLLEGE, 1393—1893.　Illustrated by
HERBERT MARSHALL. With Contributions in Prose and Verse by OLD
WYKEHAMISTS. Demy 4to., cloth, 25s. net. A few copies of the first
edition, limited to 1,000 copies, are still to be had.

'A noble volume, compiled by old Wykehamists, and illustrated by Herbert Marshall
in commemoration of the 500th anniversary of the foundation of the oldest public school
in England. Lord Selborne discourses eloquently on Wykeham's place in history. . . .
"Wykeham's Conception of a Public School," by Dr. Fearon is most interesting: the
Dean of Winchester writes of Wykeham's work in the cathedral; old traditions and
customs are treated of by T. F. Kirby, the Rev. W. P. Smith, A. K. Cook, and others,
while the Bishop of Salisbury contributes "Hymnus Wiccamicus," and the Bishop of
Southwell, Canon Moberley and other writers supply appropriate poetry, all the verses
being inspired with that intense love of his old public school which distinguishes a true
Englishman.'—*Daily Telegraph.*

PLEASURABLE POULTRY KEEPING.

By EDWARD BROWN,

Lecturer to the County Councils of Northumberland, Cumberland, Hampshire, Kent, etc.

Fully Illustrated.   One vol., crown 8vo., cloth, 2s. 6d.

' This handbook is as useful as it is comprehensive.'—*Scotsman.*

' Mr. Brown has established for himself a unique position in regard to this subject, and what he has to say is not only sound counsel, but is presented in a very readable form.'—*Nottingham Daily Guardian.*

' May be commended as a safe and useful guide.'—*Leeds Mercury.*

BY THE SAME AUTHOR.

POULTRY KEEPING AS AN INDUSTRY FOR FARMERS AND COTTAGERS.   With fourteen full-page Plates by LUDLOW, and nearly fifty other Illustrations.   One vol., demy 4to., cloth, 6s.

INDUSTRIAL POULTRY KEEPING.   Paper boards, 1s.
A small handbook chiefly intended for cottagers and allotment holders.

FARM DAIRYING.

By JASPER A. STEPHENSON,

Director of Dairying to the Northumberland County Council, etc.

Fully Illustrated.   One vol., crown 8vo., cloth, 2s. 6d.

SUCCESSFUL BEE-KEEPING.

A Guide for Amateurs.

By CHARLES NETTLESHIP WHITE,

Lecturer to the County Councils of Huntingdon, Cambridgeshire, etc.

Fully Illustrated.   One vol., crown 8vo., cloth, 2s. 6d.

The Children's Favourite Series.

A charming Series of Juvenile Books, each plentifully illustrated, and written in simple language to please young readers. Special care is taken in the choice of thoroughly wholesome matter. Handsomely bound, and designed to form an attractive and entertaining Series of gift-books for presents and prizes.

PRICE TWO SHILLINGS EACH, OR GILT EDGED, HALF A CROWN.

'A charming set of books, which will rejoice the hearts of mothers, teachers, and children.'—*Child Life.*
'Prettily bound, well illustrated, edited with much good sense, and are admirable for presents.'—*Tablet.*

THREE NEW VOLUMES.

MY BOOK OF THE SEA.

A budget of Sea-Stories which have always a special fascination for the children of Britannia.

MY BOOK OF ADVENTURES.

A collection of exploits and adventures which have become famous all over the world.

MY BOOK OF TRAVEL-STORIES.

An outline of some of the most remarkable travels and explorations by great discoverers.

MY BOOK OF FAIRY TALES.

'For children of seven or eight there could not be a better fairy-book.'—*British Weekly.*

MY BOOK OF BIBLE STORIES.

'Written so that the youngest child can understand them.'—*Saturday Review.*

MY BOOK OF HISTORY TALES.

'A splendid introduction to English history.'—*Methodist Times.*

DEEDS OF GOLD.

'A first-rate book for lads and lassies is this. Children cannot but be better for reading such splendid examples of the performance of duty as those illustrated in this book.'—*Schoolmistress.*

MY BOOK OF FABLES.

'A very good selection. The morals are rarely more than one line long, the type is large and clear, and the pictures are good.'—*Bookman.*

MY STORY-BOOK OF ANIMALS.

'This book will be found a favourite among the favourites.'—*The Lady.*

RHYMES FOR YOU AND ME.

It is sometimes thought that slovenly verse is good enough for children, so long as the sentiment and intention are right. The compiler of this volume does not think so; his choice is seldom at fault.'—*Spectator.*

WORKS OF FICTION.

THE MYSTERY OF THE RUE SOLY.

From the French of H. DE BALZAC, by Lady KNUTSFORD.

One vol., 8vo., cloth, 3s. 6d.

In her translation of this intensely exciting story of Balzac's, Lady Knutsford has endeavoured to preserve the style and character of the original, but, at the same time, has omitted or shortened several passages which have no direct bearing on the development of the tale, and would be now of little interest to English readers.

MISTHER O'RYAN.

An Incident in the History of a Nation.

By EDWARD McNULTY.

Small 8vo., elegantly bound, 3s. 6d.

'"Ould Paddy" and the "poor dark cratur" are as pathetic figures as any we have met with in recent romance, and would alone stamp their creator as a writer of real force and originality.'—*National Observer.*

'An extremely well-written satire of the possibilities of blarney and brag.'— *Pall Mall Gazette.*

'An Irish story of far more than ordinary ability.'—*Bookman.*

'A sad story, but full of racy Irish wit.'—*Church Times.*

'It is a book to circulate everywhere, a book which, by its pathos and its power, its simplicity and its vivid truth, will impress the mind as the logic and the reasoning of the statesman too rarely do.'—*Yorkshire Post.*

UNIFORM WITH THE ABOVE.

Sixteenth Thousand.

STEPHEN REMARX. The Story of a Venture in Ethics. By the Hon. and Rev. JAMES ADDERLEY, formerly Head of the Oxford House, and Christ Church Mission, Bethnal Green. Small 8vo., elegantly bound, 3s. 6d. Also in paper cover, 1s.

New and Popular Edition.

DAVE'S SWEETHEART.

By MARY GAUNT.

One vol., 8vo., cloth, 3s. 6d.

'It is interesting to watch the literature which is coming over to us from Australia, a portion of which is full of promise, but we may safely say that of all the novels that have been laid before readers in this country, "Dave's Sweetheart," in a literary point of view and as a finished production, takes a higher place than any that has yet appeared. From the opening scene to the closing page we have no hesitation in predicting that not a word will be skipped even by the most *blasé* of novel readers.'—*Spectator.*

'In every respect one of the most powerful and impressive novels of the year.'—*Daily Telegraph.*

'Essentially a strong book.' The writer has a wonderfully clean way of describing the elemental facts of life, and lets her plummet line go down deep into the depths of the sea of human tears. The book is of interest down to the last line.'—*Tablet.*

'The narrative is throughout animated and rises occasionally to heights of great dramatic power, whilst the picture of life in the diggings is delineated in a way that compels admiration.'—*Weekly Sun.*

'The action is rapid and well developed, the incidents exciting, as becomes the nature of the subject, and the human interest unusually deep.'—*Morning Post.*

THIS TROUBLESOME WORLD. A Novel. By the Authors of 'The Medicine Lady,' 'Leaves from a Doctor's Diary,' etc. In three vols., crown 8vo., 31s. 6d.

THE TUTOR'S SECRET. (Le Secret du Précepteur.) Translated from the French of VICTOR CHERBULIEZ. One vol., crown 8vo., cloth, 6s.

HARTMANN THE ANARCHIST; or, The Doom of the Great City. By E. DOUGLAS FAWCETT. With sixteen full-page and numerous smaller Illustrations by F. T. JANE. One vol., crown 8vo., cloth, 3s. 6d.

LOVE-LETTERS OF A WORLDLY WOMAN. By Mrs. W. K. CLIFFORD, Author of 'Aunt Anne,' 'Mrs. Keith's Crime,' etc. One vol., crown 8vo., cloth, 2s. 6d.

THAT FIDDLER FELLOW : A Tale of St. Andrew's. By HORACE G. HUTCHINSON, Author of 'My Wife's Politics,' 'Golf,' 'Creatures of Circumstance,' etc. Crown 8vo., cloth, 2s. 6d.

THE SNOW QUEEN, AND OTHER TALES.

By HANS ANDERSEN.

With numerous Illustrations by E. A. LEMANN.

One vol., 4to., handsomely bound in cloth gilt, 7s. 6d.

The approval which met the first series of these Tales, illustrated by Miss E. A. Lemann, has encouraged the publisher to issue a second series, with numerous illustrations by the same talented artist. This edition of 'Hans Andersen's Tales' is designed for the enjoyment of children and young people, and the illustrations are well qualified to appeal to their imagination.

Uniform with above.

TALES FROM HANS ANDERSEN. With nearly Forty original Illustrations by E. A. LEMANN. One vol., 4to., handsomely bound in cloth gilt, 7s. 6d.

'Miss E. A. Lemann has entered into the spirit of these most delightful of fairy tales, and makes the book specially attractive by its dainty and descriptive illustrations.'—*Saturday Review.*

'An enchanting gift-book for young people.'—*Lady's Pictorial.*

'The prettiest and most fascinating gift-book for a child that could well be imagined.'—*Educational Times.*

'A handsome prize and a welcome gift.'—*Church Times.*

BOOKS FOR THE YOUNG.

LAMB'S ADVENTURES OF ULYSSES. With an Introduction by ANDREW LANG. Third and Fourth Thousand. Square 8vo., cloth, 1s. 6d. Also the Prize Edition, gilt edges, 2s.

MEN OF MIGHT. Studies of Great Characters. By A. C. BENSON, M.A., and H. F. W. TATHAM, M.A., Assistant Masters at Eton College. Crown 8vo., cloth, 3s. 6d.

THE BATTLES OF FREDERICK THE GREAT ; Extracts from Carlyle's 'History of Frederick the Great.' Edited by CYRIL RANSOME, M.A., Professor of History in the Yorkshire College, Leeds. With a Map specially drawn for this work, Carlyle's original Battle-Plans, and Illustrations by ADOLPH MENZEL. Cloth, imperial 16mo., 5s.

FRIENDS OF THE OLDEN TIME. By Alice Gardner, Lecturer in History at Newnham College, Cambridge. Illustrated, square 8vo., 2s. 6d.

ETHICS FOR YOUNG PEOPLE. By C. C. Everett, Professor of Theology in Harvard University. Crown 8vo., cloth, 2s. 6d. Outline of Contents : Chaps. 1-10, Morality in General : Chaps. 11-20, Duties towards One's self; Chaps. 21-29, Duties towards Others ; Chaps. 30-36, Helps and Hindrances.

THE CHILDREN'S DICKENS. DAVID COPPERFIELD —THE OLD CURIOSITY SHOP—DOMBEY AND SON. Illustrated from the original plates, and abridged for the use of children by J. H. Yoxall. Square 8vo., cloth, 1s. 6d. each volume.

Also, specially bound for Prizes and Presents, with gilt edges, 2s. each.

TWILIGHT THOUGHTS—CLAUDE'S POPULAR FAIRY STORIES. With a Preface by Matthew Arnold. Crown 8vo cloth, 2s. 6d.

THE NINE WORLDS. Stories from Norse Mythology. By Mary E. Litchfield. Illustrated, crown 8vo., cloth, 3s.

GREAT PUBLIC SCHOOLS. Eton — Harrow — Winchester — Rugby — Westminster — Marlborough — Cheltenham — Haileybury — Clifton — Charterhouse. With nearly a hundred Illustrations by the best artists. One vol., large imperial 16mo., handsomely bound, 6s. Among the contributors to this volume are Mr. Maxwell Lyte, C.B. ; the Hon. Alfred Lyttleton, Dr. Montagu Butler, Mr. P. Thornton, M.P. ; Mr. Lees Knowles, M.P. ; his Honour Judge Thomas Hughes, Q.C. ; the Earl of Selborne, Mr. H. Lee Warner, Mr. G. R. Barker, Mr. A. G. Bradley, Mr. E. Scot Skirving, Rev. L. S. Milford, Mr. E. M. Oakley, Mr. Leonard Huxley, and Mr. Mowbray Morris.

L'AMARANTHE : Revue Littéraire, Artistique Illustrée. Dédiée aux filles de France. A monthly Magazine containing original articles by the best French writers, specially intended for the perusal of young people. 1s. monthly ; annual subscription, including postage, 14s.

Cheap Edition.   Eighth Thousand.

RIDING RECOLLECTIONS AND TURF STORIES.

By HENRY CUSTANCE, Thrice Winner of the Derby.

One vol., 8vo., cloth, 2s. 6d.

'An admirable sketch of turf history during a very interesting period, well and humorously written.'—*Sporting Life.*

VOLUMES OF REMINISCENCES.

SEVENTY YEARS OF IRISH LIFE. Being the Recollections of W. R. LE FANU. Third Edition, one vol., demy 8vo., 16s. With Portraits of the Author and J. SHERIDAN LE FANU.

' It will delight all readers—English and Scotch no less than Irish, Nationalists no less than Unionists, Roman Catholics no less than Orangemen.'—*Times.*

RECOLLECTIONS OF LIFE AND WORK. Being the Autobiography of LOUISA TWINING. One vol., 8vo., cloth, 15s. With Two Portraits of the Author.

'There is much to interest our readers in this autobiography. Miss Twining looks back over her work and the changes that have passed over society with the calm reflection won by long experience.'—*Guardian.*

ECHOES OF OLD COUNTY LIFE. Recollections of Sport, Society, Politics, and Farming in the Good Old Times. By J. K. FOWLER, of Aylesbury. Second Edition, with numerous Illustrations, 8vo., 10s. 6d.

*** Also a large-paper edition, of 200 copies only, 21s. net.

'A very entertaining volume of reminiscences, full of good stories.'—*Truth.*

THE MEMORIES OF DEAN HOLE. With the original Illustrations from sketches by LEECH and THACKERAY. New Edition, twelfth thousand, one vol., crown 8vo., 6s.

'One of the most delightful collections of reminiscences that this generation has seen.'—*Daily Chronicle.*

STUDENT AND SINGER. The Reminiscences of CHARLES SANTLEY. New Edition, crown 8vo., cloth, 6s.

'A treasury of delightful anecdote about artists, as well as of valuable pronouncements upon art.'—*Globe.*

THE BRITISH MISSION TO UGANDA IN 1893.

By the late Sir GERALD PORTAL, K.C.M.G.

Edited by RENNELL RODD, C.M.G.

With an Introduction by the Right Hon. Lord CROMER.

Illustrated from Photographs taken during the Expedition by Colonel RHODES, with a Portrait by the Marchioness of GRANBY.

One vol., demy 8vo., cloth, One Guinea.

'The subject of Uganda has for the first time been made attractive to the general reader.'—*Times.*

'In a word, his description of the expedition is one of the most deeply interesting records of East Africa ever written. The numerous illustrations in it are very well executed ; and there is an excellent map of the route to, and the countries surrounding Uganda. No one who wants to understand the East African problem can afford to neglect this book.'—*Daily News.*

'For Mr. Rodd's memoir and editing there can wait nothing but the fullest gratitude. It is a valuable monograph of an expert on countries and questions vital to British interests. Even more, perhaps, than the dead diplomatist's official report, this book is at present our most valuable document for the decision of the problems of British East Africa.'—*Pall Mall Gazette.*

BY THE SAME AUTHOR.

MY MISSION TO ABYSSINIA. By the late Sir GERALD H. PORTAL, C.B. With Map and Illustrations. Demy 8vo., 15s.

WORKS BY RENNELL RODD, C.M.G.

POEMS IN MANY LANDS. Crown 8vo., cloth, 5s.

FEDA, with other Poems, chiefly Lyrical. With an Etching by HARPER PENNINGTON. Crown 8vo., cloth, 6s.

THE UNKNOWN MADONNA, and Other Poems. With a Frontispiece by W. B. RICHMOND, A.R.A. Crown 8vo., cloth, 5s.

THE VIOLET CROWN, AND SONGS OF ENGLAND. With a Frontispiece by the MARCHIONESS OF GRANBY. Crown 8vo., cloth, 5s.

THE CUSTOMS AND LORE OF MODERN GREECE. With seven full-page Illustrations by TRISTRAM ELLIS. 8vo., cloth, 8s. 6d.

POLAR GLEAMS.

An Account of a Voyage on the Yacht 'Blencathra.'

By HELEN PEEL.

With a Preface by the Marquess of DUFFERIN and AVA, and
Contributions by Captain JOSEPH WIGGINS and
FREDERICK G. JACKSON.

With Portrait and numerous Illustrations.

One vol., demy 8vo., 15s.

'As unaffected as it is entertaining.'—*Morning Post.*

'Lord Dufferin's preface is delightfully characteristic.'—*Daily Chronicle.*

'A most delightful volume.'—*Daily Telegraph.*

'Like a fresh breeze from the sea.'—*St. James's Gazette.*

'The story is told so gaily that we should have liked more of it.'—*Pall Mall Gazette.*

Volume X. of THE ENGLISH ILLUSTRATED MAGAZINE.

October, 1892—September, 1893. With nearly one thousand pages, and one thousand Illustrations. Super-royal 8vo., handsomely bound, 8s.

Among the Contents of this Volume are two Complete short Novels by BRET HARTE and ROBERT BUCHANAN. Also short Stories by GILBERT PARKER; the Hon. EMILY LAWLESS; Mrs. LYNN LYNTON; GEORGE GISSING; MARY GAUNT; GRANT ALLEN, etc.

Among other Contributors to this Volume are: Rudyard Kipling; Henry Irving; Hon. Robert Lyttelton; Norman Gale; Duchess of Rutland; His Excellency Lord Houghton; Henry W. Lucy; Henry Holiday; Albert Chevalier; Harry Quilter; George Augustus Sala; Marquis of Lorne, K.T.; 'A Son of the Marshes'; Mrs. Russell Barrington; Lord Ribblesdale; Hon. and Rev. James Adderley, etc., etc.

Among the Artists who have contributed to this Volume are: Sir Frederick Leighton, P.R.A.; G. F. Watts, R.A.; G. Bernard Partridge; Wyke Bayliss, P.S.B.A.; T. Hope McLachlan; the late Vicat Cole, R.A.; the late Edwin Long, R.A.; G. W. Waterhouse, A.R.A.; Walter Crane; W. Biscombe Gardner: H. Ryland, etc.

Hitherto unpublished writings by Charles Kingsley, John Ruskin, and Lord Macaulay also appear in this volume.

PSYCHOLOGY FOR TEACHERS.

By Professor C. LLOYD MORGAN, F.G.S.,
Principal of University College, Bristol.

One vol., 8vo., cloth, 3s. 6d. net.

BY THE SAME AUTHOR:

ANIMAL LIFE AND INTELLIGENCE. With forty Illustrations and a photo-etched Frontispiece. Second Edition. Demy 8vo., cloth, 16s.

ANIMAL SKETCHES. With nearly forty Illustrations. New Edition, one vol., crown 8vo., cloth, 3s. 6d.

THE SPRINGS OF CONDUCT. Large crown 8vo., 3s. 6d.

THE JOURNAL OF MORPHOLOGY : A Journal of Animal Morphology, devoted principally to Embryological, Anatomical, and Histological subjects. Edited by C. O. WHITMAN, Professor of Biology in Clark University, U.S.A. Three numbers in a volume of 100 to 150 large 4to. pages, with numerous plates. Single numbers, 17s. 6d. ; subscription to the volume of three numbers, 45s. Volumes I. to IX. can now be obtained, and the first number of Volume X. is ready.

THE PHILOSOPHICAL REVIEW. Edited by J. G. SCHURMAN, Professor of Philosophy in Cornell University, U.S.A. Six Numbers a year. Single Numbers, 3s. 6d. ; Annual Subscription, 12s. 6d.

AMERICAN PHILOLOGICAL ASSOCIATION, TRANSACTIONS OF THE. Vols. I.—XXIV. Containing Papers by Specialists on Ancient and Modern Languages and Literature. The price of the volumes is 8s. 6d. each, except Volumes XV., XX., and XXIII., which are 12s. 6d. each. Volumes I. and II. are not sold separately. An Index of Authors and subjects to Vols. I.—XX. is issued, price 2s. 6d.

POPULAR EDITION.

With a Prefatory Chapter on Egypt in 1894 by the Author.

ENGLAND IN EGYPT.

By ALFRED MILNER,

Formerly Under-Secretary for Finance in Egypt.

Fifth Edition.   Large crown 8vo., with Map, cloth, 7s. 6d.

' An admirable book which should be read by those who have at heart the honour of England.'—*Times*.

' No journalist or public man ought to be permitted to write or speak about Egypt for the next five years unless he can solemnly declare that he had read it from cover to cover.'—*Daily Chronicle*.

THE POLITICAL VALUE OF HISTORY. By W. E. H.
LECKY, D.C.L., LL.D.   An Address delivered at the Midland Institute, reprinted with additions.   Crown 8vo., cloth, 2s. 6d.

THE CULTIVATION AND USE OF IMAGINATION. By
the Right Hon. GEORGE JOACHIM GOSCHEN.   Crown 8vo., cloth, 2s. 6d.

THE RIDDLE OF THE UNIVERSE.   Being an Attempt
to determine the First Principles of Metaphysics considered as an Inquiry into the Conditions and Import of Consciousness.   By EDWARD DOUGLAS FAWCETT.   One vol., demy 8vo., 14s.

LOTZE'S PHILOSOPHICAL OUTLINES. Dictated Portions
of the Latest Lectures (at Göttingen and Berlin) of Hermann Lotze. Translated and edited by GEORGE T. LADD, Professor of Philosophy in Yale College.   About 180 pages in each volume.   Crown 8vo., cloth, 4s. each.   Vol. I. Metaphysics. Vol. II. Philosophy of Religion. Vol. III. Practical Philosophy.   Vol. IV. Psychology.   Vol. V. Æsthetics. Vol. VI. Logic.

THE SOUL OF MAN.   An Investigation of the Facts of
Physiological and Experimental Psychology.   By Dr. PAUL CARUS. With 150 illustrative cuts and diagrams.   Large crown 8vo., cloth, 12s. 6d.

HOMILIES OF SCIENCE.   By Dr. PAUL CARUS, Editor of
The Open Court, Author of ' The Soul of Man.'   Large crown 8vo., cloth, 6s. 6d.

POLITICAL SCIENCE AND COMPARATIVE CONSTITU-TIONAL LAW. By JOHN W. BURGESS, Ph.D., LL.D., Dean of the University Faculty of Political Science in Columbia College, U.S.A. In two volumes. Demy 8vo., cloth, 25s.

THE MARK IN EUROPE AND AMERICA. A Review of the Discussion on Early Land Tenure. By ENOCH A. BRYAN, A.M., President of Vincennes University, Indiana. Crown 8vo., cloth, 4s. 6d.

HARVARD HISTORICAL MONOGRAPHS. Vol. I. The Veto Power: Its Origin, Development, and Function in the Government of the United States. By EDWARD CAMPBELL MASON. Demy 8vo., paper, 5s. Vol. II. An Introduction to the Study of Federal Government. By ALBERT BUSHNELL HART, Ph.D. Demy 8vo., paper, 5s.

BETTERMENT. Being the Law of Special Assessment for Benefits in America, with some observations on its adoption by the London County Council. By ARTHUR A. BAUMANN, B.A., Barrister-at-Law, formerly Member of Parliament for Peckham. Crown 8vo., cloth, 2s. 6d.

THE LAW RELATING TO SCHOOLMASTERS. A Manual for the Use of Teachers, Parents, and Governors. By HENRY W. DISNEY, B.A., Barrister-at-Law of the Inner Temple. Crown 8vo., cloth, 2s. 6d.

SIX YEARS OF UNIONIST GOVERNMENT, 1886-1892. By C. A. WHITMORE, M.P. Post 8vo., cloth, 2s. 6d.

'MODERN MEN' FROM THE 'NATIONAL OBSERVER.' Literary Portraits of the most prominent men of the day. Two volumes Crown 8vo., paper, 1s. each.

A GENERAL ASTRONOMY. By CHARLES A. YOUNG, Professor of Astronomy in the College of New Jersey, Associate of the Royal Astronomical Society, Author of *The Sun*, etc. In one vol., 550 pages, with 250 Illustrations, and supplemented with the necessary tables. Royal 8vo., half morocco, 12s. 6d.

PLANT ORGANIZATION. By R. H. WARD, Professor of Botany in the Rensselaer Polytechnic Institute. 4to., flexible boards, 4s. This volume consists of a synoptical review of the general structure and morphology of plants, clearly drawn out according to biological principles, fully illustrated, and accompanied by a set of blank forms to be filled in as exercises by the pupils.

A HISTORICAL GEOGRAPHY. By the late Dr. MORRISON. New edition, revised and largely rewritten by W. L. CARRIE, English Master at George Watson's College, Edinburgh. Crown 8vo., cloth, 3s. 6d.

A HISTORY OF ENGLISH METRE,
From the Earliest Times to the Present Day.

By Dr. JOHN LAWRENCE.

[In preparation.

No comprehensive view of this subject in English is at present in existence.

THE LIFE, ART, AND CHARACTERS OF SHAKESPEARE. By HENRY N. HUDSON, LL.D., Editor of *The Harvard Shakespeare*, etc. 969 pages, in two vols., large crown 8vo., cloth, 21s.

THE HARVARD EDITION OF SHAKESPEARE'S COMPLETE WORKS. A fine Library Edition. By HENRY N. HUDSON, LL.D., Author of 'The Life, Art, and Characters of Shakespeare.' In twenty volumes, large crown 8vo., cloth, £6. Also in ten volumes, £5.

THE BEST ELIZABETHAN PLAYS. Edited, with an Introduction, by WILLIAM R. THAYER. 612 pages, large crown 8vo., cloth, 7s. 6d.

THE DEFENSE OF POESY, otherwise known as AN APOLOGY FOR POETRY. By Sir PHILIP SIDNEY. Edited by A. S. COOK, Professor of English Literature in Yale University. Crown 8vo., cloth, 4s. 6d.

Leigh Hunt's 'WHAT IS POETRY?' An Answer to the Question, 'What is Poetry?' including Remarks on Versification. By LEIGH HUNT. Edited, with notes, by Professor A. S. COOK. Crown 8vo., cloth, 2s. 6d.

A DEFENCE OF POETRY. By PERCY BYSSHE SHELLEY. Edited, with notes and introduction, by Professor A. S. COOK. Crown 8vo., cloth, 2s. 6d.

SELECTIONS IN ENGLISH PROSE FROM ELIZABETH TO VICTORIA. Chosen and arranged by JAMES M. GARNETT, M.A., LL.D. 700 pages, large crown 8vo., cloth, 7s. 6d.

BEN JONSON'S TIMBER. Edited by Professor F. E. SCHELLING. Crown 8vo., cloth, 4s.

THE PRACTICAL ELEMENTS OF RHETORIC. By JOHN F. GENUNG, Ph.D., Professor of Rhetoric in Amherst College. Crown 8vo., cloth, 7s.

A HANDBOOK TO DANTE. By GIOVANNI A. SCARTAZZINI. Translated from the Italian, with notes and additions, by THOMAS DAVIDSON, M.A. Crown 8vo., cloth, 6s.

DANTE'S ELEVEN LETTERS. Translated and Edited by the late C. S. LATHAM. With a Preface by Professor CHARLES ELIOT NORTON. Crown 8vo., cloth, 6s.

SPANISH IDIOMS, WITH THEIR ENGLISH EQUIVALENTS. Embracing nearly 10,000 phrases. By SARAH CARY BECKER and Señor FEDERICO MORA. 8vo., cloth, 10s.

THE INTERNATIONAL EDUCATION SERIES.

NEW VOLUMES.

THE EDUCATION OF THE GREEK PEOPLE.

By THOMAS DAVIDSON.

Crown 8vo., cloth.

A scholarly treatise, showing the influence of ancient Greek education on modern civilization.

SYSTEMATIC SCIENCE TEACHING.

By EDWARD G. HOWE.

Crown 8vo., cloth.

A practical work, illustrating modern laboratory methods of instruction in all branches of science.

EVOLUTION OF THE PUBLIC SCHOOL SYSTEM IN MASSACHUSETTS.

By GEORGE H. MARTIN.

Crown 8vo., cloth.

RECENT VOLUME.

THE INFANT MIND ; or, Mental Development in the Child. Translated from the German of W. PREYER, Professor of Physiology in the University of Jena. Crown 8vo., cloth, 4s. 6d.

' Noteworthy as being the first attempt made by a scientific man to initiate the average unscientific reader into the methods of psychological observation.'—*Educational Review.*

'The theoretical parts are reasonable and intelligible, and the practical suggestions are very good.'—*Pall Mall Gazette.*

'An excellent little work, which can be studied with advantage by mothers and all interested in the development of the young.'—*Leeds Mercury.*

ENGLISH EDUCATION IN THE ELEMENTARY AND SECONDARY SCHOOLS. By ISAAC SHARPLESS, LL.D., President of Haverford College, U.S.A. Crown 8vo., cloth, 4s. 6d.

EMILE ; or, A Treatise on Education. By JEAN JACQUES ROUSSEAU. Translated and Edited by W. H. PAYNE, Ph.D., LL.D., President of the Peabody Normal College, U.S.A. Crown 8vo., cloth, 6s.

EDUCATION FROM A NATIONAL STANDPOINT. Translated from the French of ALFRED FOUILLÉE by W. J. GREENSTREET, M.A., Head Master of the Marling School, Stroud. Crown 8vo., cloth, 7s. 6d.

THE MORAL INSTRUCTION OF CHILDREN. By FELIX ADLER, President of the Ethical Society of New York. Crown 8vo., cloth, 6s.

THE PHILOSOPHY OF EDUCATION. By JOHANN KARL ROSENKRANZ, Doctor of Theology and Professor of Philosophy at Königsberg. (Translated.) Crown 8vo., cloth, 6s.

A HISTORY OF EDUCATION. By Professor F. V. N. PAINTER. Crown 8vo., 6s.

THE VENTILATION AND WARMING OF SCHOOL BUILDINGS. With Plans and Diagrams. By GILBERT B. MORRISON. Crown 8vo., 4s. 6d.

FROEBEL'S 'EDUCATION OF MAN.' Translated by W. N. HAILMAN. Crown 8vo., 6s.

ELEMENTARY PSYCHOLOGY AND EDUCATION. By Dr. J. BALDWIN. Illustrated, crown 8vo., 6s.

THE SENSES AND THE WILL. Forming Part I. of 'The Mind of the Child.' By W. PREYER, Professor of Physiology in the University of Jena. (Translated.) Crown 8vo., 6s.

THE DEVELOPMENT OF THE INTELLECT. Forming Part II. of 'The Mind of the Child.' By Professor W. PREYER. (Translated.) Crown 8vo., 6s.

HOW TO STUDY GEOGRAPHY. By FRANCIS W. PARKER. Crown 8vo., 6s.

A HISTORY OF EDUCATION IN THE UNITED STATES. By RICHARD A. BOONE, Professor of Pedagogy in Indiana University. Crown 8vo., 6s.

EUROPEAN SCHOOLS; or, What I Saw in the Schools of Germany, France, Austria, and Switzerland. By L. R. KLEMM, Ph.D. With numerous Illustrations. Crown 8vo., 8s. 6d.

PRACTICAL HINTS FOR TEACHERS. By GEORGE HOWLAND, Superintendent of the Chicago Schools, Crown 8vo., 4s. 6d.

SCHOOL SUPERVISION. By J. L. PICKARD. 4s. 6d.

HIGHER EDUCATION OF WOMEN IN EUROPE. By HELENE LANGE. 4s. 6d.

HERBART'S TEXT-BOOK IN PSYCHOLOGY. By M. K. SMITH. 4s. 6d.

PSYCHOLOGY APPLIED TO THE ART OF TEACHING. By Dr. J. BALDWIN. 6s.

A NEW SCHOOL HISTORY OF ENGLAND.

By C. W. OMAN, M.A.,

All Souls' College, Oxford, Author of ' Warwick the King-maker,' etc.

A History of England, from the Earliest Times to the Present Day. Fully furnished with Maps, Plans of the Principal Battle-fields, and Genealogical Tables.

Crown 8vo., cloth.

Mr. Oman's object has been to tell the story of the English nation as a whole ; he has avoided, of set purpose, the method of dealing with any portion of it apart from the rest, in the dry isolation of a separate section, and has grappled with the more difficult task of blending the various elements—political, religious, economic, etc.—that make up English history, into a single perspicuous and consecutive narrative. Mr. Oman's familiarity with the principles and details of warfare in all ages is well-known, and his accounts of campaigns and battles are none the less interesting because they are intelligible. Most schoolboys are attracted to history by its dramatic and personal side ; Mr. Oman's treatment of it appeals to this sentiment, while at the same time he introduces his readers, almost without their knowing it, to the important matters which lie behind.

ARNOLD'S SCHOOL SHAKESPEARE.

General Editor : J. CHURTON COLLINS, M.A. Assisted by special editors in the preparation of the different plays.

Crown 8vo., each Play One Shilling net.

MACBETH. By R. F. CHOLMELEY, M.A., Assistant Master at St. Paul's School.

MIDSUMMER NIGHT'S DREAM. By R. BRIMLEY JOHNSON, Editor of Jane Austen's Novels, etc.

HENRY V. By J. H. F. PEILE, M.A., Headmaster of Bury St. Edmund's School, late Assistant Master at St. Paul's School.

KING LEAR. By the Rev. D. C. TOVEY, M.A., late Assistant Master at Eton College.

THE MERCHANT OF VENICE. By C. H. GIBSON, M.A., Assistant Master at Merchant Taylor's School.

HAMLET. By W. HALL GRIFFIN, Professor of English Literature at Queen's College, London.

THE TEMPEST. By E. L. VAUGHAN, M.A., Assistant Master at Eton College.

RICHARD II. By R. BRIMLEY JOHNSON.

KING HORN.

Edited, with Introduction, Text, Notes, and Glossary, by
JOSEPH HALL, M.A.
Headmaster of the Hulme Grammar School, Manchester.

[In preparation.

THE LIBRARY OF ANGLO-SAXON POETRY.

CYNEWULF'S PHŒNIX. (*New Volume.*)   Edited, with
Introduction, Text, and Critical Notes, by Professor W. S.
CURRELL, Ph.D., of Davidson College, N.C.

BEOWULF, AND THE FIGHT AT FINNSBURH.
Edited, with Text and Glossary, by JAMES A. HARRISON and ROBERT
SHARP.   Third Edition, revised.   Crown 8vo., cloth, 6s.

CÆDMON'S EXODUS AND DANIEL.   Edited, with In-
troduction, Text, and Glossary, by THEODORE W. HUNT, Professor of
Rhetoric and English Language in Princeton College.   Revised Edition.
Crown 8vo., cloth, 3s. 6d.

CYNEWULF'S ELENE.   Edited with Introduction, Text,
Notes, and Glossary, by CHARLES W. KENT, Professor of English in the
University of Tennessee.   Crown 8vo., cloth, 3s. 6d.

ANDREAS: A LEGEND OF ST. ANDREW.   Edited, with
Introduction, Text, and Critical Notes, by W. M. BASKERVILLE, Ph.D.,
(Lips.), Professor of English Language and Literature in the Vanderbilt
University.   1s. 6d.

ELENE; AND OTHER ANGLO-SAXON POEMS.   Trans-
lated into English by JAMES M. GARNETT, M.A., LL.D., Professor of the
English Language and Literature in the University of Virginia.   4to.,
cloth, 5s

ORIENTAL LITERATURE.

OMARAH'S HISTORY OF YAMAN. The Arabic Text, edited, with a translation, by HENRY CASSELS KAY, Member of the Royal Asiatic Society. Demy 8vo., cloth, 17s. 6d. net.

LANMAN'S SANSKRIT READER. New Edition, with Vocabulary and Notes. By CHARLES ROCKWELL LANMAN, Professor of Sanskrit in Harvard College. For use in colleges and for private study. Royal 8vo., cloth, 10s. 6d. For the convenience of those who possess the old edition, the Notes are also issued separately. 5s.

HARVARD ORIENTAL SERIES. Edited, with the co-operation of various Scholars, by CHARLES ROCKWELL LANMAN, Professor of Sanskrit in the Harvard University. Vol. I.—The Jātaka-Mālā ; or, Bodhisattvāvadāna-Mālā. By ARYA-CŪRA. Edited by Dr. HENDRIK KERN, Professor in the University of Leyden, with Preface, Text, and Various Readings. Royal 8vo., cloth, 6s. net.

Vol. II.—Kapila's Aphorisms of the Sāmkhya Philosophy, with the commentary of Vijñāna-bhiksu. Edited in the original Sanskrit by RICHARD GARBE, Professor in the University of Königsberg. [*In the press.*

A SANSKRIT PRIMER. Based on the *Leitfaden für den Elementarcursus des Sanskrit* of Professor Georg Bühler of Vienna. With Exercises and Vocabularies by EDWARD DELAVAN PERRY, Ph.D., of Columbia College, New York. 8vo., cloth, 8s.

THE RIGVEDA. The oldest literature of the Indians. By ADOLF KAEGI, Professor in the University of Zürich. Authorised translation by R. ARROWSMITH, Ph.D. 8vo., cloth, 7s. 6d.

PUBLICATIONS OF THE INDIA OFFICE AND OF THE GOVERNMENT OF INDIA.

Mr. EDWARD ARNOLD, having been appointed Publisher to the Secretary of State for India in Council, has now on sale the above publications at 37 Bedford Street, Strand, and is prepared to supply full information concerning them on application.

INDIAN GOVERNMENT MAPS.

Any of the Maps in this magnificent series can now be obtained at the shortest notice from Mr. EDWARD ARNOLD, Publisher to the India Office.

ENGLISH CLASSICS FOR THE YOUNG.

PUBLISHED IN AMERICA BY MESSRS. GINN AND CO.

ROBINSON CRUSOE.   Edited by W. H. LAMBERT. Cloth, 2s.

ARABIAN NIGHTS (Selections).   Illustrated.   Boards, 2s. 6d. ; cloth, 3s.

GULLIVER'S TRAVELS.   Boards, 2s. ; cloth, 2s. 6d.

VICAR OF WAKEFIELD.   Boards, 2s. ; cloth, 2s. 6d.

RASSELAS, PRINCE OF ABYSSINIA.   Boards, 2s. ; cloth, 2s. 6d.

LAMB'S TALES FROM SHAKESPEARE.   Boards, 2s. 6d.; cloth, 3s.

SCOTT'S TALES OF A GRANDFATHER.   Boards, 2s. 6d. ; cloth, 3s.

PLUTARCH'S LIVES (Selections).   Boards, 2s. 6d. ; cloth, 3s.

IRVING'S SKETCH BOOK (Selections).   Boards, 2s. ; cloth, 2s. 6d.

BENJAMIN FRANKLIN'S AUTOBIOGRAPHY.   Boards, 2s. 6d. ; cloth, 3s.

THE PILGRIM'S PROGRESS (Selections).   Boards, 2s. ; cloth, 2s. 6d.

OLD MORTALITY.   Boards, 3s. 6d. ; cloth, 4s.

IRVING'S ALHAMBRA.   Boards, 2s. 6d. ; cloth, 3s.

Miss CHARLOTTE M. YONGE, Author of 'The Heir of Redclyffe,' etc., has written Introductions to the following volumes in this series :

QUENTIN DURWARD.   Boards, 2s. 6d. ; cloth, 3s.

THE TALISMAN.   Boards, 3s. ; cloth, 3s. 6d.

ROB ROY.   Boards, 3s. 6d. ; cloth, 4s.

GUY MANNERING.   Boards, 3s. 6d. ; cloth, 4s.

IVANHOE.   Boards, 3s. 6d. ; cloth, 4s.

THE NATIONAL REVIEW.

The leading Political Review.

Price 2s. 6d. monthly.

Among a few of the important articles which have appeared during 1894 are the following : *January.* ' W. H. Smith as a Colleague,' by Lord Ashbourne ; ' The Garden that I Love,' by Alfred Austin ; and articles by T. Mackay, Lady Frances Balfour, Mrs. Asquith, etc.—*February.* ' The Life of Arthur Stanley,' by Sir Mountstuart Grant-Duff, G.C.S.I.; ' Edward Stanhope,' by the Hon. St. John Brodrick, M.P.; and articles by Hugh Bell, E. J. Cook, etc.—*March.* ' Luxury,' by Leslie Stephen ; ' The Referendum,' by Prof. A. V. Dicey, Hon. George Curzon, M.P., Earl Grey, K.G. ;. A Family Budget by a Family Man ; and articles by H. D. Traill, Miss Taylor, Lord Stanley of Alderley, etc.—*April.* ' Foresight and Patience,' a poem, by George Meredith ; ' The Art of Reading Books,' by the Rev. J. E. C. Welldon; ' The Matabele War,' by F. C. Selous ; and articles by Lord Lilford, T. W. Russell, M.P., George Gissing, etc.—*May.* ' The Home Rule Campaign,' by the Right Hon. J. Chamberlain, M.P. ; ' The Duties of Authors,' by Leslie Stephen ; ' Another Family Budget '; ' Eton Cricket,' by the Hon. R. H. Lyttelton ; and articles by H. O. Arnold-Forster, M.P., Sir Herbert Maxwell, Bart., M.P., etc.—*June.* ' The Attack on the Church,' by Sir Richard Webster, Q.C., M.P. ; ' Ocean Highways,' by the Right Hon. Lord George Hamilton, M.P.; ' The Great Conspiracy,' by the Rev. Athelstan Riley ; ' Developments of Tennis,' by J. M. Heathcote.—*July.* ' The Colonies and Maritime Defence,' by the Imperial Federation Committee ; ' An Irish Landlord's Budget '; ' Harrow Cricket,' by Spencer W. Gore ; and articles by J. L. Mahon, Sir David Barbour, K.C.S.I., etc.—*August.* ' Lords and Commons,' by H. D. Traill ; ' Human Evolution,' by Francis Galton, F.R.S., and Benjamin Kidd ; ' Sleeplessness,' by A. Symons Eccles, M.B. ; and articles by T. W. Russell, M.P. ; A. C. Benson, the Author of ' A Study in Colour,' etc., etc.

THE FORUM.

The famous American Review.

1s. 3d. monthly ; annual subscription, post free, 15s.

Index to Authors.

ADDERLEY.—Stephen Remarx . 12
ADLER.—Instruction of Children . 24
AMARANTHE (L') 15
AMERICAN PHILOLOGICAL ASSO-
    CIATION 19
ANGLO-SAXON POETRY, Library of 26
ARROWSMITH.—Rigveda . . 27

BAUMANN.—Betterment . . 21
BELL.—Poems 9
  ,,   Name above every Name 9
  ,,   Diana's Looking-glass . 9
BENSON.—Men of Might . . 14
BOYLE.—Recollections of the Dean
    of Salisbury 3
BROWN. -- Pleasurable Poultry
    Keeping . . 10
  ,,   Poultry Keeping as
    an Industry . . 10
  ,,   Industrial Poultry
    Keeping . . 10
BURBIDGE.—Wild Flowers in Art
    and Nature 8
BURGESS.—Political Science . 21
BUTLER.—Select Essays of Sainte
    Beuve 6

CARUS.—Soul of Man . . . 20
  ,,   Homilies of Science . 20
CHERBULIEZ.—The Tutor's Secret 13
CHILDREN'S FAVOURITE SERIES. 11
CLAUDE.—Twilight Thoughts . 15
CLIFFORD.—Love Letters . . 13
CLOWES.—Double Emperor . 7
COLLINS.—School Shakespeare . 25
COOK.—Sidney's Defense of Poesy 22
  ,,   Shelley's Defence of Poetry 22
CUSTANCE.—Riding Recollections 16

DAVIDSON—Handbook to Dante . 22
  ,,   Education of Greek
    People 23
DICKENS, CHILDREN'S . . 15

DISNEY.—Law relating to School
    masters . . . 21
ENGLISH CLASSICS FOR THE
    YOUNG 28
ENGLISH ILLUSTRATED MAGA-
    ZINE 18
EVERETT.—Ethics for Young
    People . . . 15

FAWCETT.—Hartmann the Anar-
    chist . . . 13
  ,,   Riddle of the Uni-
    verse . . . 20
  ,,   Swallowed by an
    Earthquake . . 7
FORUM 29
FOWLER.—Old County Life . 16

GARDNER.—Friends of Olden
    Time . . . 15
GARBE—Kapila's Aphorisms . 27
GARNETT.—English Prose Selec-
    tions . . . 22
GAUNT.—Dave's Sweetheart . 13
GOSCHEN.—Use of Imagination , 20
GOSSIP.—Chess Manual . . 6
GREAT PUBLIC SCHOOLS . . 15
GREENSTREET.—Fouillée's Educa-
    tion . . 24

HALL.—King Horn . . . 26
HANS ANDERSEN.—Tales from 14
  ,,   ,,   Snow Queen 14
HARE.—Life and Letters of Maria
    Edgeworth 2
HARTSHORNE. — Glasses and
    Goblets . 9
HARVARD. — Historical Mono-
    graphs . . . 21
  ,,   Oriental Series . 27
HERBERT.—Fifty Breakfasts . 5
  ,,   Common-sense Cookery 5

PAGE

HERVEY.—Reef of Gold . . 7
HOLE.—Little Tour in Ireland . 4
  ,,   Addresses to Working
     Men 4
  ,,   Memories . . . 4
  ,,   More Memories . . 4
  ,,   Book about Garden . 4
     Book about Roses . . 4
HOWE.—Science Teaching . . 23
HUDSON.—Characters of Shake-
     speare . . . 22
  ,,   Harvard Shakespeare 22
HUNT.—What is Poetry ? . . 22
HUTCHINSON. — That Fiddler
     Fellow . . 13

INDIA OFFICE PUBLICATIONS . 27
INTERNATIONAL EDUCATION
    SERIES 23

JOHNSON.—Richard II. . . 25
  ,,   Midsummer Night's
     Dream . . . 25

KAY.—Omarah's Yaman . . 27
KERN.—Jātaka Mālā . . . 27
KNUTSFORD.—Mystery Rue Soly 12

LAMB.—Adventures of Ulysses . 14
LANMAN.—Sanskrit Reader . 27
LATHAM.—Dante's Letters . . 22
LAWRENCE.—English Metre . 22
LECKY.—Value of History . . 20
LE FANU.—Irish Life . . . 16
LOTZE.—Philosophical Outlines . 20

MARTIN.—Public School System . 23
McNULTY.—Misther O'Ryan . 12
' MEDICINE LADY, THE,' authors
  of.—This Troublesome World 13
MILNER.—England in Egypt . 20
Modern Men 21
MORGAN.—Animal Life . . 19
  ,,   Animal Sketches . 19
MORGAN.—Springs of Conduct . 19
  ,,   Psychology for Teach-
     ers . . . 19
MORPHOLOGY, JOURNAL OF . 19

PAGE

MORRISON.—Historical Geography 21

NASH.—Barerock . . . 7
NATIONAL REVIEW . . . 29

OMAN.—History of England . 25

PAYNE.—Rosseau's Emile . . 24
PEEL.—Polar Gleams . . . 18
PERRY.—Sanskrit Primer . . 27
PHILOSOPHICAL REVIEW . . 19
POPE.—Memoirs of Sir John Mac-
    donald 1
PORTAL.—Mission to Abyssinia . 17
  ,,   Mission to Uganda . 17
PREYER.—Infant Mind . . 23

RANSOME.—Battles of Frederick
     the Great . . 14
RODD.—Poems 17
  ,,   Feda 17
  ,,   Unknown Madonna . 17
  ,,   Violet Crown . . . 17
  ,,   Customs of Modern Greece 17

SANTLEY.—Student and Singer . 16
SCARTAZZINI. — Handbook to
     Dante . . 22
SCHELLING.—Jonson's Timber . 22
SHARPLESS.—English Education . 23
SHELLEY.—Defence of Poetry . 22
SHERARD.—Alphonse Daudet . 3
SIDNEY.—Defense of Poesy . . 22
SPARKES.—Wild Flowers in Art . 8
STEPHENSON.—Farm Dairying . 10

TATHAM.—Men of Might . . 14
THAYER.—Elizabethan Plays . 22
TWINING. — Recollections of a
     Social Worker . 16

WHITE.—Bee-Keeping . . 10
WHITMORE.—Unionist Govern-
     ment . . . 21
Winchester College . . . 9

YONGE.—Classics for the Young . 28
YOUNG.—General Astronomy . 21